Acclaim for J.M. Redmann's Micky Knight Series

Death by the Riverside and

"Maybe we should call J.M. Redmann 'Lady Spillane.' When this woman puts up her dukes, you'll put everything else down to follow her."—Vicki P. McConnell, author of the Nyla Wade mystery series

"One of the best mystery debuts of this or any year, J.M. Redmann's page-turning *Death by the Riverside*, featuring a fabulously sexual, all too fiercely independent lady dick to rival any hetero or homo counterpart on the market, female or male."—Helen Eisenbach, *QW*

"J.M. Redmann once again keeps you at the edge of your seat. A gutsy, fast-thinking PI in the Raymond Chandler tradition, Micky Knight is a detective mystery fans both gay and straight will want to see again and again."—*Booklist*

"Fine, hard-boiled tale-telling."—*Washington Post Book World*

"Imagine Kinsey Millhone as a lesbian and you've got Micky Knight."—*The Nation*

The Intersection of Law and Desire

"A gritty, involving mystery. Pretty good for a woman!"—(Sneaky Pie Brown) Rite Mae Brown

"J.M. Redmann is simply a wonderful writer. And Micky Knight is a terrific character. I enjoyed this book immensely."—Sandra Scoppettone, author of the Lauren Laurano series

"J.M. Redmann's new mystery is an unbeatable combination of high-stakes thriller and believable love story, which takes on the issue of child sexual abuse and explores it with insight and outrage. Best of all, its hero Micky Knight is a smart, generous, in-your-face dyke detective that any of us in trouble would want on our side. I guarantee you, you'll stay up late with this one."—Barbara Wilson, author of *Trouble in Transylvania*

"Superbly crafted, multi-layered…One of the most hard boiled and complex female detectives in print today."—*San Francisco Chronicle* (An Editor's Choice selection for 1995)

"An edge-of-the-seat, action-packed New Orleans adventure…Micky Knight is a fast-moving, fearless, fascinating character…*The Intersection of Law and Desire* will win Redmann lots more fans."—*New Orleans Times-Picayune*

"Crackling with tension…an uncommonly rich book…Redmann has the making of a landmark series."— *Kirkus Review*

"Perceptive, sensitive prose; in-depth characterization; and pensive, wry wit add up to a memorable and compelling read."—*Library Journal*

"Powerful and page turning…A rip-roaring read, as randy is it is reflective… Micky Knight is a to-die-for creation…a Cajun firebrand with the proverbial quick wit, fast tongue and heavy heart."—*Lambda Book Report*

Lost Daughters

"Micky Knight is exotic and down-to-earth, tough and funny—and *Lost Daughters* is the best in a series that just keeps getting better and better." —Kevin Allman, author of *Tight Shot* and *Hot Shot*

"When Micky Knight takes a case, she takes on herself, and she couldn't find a more stubborn, gritty opponent. The only sure winner is the reader; *Lost Daughters*, with Micky as exacting, angry, and engrossing as ever, is the perfect Redmann tale."—Linnea Due, author of *Life Savings*

"Few writers understand the human heart as well as J.M. Redmann. *Lost Daughters* manages the rare trick of being a mystery packed with surprises as well as a moving exploration of the pain of loss between parents and children."—Val McDermid, Gold Dagger–winning author of *The Mermaids Singing*

"As tightly plotted a page-turner as they come…One of the pleasures of *Lost Daughters* is its highly accurate portrayal of the real work of private detection…and Knight is a competent, tightly wound, sardonic, passionate detective with a keen eye for detail and a spine made of steel."—*San Francisco Chronicle*

"For finely delineated characters, unerring timing, and page-turning action, Redmann deserves the widest possible audience"—*Booklist*, starred review

"…tastefully sexy…"—*USA Today*

"Like fine wine, J.M. Redmann's private eye has developed interesting depths and nuances with age…Redmann continues to write some of the fastest-moving action scenes in the business"—*New Orleans Times-Picayune*

"An admirable, tough PI with an eye for detail and the courage, finally, to confront her own fear. Recommended."—*Library Journal*

"The best mysteries are character-driven and still have great moments of atmosphere and a tightly wound plot. J.M. Redmann succeeds on all three counts."—*Outsmart*

The Intersection of Law and Desire

by

J.M. Redmann

2009

THE INTERSECTION OF LAW AND DESIRE

ISBN 13: 978-1-60282-090-6
ISBN 10: 1-60282-090-2

THIS BOOK IS PUBLISHED BY
BOLD STROKES BOOKS, INC.
P.O. BOX 249
VALLEY FALLS, NY 12185

FIRST BOLD STROKES EDITION: MARCH 2009

CREDITS
PRODUCTION DESIGN: STACIA SEAMAN
COVER DESIGN BY BOLD STROKES BOOKS GRAPHICS

CHAPTER 1

I cursed myself for being a good girl and promised that little old ladies would get no more favors from me. It was now 4:54 p.m. At three o'clock, I had been beyond ready to admit that business was slower than a dead turtle. Good girl or no, at five exactly I would be closed for the business day. I wouldn't be gone because I lived here. I could have been the kind of detective who earned enough to afford both an office and an apartment, but that would require taking too many of what I called the "Oh, shit" cases—husbands looking for wives who where probably in the local women's shelter, bosses who wanted to make sure their no-insurance, minimum wage employees didn't cheat them. So I now sat in my office/living room waiting for six minutes to slowly tick by. Sara Clavish, who had the other office (Cajun cookbooks) on this floor had asked if I could accept a package for her. I certainly owed her the favor. Ms. Clavish was a woman in her early sixties who still occasionally wore white gloves. Besides the cat feeding I could always depend on her for, a client had had some exotic toys shipped to me. I wasn't around, so the delivery person left them with Ms. Clavish. To claim that a package from Mons of Venus, Inc., wasn't for me would sound unbelievable, so I didn't. Ms. Clavish had handed it to me without even the hint of a lifted eyebrow. But I hadn't thought that her noon-ish request would trap me in the office until the dregs of the afternoon.

My clock-watching was interrupted by the phone. "Hello," I answered, skipping the "M. Knight Detective Agency" routine, since I assumed that it was too late in the day for clients.

"Hi…uh…Micky?" replied a hesitant young boy's voice.

"Patrick, how are you?"

"I'm fine, thank you," he answered, his voice relaxing as he was recognized.

I hadn't seen Patrick, a twelve-year-old boy, in about a month. His mother Barbara and I were friends. While she had been doing physical therapy, I had insisted on being at the top of the list of people to stay with Patrick and Cissy, her kids. She needed physical therapy because she had been shot in the head. I had been with her when it happened. And although Barbara insists that I had saved her life, I still feel guilty that she almost died while I escaped with only cuts and bruises. She finished about five weeks ago. I had seen her a few times recently, but, my babysitting duty over, I hadn't seen Patrick or Cissy since.

"So, what's up? You miss me so much, you can't survive without hearing my dulcet tones?" I kidded Patrick.

"Well…no. I want to hire you." His voice was serious.

"Hire me?" I was caught off guard both by his request and his earnestness.

"Yes. That's if you're not too busy or anything."

"I might be able to work you in," I agreed. Busy was not a major problem.

"Maybe we can meet to discuss it?" he asked, trying his best to sound adult and businesslike.

After maneuvering around Little League and the like, we worked out a time. In the middle of this, my buzzer rang. I assumed it to be Ms. Clavish's tardy package, so without interrupting my conversation with Patrick, I buzzed open the downstairs door. The delivery person could huff and puff up three flights of stairs.

"You don't want to tell me what this is about?" I asked Patrick.

"Well," he hesitated for a moment, "it's sort of about Cissy. But I don't want to talk over the phone." Cissy was two and a half years younger than he was. For a brother and a sister, they were fairly close.

"Okay." I didn't push.

"Please don't tell my mom," was his final request.

My door swung open. For a moment I thought it was a rude delivery person, until I realized that it wasn't a package courier framed in my doorway.

As usual, her clothes were expensive, her hair perfectly styled, a shade of blond that I would have taken for natural if Cordelia hadn't shown me a picture of them as children at a family reunion. Her eyes were a blue that was enhanced by perfectly applied makeup. She had the self-assured poise of someone who has always had enough money to buy whatever she wanted.

"Karen Holloway," I said. "How nice to see you again. Don't tell me you've come to apologize for all the trouble you caused me."

My sarcasm was lost on her. "Micky, I want to hire you."

"Pity. I'm closed for the day." I stood up like I was about to leave.

"I'm serious. I do need your help." Then she added, "I'll pay you well for your time."

If I were Nancy Drew, this would be the Case of the Boy and the Blond Bitch. Cases, that is. And a grown-up Nancy Drew to be using words that rhymed with witch. Timing and alliteration were the only links between the Boy and the Blond Bitch.

Karen had her checkbook out and was writing a check.

"You need my help? Well, my prayers have been answered," I finally replied.

"Don't you want this check?" Karen asked as she walked by me. She waved it in my face. It was for $5,000.

"What are you doing here?" I countered. I sat down behind my desk, putting as much distance as I could between us.

I first met Karen last January when she had hired me, ostensibly to find her lost fiancé. The assignment was easy—he was working as a dancer in a gay bar. But, of course, Harry wasn't her fiancé; he was her brother, and a few pictures of him dancing for the boys was enough to get him kicked out of rich grandpapa's will. I decided that fair was fair and took advantage of Karen's interest in my body to get some equally compromising pictures to hand over to her grandfather. I winced at the memory. I hadn't actually handed them to him, but to his other granddaughter, Cordelia James.

I shook my head to clear the memory. It wasn't one I was proud of. I reminded myself that at least Cordelia had had some idea of what I was when she became involved with me. It still seemed improbable that we were lovers.

"Will you help me?" Karen asked, making herself comfortable on my couch.

I sat at my desk, trying to answer that age-old question, "Now what?" I knew that Karen and Cordelia, who were first cousins, maintained a polite, if distant relationship. They didn't run in the same circles, but occasionally Cordelia would make a token appearance at Karen's uptown parties. However, I wasn't sure what Cordelia really thought of Karen. What she might think of me for working for Karen, I was even less sure.

"You can't seriously expect me to do anything for you, can you?" I told her. There, that should be blunt enough.

She could and it wasn't. "Yes, I can. I'm asking you to help me and paying you good money for it," she informed me. She put the check on my desk.

The money was, unfortunately, a major temptation. Cordelia had been the only grandkid without compromising pictures, and, despite her not wanting it, she had gotten the bulk of her grandfather's estate. She was also a doctor, and, although she was a low-priced internist, she still made a lot more than I did.

Conceding to reality that Karen was here, I said, "What help do you want?" I was also, I had to admit, just a bit curious about what Karen was up to that would lead her back to my office.

"So, you'll do it?" It was just barely a query.

"Check ain't cleared yet." I put my feet up on the desk and leaned back, refusing to be budged by her haste. Karen wasn't giving me much time to think about my original problem—did I really need the money enough to get tangled up with her again? My only other case, Patrick, didn't appear to be a real money maker. I reached one of those pragmatic compromises with myself—to take the money. It would buy Karen the time I spent listening to her and my effort in figuring out who to palm her off on.

"Call my bank. They'll vouch that it's good."

"Like last time?"

"I paid you."

"Eventually. And under duress," I reminded her.

"Why don't we go to the bank right now? I'll give it to you in cash."

"Why don't you go and get the cash and come back here?"

"Because I don't want to be carrying five thousand dollars in cash on me."

"Oh? But it's all right if I do?" I retorted. "Thanks, but no thanks, Karen. I'll let you know when it's cleared," I finished, a clear dismissal.

To anyone but Karen. "Please, I really do need your help. I don't know who else to turn to," she pleaded, an almost real sound of desperation in her tone.

"All right, Karen," I cut in. "What's your problem?" I asked brusquely.

"I lent some money out."

"And you want me to get it back?"

"No, not really. I don't care about the money. Much."

"So what's the problem?"

"He wants more money."

"Say no, Karen. Just say no."

"I can't. I sort of…made a deal."

"Yes?" I prompted.

"He promised a very good return on my money. I just had to commit to a certain amount up front. And he has some collateral that I want back."

"Karen," I said as patiently as I could, "when you loan someone money, you don't give them collateral, they give you collateral."

"I know that. I'm out this money and I don't want to lose any more."

"Then maybe you should talk to your financial planner instead of me."

"I can't. It's all…a bit irregular."

"How irregular?" I demanded.

"Informal would be a better way to put it."

"How informal?"

"I met him through the friend of a friend one night."

"One night?"

"At a club."

"A bar?" I asked sarcastically.

"No, of course not. A very nice private club," Karen defended.

"Nice, huh?" As usual, it was going to be a struggle getting the truth out of Karen. I would, it appeared, earn the five thousand.

"Exclusive. Expensive. Only the right people go there."

"How could the 'right people' do you wrong?" I asked rhetorically, then continued, "How informal was this investment? Did you sign anything?"

"No."

"Did you agree to specific terms in front of witnesses?"

"No."

"Karen," I said, "you, of all people, would not pay me good money just to tell me that you made a bad and probably stupid loan. What do they have on you that makes you think you require my services?"

"Well," she hedged, "nothing. Really, I don't know."

I let her sit in silence for a few moments before repeating, "What do they have on you?"

Karen crossed her legs, then opened her purse, taking as long as she could to dig out her lighter and cigarettes. "Smoke?" she offered.

"I don't. And if you want to, you have to go outside. My cat's allergic."

"Oh." She stopped in mid-cigarette light. Then took as long to put them back into her purse as she had taking them out.

"So, what do they have that you want back?" I questioned again, looking pointedly at my watch to indicate that she was running out of time and I was running out of patience.

"A picture," was her less than elaborate answer.

"A picture? Rembrandt? Degas? Polaroid? Can we be a bit more specific?"

"Of me."

"Of you doing what?" I asked pointedly.

"I'd…rather not say. It's embarrassing."

"Uh-huh." Now we were getting down to it. "Let me indulge in some wild speculation. Is there any possibility you want me to get this picture back for you?"

"Yes, yes, that's it. You will help me, won't you?"

"You know, Karen," I replied, "it would be impossible for me to recover a picture if I didn't know what it was of."

She sat still, a slight furrow of her brow the only sign of all the mental squirming she was doing. "I'm with a woman," she finally conceded.

"Discussing Hannah Arendt's concept of the banality of evil, I'm sure."

"What?" Karen evidently didn't read much philosophy.

"What are you and this female person doing?"

"Kissing and, well…" She trailed off ever so coyly.

"Karen," I said, getting exasperated. "You don't work, so you can't get fired, and you own your own property, so you can't get evicted. It can't really hurt you if people find out that you kiss girls."

"That's sort of the problem," she replied softly.

"Sort of?"

"I thought she was nineteen."

"You what?" I demanded as I got the picture (pun intended). "How old is she?"

"Uh…sixteen. In a few weeks," Karen added sotto voce.

"Karen!" I said sternly, standing up. But I couldn't think of anyplace to go, so I sat back down again, scowling at her across my desk. "Literally a girl, huh?" I snarled. "I know you don't have any morals; but, tell me, do you even have a concept of what one might be?"

"Look, I met her in the club," Karen defended, ignoring my very pointed aspersion. "How could she have gotten in there if she wasn't over eighteen? She told me she was a college student. What was I supposed to do? Card her? Besides, she started it."

"How far did 'it'go?"

"As far…as it usually goes."

"You had sex with a fifteen-year-old?"

"It wasn't my idea. She did start it."

"How did she start it?"

"Want me to show you?" Karen offered.

"No, words only," I countered from behind the safety of my desk.

"She put her hand on my knee and told me she thought I was an attractive and intelligent woman. Then she suggested we go to one of the private rooms at the club. For when you really want to keep the riffraff out."

"Unless they have cameras," I observed.

"They didn't take my picture there," Karen told me. "Then she took off my bra and started sucking my tits and then I…"

"Karen," I cut in, "skip the prurient details. When did they take your picture?"

"Oh," she said, seeming to have enjoyed telling me the prurient details and disappointed that she was deprived of the chance. "We left the club and went to her place. They took a picture of us on her couch."

"In flagrante delicto?"

"Ah…yes. She had her shirt off and I was kissing her breasts."

"That's a big uh-uh in this state."

"Like a…felony?" Karen asked, a trace of fear edging into her voice. Her trust funds were tied to the lack of a criminal record.

"Yeah. Just for having sex with a woman. Let alone a minor."

"Oh." Then again, "Oh. Can you get the picture back?"

"No."

"Oh. But…what will I do?"

"Frankly, my dear, I don't give a damn." I couldn't resist.

"Damn it, Micky, help me," she burst out, truly scared that she might lose her trust funds. "I have to meet Joey tomorrow night. What am I going to do?"

"You do have a few options. For example, you could go to the police and tell them you're being blackmailed."

"No, I can't. If they see the photo, they would arrest me."

"Maybe. That leaves two other choices."

"Yes?"

"You could give Joey the money."

"What's the other choice?" Karen obviously didn't like that one.

"Call his bluff. It's not likely he'll go to the cops and admit he was blackmailing you. And if he does…hire a good lawyer. Hope they believe that you really were set up."

"Thanks," she said disgustedly. "Those aren't very good choices."

"They're the only ones you have as far as I'm concerned. I'm not going to risk a breaking-and-entering charge to save you from the consequences of pawing a fifteen-year-old."

"Damn it," she said in exasperation, reaching in her purse for her cigarettes, then catching herself and tossing them back down. "All right."

"All right what?" I prompted.

"I'll call his bluff. Will you go with me?"

"Do what?"

"Go with me tomorrow night. You should do something to earn your money."

"I have done something to earn my money. Getting a semblance of the truth out of you is a major achievement."

"Please, Micky. I'd feel a lot safer if you were there."

"Okay," I tersely agreed, less out of concern for her safety than to ensure she did the right thing. Not to mention that I couldn't come up with anyone to foist this off onto.

We sorted out where and when to meet, and Karen outlined the dress code for me so I would fit in with the "right" people. Then, with repeated iterations of how busy I was, I hustled her out of my office.

After giving Karen enough time to get safely out of my neighborhood, I headed out. A package slip was stuck on the door. The delivery man didn't even ring once. I got in my car, went to the bank machine, and deposited her check. I'd wasted my restful afternoon with Karen Holloway. I was not looking forward to tomorrow night. I've never hung around with the "right" people.

CHAPTER 2

The most unpleasant task of the Case of the Blond Bitch awaited me when I got back to my office—calling Cordelia to tell her I would be elsewhere on Friday night. I puttered around for a bit, delaying the disagreeable. Just as I was reaching for the phone to do my duty, it rang. "M. Knight Detective Agency," I answered automatically.

"Right. And I'm the attorney general." It was Danielle Clayton, one of my closest friends and an assistant district attorney for Orleans Parish. We had gone to college together, a black and a Cajun from the Pelican State, and, after moving back to the Big Easy, lived together. First as roommates, then as lovers. I broke us up, sleeping around on Danny. I knew love didn't last, and I had to prove it. Somehow, we had remained friends. I was twenty-two then. By the time I had turned thirty, last February, I had finally realized that perhaps love could have stayed, but Danny hadn't been waiting for me.

"Elly and I are joining you this weekend," she said. "I can't wait to see you sweating around Lake Pontchartrain." Elly was her lover. She and Danny had been together for close to three years.

Cordelia had a tradition of biking with friends along the lakefront. As I was now spending weekends with Cordelia, I was part of the party. I don't own a bike. Cordelia had offered to buy me one, but I was too proud to accept. I was also unwilling to spoil their fun by sitting bereft and bikeless. So I bought a cheap pair of running shoes and insisted I preferred jogging. I hate it. Some days I thought about breaking a leg just to get out of it.

"So how's Cordelia?" Danny asked, getting to her real point.

"She's fine."

"Good. Are you behaving?"

"Me? Absolutely."

"I can't believe you've lasted two whole months. And with someone like Cordelia," she finished.

"What's wrong with Cordelia?" I countered, although I knew Danny was commenting more on me than on Cordelia.

"Nothing's wrong with Cordelia," Danny responded. "I just don't want to see her get hurt." She didn't add "the way you hurt me."

"I know, Danno. But I'm not that person anymore. At least I hope not."

"No, but I've known you, what, twelve years, and you've only spent the last six months sober. It's an adjustment." Without pausing, she continued, "When are you moving in with her?" Danny had a lawyer-like ability to stick to the point she wanted to make.

"Live together?"

"Yeah. You know, same bed seven nights a week."

"She hasn't asked me yet," I replied. "And..."

"And?"

"There are a few practical problems to be worked out."

"Such as? You could ask her, you know."

"Such as, I don't think she'd want to move into my hovel, and I can't afford her place." I ignored Danny's second comment. There were any number of reasons for my not asking Cordelia to live with me, the most potent being that she might say no. The second most potent being that she might say yes.

"That's a pretty stupid argument," Danny said bluntly.

"Anyway, we're not at that point yet," I backed off.

"Just checking," Danny said amiably. "See you Saturday. I'm bringing a camera."

"Be sure and take pictures of all your bike wrecks." After we rang off, I put down the phone only long enough to get a dial tone, then I dialed Cordelia's office number.

"Cordelia James," she answered in her brisk professional manner.

"Hi, it's Micky."

"Hi. How are you?" The change in her tone made me smile.

"Fine. But I have some bad news. I have to work Friday night."

"But that's good."

"I won't be able to see you then."

"Then that is bad news, but I'm glad things are picking up for you."

"You're not upset?"

"No, of course not. I'll miss you, but we work around my schedule so much, turnabout's only fair."

"I guess. Do you want to set a time for Saturday?"

"You've got keys. Why don't you just come over when you're finished on Friday?"

"It might be late."

"Um. It was a thought," she replied distractedly, then paused. I waited, knowing she was going to say something more. "You know, Micky, it's okay if you just show up. That'd be…okay," she continued diffidently.

"Just show up?"

"Well…yeah. What's wrong with that?"

"I wouldn't want to disturb you. Or catch you…doing whatever."

"Whatever would I be doing?"

"I don't know. Scratching your ass or something."

Cordelia laughed. "Let's see. The worst thing I can imagine would be you showing up with the place a mess, cat litter unchanged, and…me sitting on the toilet reading some trashy lesbian novel. I'd survive that."

"I would hope so," I agreed, laughing at the image and admiring the ease with which she had conjured it up.

"What would I catch you at?" she asked cajolingly.

"You really want to know?" I stalled, thinking of too many things.

"Yeah."

I hesitated for a second, embarrassed at what came to mind. "Oh, hell. Jerking off," I finally admitted.

"You do that?"

"Don't you?" I asked, suddenly uneasy, wondering if I was revealing something.

"Of course," she answered easily.

"Oh, good. I thought I was perverted or something."

"My kind of pervert," she replied, then added, "I'd love to watch."

Desire suddenly appeared. Are we going to do this over the phone? I thought, aroused at the idea of her watching me. "Then I'll have to let you catch me sometime."

"On your back or on your stomach?"

"Both. Which do you prefer?"

"On your back," she murmured. "I think. I'm imagining both ways." Then, her voice low and intimate, she said, "I want you."

I felt a touch of slickness between my legs. "I'm wet," I acknowledged.

"I am, too, I think." Then she let out an embarrassed chuckle, saying, "I can't believe I'm really doing this on the phone. I used to be such a nice girl."

"Sorry. Didn't mean to get you going," I answered ruefully.

"I had a part in this, too, remember?" She continued, "Oh, hell, when am I going to see you? By the time I get finished with this meeting tonight, the best I could do is jump on you for some perfunctory… Okay, I'll be with you in a minute," she said to someone else. "Tomorrow?" she returned to me.

"I'm working. You'll be asleep when I'm finished."

"And I have the clinic Saturday morning. So, it's Saturday night, I guess," she said with a sigh.

"Looks that way. Until then, I guess we…"

"Don't get me thinking about that again," she cut in with a laugh.

"…take cold showers."

"Right." Then she paused. "It would be nice…if sometime…you have keys…if you were there when I got home." A tentativeness appeared, the diffidence she showed when she suggested something that she thought might make me uncomfortable. Perhaps because she had seen some of my moments of utter panic at the idea of intimacy, of finally really letting someone know me. She had, early on, casually handed me the keys to her apartment. My immediate reaction was to want to give them back and say, "You're a very nice woman, Cordelia James, but I'm not ready to have this kind of access to your life." I'd thanked her and put them in a desk drawer, wondering if I would ever use them. It took me over a week to get my keys duplicated, so I could give her a set in return.

"I will. Someday," I assured her, wanting to ease her uncertainty, but unwilling to commit myself. "When you least expect it."

"I'd…like that." Then her tone changed; someone was within earshot. "So let's plan on Saturday, then. I'll get back to you about the time."

"Okay," I answered. "Cordelia, I love you." I could say it, even if she couldn't without risking someone overhearing.

"I know." Then there was a moment's hesitation and, I realized, a decision made. "I love you, too. Talk to you soon."

We hung up. I wondered who had been listening to Cordelia and why she had decided it didn't matter if they overheard her. Reason told me it was because she'd looked up and seen it was Elly, who worked at the clinic. But something hinted at her wanting to acknowledge…me? That she loved someone? That acknowledgment deepened her commitment, a thought that both pleased and frightened me.

We were an odd coupling. "Unexpected" was the polite term people would use when they heard that we were together. When I first met Cordelia, handing her those tawdry pictures of Karen and me, I had resented her. She came from a world of privilege, surrounded by the comforts that money guarantees.

But Karen getting her brother disinherited went beyond a bizarre sibling rivalry into the kind of greed that doesn't look where it's going. Karen had gotten tangled up with some men for whom avarice was a mere venal sin. Karen getting the estate fit into their plans. Cordelia getting it didn't.

Greed and its attendant necessities are never pretty or neat. Barbara Selby, too, had become caught in the net, disposable flotsam. She worked for an export company that was shipping more than just Mardi Gras trinkets. The owner of the company wanted Grandfather Holloway's secluded estate so he could conduct his business there. Barbara saw too much to be left alive. We spent a long night together, tied up in a dirty basement. In the morning she had been shot, left to die. Though bruised and battered, I had escaped.

In the emergency room, Cordelia had seen to me. Rather than let me go home alone, she had taken me to her apartment. During that night, I realized that Cordelia was the rare person whose first instinct is to be kind, as if that's the way she sees the world.

When ruthless men decided to remove the obstacle that Cordelia had become, I led them away from her, forcing them to chase me into a swamp that had no intention of letting any of us escape. As we parted, I had kissed her and told her that I loved her.

Love has many levels and degrees. What I really meant was that I could love her if she would let me.

Cordelia acknowledged the connection that had grown between us, but was ambivalent about it. Danny was her friend and had told Cordelia about how I had treated her when we were lovers. I drank a lot, besides sleeping around on Danny. She had watched me repeat that pattern over and over again and was blunt in her opinion that a not very sober lesbian tomcat and a woman who had never had a one-night stand in her life didn't stand a chance of making it together.

Cordelia and I had parted, she said she needed time to think. I sobered myself up after she left me. I wanted her and I knew I had no chance if I didn't change. But I really did it for myself. I wanted to find out who I was and who I could be.

Several months later Cordelia had hired me as a private investigator. She had started her own clinic, using the estate money to do what she wanted to do, which was offer medical services to those bypassed by the for-profit care system. The clinic was getting threatening letters. She later admitted that one of the reasons that she had chosen me was to see if any connection between us remained. She was still unsure of what she wanted. Given what Danny, and others, had told her, she didn't trust that I really loved her. She was afraid to call me up and say let's go out, apprehensive that my desire for her was ephemeral, that she would reach out for it and it wouldn't be there. She thought of herself as the "best friend," a "nice girl," a woman who watched passion from a distance. In hiring me, Cordelia had settled for the safe boundaries of a professional relationship.

I was still in love with her, but I couldn't imagine what nice, respectable, Cordelia James would want with bayou trash like me. We did an awkward dance, her shyness, my insecurities, always stumbling over one or the other. Finally, my ability to speak without thinking of the consequences found a use. I managed to blurt out that I wanted more than just friendship, before my terror silenced me. That was less than three months ago. I looked out the window, noting that the light had changed, giving the first hint of the turning season. We had first met in winter, become lovers in summer, and now it was barely fall.

It was time to get back to business, of a sort. I called my cousin, Torbin.

"Answer the phone, Torbin Robedeaux," I told his answering machine, knowing that he was probably in. He was actually one of many cousins, but he and I were both queer, the lavender sheep of the family. He was now a very popular drag act in the French Quarter. For me, he was the only family member I felt I could rely on. Enough times to have made me ashamed, Torbin had hauled me home after a long night in the bars. I knew a couple of his uptown friends had questioned his bothering with a drunken dyke. Torbin had just shrugged and said, "That lavender blood runs thick." His only comment to me would be, "You might think about this," a few days later. But I hadn't wanted to think about my drinking and sleeping around, so I had ignored Torbin.

"Come on," I said into the phone, "get your fat ass out of bed."

"I do not have a fat ass." Torbin couldn't resist the bait.

"Stay in bed all day and you will."

"I work nights, remember? And speaking of staying in bed, I hear you've been racking up time on someone's mattress."

"Vicious lies," I bantered. "It was under the kitchen table."

"Too busy to call me up with the glorious news, I notice. So when do I get to meet this paragon of earthly delights?"

"When you can behave."

"Ah-ah. You have to set a time before we can discuss what it is that you want to borrow this go-around."

"I don't know, Tor. It's kind of…new right now."

"I'll bet it is. Micky, dear, darling, dyke cousin of mine, I love you immensely, but you have single-handedly kept me in confusion about what it is lesbians really want. I've always heard you girls desire a significant other and two cats at the fireside to be happy, but you've always confounded those notions totally. However, I guess even the mighty fall. Do I hear the crackling of a fire and the mewling of kittens in the background?"

"Hell, Torbin, I don't know," I replied, uncharacteristically flustered by his blather.

"Let's break it down. Has it gone beyond the 'Don't-talk-to-me-just-fuck-me' stage?"

"Torbin," I cautioned.

"Has it?" he persisted.

"Of course. Sort of."

"On to the real four-letter-word stage?"

"Which is?"

"Love."

"Oh, that."

"Well?" he insisted.

"Yes. I'm in love with her," I admitted.

"Oh, Micky," Torbin said, unexpectedly serious. "I've watched you chase shadows for so long. I hope this one's real."

"Yeah, Tor, me, too," I replied, caught unprepared for his sobriety. "I just…I don't know."

"As you well know, I have regretted many things in my life and add more daily, but I have never regretted walking over to that skinny boy with glasses and saying, 'Excuse me, but if I press this button, will it blow up?' And, if you can believe your old cousin Tor, it's been over five years now and it just gets better. There, that's my glorious love speech," Torbin said, then continued, "So when do I meet her?"

"Well, you saw her at Emma Auerbach's party last May. The tall one."

"The real tall one? Titian-haired, blue eyes to die for?"

"That's the one."

"Um. So when?"

"She has a very busy schedule…"

"I can serve breakfast in bed, if need be."

"Why don't you and Andy bike along the lake starting around two-ish on Saturday."

"I love spontaneous prearranged dates. When did you get a bike?"

"I don't have one. I jog."

"You hate jogging. Beyond hate, you abhor it."

"I know. But don't tell her that."

"Tut-tut. Deception so early."

"She offered to buy me a bike," I explained.

"So?" Torbin didn't get it.

"She's rich," I clarified.

"Still, so? When is that ever a problem?"

"I can't have her paying my way all the time."

"Why not?" Torbin asked, still not understanding. "If she can afford it?"

"It would compromise my independence."

"Oh, so that's it. In that case, I wish Andy would do a better job of compromising my independence. He's compromised everything else. Not that Andrew boy can't make money. He just has such enormous equipment needs. Don't even think it. You know I meant computers, dear. I am more than adequate below the waist."

"So you say. I'm no judge of it."

"Okay. So it's set. I will meet this good-looking, very tall, rich woman on Saturday. She and I will spend some time whizzing about on bikes, while you sweat, turn red, and jostle your guts to the point of puking. I am truly looking forward to it."

I was finally able to steer Torbin around to the real point of my call—my need to borrow something to wear to meet the "right" people in. He and I were close enough to the same size that this exchange usually worked.

"The Sans Pareil Club? My, my," he clucked when he heard my destination.

"Nulli secundus."

"Don't flaunt your education, Miss Mick. How about a little strapless thing?"

I insisted on sedate, and, after our usual haggling ("Don't come to a drag queen if you insist on sensible shoes"), Torbin made me an acceptable offer and a time to come by for it on Friday afternoon.

After that I would have closed up shop for the day and gone home if I hadn't already been there.

CHAPTER 3

High heels in the rain are enough to make me confess to murder. That I was wearing them at Karen Holloway's behest only put me in the mood to commit a murder so that I might confess it. She was late, of course. She hadn't wanted to come all the way downtown to get me, so we had agreed to meet on Canal Street. ("The nice part," Karen had insisted, "Near Saks.") I finally caught sight of her red BMW nosing through traffic. I stayed under my scanty shelter, pretending I didn't see her until she got a few well-deserved honks.

"Sorry I'm late," she apologized as I slid into the front seat.

I brushed some of the water out of my hair, hoping it would spot her leather interior and muttered, "Whoever said, 'Better late than never'?"

"What?"

"Never mind."

We headed uptown to the club. It annoyed me no end that Karen was an excellent driver, skillfully maneuvering through the slick streets and the insanity that rain inspires in this town.

"I don't think Joey will be there until later," Karen said. "I didn't have time to call you," she lied.

"What a busy life you lead."

"I could cook something at my place, a nice, quiet dinner."

"You cook? You're not paying me enough for that kind of risk."

"I can cook. We summered in France, and Mama," the accent was on the second syllable, "insisted I learn."

"I'm not hungry," I informed her.

"You don't like me," Karen very perceptibly noted. "Why?"

"To begin, you're a shallow, vain, greedy, hypocritical, self-centered woman. Shall I go on?"

"Why must you always be funny?" Karen asked, attempting to save face.

She turned into the entrance to the Sans Pareil Club, a long drive overhung with picture-perfect live oaks draped with Spanish moss. The club oozed aristocratic presumptions—lofty white columns twined with perfectly clipped ivy and an entrance ablaze through leaded crystal. Two doormen with oversized umbrellas were instantly upon the car, escorting us safely through the torrent.

"Even with your money, can you afford this?" I asked Karen as we walked down the oak-panelled foyer.

"I don't know. Fortunately, I've never had to find out. I'm paid for. Anthony Colombé."

"Why?" I recognized the name, although I had never seen the man. The sights of such Olympic gods were not meant for rabble like myself.

"Why do you think?" she answered, as we waited for the maître d' to attend to us.

"Sex?"

"The illusion of it. We have similar interests. He likes boys and I like girls. There are no messy expectations on my part."

"Like a straight woman might have."

Karen nodded as the maître d' led us to our seats. It was all very swank, plush royal blue and gleaming brass, real crystal chandeliers with antique gas wall sconces to give the club a warm, rich (very rich) glow.

After we were seated, Karen said, "They have an excellent wine list here. Would you care to see it?"

"I'm not drinking."

"Something other than wine? Scotch?"

"I'll have a club soda, thank you," was my terse reply.

A sommelier came by, but Karen waved him away impatiently.

"What would it cost," Karen asked disdainfully, "for you to be nice to me?"

"A lot."

She nodded slowly, then ordered our drinks from a tuxedoed waiter, giving me a cool, appraising look as she did.

"What would it cost to get you to spend the night with me?" She lit a cigarette, waiting for my answer.

"A lot more."

"Fifty?" she asked.

It took me a second or two to realize she didn't mean fifty dollars. I shook my head, trying not to think what fifty thousand dollars could buy. Then telling myself it didn't matter, because Karen had no intention of paying fifty thousand to have sex with me.

"Seventy?" she persisted.

"Let's not play this game," I answered.

The waiter brought our drinks.

Karen took a sip of her Scotch before saying, "Why not? You could use the money, couldn't you?"

"Most people could use that kind of money," I answered. "If they got it, that is."

"What if you did? Interested?"

I hesitated, then shook my head no.

"I'd forgotten what a noble character you are. Can't buy Micky Knight," Karen said condescendingly.

"No, you can't."

"So for five thousand dollars you'll sit here all night and let everyone in this place assume we're sleeping together, but for seventy thousand dollars you won't really do it? Why? What the hell's the difference?"

"About sixty-five thousand. And my integrity."

"Well, let's hear it for all the 'noble' people in the world." She took a belt of Scotch. Karen shook her head and sighed. "You're as bad as my cousin. The altruistic doctor."

"Altruism has its benefits. She did get your grandfather's fortune."

Karen shot me a glance. "Oh, that's right. You've met her. I suppose she's the type you would sleep with. Even though she's…" Karen remarked sourly, her expression indicating what she thought.

"She's…?" I gathered Cordelia hadn't told Karen about us yet. To my knowledge they had not seen each other since we'd become lovers.

"You know—straightlaced. Ever so moral. Sort of…quaint," Karen finished.

"Yeah, I'd sleep with her," I answered. "For free," I baited her.

Karen gave me an annoyed look. "Why?" she countered. "She's not that good-looking."

"I respect Cordelia," I said slowly and distinctly.

Karen got the comparison. And I saw the flicker of a genuine emotion cross her brow—shame, but it was something.

She recovered quickly, though. "I'll pass along her good fortune. Should I give her your phone number?"

"Why don't you?" I replied smoothly, enjoying Karen's discomfort.

Karen made no answer, taking a drink of Scotch, then lighting a cigarette. We sat in silence for a while. She ordered another round, although I had plenty of club soda left. At some point, Karen reinstalled idle chatter, pointing out prominent names among the "right people." I replied with cool but polite answers.

A woman I recognized from the society pages wiggled in beside

Karen. She was a Mrs. Martin Essex Vandersnide Higglesworth III type, preserved and packed in by plastic surgery and private aerobics classes.

"Karen, darling, how divine to see you," she oozed, taking Karen's head between her hands and forcing a lip-to-lip kiss.

While Karen introduced us, Mrs. Whoever-the-III, fixed Karen's cleavage with the look a hungry python might have given a baby lamb. To be fair, Karen was showing a lot of it. But I had to give her a few points for panache. She gave Mrs. Mansion-on-St.-Charles-Avenue a very gracious smile, murmured some chatty and polite drivel, then casually reached across the table, took my hand, and told Mrs. Van-Very-Rich that she had other plans for the evening. Mrs. The-III looked at me, a direct glance like I was some object to be appraised and her appraisal was very low. She didn't have the aplomb to return Karen's radiant smile or even hide her distaste. She wiggled her way out of our booth and went off in search of other sexual prey.

Karen held my hand for a moment longer, then, rather than allow me to snatch it away, let go.

Variations of this little scene were repeated several times. Karen, it appeared, was a sought-after (and lusted-after) woman. Not all of the would-be suitors were as repulsive as Mrs. Wigglesworthless III. Some, in fact, were quite handsome and personable, of both sexes. Karen had, it seemed, gotten the fabled family charm. It's galling to have someone you want to hate have a few saving graces.

Then a man in a very expensive suit joined us. He wasn't handsome in the strict sense, but his looks and clothes were the best money could buy, his glossy brown hair combed straight back and perfectly in place. His skin was pale, from days of sleeping and nights of partying. He reminded me of a sleek racing dog, his face narrow, his build lithe and compact, his clothes fit perfectly, but his eyes glittered with a nervous watchfulness as if he were ready and waiting for the starter's gun.

"Joey," Karen greeted him, giving him the standard hello kiss.

After the usual pleasantries, he suggested adjourning to a back room. Karen took my arm as we followed him to one of a series of posh private rooms.

I wondered if Joey was carrying a gun and braced myself for something that would be, at best, unpleasant. Karen licked her lips distractedly, then catching herself, redid her lipstick as if she had planned it.

"First of all," Joey began with an easy smile, "I want to thank you for your loan. It saved us all a considerable amount of inconvenience. Now," he continued, placing an expensive leather briefcase on the table, "the only thing left to do is pay you back."

With that he opened the briefcase. It contained some papers, notepads, pens. And more than a few stacks of one hundred dollar bills. So much for unpleasantness.

"I owe you seventy thousand, right?" he said and began counting out the hundreds in piles of ten.

I stood transfixed as the money piled up. I knew that Cordelia was worth considerably more, but her wealth was abstract; this was very real.

Joey actually counted out seventy thousand dollars in one hundred bills. Karen looked from the money to him, then to me. I just looked at the money.

"That's it," he said, his elegant smile still firmly in place. "You can take it now and say good-bye. However, there's a lot more money to be made here."

Karen nodded, looked at me again, then said, "Let me discuss it with my associate. Could you wait outside for a moment?"

"No problem," he still smiled. "Counting's thirsty work. Can I get you ladies anything?"

Karen demurred for both of us. Then Joey disappeared, leaving me alone with Karen and the money. She walked slowly around the table until she was facing me.

"How about it?" Karen asked seductively. "Seventy thousand dollars in cash." She looked at me calmly, daring me to refuse.

She was, I noticed, wearing a very expensive and subtle perfume. I glanced at the money, then back to her, aware of how close she was standing, her breasts under mine, almost touching. One night. Karen was far from unattractive. I also had to admit, not that I liked to, that during our earlier encounter she had been a skilled and attentive lover, even if it was all just part of the performance.

She put her arms around my neck. One night.

I would be seeing Cordelia tomorrow, I suddenly realized. And myself in the mirror later tonight. I gently removed Karen's arms from around my neck.

"Sorry, Karen, I guess my self-respect has a much higher price than anything you can come up with." I stepped away from her.

"Damn you," she hissed, furious at my rejection. Then she stalked out of the room. I was probably one of the few shopping challenges left her.

After a few minutes she returned, smiling and laughing with Joey.

"I'm so glad you've decided to reinvest," I heard him say as they entered.

"It seemed the only logical thing to do. I am, after all, a capitalist at heart," she laughed. I noticed her tucking a small, picture-sized envelope in her clutch purse.

"So, why don't we plan to meet here again next month, around the same time," he suggested as he put the money back in his briefcase.

"That'd be fine," Karen purred, acting like nothing in the world could go wrong.

We returned to the main part of the club. Karen bid Joey farewell, and, after the obligatory air kiss, she turned to me and said, "Shall we?"

I nodded agreement. She took my arm, daring me to protest, asserting some small claim to my services for this evening.

"I can call a cab," I said as we moved down the entryway.

"They don't allow cabs here," Karen retorted. Mere cabs.

Her car was waiting for us as if it had never been moved. Again the two doormen escorted us efficiently and unobtrusively to its doors.

"I'll take you home," Karen said as we left the wrought iron portals of the Sans Pareil.

"That's not necessary."

"No, it's not." But she didn't stop, instead swiftly maneuvering through the sparse traffic, heading downtown.

I took my watch out of her glove compartment where she'd insisted I hide its less than fashionable face from the "right people." A little past three in the morning. My legs were already aching from the idea of jogging tomorrow.

"Are you involved with someone?" Karen asked abruptly.

I wondered what she'd do if I asked her to drop me off at Cordelia's. But I hadn't brought her extra set of keys and I knew she would be asleep by this hour.

"Yes. I would have turned you down anyway."

"No doubt," Karen replied. "Is she…attractive?"

"Very."

Karen didn't seem to need any directions to my apartment, so I didn't give her any.

"Of course. And a kind, generous, respectable sort, needless to say."

"Yes, that, too."

Karen stopped in front of my place.

"And good in bed, of course," she said, not really seeking an answer.

"Very good." I opened the door of her car. "Good night, Karen."

"'Night, Micky," Karen replied politely. Then she said, "Interested in next month?"

"For your meeting with Joey? Why? To watch him count out even more money? Will you get the negatives back next time?"

"I got everything this time. Joey said it was all a mistake."

"A mistake? On his part or yours?" If Joey gave Karen the picture back, it meant that he didn't need it anymore. Maybe he realized that Karen's greed didn't require that kind of coercion.

"Will you go with me? It's another easy five grand."

I was suddenly curious about something. "Karen, how much was your initial amount?"

"Fifty," she answered casually.

"A month ago?"

She nodded. "Will you go with me? You're very good at helping me avoid unwanted advances."

"What? Imitation sex for you, too? You front for Colombé, I front for you? Nothing real. A rather sordid façade, don't you think?"

Her jaw clenched for a moment, then she retorted, "I can get the real thing whenever I want it. For free."

"Call me next month. I might be available. And stick to women over twenty-one."

I got out of her car, turning my back as Karen squealed away in the night.

Nothing I could think of would earn that kind of money that quickly. I would have to find out what it was, I sighed as I climbed my stairs. Not just for my curiosity's sake (and I was pretty curious), but because if it involved Karen, it might involve Cordelia.

I went to bed praying for rain.

CHAPTER 4

The sun was shining brightly when the phone rudely pulled me from my slumbers. "Yeah?" I rasped out, my throat still clogged from the late night and its smoky atmosphere.

"Good morning. How are you?" Cordelia replied cheerily. "Did I wake you?"

"What time is it?" I mumbled grouchily.

"Oops, guess I did. It's ten-thirty."

I grunted. As politely as I could, mind you. I hadn't been in bed with the lights out until after four. And had lain awake until dawn's early light wondering just what I'd gotten involved in and what I was going to do about it.

"I just wanted to arrange today," Cordelia continued. "Why don't you go back to bed? I'll load my bike and come by and get you. Say around one-thirty?"

"Yeah, that's fine," I replied, not yet awake. I went back to bed, trying to take Cordelia's advice. Then got up to set the alarm clock so I wouldn't oversleep. I set the clock for noon, then lay back down. But didn't fall asleep; instead I alternated between worrying about what Karen was up to and wondering what Torbin would say to Cordelia. And then worrying that she might find him too—well, you know, flamboyant. Somewhere in all this worry, I realized that if I did ever fall back asleep it would be so close to the time I had to get up as to be useless.

Conceding reality, I got up and took my shower, washing off all the "right" odors from last night. My drying off was rudely interrupted by my alarm clock going off. My progress to turn off my alarm clock was rudely interrupted by a cat who wanted to test the lengths to which I would go not to step on her and break her back. It was, I thought as I finally slapped off my alarm clock, shaping up to be a very rude day.

I got dressed, left, and walked purposefully to the Quarter to meet

Cordelia at her place. If she picked me up, she wouldn't be able to leave her bike unattended to come up and give me the hug and kiss I wanted. And deserved.

I scanned Ursulines for her car, but didn't see it, then rang her buzzer in case she had ended up in the parking garage. However, it appeared that the most likely possibility, her not being here yet, was the case.

Saturday afternoon in the Quarter is prime tourist time. I loitered at Cordelia's doorstep trying to look like I wasn't some miscreant, but merely a pinko communist queer. You could have brought her keys and spared yourself this, I thought, as the third hetero couple in a row walked by me, kissing and cooing, flaunting their sexuality.

I wondered why I hadn't. I was harried and in a hurry, I told myself. And I couldn't just arbitrarily change plans and surprise her on her living room couch, I rationalized.

It took me a couple of seconds to realize that the car that had just pulled up in front of me was hers. I wasn't used to her in her new burgundy car. Cordelia is tall, a little taller than me. She is also three years older. She still retains some of that awkwardness that women who are too tall, too big sometimes have. Her eyes were a deep blue, at times shading into blue-gray, always clear and purposeful. Her hair was a rich auburn; at a distance it could look almost black. She kept it in a practical short cut, as if saying she knew she couldn't be beautiful, but she could be smart and hardworking. At times I tried to tell her how strikingly handsome I found her, but she usually laughed it off with a comment about how lovers are supposed to feel that way.

"Hi," Cordelia said as she got out. "This is a surprise."

"I couldn't get back to sleep. I thought I'd help you load your bike."

"Sorry. I'm glad to see you, though." She smiled at me, then turned and opened the gate into the courtyard. I followed her, glad to be away from the prying eyes of the tourists. There are some things you can't hide. Like the happy way I had to be smiling back at her. Okay, also lust.

She led the way up the stairs. Nice ass, I thought for the umpteenth time as I followed it closely. Cordelia lived in one of the old Quarter buildings, with a courtyard hidden behind wrought iron gates. An inner balcony circled it, leading to the apartments. Hers was a comfortable two-bedroom on the second floor, overlooking the street.

"You're quiet," she said as she opened the door.

"Thinking."

"About?"

"Your ass," I answered as I shut the door, making it safe to voice my preoccupation.

"And here I thought it was something profound," she said with a self-deprecating laugh.

"Ms. James, how can you doubt the profanity of my thoughts?" I asked.

"Very easily," she replied as she started taking off her clothes. "Where is my helmet?" she asked distractedly. "Could you look in the other room?"

"Not until you at least kiss me hello," I insisted. Then immediately wondered at my presumption. What if she said, "Not now," or any of the other minor rejections?

She looked at me for a moment as if deciding between me and finding her helmet, then reached out and grabbed my wrists, pulling me to her. "I'll kiss you all right." She did.

"What time are we meeting…whoever it is we're meeting?" I asked a few minutes later.

"There's not time," Cordelia replied, answering the question I had really asked. "I'd be late. Or not even show up, but Joanne and I are planning Alex's birthday party while Danny and Elly keep her busy." Alex was Joanne's lover.

"Damn," I muttered. "There's a marvelous new invention. It's called a telephone."

Cordelia laughed, gave me one more quick kiss and pulled away. "Come on. Help me find my helmet. Yes, I know about phones, but Joanne and I are both too caught up at work to do any serious planning. And I can't call her at home, not with Alex there." Joanne Ranson was a detective sergeant in the NOPD and usually very busy at work.

"I guess," I answered, feeling less like jogging then ever. (Particularly my thighs.)

"But," Cordelia said, as she threw on a T-shirt suitable for biking, "tonight, when we're alone, I am going to…"

The phone rang. So much for marvelous. Cordelia answered it. "Hello?…Oh, hi, how are you?…She's here…Emma says hello," Cordelia said to me. Then a series of uh-huhs, as Emma explained whatever it was she was calling about. "Tonight?…You really think I should?…Okay…" I made a face. Cordelia gave a helpless shrug. "Micky'll be devastated—"

"I will not," I interjected. Just highly disappointed. I went to find Cordelia's helmet while she finished up.

"Sorry," Cordelia said as she joined me. "I hate to do this to you but…Emma thinks—and I agree—that the more endowed the clinic is at this point the better. With the new building on the drawing board and…"

Emma Auerbach was the chair of the clinic's board of directors and one of its chief supporters.

"You don't need to explain to me." I waved her off. "Remember, I've been hearing your plans and hopes for a while now."

"Anyway," she continued, "Emma has some moneyed types who are interested and probably good for a couple hundred thousand a piece—do I sound crass?—and she wants me to meet them."

"Lucky you," I said, tossing her her helmet. She threw it back at me to look for her shorts.

"I don't like the political stuff. I don't...I'm not very good at it. Emma helps a lot, she has such social grace." Cordelia found her shorts and put them on. "I hope you know I'd really rather be here with you. And..."

"Cordelia, if you spend all afternoon apologizing, you'll never get Alex's party planned. And that'll only make you feel worse," I cut in.

"You're right," she said with a rueful half-smile. "I just wish...I could do the right thing for everyone. Oh, boy, we're late, aren't we," she finished with a hurried look at her watch.

I picked up her bike rack and my duffel bag with my oh so beloved running shoes, while Cordelia managed her bike and gear. After locking up, we headed down to put the bike on her car.

"Lakeward-ho. Let's not be late or Danny will make tacky jokes about the sex we didn't have," I commented as I got in her car.

We headed off, Cordelia to the bliss of bicycling and me to the joylessness of jogging.

"You know," she said as we got caught at a light, "I wish you could go with me. I'm tired of...I don't know. Pretense, denial. I'm not...Don't even think that I wouldn't be proud to be seen with you. Anywhere." She looked at me, then back to traffic as the light changed.

"No, I don't," I answered quickly.

"I do mean that."

"How about your mother?" I asked. "Would you be proud of me in front of her?"

"How about your father?" Cordelia asked.

That stopped me short. "Touché," I replied, realizing I had an answer but not one I was sure was honest. My dad had been a wonderful, kind, understanding man. Who had grown up in a small town out in bayou country and, after the Second World War, gone back there to live. He had died when I was ten, and there was a tremendous gap between my bucolic childhood and the life I now lived. I wondered if he could have actually bridged it or if I just wanted to believe he could.

"I'm sorry," Cordelia said. "That wasn't fair. I have no problem taking you home to meet Mom. She suggested to me that I was a lesbian even before I knew I was."

"Now that I think about it, Aunt Greta suggested that I was a lesbian before I knew I was."

"Really?" Cordelia said, very surprised. She had met my Aunt Greta.

"Yeah. She knew there was something wrong with me, she just didn't know what. I think being queer exceeded her wildest expectations."

"That must have been so hard for you, living in that house. Sometimes I think the self-righteous do more harm than any other sinners."

"I've always favored the hypocrites myself. Those and…the betrayers. Those who violate trust."

"Isn't that what your aunt did?" she asked softly.

"No, not Aunt Greta. I never trusted her," I commented with a derisive laugh.

"Who betrayed you, then?"

"No one. I meant in general. Hey, isn't that Danny's car up there?"

"Looks like it," Cordelia agreed.

"They seem to be holding hands," Cordelia said.

"Elly's head is above seat level, they can't be doing much else," I commented.

"Not in this traffic. It might be dangerous to even hold hands in this mess."

"For two women, you mean."

"Well, yeah. There are certain things we can't take for granted."

"Like being adults in our thirties and not able to hold hands on a Saturday afternoon," I replied sarcastically.

"I don't like it."

"Proud, huh?" I nettled, a bit peeved by her slight rebuff.

"I can't fight all the battles all the time," she replied quietly.

"Holding hands in a car is one of the big ones, I must admit."

Cordelia gave me a look that was partly exasperated and partly challenging, but the light changed and she had to shift again, then again to get up to speed.

"You know, Micky," she said slowly and thoughtfully, "If those people I'm going to meet tonight knew I slept with women, they wouldn't give me a penny."

I turned sharply around to scan the road. "Nope. Not a Rolls in sight.

The snootiest car visible is a Cadillac. And it's not even this year's model. I don't think they're watching you right now."

"Oh, I get it. You're testing my limits: Do I love you enough to hold your hand on the way to the lake?"

"Don't psychoanalyze me," I retorted.

"But, Micky, it's so tempting," Cordelia replied, smiling at me to signal the end of the dispute.

"Never get involved with a thoroughly neurotic person."

We stopped at another light. I glanced at Cordelia, she was leaning toward me. She took my face between her hands and kissed me on the lips, leaving me surprised and flustered, not to mention suddenly paranoid about who was in the car next to us.

"Now, why do you think I'm thoroughly neurotic?" Cordelia asked me as we started again.

"Not you. Me. Of course. Now I'm the one worried about the people around us. Isn't that a 'Kill A Commie Queer for Lent' bumper sticker up there?"

"No. 'Save Our Lake,' and it's on Danny's car. I did think you meant me. That I'm being neurotic about being out."

"No, you're being reasonable. I don't have much to lose. I work for myself. My landlord knows I'm gay and isn't going to kick me out, because she knows there aren't that many people foolish enough to live there anyway. And I'm not...well, my social stratum is Gertie's bar. I don't get frequent invitations to meet moneyed people."

"I don't want them. You know this is because Emma is doing her best to help me and the clinic." Cordelia continued, "Are you upset about tonight? I could cancel."

"No," I replied. "Don't cancel. Maybe I'm a little upset, but you're right, the bigotry is there. Losing the funding to the orphaned children's wing is not worth holding my hand on Elysian Fields. And I will try not to put any more asinine tests in your way today."

Cordelia followed Danny's car as it turned into the parking area. Alex and Joanne were already there with their bikes. After a round of hellos, I set myself to the unpleasant task of putting on my jogging shoes.

"Michele, dear, it's so good to see you. And so unexpected, too," Torbin's voice rang across the parking lot. He didn't waste any time. "How do you do. I'm Torbin Robedeaux," he said as he walked directly to Cordelia. "You must be the woman who's keeping the Crescent City rumor mills ablaze. You can't imagine how tongues are wagging with questions concerning the woman who has finally taken Micky Knight out of circulation."

"Torbin," I threatened.

He ignored me. "Hearts have been broken from Texas to Florida. The president should declare it a national disaster area, but he doesn't dare admit there are that many lesbians out there."

"Torbin," I threatened again.

Torbin continued, "And this is my significant other of a significant number of years, Andrew Beaumont."

"How do you do?" Cordelia replied as she shook their hands. "Biking on the lake?"

"Yes, what a coincidence," Torbin answered. "You and I must pedal together for a bit and exchange pertinent information. I know a few interesting tidbits about your amour."

Danny came up to say hello to Torbin, and then Joanne, Alex, and Elly were introduced. As the lucky non-joggers prepared, I got just a moment to grab Torbin's arm and mutter, "Behave."

"Not on your life," he answered and they were off.

I watched them as they pedaled away, Torbin riding abreast with Cordelia. She was nodding her head to something he was saying. Then a line of trees hid them from my view.

A marathon or two later, I looked at my watch and realized it must have stopped. Not enough time had passed for my stomach to feel like it had loosened all its moorings.

As I was slowing, I noticed Joanne riding back in my direction. But instead of passing by as I had expected, she turned and rode beside me.

"I wanted to talk to you about Alex's birthday," she said, slowing to my speed. Joanne is in her late thirties, her hair marked by gray, the lines at her eyes and nose permanently etched into her face. Her aviator-style glasses masked her constantly observing eyes. She had an intensity that I found both compelling and forbidding. That attraction had flared into an affair, but not one that could last, caught as we were between our barely controlled tempers. Now we were trying to find our way back into friendship.

"Uh-huh," I panted in response to her.

"It's going to be a night on the town for all of us."

The only response I could manage was a grunt.

"Cordelia's paying for most of it," Joanne continued, oblivious to my discomfort. "And I know you can be persnickety about that."

I stopped. Clearly we needed to have more than a one-sided conversation. Joanne looped back to me.

"Now, what," I gasped, "is that," another breath, "supposed to mean?"

She stopped and dismounted her bike.

"And who the hell," I continued, having taken a few breaths in the interval, "told you I was 'persnickety'?"

"Alex. Via Cordelia."

"Great, so Cordelia's discussing our disagreements with the whole world?"

"Calm down, Mick," Joanne said. "Alex and Cordelia are close friends. They're going to discuss us. Come on, let's walk. I don't want to stand here and cool down."

"I don't like this, I feel used," I said as we started walking.

"Get over it. There are always little adjustments. This is one," Joanne said bluntly, obviously not in one of her more charitable moods. I liked Joanne, on some level even loved her, but not for the gentility of her temper. "Alex's birthday. Be there and behave."

"Don't order me about."

"Take it as a request, then. This matters to me, Mick," Joanne told me. She looked directly at me. "Alex is taking this birthday hard. I want her to have a great time."

"Okay, Joanne," I relented. "I'll be a good girl."

"Thanks," she said, giving me one of her rare smiles. Then she got on her bike and headed off again.

I faked jogging until she was out of sight, then slowed, trying to figure out whether I should be annoyed because of Joanne's lecturing me, angry because of Cordelia passing along things that I felt should be just between us, or vaguely pleased that Joanne thought my presence could be that important at Alex's party.

Despite my slowed pace, sweat was running off my nose and into my eyes, finally deciding the battle on the annoyed and angry side. Nor was my budding foul mood assuaged by my bicycling buddies returning a good half an hour later than expected, leaving me sitting on the hood of Cordelia's car, locked away from my towel and water bottle.

They were laughing and having a good time, Torbin and Andy still with them. Danny took it onto herself to enlighten me as to what a wonderful time they had. They were late because Torbin had been so funny, yadda, yadda, yadda. I nodded and grunted ever so politely.

"I'm sorry," Cordelia said as she finally tore herself away from some hilarious story Torbin was telling. "I didn't mean to strand you here."

I shrugged noncommittally.

"Are you okay?" she asked.

"Me? Oh, I'm fine," I answered, shrugging yet again.

She started to say something else, but was interrupted by Torbin.

"Is it a quarter to seven or eight?" he asked.

"To seven," Cordelia answered. "We're supposed to be there at seven."

"Tonight?" I questioned, looking from Torbin to Cordelia.

"Yes, tonight," Torbin informed me. "I could hardly enlighten the delightful Dr. James about all your foibles on a mere bike trip. Ergo, I'm doing my John Wayne imitation, well, perhaps, Noel Coward, and escorting Cordelia tonight."

Cordelia gave me a slight smile and a shrug.

"I must be off," Torbin continued. "Shower, shave, and all that good stuff. The hard part, of course, will be finding all those boy things to wear." Torbin gave me a quick kiss, then hastened off to help Andy put their bikes on his car.

"Are you upset?" Cordelia asked.

"Me? No. Why should I be upset?"

"I don't know. You seem upset."

We were interrupted by good-byes from Danny and Elly.

"I need to get showered and changed for the ordeal tonight," Cordelia said with a rueful smile.

I nodded as I waited by the passenger door for her to open it.

"I think I'm tired," I said to explain my shortness.

"I guess you're surprised about Torbin going with me," Cordelia said. "Do you think I'm a hypocrite?" she asked abruptly.

"No. Do you?"

"Maybe. I feel…disloyal. I should take you and damn them all."

"I don't know. I don't know what the hell the answer is," I replied quietly.

"Torbin reminds me of you."

"How?" I asked, surprised. "Torbin's a good-looking blond. With blue eyes."

"Not physically. But your, I guess, sensibility. And I can talk to him about you."

"Yes?" I inquired sarcastically.

"Not like that. I mean, admit that…well…we're lovers. And he's a safeguard against the thing I hate most about these kinds of parties—unwanted male attention. I won't end up by myself in the corner. I can be… quite inept socially."

"It's okay," I said, reaching over and hooking my hand in her pocket. "I suppose if you're not going to be with me, I prefer you be with Torbin. I can be sure he doesn't have any lascivious designs on you."

"Thanks," she said, smiling at me. She covered my hand with hers. "Will you…will I see you tonight? I'll try not to be too late."

"You'll see me," I reassured her.

Cordelia let go of my hand for a moment to shift. "Next car I get will be an automatic," she told me as she took my hand again.

As we drove into the French Quarter Cordelia asked, "Can I stick you with taking my bike and stuff up while I park the car?"

"Sure," I replied. "But you'll have to give me your keys."

She nodded, but didn't say anything. We pulled in front of her apartment. She took two keys off her key ring and handed them to me. It took me a little juggling but I managed to get the bike, et cetera, upstairs in one trip. I had just gotten them in their proper places when Cordelia arrived.

She glanced at her watch, sighed, and, with a quick smile in my direction, headed for the shower. She emerged several minutes later, with a towel wrapped around her and that distracted look she got when she was rushed and late.

"The royal blue," I advised.

"You think?" she asked, taking the dress out. "It's not too low-cut?"

"No, it brings out your eyes. Besides, your cleavage should be worth a few bucks."

"Right," she replied, "Let's hope it doesn't come to that." Cordelia hastily dressed, slip, hose, grousing, "This is supposed to be my night off," as I hooked her bra. She surveyed herself in the mirror. "Have I got everything?" she asked with a quick glance at her watch.

"You look stunning," I told her.

She smiled at me, the distracted look disappearing. "I have forgotten something." She put her arms around me. "Thank you."

"For what?"

"I don't know…understanding…helping. Telling me I look beautiful." She gently kissed me for a moment, breaking it off, but still keeping her arms around me.

"Thank you," I replied. "For holding me when you're late and in a hurry."

"I know what's important. I love you, Micky."

"Me, too," I responded, then clarified, "I love you, too."

"You'll be here when I get back?" she asked as she picked up her keys and purse.

"In your bed. With my legs spread."

"Yes, I like that," Cordelia answered, grinning at me, "I am turning into a sex fiend." She gave me one more quick kiss and left.

I took a long shower to pass the time. When I stepped out, I was confronted with an image of myself in a full length mirror. Not too bad, I thought, for halfway through my thirtieth year. I was tall. Thin, particularly since I lost the alcohol bloat. If you got close and looked very hard you could find a few gray strands, but my hair was still basically a raffish mess of black curls. I looked at my naked body in the mirror, absentmindedly running my hand down my stomach to my thighs, then brushing a few stray water droplets off my pubic hair. I didn't feel sexual at the moment.

I tried to read, but I realized I was still upset at Cordelia for complaining about me to Alex. I didn't know that I felt like making love with her. Actually, I did feel like making love with her, but I knew I would be holding some part of myself back from her and I didn't want to do that. Talk to her, I told myself. Coolly and dispassionately, yet assertively would be the best approach. I was still trying to think of what to say when I heard her key in the lock.

"Hi," I heard her call. "You still here?"

"Yeah, in here," I answered from her bedroom. I was sitting at her desk pretending to read, wrapped in her bathrobe, not in bed like I had promised.

"Well, I survived that," Cordelia announced as she entered the room. She kicked off her shoes, then pulled her dress and slip over her head with one motion. "Will you do the honors?" she asked, turning her back to me.

I reached up and unhooked her bra.

"Ah, comfort," she said slipping it off. "Torbin was a major hit. I even had some of those painted dolls looking at me and wondering how I'd managed to get someone as handsome as he is."

"I'm glad he was such a good cover."

"You sound upset about something."

"I'm not. Tired, probably," I evaded.

"You didn't need to wait up, you know. I'm sorry. I guess it is kind of late."

She sat down on the edge of the bed. I remained seated at her desk.

For a moment there was an awkward silence. Then I abruptly said, "Joanne and I talked today. Or I should say Joanne gave me a talking to. She told me that Alex told her that you said I have a problem with money."

"Is that what's bothering you?"

"No, why should that bother me? I like having the things I say to you in bed repeated to me on the jogging trails of City Park." So much for cool and dispassionate.

"I was going to talk to you about that."

"Well, you needn't bother. Joanne got there first."

"Then I'll have to talk to Joanne. She shouldn't be using a sledgehammer to destroy a molehill."

"Joanne shouldn't be privy to our private conversations. Don't you think that would be a better solution?" I retorted.

"It's not quite like that," Cordelia said calmly. "I think I mentioned, in passing, that you weren't comfortable with my spending money on you. And," she put up a hand to forestall the comment I was going to make, "and I only said that to be fair. Alex had given me the details of an argument that she and Joanne were having. At some point she got exasperated with my telling her how wonderful you were and demanded a fault."

"So you told her I had problems with money?"

"I told her it was the one area we were not perfectly agreeable about."

"What were she and Joanne fighting about?" I asked. Then added, "You don't have to tell me. I don't guess it's any of my business."

"Alex can't expect me not to pass on things if she does," Cordelia replied. "Joanne was supposed to get a brake tag inspection. She called Alex at the last minute and asked her to do it. Alex agreed, then she got caught up, resented being stuck with it, and didn't get it done. Joanne had to get up very early the next morning to get the car inspected, woke up Alex in the process, and then stomped out without saying good-bye. It was after that, that I mentioned that you sometimes objected to my taking you out to dinner."

"Oh," I said. I was beginning to understand this was not the major transgression I had imagined.

Cordelia gave me a tentative smile, then extended her hand. "Am I forgiven?"

I nodded. "Of course." I stood up, then reached out and took her hand, holding it for a moment before I stepped in to where she was sitting on the bed. She kissed my hand and put her other arm around my waist.

After holding me like that for a moment or so, Cordelia let go of my hand.

"Can I?" she asked as she started to unloosen the robe. I didn't object, letting the robe fall open as she undid the belt. She kissed my stomach, then slid her arms inside the robe to hold me. She kissed my stomach again, moving up until she was kissing the underside of my breasts. I let go of her long enough to slip off the robe and throw it in the direction of a chair.

Cordelia lay back, pulling me on top of her, still kissing my breasts, now the nipples, tightening her arms around my waist.

My response was slow, not as immediate as I wanted it to be. I did want her to make love to me. I wanted her to love me. I wanted some small reassurance that I didn't know how to ask for and that she had no way of knowing to give.

Her hand moved down my back, then around my hip. I took my breast away from her mouth, sliding down to kiss her on the lips, moving on to run my tongue down her neck to her already erect nipples. I would make love to her first to slow the pace and as an oblique apology for my anger.

"Oh, yes," Cordelia responded to my tongue on her nipple. Her hands were in my hair, pressing me close.

I began kissing my way down, but a slight pressure from her hands stopped me.

"Um, no," she murmured. "I want you beside me."

We rearranged ourselves on the bed, Cordelia on her back, me lying next to her. We kissed as my hand moved to where my tongue had been going. Cordelia broke off our kiss to gasp as my fingers entered her.

It had been easy for her to ask for what she wanted. Why hadn't I? Why had I been unwilling—scared?—to simply say, "Just hold me for a minute more, then kiss me softly and slowly and I'll be ready?" Didn't I think I had a right to my small requests? Was there any possibility she would refuse me? I pushed these questions aside.

I had always been amazed and delighted by Cordelia's quick and unbridled response when we made love. Her hesitancy and awkwardness disappeared. In some ways, it was consistent with her everyday self. She made decisions slowly and thoughtfully, but once decided, the doubt was gone and no hesitancy reappeared to plague her.

After we had agreed to be lovers, to make love, and done so time and again, a covenant had been reached. Her body was open and responsive to me. Unconditionally. It thrilled me. And in odd moments, scared me. I was slow to respond, at root, slower to trust.

Sex had been, at times, problematical for me. Consent sometimes so shifting and muddled that I was left with only a vaguely uneasy feeling in the morning and no clear way or place to have said no, but unsure if I had really meant yes.

Cordelia hadn't had that many lovers. Not compared to me and my list of one- or two-night stands. Hadn't traded sex off for small kindnesses, clutching at it for its resemblance to love as I too often had.

And hadn't, finally, used people as I had, sleeping with them indiscriminately for any number of reasons—lust, boredom, and, ultimately, for the sheer power of the erotic. Making women want me because I could, because it gave me control over them. I became not only the betrayed but the betrayer, burdened with the shame of the victim and the guilt of the user.

I had hoped that with Cordelia, with someone with whom I finally connected and touched as a person, not as a shadow or an object, I could walk away from what I had been. With the shining newness of our passion, it had seemed possible; in the initial exhilaration, anything had seemed possible. I was different. I was better than I had ever been, and my demons, as in a fairly tale, had been permanently vanquished.

I was upset, angry even, at my unsureness and hesitation now. And at the one possibility that I hadn't considered—that my demons were slowly creeping back, tainting my bright and shining love.

I hoped that she wouldn't notice, that, touching her as closely as I was, I could still hide a part of myself. And that the morning would drive away all doubt and confusion.

I felt her arms around me, holding fiercely to me, as if some deep part of her trusted absolutely that I would be there, that I had no doubts about loving and wanting her.

I watched Cordelia's face closely as I stroked her, one arm returning her tight embrace. She was close to coming; I could feel that tautness in her breath. She moaned softly, her hand clutching, control gone or let go of. I watched until I saw it, the absolute nakedness possible only in these fleeting moments. Take me as I am, beggar, fool, sinner, saint, touch me as I am. What more could you risk?

I held her tightly, protectively as her face contorted and body arched. She had no control. Trust so deep should not be betrayed. The moment passed, we lay together quietly, her breath warm on my cheek.

We spoke no words as I let her go down on me, not wanting her eyes next to mine, looking into them. My body responded, finally succumbed to the flow and sway of her touch.

“God, I’m tired,” Cordelia said after I had come and she was lying next to me. “Do you mind if I just roll over and go to sleep?”

“Mind? No, of course not.”

“Sorry, I feel rude doing this.” She disentangled herself from me, then rolled over on her side. We were no longer touching.

“You’re not rude. If you’re tired, you’re tired.” Cordelia’s only reply was steady, even breathing. I watched her for a moment, relaxed in sleep, then turned away, willing sleep to come.

CHAPTER 5

Hordes of parents were awaiting their progeny. I scanned the joyous faces of the just released children, searching for Patrick Selby. Today was the day we were to meet.

"Micky," Patrick called, spotting me first. I waved in his direction. He looked like his mother. His dark brown hair would be the color of Barbara's if she didn't keep hers ash blond. His eyes were a dark brown, also hers. And like hers, his face was rounded, chin and nose with no sharp lines.

"Cissy will be here in a minute," Patrick informed me as he got near. We settled on going to a local burger-thing to have our meeting.

"Hi, Cissy," I called when I saw her. She glanced over her shoulders, then started running for us as if she'd caught sight of some demon behind her. Cissy's looks brought reminders of their absent father back into the family. Her hair was much lighter, streaks of blond that would follow her into adulthood. Her eyes were green, the shape of her face sharper, her nose a straight line.

"Hey, what's up?" I asked as she came to a stop in front of us.

"Nothin'."

"So why are you running?"

"Just wanted to," Cissy answered with a shrug.

Two chocolate shakes and a small Coke sat before us on the far corner table Patrick had selected. The shakes looked good, but Patrick had insisted on buying.

"What's going on?" I asked, scanning the two faces opposite me.

"Judy Douglas," Patrick said. "She was a girl in Cissy's class. She died about a month ago. Cissy thinks she was murdered."

"Why do you think that?" I asked Cissy.

"I dunno. Some girls said so." She shrugged and started sucking on her milkshake.

"What girls?"

"Just some girls," she answered, barely letting the straw out of her mouth.

"Why do they think she was murdered?"

This time all I got was a shrug, the straw didn't move.

"How did she die?"

Patrick answered. "They say it was an accident. That she fell and hit her head. Maybe the grownups aren't telling us anything."

"Have you talked to your Mom about this?" I asked.

"No." It was Cissy who replied. "There's no reason to tell her," she added.

"Well, I mentioned it to her," Patrick started.

"I told you not to," Cissy cut in.

"Why are you upset about it?" I asked to forestall a sibling argument.

"I'm not upset," she said, slamming down her milkshake. "I just don't like Pattie doing things I ask him not to. Mr. Know-It-All." The last was directed to Patrick.

"Don't call me Pattie."

"Will if I want to."

"Patrick," I said, "Could you please get me another Coke?" I pulled a crumpled bill out of my pocket and handed it to him. He glanced at Cissy, rolled his eyes, then took my dollar and headed to the counter.

"Were you and Judy good friends?" I asked Cissy.

"No, uh-uh. Sometimes she'd beg rides home with us and complain 'cause no one picked her up. She had to take the bus."

"It's scary when people we know die, even if we don't know them very well."

Cissy just nodded.

"Are you scared that it might happen to you?"

She shrugged. "Good girls don't get hurt." It sounded like whistling in a dark cemetery to me.

"Was Judy a bad girl?"

Cissy gave me another of her shrugs, then mumbled, "I guess."

"What did she do that was bad?"

"I dunno." The straw was back in her mouth. I didn't say anything, letting her answer hang. Cissy finally added, "She talked a lot."

"What did she talk about?"

"Just things." The straw made a loud slurping noise.

"Cissy, sometimes bad things happen. I don't want you to be scared. Telling doesn't hurt anyone. Is there something you want to talk about?"

"No." Another loud slurp. Then she added, "Judy told secrets. She wasn't supposed to."

Patrick returned with my Coke. I didn't get anything more out of Cissy. Even if Patrick hadn't been there, I don't know if she would have told me anything else.

After I drove them home, Patrick remained behind as Cissy went into their house. "Cissy told me that Judy was murdered," he informed me. "That's why I wanted to hire you." He added, "I can pay you. I've been saving up my paper route money."

"I can make a few inquiries," I answered. "Then we can discuss money." I wasn't going to take his paper-tossing pennies.

"She's been acting real strange ever since," he added. "I think someone needs to get to the bottom of this."

I grinned at his use of TV cop show cliché, then said, "I'll do what I can. I'll call you as soon as I've got something to report."

"Okay. Wait, maybe I'd better call you. Mom might wonder. Cissy's upset about this and doesn't want her to know."

"You're the boss," I told him. I returned to my car, waved one last time to Patrick, then drove away.

Had Judy Douglas been murdered? It was possible that to avoid scaring the kids, parents and teachers had concocted the accident story. I decided the newspaper room at the library might hold a few basic answers. The public library was about to close, so I gritted my teeth and headed uptown to Tulane. In just under an hour of searching I found what I was looking for—a brief article in the Metro section of the *Times-Picayune*.

Judy Sullivan Douglas had been playing in the local football bleachers with several other kids after school. She was jumping from seat to seat, tripped, and hit her head on the corner of a bleacher. The blow had killed her. Nothing in the article hinted at foul play, just a tragic accident. But papers don't always tell you everything, either.

Back in my car, I got out a map and figured out which precinct was closest to the accident site. I thought about calling Joanne to see if she could grease a few wheels, but decided against it. I wasn't up to dealing with her.

I didn't recognize the desk sergeant. I introduced myself, then bantered a bit about the Saints' chances for the playoffs this year.

"Judy Douglas. Yeah, I remember that one," he said. "Real sad. Hey, Bill. This little lady's looking into that little girl's accident. The one that bashed her head in," he called out to a middle-aged man across the room. "Bill took the accident report," he confided to me.

Bill sauntered over to us, holding out his hand to shake. His hair was dark brown, going to grey, his hairline sparse, the lines in his face those of a man who had spent too much of his youth in the sun.

Bill waved me back to his cramped cubicle. "Why are you interested in Judy Douglas?" he asked after offering me some industrial-strength coffee.

"You know how parents are about their kids. Particularly uptown parents. They want to make sure that what happened to Judy doesn't happen to their Susie or Johnny."

Bill nodded. "Well, Ms. Knight, I don't usually talk about official police business with non-police, but I'm a parent myself so I'm willing to do you a favor." Bill looked at me. I nodded. Quid pro quo. A New Orleans tradition.

He pulled a file out of a battered gray file cabinet. Opening it, he read, "Judy Douglas, age nine years, seven months, died from head trauma caused by an accidental fall."

"Was it definitely an accident?" I asked.

Bill glanced at me. "You have some imaginative parents. A couple of teachers were in the stands. The junior high band was practicing on the field." He looked again at the file. "No one was within fifteen feet of her. She tripped and hit her head. Brain dead by the time she reached the hospital. She passed several hours later. Tragic, yes, but not suspicious." He handed the file to me.

I opened it and started reading, although I knew it would back him up. Bill did paperwork until I decided I had read all of the autopsy report that I cared to. I handed the file back to him.

"Thanks," I said. "You know how parents can be." I got up to leave. But something caused me to turn and ask, "What do you know about the Sans Pareil Club?"

"Nothing," Bill replied, then added, "Nothing that you don't already know. Any problems, they take care of them. No grubby police presence to disturb the clientele," he finished, shaking his head. "Why do you ask?"

"Curiosity."

"Which has killed better cats than you, Ms. Knight," Bill replied.

"Someone invests fifty thousand dollars and a month later gets seventy thousand back. Wouldn't that make you curious?"

Bill let out a low whistle, then nodded.

"Could that be legit?" I asked.

"Only if I could be the pope, and I'm Jewish. Drugs most likely. How did you hear about this?"

"An acquaintance."

"In the Sans Pareil Club?"

"Possibly."

"Wouldn't want to give me any names, would you?" Bill asked.

"Client confidentiality."

"Of course. Why don't you ask your client?"

"Because my client doesn't know. And if he (I deliberately changed the pronoun) did, he'd lie. You might try a search warrant."

"For the Sans Pareil Club? No thanks, I need to be able to work in this town at least until my kids finish school."

"Are they that far beyond the law?" I asked.

Bill grimaced, then shrugged, and said, "Maybe. I wouldn't want to be the one to put it to a test."

"Thanks, I'll keep that in mind." I stood to go.

"Ms. Knight. Tread lightly. To men like Anthony Colombé, you and I are just insects. He'll slap you like a gnat."

"So I've heard," I said as I walked away. I didn't enlighten Bill that I had no intention of tangling with Anthony Colombé.

Well, I thought as I got into my car, I've solved one case. Judy Douglas hadn't been murdered. But I knew the real solution would be ridding Cissy of her fears. And I wasn't very sure I would succeed there.

Chapter 6

The next few days I was busy doing some industrial spying. One Mardi Gras krewe had hired me to check out how another krewe's floats would be decorated.

Karen left messages twice, but I ignored them. I would call her back when I felt like it. I was hoping that Patrick would call so I could tell him and Cissy what I had discovered.

The best thing that happened all week was that it rained from Saturday morning to late Sunday afternoon. Instead of jogging in misery, I spent Sunday in the ecstasy of a long, lingering brunch, then sitting on Cordelia's balcony watching the rain and holding hands until handholding became a woefully inadequate form of physical contact.

I realized later, as I lay beside Cordelia watching her sleep in the dim reflected light from the street, that I had lost my hesitancy and ambivalence from last week. The demons were gone. And, I assured myself, they would not come back.

On Monday afternoon Patrick called. I told him I had some information for them, and we arranged to meet the next day after school.

Instead of going to the local burger-thing, we got snowballs and found a shady spot in City Park.

"I saw the official police report on Judy Douglas," I started as soon as we were comfortably settled. "Her death was accidental. She tripped and hit her head against the corner of a bleacher. Most kids who fall don't get hurt like she did." I looked from Patrick to Cissy. Cissy wasn't looking at me, her eyes downcast. She was putting a lot of attention into eating her snowball. "So you see," I continued, "You don't have anything to worry about." I put my hand on her forearm to reassure her.

"I told you it was okay," Patrick added.

Cissy just gave a quick nod of her head, then another one of her shrugs.

"You look like you don't believe me," I said, still keeping my hand on her arm.

"I believe you," she said with a quick look at me, then down to her snowball again. "It's just that maybe other things can happen. Maybe Judy got shot with a ray gun or something like that."

"You mean aliens attacking us with unknown weapons?"

"That's silly," Patrick interjected.

"Perhaps not silly," I said, "but certainly unlikely."

"It's silly," Cissy said. "Patrick's right."

"See, it's all okay," he added, the triumph of a brother being acknowledged right by a younger sister.

"I'll make it as okay as I can," I said quietly, trying as best I could to reassure this young girl with her downcast eyes. I gave her arm a reassuring squeeze then let go of her.

Cissy grabbed my hand, her small child's fingers wrapped around mine, holding fiercely. In her eyes I saw a moment of terror. Abruptly it was gone. "Thanks, Micky," she said, and just as suddenly let go of me, her eyes again opaque and downcast.

What terrifies you so much, I wanted to ask, but realized that Cissy would not, perhaps could not, answer that question.

We got into my car, and Patrick and I chatted about school, how he was looking forward to junior high next year. I pulled into the driveway just moments after Barbara Selby did. She was taking groceries out of the trunk of her car.

"Hi, Micky," she called out. "C'mon, kids, help with this stuff." Barbara cheerfully admitted that she was on the wrong side of forty and a size fourteen. She wore tortoiseshell glasses that kept sliding down her nose. Her eyes were a deep brown, alert and alive, the kind of eyes that proclaimed that this was an intelligent and exuberant woman.

Patrick grabbed two bags, then, seeing that I was coming around to help, handed them to Cissy, saying, "Here, these are light, you can take them."

Cissy took the bags, rolled her eyes, and headed into the house. Patrick reached into the trunk and got four bags, two in each hand. He tottered a bit as he swung the bags out, then steadied himself and muscled the heavy bags into the house.

"Those four bags were for your benefit," Barbara said as she closed the trunk. "He's never that ambitious when it's just me. How does it feel to have a twelve-year-old boy have a crush on you?"

"Decidedly odd. I'm not his type." Barbara knew I was a lesbian.

"I think it's cute," Barbara replied, taking one of the bags I was holding and heading for the door.

"Would you still think it's cute if it were Cissy?" I asked.

Barbara turned back to face me, an unfamiliar look on her face. She shifted the groceries in her arms, looked away for a moment, then back at me. "Well, that caught me out, didn't it?"

"Don't worry," I said brusquely, "I'm sure Cissy will grow up to be heterosexual and live happily ever after, just like you have." Barbara's husband had left her and her kids.

"Ouch," Barbara said. "I didn't mean to offend you. It's hard for mothers to conceive of their children as sexual. You've just blindsided me with not only the concept of my nine-year-old daughter's sexuality, but the possibility that she could be gay. Give me a few seconds to adjust before you bite my head off."

"Sorry," I said. "It's been a long day." *Your daughter's terrified of something*, I wanted to say. *If you were a better mother, you'd have done a better job of protecting her*. I didn't want Cissy's terrors weighting on my conscience. Or the promise I'd made to Patrick not to tell Barbara about Cissy's fears.

"Sorry," I said again. "I'm probably just angry at the world. Or my mother." I remembered my mother, how tired she was when I had woken her with my nameless terrors, sinister shapes in the shadows of a dim moon.

"Does your mother know you're gay?" Barbara asked.

"My mother doesn't know I'm alive," I answered, then elaborated, "She left when I was five. I've never heard from her."

"I'm sorry," Barbara said. "Why don't you come in and have supper with us? Patrick can practice his fledgling flirting skills with you."

"Thanks, but…"

"Oh, hell, Cissy can even have a crush and flirt with you," Barbara said as she led the way to her kitchen. Patrick and Cissy were already in the living room watching TV.

"I'm sorry I snapped at you just now."

"It's okay, Micky," Barbara replied. "I'm just worried about Cissy, she's been in such a sullen mood lately. I keep hoping that it's just early adolescence. The hope being that if it starts early, it ends early."

"Wasn't there a girl in her class who died recently? Could that be upsetting her?"

"Maybe, but she didn't seem upset at the time. Who knows with kids these days? So, how about supper?"

"Thanks, but I have a previous engagement." For a moment I thought of breaking my promise to Patrick and telling Barbara about Cissy's apprehension. But maybe it would pass and attention to her fears could cause them to linger.

"Anyone I know?" Barbara asked.

"I doubt it," I replied. "A friend of Alex's."

"By the way, let me thank you again for telling me about this job. Alex is a great boss. So which friend is it? She seems to have tons of them."

"Cordelia James," I said, after a moment's hesitation, wondering how much claim I could lay on her. And how much I wanted to. "She and Alex have been friends since high school," I explained.

"So what does Cordelia do?" Barbara asked as she put on some rice.

"Are you one of those people who judge a person by their job?" I asked.

"No, just curious. Is she unemployed? Believe me, I understand that."

"No, she works."

"As? Come on, Micky. What is she, a dishwasher?"

"No. She's a doctor."

"A doctor? That's nothing to be ashamed of."

"I wouldn't be ashamed of her if she were a dishwasher," I answered sharply. "And there are doctors I would be ashamed of."

"Micky, have you had a rough day?"

"No. Yes. It doesn't matter. Why assume that doctors are automatically better than dishwashers? It's an ugly form of classism."

"I suppose," Barbara sighed. "But raising two kids as a single mother gives one an appreciation of a doctor's income."

"Having money is just luck and privilege. That's all."

"Going to medical school is a bit more than just luck. Occasionally studying, for example. However, I have to feed two starving children. Cordelia will not like me if I keep you here arguing or send you off in a cantankerous mood."

"Sorry, Barbara," I replied for the umpteenth time.

"Do come by for supper sometime. It will probably inspire Patrick to help out in the kitchen without grumbling or dawdling." Barbara gave me a hug good-bye. I gave her a quick hug in return, called out a farewell to Cissy and Patrick, then headed out.

CHAPTER 7

I had spent the night with Cordelia, then got up at a brutal hour to take her to the airport. She was going to a doctors' convention in Boston. When I got back to my place it was still a forbiddingly early hour as far as I was concerned, but I was too awake to go back to bed. I did chores until what I called morning arrived, then started on my latest paying job. I had been hired to get the recipe for crawfish jambalaya that a new restaurant, Aunt Eula's Cajunfest, was packing them in with. My client suspected that they had stolen her recipe and wanted it back or at least a cut of the profits. I spent most of the day loitering in a French Quarter alley, noting down what was delivered to the restaurant.

It was late, and the day had advanced to the grand master level of humidity by the time I got back to my place. The phone rang, but I wasn't in the mood to answer it, so I let my machine pick it up.

"Micky, please call me. It's very important." It was Karen. "I have to see Joey tonight and I'd really like your company. Paid, of course," she added, quite necessarily.

"Better leave your phone number. I seem to have misplaced it," I told her disembodied voice.

"This is Karen," she continued.

"I know that," I growled.

And then she left her phone number.

I let an entire hour pass before I called her back. I got her answering machine, which made me happy. "Karen, this is Micky Knight returning your phone call."

"Micky, I'm so glad you called back." Karen had been screening her calls and picked up the phone. "I'm meeting Joey at the club again tonight. Will you go?"

"Same price as last time?" I coolly responded.

She paused for a moment before replying, "Yes, the same amount.

I'll give it to you in cash. That way, you won't need to declare it on your taxes."

"Are you suggesting I cheat on my income taxes?" I baited her.

"Well, uh, no. I'll pay you by check if you prefer."

"Cash will be fine, but I will give you a receipt," I answered.

"Good, I'll pick you up around seven."

"Yeah, around seven," I answered and then hung up.

I only left the office long enough to swing by Torbin's to pick up a basic black dressy thing, with enough time to take a shower, before Karen came to pick me up. She was willing to come downtown to my neighborhood, a major concession on her part.

"You look good in black, Micky," she told me after safely power-locking all the doors.

"It probably suits the evening to have me in black and you in blue," I commented. Karen was dressed in an elegant silk dress, its cobalt blue matching her eyes, bringing them out better than the discreet amount of makeup she had applied.

I turned away from her, annoyed that I had to acknowledge that Karen was an attractive woman with good taste in clothes. She didn't bother with small talk as we drove uptown.

The Sans Pareil Club was as opulent as ever. Even more so, since it was no longer enshrouded by rain and mist. The massive front columns, with their perfectly trimmed ivy, rose to a wide balcony surrounded by an intricate lacework of wrought iron. This antebellum mansion had been built with money and maintained with money over its long life.

Karen led the way to a secluded table in the back.

"What will you have?" she inquired of me, a waiter hovering instantly.

"Club soda," I answered.

"The same," she instructed the waiter.

She remained silent until he returned with our drinks. It was only after he left that she looked at me and said, "Thank you for coming. I know you didn't want to."

"Money and curiosity. Not very high-minded reasons."

"Perhaps. Joey makes me nervous. He…" She paused. "He called and suggested I reinvest my money again." She paused again. "It wasn't much of a suggestion. More like a…" She stopped.

I didn't need to look around to know that Joey had arrived.

"Karen, darling," he said, leaning to give her the obligatory air kiss. Turning to me he said, "Micky, good to see you again." We settled for shaking hands. He was too smooth for me to be able to guess whether he really didn't want me here, whether he didn't care, or, least likely, he really was glad to see me.

We followed him back into the same private room in which he'd last counted out the money. Joey set his briefcase on the table, but didn't open it. He got down to business.

"So, Karen, as I mentioned in our phone call, we'd really appreciate it if you'd roll over your investment once again."

Karen licked her lips nervously, then glanced at me.

"What's this investment in?" I asked. For five thousand dollars I might do more than be a piece of movable furniture.

"Some offshore work," Joey replied.

"Can you be more specific?" I returned.

"Trade secret," was his answer. He tried to give me a disarming smile, but the edge of his irritation was showing.

"So you want Karen to invest in something about which you'll only reveal that it takes place in the water?" I said.

"She also knows she makes money off of it," Joey replied. "That's usually the most important thing."

"Is this offshore thing legal?" I demanded.

"Who is this lady, anyway?" Joey asked, turning to Karen, trying his disarming smile on her.

"Michele Knight. She's a financial advisor," Karen answered.

"Financial advisor?" Joey turned to me. "When did you stop being a private eye?" He didn't bother smiling.

"This is an unusual investment. Karen felt she needed an unusual type of advisor," I replied. In the Sans Pareil Club, Joey's tough act could only go so far.

"Unusual, yeah. A dyke dick from downtown," Joey responded, giving me a hard look.

"Oh, Joey, don't be parochial," Karen cut in. "Anthony has no problem with her being here. You shouldn't." Anthony was Anthony Colombé. Joey had been put on notice that Karen was on first-name terms with one of the most powerful men in town. Whatever Karen's involvement with him, she had no problem using it. With Karen hanging on his arm, Colombé projected the image of a virile man, able to satisfy young, attractive women. It was an impression that he obviously cared a great deal about. Karen, in turn, was treated as one of his inner circle, although I suspected that if she really were a true intimate of his instead of just someone he found very useful, she wouldn't need my help in dealing with Joey and his unnamed friends.

"Sorry," Joey answered. "No offense meant."

"So what is it, Joey? Drugs?" I asked. "I'm not the cops. I just want to know what my client's getting into."

"Not drugs. I can promise you that," he replied.

"Yeah? What else earns money like this?" I returned.

"Come on, Karen. Call off your attack dog," he appealed to her. "I can't really tell you what it is. I can promise you it's not illegal drugs. Not even legal drugs. It's just a real good and easy way for you to earn money."

"How do you turn a profit so quickly?" I asked.

Joey didn't answer my question. He continued speaking to Karen. "I'll give you some more information next time, but I'm late for another meeting. Yes or no?" he finished with a nod at the briefcase.

"What if she says no?" I asked.

He faked a nonchalant shrug. "If the lady says no, the lady says no. It would, however, come at an inconvenient time. We would really appreciate your continued support." Joey had his hand on the briefcase.

"I think I'd prefer not to—" Karen started.

"The lady says yes," I cut in. It wasn't much of a threat. It didn't need to be. One person's inconvenience is another person's already dug grave.

Joey wasted no time in snatching up his briefcase and smiling ever so pleasantly as he said, "Thanks, ladies. I assume I'll see you both next time." Then he was gone.

Karen turned from the just closed door to me and said. "Micky, what the hell was that about? I thought you wanted me out of this?"

"I do," I retorted. "I'd just prefer you get out of it alive rather than dead."

"What? Oh, be serious. Joey's not going to—"

"Karen, I am serious. Don't let his smooth and pleasant exterior fool you. These are not men you inconvenience. Whatever you cost them, it will cost you more. Understand?"

"I guess. But I—"

We were interrupted by a discreet knock on the door.

"Come in," Karen said, then, "Hello, Francois," to the man who entered. He was tall, still handsome, but the long, late nights were beginning to show. His dark hair was receding, the bags under his eyes needed the soft light of evening to remain imperceptible. Their gray color matched his distant expression.

"Miss Holloway, Mr. Colombé wishes your company, if it is convenient for you." Mr. Colombé wanted his façade in place.

"Of course," she replied, then to me, "I'll call you later." Karen turned and followed Francois out of the room. I trailed behind.

As it was clear that I wasn't included in the invitation (not that I wanted to be), I told Karen, "I'll find my own way home."

"That's not necessary," she replied, giving me a quick social kiss on the cheek. It wouldn't do for our parting to be too businesslike in the Sans Pareil Club. "Francois, please see to Micky," Karen instructed, then left us for Anthony Colombé.

"If you'll follow me, Ms. Knight," Francois said.

Impressive, I thought, as I followed Francois to the entryway, his smooth transition from Miss to Ms., knowing automatically which I would prefer. It was a skill a man like Anthony Colombé could afford.

"Charles," Francois said softly. One of the doormen snapped to attention despite several other people vying for his services.

I noticed a black Porsche turning down the long drive of the club. Joey. Of course, he would have a Porsche. And, I noted, a vanity plate: ET OR B E10. "Eat or Be Eaten"—the perfect sentiment for a shark.

"Please bring one of Mr. Colombé's cars for Ms. Knight," Francois instructed the doorman. "The Mercedes, I think."

"Thank you," I told Francois. He nodded briefly and reentered the club.

The car was a vintage Mercedes driven by a strikingly good-looking woman. I gave her my address, then offered directions, which she declined. "That's beyond Desire, isn't it?" she asked, her smile full lipped and sensual. Anthony Colombé probably required his drivers to memorize the streets of the greater New Orleans area.

"Will there be anything else?" she asked as she pulled in front of my place.

I thought about asking her if she was flirting with me because she wanted to or if it was part of the job. I also thought of inviting her upstairs and pumping her about Anthony Colombé, but knew she was too well trained and well paid to divulge anything.

"No, nothing," I replied. "Thanks for the ride."

"My pleasure," was her well-trained answer.

I got out of the Mercedes, which looked drastically out of place on my run-down block. The car disappeared, its engine a bare purr. I entered my building and climbed the three flights of stairs to my apartment.

Cordelia had left a message. She was just going to bed when I returned her call; I had forgotten it was an hour later in Boston. We chatted for a bit, I agreed to pick her up at the airport, and then I let her go on to bed, as she had to give a presentation in the morning.

I prowled around my apartment for a while, doing a few necessary and neglected chores like dealing with Hepplewhite's lovely litter box. I was trying to figure out the best approach to get Karen out of the deep shit she had done a swan dive into. Nothing elegant and easy came to mind.

I went to bed. But it wasn't Karen and her troubles that drifted by as I began to fall asleep. Instead it was Cissy, with her downcast and hidden eyes.

CHAPTER 8

I had been awakened sometime past midnight by the lash of rain and the boom of close thunder. The storm had gone nowhere during the night and was still pouring rain with a vengeance when my alarm clock goaded me out of bed.

Already in an irritable mood, I decided to compound it by calling Karen. All I got was her answering machine. I left a message telling her to call me. I had a few questions I wanted answered.

Karen didn't call back until late in the afternoon.

"About time," I greeted her.

"I just got in," she defended. "I spent the night at Anthony's."

"And, of course, cooed and aahed at breakfast as if you'd really had sex."

"All right, Micky, what do you want?"

"Answers. Honest answers. How did you get involved with Joey?"

"I've already told you that. I met him at the Sans Pareil Club."

"So you met this guy, he said, 'Yo, babe, want to earn some money' and you just coughed up, what? Fifty?"

"No. I met him several times. And I started out with five."

"Five?" Another lie she had told me. "How long has this been going on?" I demanded.

"Uh, I guess about eight months."

I let my disapproval hang in the silence for a long moment. "Eight months? And you're just now wondering about it?"

"No, I tried to get out before. That's when Joey mentioned the picture."

"Oh, yes, the picture. Karen, what's Joey's last name?"

"Boudreaux."

"Great, the Cajun version of 'Smith.' Do you have an address or phone number?"

"I have an address." It was a post office box.

"Karen, there is a remote possibility that Joey and his cohorts are merely paranoid businessmen. The only other choice is that what they're doing is illegal—drugs, dumping toxic waste, whatever. If that's the case, there's no nice way out for you. Be prepared to go to the police."

"I guess," she reluctantly agreed.

"And, Karen," I added, "count yourself lucky if you get out of this one without getting hurt. If you hear from Joey again, call me. If you can get any information, great. But don't push him. Don't agree to meet him unless you tell me. All right?"

"All right," she answered. "Micky? I don't know how to thank you."

"Pay my bill promptly when it arrives." With that I hung up.

I rubbed my forehead. Between the incessant rain and Karen's mess, I was getting a headache.

The phone rang. It was Barbara Selby. "Micky, I need a real big favor," she said. "My Aunt Josselyn has fractured her hip and my mother is going to stay with her. The problem is that Aunt Joss lives in Jacksonville, Florida. I can drive Mom if I can find someone to sit with the kids for a day or two while I'm gone. They don't really need babysitting, just someone adult and stable in the vicinity."

It took me a second to realize that I qualified as "adult and stable." "I'd be glad to," I replied. "I'd love to have a day or two to corrupt, I mean, hang out with Patrick and Cissy."

"I do have one request," she said seriously. "No overnight guests."

"Not to worry. She's at some docs' conference in Boston. I'll behave," I promised.

"Thanks, Micky. I really do appreciate this. I'm leaving tomorrow after work and I hope to be back Saturday." After settling the logistics, she thanked me again, then we rang off.

I was glad to do the favor for Barbara. And with a few days together, Cissy might open up to me. Maybe I could bring the Case of the Boy to a happy ending. Which left the Case of the Blond Bitch. Perhaps my favorite gossip monger would have some tidbits, I thought as I dialed Torbin's number.

"Robedeaux's Pool Hall. Our motto is 'Rack 'em, stack 'em, and shoot 'em hard,'" he greeted.

"But do you pick up the pieces in the morning?" I returned.

"Forget it, all my clothes are at the cleaners," Torbin said.

"Nothing to wear," I reassured him. "A gossip test. Do you know who Anthony Colombé is?"

"Do I know which general Lee Circle is named after? Next question, please."

"Do you know he likes boys?"

Torbin was silent long enough to tell me that he didn't know this. "Well, shut my mouth," he finally exclaimed. "Me, a gossip test flunkout. Are you sure?"

"Reasonably. Short of being in his bedroom."

"Holy shit, Batman. Anthony Colombé is a fag."

"You're no help," I scolded him. "I need to be getting more information, not giving out what little I have."

"How about if your devoted cousin Tor promises to keep his ears peeled, sliced, and diced for any juicy tales?"

"It'll help."

"But you must tell me how you unearthed this well-hidden detail."

"Client confidentiality."

"Remove all names and identifying data. Come on, I know you can do it."

"Torbin…"

"I'll lend you my colorized version of *Madchen in Uniform* with explicit lesbian sex scenes spliced in at the appropriate moments."

"Torbin…"

"What if I throw in a pale lavender dildo? Guaranteed to spice up any lesbo's love life?"

"Pale lavender is too femme for me."

"Okay, deep purple. With all the studs you could want."

"Forget the studs. Girls don't like studs. Add a harness of deep red leather and you're in the ballpark."

I finally gave Torbin a few of the details. In return, I got a promise from him that he would make a serious attempt to ferret out more about Anthony Colombé's hidden life. If nothing else, how he had managed to keep so perfectly closeted in a city with long hot summers in which the only possible activity is the passing, and often embellishing, of rumor and scandal.

It was still raining when I went to bed.

CHAPTER 9

Barbara called me at a little after four. "Alex let me out early so I could pack and get going," she told me.

"I'm ready to whisk out the door," I answered. After dumping extra rations in Hepplewhite's direction I headed over to Barbara's.

She was putting a suitcase into the trunk of her car when I arrived.

"Anything I can do?" I asked as I approached.

"Not that I can think of," she replied. "Keep pandemonium to a minimum."

"'Min. pan.'—will do."

Barbara's mother came out of the house. I tried to look as "adult and stable" as I possibly could, at least until Barbara's mother was safely on her way. Barbara gave Cissy and Patrick one last hug, then they were gone.

I had been briefed on the household routine—TV, checking homework, bedtimes, and the like. Pizza for dinner instead of leftovers was my one concession to the disrupted routine. Homework, baths, and bedtime remained firmly on schedule. Ten p.m. was bedtime. By ten fifteen Patrick and Cissy were behind closed doors with the lights out. I might make a decent mom after all, I thought.

Using my phone card, I called Cordelia to let her know what I was up to and that I would pick her up Sunday evening at the airport. We didn't talk long. Cordelia was going on rounds with her friend Lynn early in the morning, and my phone card wasn't up to much long-distance usage.

After turning out all the lights but a small night-light in the hallway, I retreated to Barbara's bedroom. I wasn't very sleepy—I'm not an early to bed, early to rise type of gal. I sat cross-legged on Barbara's bed, attending to my long neglected letter-writing duties. I don't like writing, the irretrievable art of putting words on paper. Nonetheless, I had managed to eke out two letters and four postcards when I heard the soft opening of a bedroom door.

Patrick or Cissy on a bathroom run. I wouldn't get concerned unless I heard the TV turn on or the liquor cabinet open. I finished another postcard—a picture of three hoop-skirted belles—to a radical lesbian living in a women-only commune in Oregon. I still hadn't heard my nocturnal roamer return to bed. I gave it another postcard and finally decided to stick my head into the hallway. Very carefully opening the bedroom door (I didn't want to be responsible for causing a trauma in Patrick's life—nothing like a female guest catching you in your first sexual explorations), I peered into the dimly lit hallway.

Cissy was sitting on the floor next to the night-light, watching me. She looked down when she realized I had seen her.

"Cissy," I said as I went over and knelt beside her. "Are you okay?"

"Can't sleep," she whispered in reply.

"Are you scared of something?"

"Maybe." Then in a very soft voice that I could barely hear, "I heard something outside my window."

"Do you want me to go check?" I asked. I had been awake, if it was anything other than a squirrel I would have heard it. "I'll go outside and look around."

"No, don't." She grabbed my hand. "They might hurt you."

"Who? Who can hurt us?"

"I dunno," she answered, her eyes again firmly focused on the floor. "Whatever's out there."

"What do you think it might be?" I tried again.

"I dunno. Monsters maybe." She still didn't look up at me.

"I didn't hear any monsters, and I was listening."

"Maybe…quiet monsters," she answered softly. I doubted she literally meant monsters, like vampires and werewolves, but something or someone for which "monster" was the only word she could think of.

"They can't hurt me," I told her. The squirrels couldn't, at any rate. "And I won't let them hurt you." I stood up. "You stay here. I'm going to check outside. I'll be right back."

I let myself out the front door, locking it after me. Barbara lived in a quiet block near the lake. A few blocks away a dog was barking, but all was silent here. I walked around the house, letting the light from the street guide me. My main worry was stepping in dog shit. If Cissy had heard anything, it was in her dreams. Sometimes, I thought, as I passed her window, that can be the most terrifying place.

There was nothing out here, save for wet, dewy grass. I wiped my feet thoroughly on the scratchy welcome mat before letting myself back into the house.

Cissy was still in the hallway, huddled next to the night-light.

"It's all okay," I told her. "Nothing's out there." I sat next to her on the floor. I didn't want to just hustle her back to bed, because unless she told me what terrified her, my walking around the house would only keep the monsters away for a little while.

Cissy didn't say anything. She leaned her head against my arm, then curled into me as I put my arm around her thin shoulders.

"What did you hear?" I asked.

"Nothin', I guess. I guess I dreamed it."

"What are you afraid it might have been?" I asked, then before she could shrug another denial, "I can help you if you tell me. Don't fight your battles alone, Cissy."

She didn't reply. Instead she rubbed her face into my shirt like a kitten burrowing for warmth against a momma cat. Finally, she repeated, "I guess I must've dreamed it."

We sat in silence for a few minutes until I realized that she was falling asleep in my arms. "Let's go to bed," I said, gently lifting her to her feet.

Cissy rubbed her eyes sleepily, then asked, "Can I sleep with you?"

Her request caught my unprepared. Was Barbara really liberal enough to be okay about Cissy sleeping with me?

"Come on, let's go to your room," I heard myself saying. "I'll sit with you while you sleep. Okay?"

"Okay," Cissy agreed, taking my hand as I led her back to her bed. "I like the light in the hallway," she said as we entered her darkened bedroom.

"Tomorrow, I'll get you a night-light for your room."

"Okay," she mumbled sleepily as I tucked her in. She clung to my hand, only letting go long enough for me to get a chair and drag it next to her bed. It took the deep rhythms of sleep for her fingers to finally loosen their grip.

I sat with Cissy until almost four o'clock. I had implied that I would stay with her all night, not just until she fell asleep. I didn't like misleading her, making one of those adult half-promises, but I needed some sleep.

Finally, I got up and trudged back to Barbara's bedroom. I left the door ajar, telling myself I would hear her if she woke up. Then I set my alarm clock for fifteen minutes before Cissy was supposed to get up.

I must have slapped off the snooze button without knowing it. Or mis-set Barbara's unfamiliar alarm clock. I could hear Patrick's voice in the hallway talking to Cissy. I jumped out of bed and hastily threw on some clothes, out of sightline of the still ajar door.

"Good morning," I said to Cissy as I came out of the bedroom. "How are you?"

"Fine," she answered automatically.

"I stayed with you until the sun came up." I almost had. "I'll get you the night-light today," I offered by way of apology.

"Okay. Thanks," was her reply, then she gathered her things for school.

After dropping them off, I headed downtown to my place. I decided the first order of business was to go back to bed. Tonight might be a long night.

I woke up in the early afternoon. After some paperwork and a few moral dilemmas—should I keep a copy of the famous jambalaya recipe (yes, but only for my records), it was time to pick up Patrick and Cissy from school. I stopped on the way to pick up Cissy's promised night-light.

I got there about ten minutes early, getting a parking space that a big, family-sized car had to give up on. Other parents were there, most of them familiarly chatting. This was a daily ritual for them. I stood off to one side, by myself.

"Hello. Are you a new parent?" a man in his mid-forties asked as he approached.

"Hi," I answered. "No, I'm not. I'm not a parent at all."

"I'm Warren Kessler," he said, extending his hand. "I'm the principal here." He had on a loosened tie with his shirt sleeves rolled up, and an ease and assurance that indicated he belonged here. His hair only had enough gray in the reddish brown to give weight and maturity to a boyish face. His teeth were even and white, from good genes because they were not quite perfect enough to be from expensive dental work.

"Michele Knight," I answered, taking his hand. He had a warm, firm grip. "I'm here to pick up some kids for a friend of mine."

"Whose kids?" It came across as a friendly inquiry, not an interrogation, although I knew he was checking up on me, which I found reassuring. Someone here should be checking up on the where the kids went and with whom.

"Barbara Selby. Her kids Patrick and Cissy."

"Oh, yes, I've met Mrs. Selby a few times. Patrick and Cissy are good kids, so I don't see her that often."

"Yes, they are good kids," I echoed, then added, "Although Cissy has gotten awfully quiet lately. I'm a little worried about her."

"Has she? Any idea why?"

"I'm not sure. Possibly the death of that girl in her class."

"Judy Douglas." He knew her name without having to think. "A horrible tragedy. A single mother, her only child. It's understandable that Cissy would be upset. She's being raised by just her mother, isn't she?"

"Yes, she is," I confirmed. "I guess Judy's death could seem very close to home."

"Of course, we're a public school, and we don't have enough counselors for everyday events, let alone incidents like this, but I'll see if I can get Cissy in to see one of them sometime soon. And make up some routine reason for doing it."

"Good idea." Let the professionals take care of Cissy, I thought. But I'm a detective and I ask questions, so I did. "Could it be something else?"

"Possibly," Warren Kessler answered. "Different things affect us differently. Maybe she's really upset because her best friend is playing hopscotch with someone else. It can run the gamut from getting a math problem wrong to…" He trailed off with a shrug.

"To?"

"The ones we don't like to think about."

"Violence?"

He nodded.

"Sexual abuse?"

Again, he nodded, then asked, "Do you have any reason to suspect that Cissy is being abused?"

"No, nothing other than that she's gotten very quiet and seems to be scared of something," I admitted.

"If you find anything, even if it's not so-called hard evidence, you should probably go to Mrs. Selby—but if you don't feel comfortable doing that, you can always come to me."

"I hope it doesn't come to that."

"Me, too. Even if there's something you're unsure of or not comfortable with, you can tell me. I might be easier to talk to than Mrs. Selby. Parents are either very emotional about these things or…" He trailed off.

"Or?"

"The ones responsible."

The end-of-school bell rang.

"Let me get to where I'm supposed to be," Warren Kessler said with a quick laugh. "It's been good talking to you, Ms.…Knight, is it?"

"Let me give you my card," I offered, pulling one out of my wallet and giving it to him.

He glanced at it. "A private detective? Good, now I'll know where to find one. You don't do truants, do you?" he added jokingly.

"No, I don't."

He shook my hand one more time, then headed in the direction of a teacher calling his name.

Patrick and Cissy both came out different doors at the same time. I let Cissy have the front seat since Patrick had had it in the morning.

After dinner, during a bland hour of TV, the phone rang. Patrick answered it. His "Hi, Mom," told me it was Barbara. He chatted for a bit, then handed the phone to me to give Barbara the "adult and stable" version of the last day or so.

"Hi, Micky, how's it going?" she greeted me.

"We're still alive. Is that good enough?" I answered. I picked up the phone and moved into another room, shutting the door to close out the TV noise.

"They haven't been acting up, have they?"

"No," I answered. "But…has Cissy had problems sleeping?"

"She's had some bad dreams, but not in a while. Maybe she's upset because I'm not around."

"Maybe," I answered, taking some irrational offense at Barbara's implication that I had allowed Cissy's night fears to return. "Or maybe you've been asleep and haven't noticed her wakefulness."

"That's possible," she answered slowly, clearly not liking my implication any more than I liked hers.

I decided that sniping at each other wasn't going to be helpful. "What do you do to calm her fears?"

"It depends," Barbara replied. "Sometimes, unfortunately, on how tired I am. Sometimes I sit and talk with her, turn on lights in her room, show her there's nothing there. Sometimes I just let her sleep in my room. That's her preference."

"I know. She asked if she could join me."

"So, what did you do?"

"I didn't know if you'd approve of your daughter in bed with me."

"I'm trying to get her to be able to sleep by herself."

"Well, that's a direct answer."

"Micky, of course, it's all right. I'd hardly let you stay with my kids if

I didn't trust you. If you told me Cissy had crawled into bed with you last night, I wouldn't be upset. But still…" She let it hang. Then changed the subject. "Anyway, I'm leaving tomorrow morning. I should be in around five or six. Thanks again for doing this, Micky."

"No problem," I answered, not quite truthfully.

I installed the night-light next to Cissy's bed, then stayed up reading until a little after three, but no one stirred. Maybe the night-light would keep away Cissy's fears.

CHAPTER 10

Barbara got home a little after five, tired from the long drive. She thanked me again and even offered dinner, but I declined. It was time for Barbara to be with her kids and for me to be by myself.

The next day, I went to the airport. Cordelia's plane was only a few minutes late—a minor miracle. Moisant Field, better known as New Orleans International Airport, is located in the far reaches of Kenner, a New Orleans suburb beyond Metairie. Except for the grossly overpriced pralines and crawfish-to-go, it is an airport like any other airport. In the twenty minutes that I waited I saw one definite gay male couple, one highly possible dyke, and a maybe lipstick lesbian. The rest were hetero or well hidden.

I call it my count-the-queers game, but the underlying intent is to fight the alienation and, yes, even paranoia, that hits me whenever I am at some so-called mainstream place. (Danny claims that once you take out the people of color, the queers, the women, the poor, the disabled, the Jews, Buddhists, and other non-Christian religions, the mainstream turns into a trickle of privilege.)

I spotted Cordelia walking down the concourse. I watched her for a moment. She looked tired, subdued, as if she'd spent too many hours confined with strangers and the attendant strains of superficial chatter.

Then she saw me, a radiant smile breaking through the weariness on her face. Her smile stayed in place as she made her way through the crowd to me.

"Hi," she said, "I wasn't sure you'd come all the way out here for me." With the awkwardness of absence, she hugged me.

"Welcome back," I replied as I returned her hug. "And you should know I'd come for you anywhere," I whispered in her ear. Then we broke our embrace, in too public a place to risk more than an ambiguous hug.

"Can I help you with something?" I asked as we headed down the terminal.

"Here, take this." Cordelia handed me a very stuffed backpack.

We chatted a bit about the conference, her flight, and the like.

"I do appreciate your doing this," Cordelia said as we got into my car. "I feel like it's a wonderful luxury to be met by someone."

"You say that now. Pretty soon you'll take my schlepping you around for granted."

"I'll never take you for granted," Cordelia replied, looking directly at me.

"I hope not. It is quite a sacrifice for me to come this far out in the 'burbs," I answered, ignoring her seriousness.

"I know," she said, matching my tone. "What have you been up to while I've been gone?"

I gave her a quick rundown while driving out of the airport maze. Then I asked the question I had been wanting to ask. "What do you know about child psychology?"

"Child psych? I know kids don't like getting stuck with needles. For more in-depth insight you'd have to ask someone else. It's not my field. Why do you want to know?"

"A case. A kid who's scared of something, but won't talk about it."

"That could be anything. I can give you some names if you think it would help."

"Thanks. It might." I merged into the interstate traffic, then with my gear-shifting over until we got to the French Quarter, I reached over and took Cordelia's hand. She returned my grasp, her hand firm and warm.

We said little, Cordelia even closed her eyes for a while, avoiding most of Metairie.

After letting her get out, it took me about fifteen minutes and much cursing at stupid tourist parking before I finally found a place to park.

Cordelia was still looking through her mail when I came in. "There's something about traveling that makes me feel like I really need to wash it off," she said as I entered. She put her arms on my shoulders. "Thanks. I do appreciate your being here. I…like your company…" She trailed off, then pulled me to her, an awkward embrace, as if she wasn't quite sure what my reaction would be or how far she should commit herself.

I kissed her. Cordelia instantly responded, kissing me back, as if her only hesitancy had been an unwillingness to push against my reticence. I opened my mouth, inviting her to kiss me deeply. Her response was again immediate, her tongue against mine. Her arms tightened around me.

I broke it off. "Go take your shower," I whispered in her ear, then kissed her cheek, not wanting our break to seem too abrupt.

"Yeah, I guess I do need to do that," she said, her eyes still half closed, then she added, "Would you like to join me?"

"I took a bath just before I went to get you. And I want you to take a quick shower."

"Your wish is my command," Cordelia said as she headed for the bathroom.

I sat down on her couch, glancing distractedly at a magazine from her accumulated mail. Is this how it goes, this awkward dance to intimacy—halting, jerking, shying at any obstacle? I had needed to pull away from her. I didn't know why I felt so threatened.

Fuck analysis, I thought, it only leads to more questions. I opened the magazine and forced myself to read a story about the rain forests.

Cordelia reappeared three pages into the rain forests, wrapped in a towel, her hair wet. "God, I feel much better," she said, running her fingers through her hair to help dry it.

"You still look the same. Fabulous."

She flashed me a quick smile as if to say, "Thanks, I almost believe you." I remember her telling me of once overhearing her grandfather say, "Cordelia got the brains, but Karen got the looks." I wondered how disappointed her grandfather, father, and, perhaps, even her mother were that she wasn't ever going to be blond, petite, and pretty.

She was tall and big-boned, her breasts full, voluptuous, her stomach rounded and soft, and her hips wide, the center of her gravity. It was one thing I wanted very much to give to Cordelia, the belief that in her very special and unique way, she was strikingly beautiful.

"Should I bother putting on clothes for you to take off?" she asked.

"No need. But keep your towel on for a bit." I put the magazine down. "I want to see what your erect nipples look like under terry cloth."

"The bedroom?" she inquired, holding out her hand for me.

"The bed, even," I said as I took her hand, then stood to follow her into the bedroom. But as we got in the door, I said, "Cordelia, not to be too disruptive, but do you have any of those child psych names?"

"Oh, of course," she said, letting go of my hand. She had a desk in the corner of her bedroom, a secretary that had come down from several generations. It was where she kept her personal correspondence and things related to family or friends. Out in the living room was her large, practical desk, which contained her bills, checks, medical journals, and the like. Cordelia went to the secretary and opened one of the small drawers in the desk section. Pulling out a stack of miscellaneous papers from the drawer, she took a card off the top, flipped quickly through the rest of the papers, but took nothing else. She put them back into the drawer, keeping only the card.

Then she turned back to me and handed me the card. I glanced at it. "Lindsey McNeil, M.D. By appointment only" and a phone number were all that was on it. It was typeset on expensive gray card stock.

"Lindsey's very good," Cordelia said by way of explanation. "Mention my name when you call. Tell Lindsey that…she owes me this one."

"How do you know her?" I asked, catching a shadow passing in her voice.

"Residency. She was chief resident in pysch when I rotated through." Cordelia changed the subject. "When do I get to take this towel off?"

"Not yet," I answered, putting the card in my wallet. "Sit on the bed," I told her.

I stood in front of her, still fully dressed. Her legs were between mine. She started to put her arms around me, but I shook my head. I brushed her hair back, then bent over to run my tongue along the rim on her ear. I moved my weight onto the bed, sitting in Cordelia's lap, straddling her. She took a sharp breath as I began softly kissing her neck, using both my lips and tongue.

"Lie down," I instructed as I moved away from her neck.

"I should go away more often," she said as she lay back, her arms above her head.

"No, you should come back more often," I amended.

Somehow I had to be in control tonight, to be the one setting the pace, the intensity. For a moment, I realized that not to have control frightened me. But I didn't know why and I didn't want to think about it.

I pulled the towel off Cordelia.

Chapter 11

Lindsey McNeil. I looked at the card. I wondered what she might tell me about Cordelia. More importantly, I reminded myself, could she help with Cissy?

First, another cup of coffee. I was at my place, trying to wake up. I hadn't gotten much sleep. Neither had Cordelia, but I assumed that life-and-death crises would keep her alert. I, on the other hand, was sitting at my desk with only a sleeping cat and a few unpaid bills to liven things up.

With a full cup of coffee in front of me, I braced myself for the usual runaround of "not in, busy, in a meeting" and promises of being called back sometime before the turn of the century, and dialed the number on the card.

An efficient secretary answered the phone. So far the usual, I thought, after being put on hold before I even got to say who I was.

I amused myself by timing my holding pattern. Ms. Efficient came back on the line exactly fifty-nine seconds later. I told her who I was and that, "Dr. Cordelia James gave me Dr. McNeil's name. She suggested that Dr. McNeil might answer some questions I have about child psychology." I added, "Cordelia said to tell Lindsey that she owed her this one."

Ms. E. put me on hold again, which I took as a good sign. It meant that instead of just brushing me off, she was checking with the great doctor herself. It was forty-five seconds this time.

"Dr. McNeil wants to know if you have some free time this afternoon. She can see you around four thirty, if that's convenient."

I told Ms. E. that it was, and she gave me the address, a comfortable uptown block, not St. Charles Avenue, but Prytania, the next street over. Well, did Dr. McNeil have a cancellation and just happen to be bored enough to talk to an unknown P.I.? Or was her sudden availability a measure of what she owed Cordelia?

I got another cup of coffee and wrote out checks to cover the bills that demanded attention. With the money Karen was giving me, I could afford to pay them in a timely manner, thereby preserving truth, beauty, and the American way, at least as far as capitalism was concerned.

Midway through the final bill, the phone rang. It was Karen. "Micky," she said. "Joey called."

"What did he want?"

"He didn't say. He just left a message," was her less than helpful elaboration.

"What did the message say?"

"That he would call back later."

"That's it?" I demanded.

"Well, so far. You did tell me to call you if he called," Karen defended.

I had. Somehow, I didn't think she would take it so literally. "Okay," I replied, "if he calls back, let me know."

"Uh…sure. You could come over here and wait for his call, you know."

For a moment, I thought I noticed uncertainty in Karen's voice. Not possible, I told myself. But I did bite back my first reply—"I can, but I won't"—and instead answered, "I know, but I've got a lot of things I need to do. You'll be okay."

"Yeah, I guess."

"I'll talk to you soon, Karen." That seemed to cheer her and we hung up.

Busy turned out to be doing my laundry. Clean clothes sounded like the order of the day to meet Dr. McNeil. I headed uptown a little before four. I wanted to be safely through the CBD (Central Business District, a sporadic hodgepodge of tall buildings on the uptown side of Canal Street) before the narrow streets became engorged with fleeing suits and dresses with high heels—ever so boringly on men and women, respectively.

At around four twenty I arrived at the address Ms. Efficiency had given me. It was a house, one of several well-preserved Victorians in the area. Other than it being the corner house and having some extra parking spaces opened up next to the drive, nothing differentiated this house from the others on the block.

I pulled into the driveway, parking toward the back, next to a fairly new Toyota Celica. On the other side of it was a red Jaguar. Parked nearer the driveway entrance was a boxy Cadillac with one of those obnoxious furry things stuck to its back window.

The front door opened and an uptown lady and her pouty teenaged daughter came out. With a quick glance and dismissal of my out-of-date

Datsun, they got into the Cadillac. I wondered if the daughter was getting enough therapy to realize that, despite all her rebellion, she was turning into her mother. They pulled out and drove away.

That, I surmised, left the other two cars for the doctor and Ms. Efficiency, and I doubted that Ms. E.'s was the Jag. What kind of child psychiatrist drives a red Jaguar, I wondered. Time to find out. There was a small brass plaque next to the door that read, "L. McNeil, M.D.," but you had to be on the porch before you could read it. Very discreet. For a moment, I wondered if Dr. McNeil was a lesbian, then I rang the buzzer, announcing my presence to Ms. E. She responded by buzzing me in.

I entered a comfortable and tasteful waiting room. Its main focus, and diversion for the kids, was a large and well-stocked aquarium. I found myself drawn to its flashes of gold and silver cavorting about, an iridescent blue flickering behind them.

"Ms. Knight?" a voice called me away.

"Yes," I replied, turning to face Ms. Efficiency. She was a tall, striking black woman, dressed elegantly but comfortably in a bright turquoise jumpsuit. It was a style and color I could never pull off. I wondered how Dr. McNeil's uptown trade liked being put on hold by this woman. Then I realized that Lindsey McNeil, with her red Jaguar, probably didn't care.

"Dr. McNeil will be with you in just a moment," she said. A small brass plate, similar to the one outside, announced that she was Amanda Jackson. "Time to feed the fishes," she continued, coming around the partition that divided her area from the waiting room. "Want to help?" She flashed a broad smile.

A child would be enchanted. But I wasn't a child. "No, no thanks," I replied. "I'd probably overfeed them or something."

Amanda showed no such reticence. She poured a layer of fish treats on the water. "Come and get it. Don't hide behind the rock, Erato. Thalia, you're overeating again."

"You name the fish?"

"How else would you know what to call them?" Amanda Jackson replied.

A soft chime on her desk sounded. "Dr. McNeil will see you now," she said, motioning me before her.

I went around the reception area, then down a hallway. Amanda pointed me toward an open door.

"Thank you," I said to her retreating figure.

I entered Dr. McNeil's office. It was a large, yet friendly room, an oak bookcase in one corner, a deep blue Oriental rug on the floor, a couch, its material matching the rug, several other chairs, and, off-center enough so that it didn't dominate the room, an antique desk. Lindsey McNeil was seated behind it.

"You're Michele Knight, I presume," she said.

"Yes, I am," I answered. She was classically beautiful—nose, eyes, jaw, all in perfect proportion. Her lips were full, adding sensuality to a face that could have been austere without a hint of licentiousness. Her eyes were blue-gray, confident and direct, a contrast to her playful, sensual mouth. This was definitely a woman who would be a child psychiatrist and drive an expensive red sports car. She was also, I suspected a woman who could give the illusion that you knew her well, when, in fact, you knew only a small part of her. Her hair was full, chestnut brown, cut casually short. A pair of glasses was perched on the top of her head. I wondered if she really needed them or just used the studiousness glasses implied to counterbalance her looks. She also had, I couldn't help noticing, perfect breasts, high and round, just large enough that attention had to be paid, but not so huge as to be overwhelming. I quickly looked back at her face, not wanting her to catch me staring at her breasts. Her slight smile gave no clue as to whether or not she had seen where my attention had been briefly focused.

"And you, of course, are Dr. McNeil," I said, stating the obvious.

"Please sit," she said, not offering to let me call her Lindsey, I noted. She indicated a chair beside her desk. "So what can I do for you, Ms. Knight?"

I didn't offer to let her call me Micky, either.

I began by asking a few questions, getting a basic introduction to development in prepubescent girls as an answer. Lindsey McNeil seemed willing to take the time to answer my questions with a broad range of information. Clearly, she wasn't going to stint or hurry this interview. Again, I couldn't help but wonder if her generosity with her time was related to what she owed Cordelia. I finally got to my main purpose and gave her a brief description of Cissy and what was going on.

"It's hard to say," Lindsey replied, "without having seen the child or her mother. This is all speculation."

"What do you speculate?"

"The usual suspects. No bruises, scars, or broken bones makes physical abuse less likely. That leaves either psychological abuse or sexual abuse. A young girl with an often absent mother is a prime candidate for sexual abuse. That's my best guess. Again, this is just speculation," she emphasized.

"That's it?" I questioned, somehow annoyed that it so quickly came down to this.

"Best guess. I gather you don't like it."

"Why should I like the idea of a nine-year-old girl being—that," I broke off, needing to get my sudden anger under control.

"There are other possibilities, of course," she said calmly. "And we can hope her behavior change is only due to one of those many rough patches on the way to growing up." Lindsey looked directly at me, "But I do want to be honest with you."

"Yes, be honest," I affirmed.

She nodded, then said, "It's not easy to confront the possibility that someone we care about is being sexually molested."

I shrugged, met her gaze for a moment, then looked away. "What do we do?" I demanded.

"What would you like to do?" Lindsey asked quietly.

"Stop it. Make it stop," I answered.

"For your friend?"

"Yes, of course," I retorted fiercely. "Who else?"

Lindsey didn't reply, she didn't need to. We both knew what I had just revealed.

"It's getting late," I said. "Thank you for your time. I've taken too much of it."

"Not at all. I hope I've been of some help," Lindsey had the grace to reply.

"Yes, thank you, you have," I answered distractedly, standing to go.

"Can I ask you to walk me to my car?" she asked.

"Yes, of course," I said, hiding my surprise that a woman who drove a red Jaguar needed to be walked to it.

"Just a moment," she said, as she cleared her desk.

I stood gazing out the window to avoid looking at her while she packed up.

Lindsey closed her briefcase with a snap, then slowly stood up. Suddenly, she grimaced with pain, then used her hands to catch herself.

"Can I help?" I asked, moving toward her.

"It's okay," she said. "My legs get stiff after sitting for a while. Particularly at the end of the day." She reached to the far side of her desk and got a cane. "I'm okay," she reassured me.

"Would you like me to carry your briefcase?" I offered.

"No, I've got it," she replied, adding, "I'm used to it." Taking the cane in her left hand, she grasped the briefcase in her right. "You can, however," she said as she walked across the room, "shut the door and catch the light."

I obeyed, following her out. The reception area was dim, most of the lights were out. Ms. Jackson had gone. The aquarium glowed ethereally at one side of the waiting room.

Lindsey led the way out the front door, then turning to lock it, she handed her briefcase to me while she fumbled with the keys.

It wasn't recent or temporary, I thought. The cane, the limp, the accommodations had all been accepted a long time ago. She knew how much assistance she needed; there was no trial and error in what she could or couldn't do.

The door locked, Lindsey took the briefcase from me. She crossed the porch, took one step down and stopped, a look of pain on her face. She shook her head, as if to clear it.

"The changing weather. It seems to make things worse. Or maybe it's just that the days darken so quickly," Lindsey said. With a wry smile, she handed the briefcase back to me, then using both the cane and the stair rail, she made her way down. She didn't take the briefcase back this time.

"What do you do if no one's here?" I asked, curiosity overcoming my reticence.

"When I'm seeing patients, Amanda usually stays until they're gone and she locks up. If I have to, I can manage by myself. I could probably crawl from my office to my car if I had to. But it's easier if you help me. You don't mind, do you?"

"No, of course not," I answered quickly. My legs weren't permanently twisted.

We walked past my car to hers. She unlocked her door, letting me stand and hold her briefcase.

"It was a car accident," Lindsey stated. "Now, can I ask you a question?"

I nodded yes.

"Are you and Cordelia lovers?" She looked directly at me, but her glasses covered the intent behind her gaze.

"Yes," I answered. "Yes, we are."

Lindsey said nothing, but reached out and took her briefcase from me. Her hand lingered for just a moment against mine. I couldn't fathom the gesture.

"I wondered," Lindsey replied, as she stowed her briefcase in her car. "Tell Cordelia…that I'll call her sometime." She added, "And if I can help you, let me know." Her offer seemed genuine.

"Will you talk to the girl?"

"I could. But if she hasn't told you anything, it will probably take a while to get her to trust me. If ever."

"Would you try?" I pushed.

Lindsey slowly nodded, then said, "My fee is one hundred and fifty dollars an hour. In a few cases, I will do sliding scale, but only if the situation merits it."

I thought for a moment. Barbara Selby couldn't afford anything like it. Then I remembered the money Karen was paying me.

"Okay," I agreed.

"I'll need to meet the mother and get her permission."

"All right. But I'll pay the bills. Don't discuss money with Cissy's mother."

"Okay. I can't make any promises that Cissy will tell me anything. And even if she does, that I can tell you."

"I know. But I can't..." I didn't finish the sentence.

Lindsey nodded. She got in her car. "Goodbye, Micky. It was intriguing to meet you." She gave me an enigmatic smile, then started her car and pulled out.

Seated in her car, she seemed very confident and in command, a woman who should be driving a red Jaguar, I thought as I got into my not-very-late model, faded lime green Datsun. She had, I realized, controlled the entire interview. I only knew what she had intended to reveal, nothing beyond that, and I had given away things I never intended to let escape.

I sat in my car, remembering that ugly yellow brick house in Metairie where I had lived with my aunt and uncle after my father had died. I had been ten years old when I first moved there, eighteen when I'd walked out, vowing never to return. Never to see my Aunt Greta, Uncle Claude, and their three children, Bayard, Mary Theresa, and Augustine, again. Gus was a year younger than me, always a little slow and glad that I was the new "whipping boy" in the family, but he was never malicious or mean. Mary Theresa, into boys and makeup, had no interest in a tomboy cousin from the backward bayous, a few years younger than she was. Bayard was five years older than I was. And he had an interest in me.

But that was the past. It was gone. I started my car and drove away.

Chapter 12

After I had gotten home yesterday from my talk with Lindsey McNeil, I had turned down my phone and answering machine. I didn't remember to turn the volume back up until midafternoon when I noticed the message light blinking. Cordelia had called, her message was short—she had just called to say hi and that she was going to bed early. There were two name-and-phone-number messages from Joanne, both from earlier today. I wondered what she wanted. I didn't have to wonder long. The phone rang and it was her.

"You're hard to get a hold of," was her greeting.

"Sorry, I occasionally have to go out and work for a living."

"But not as hard to reach as Cordelia. So you get to be the message bearer. Alex's party is a surprise. Tell Cordelia that I've gotten reservations at Commander's."

"La-di-da," I interjected at the name of the Garden District restaurant. "I don't know if I have anything that will pass their dress code."

"You have a little over a week to beg, borrow, or steal something."

"An officer of the law advising me to steal?"

"Beg or borrow, then. We need to get Alex there without her suspecting. Pass this on to Cordelia and discuss it. I'll call you later in the week."

"Okay, I will."

"And check your answering machine more often. Bye." She hung up.

"Nice talking to you, too, Joanne," I said to the receiver still in my hand.

I decided to do some work on my one paying case and dialed Torbin's number.

"Sisters of the Sacred Crawdad. We bless sucking heads, pinching tails, and eating the meat," he answered the phone.

"Torbin, someday you will get into trouble."

"Oh, Micky, darling, trust me, I already have. Your favorite aunt and mine, Greta, was the first person to hear that particular little salutation. Her involuntary screech of outrage, at least an A above high C, was worth the twenty-minute sermon I got on blasphemy. I used the time wisely to pick up the shattered glassware."

"The Robedeaux Family Follies, I can't wait for the musical. However, my call has a serious purpose. What have you found out so far?"

"Not much. This book isn't just closed, it's locked in the vault," he admitted. "Pillar of the community, family man, the same refrain over and over again. The only faint whiff is that he donates a discreet amount of money to local AIDS organizations."

"That doesn't mean much. Decent people donated five years ago, even the merely respectable are doing it today."

"True," Torbin answered, then continued, "And, I don't like this. It's not from a reliable source. Actually, a rather disgusting source. A less-than-gentleman trying to pick me up at a urinal."

"Don't give me the details of your sex life."

"No, no, I'm not. Peeing was my only purpose for being at that urinal. Anyway, this man, one of those types with scruffy facial hair and oh-so-sexually attractive beer belly bulging over a commercially distressed black leather belt, suddenly appeared and scared the piss back into me. While I was attempting to get it started again, he proceeded to regale me with his sexual exploits. As I said, not the most reliable of sources."

"So, what did this source reveal?"

"He claimed that, in his younger days, he procured for Colombé. Men, sometimes women, usually eighteen or nineteen, and that Colombé liked to play rough with them."

"How rough?"

"The usual stuff, fisting, whips, chained down or up. The ugly twist is that these procured young kids didn't really consent, they were coerced. They were poor, they needed the money. My source said that the more desperate they were, the more Colombé liked it."

"If it's true, it's ugly."

"But remember the source."

"How did you escape?"

"Using my wits. And zipping my pants quickly. I told him to meet me at 334 Royal Street at the new bar there."

"Torbin, that's the Vieux Carr police station."

"And I'm sure he had a much more interesting night than I ever could have given him. Besides, he looked like the type who would like men in uniform."

"I'll bet. Nothing else on Colombé?"

"*Nada*. Nil. None. A nadir."

"Enough. Let me know if you hear anything."

"Will do. When are you and that lovely lady friend of yours going to come over?"

"Sometime, Tor. We're both a bit busy at the moment."

"With each other, I hope."

"Do you know someone by the name of Lindsey McNeil?"

"Mick, I'd expect more subtlety from you in changing the subject," Torbin caught me, then he bit. "Male or female?"

"Female."

"Actually, I don't know anyone with that name, male or female. Why do you ask?"

"I met her yesterday. I'm just curious."

"You're not supposed to be curious about other women, at least not yet."

"Another case I'm working on. It'd be helpful to know a few more things about her."

"Like her sexuality?"

"It might be useful to know."

"If I hear anything, I'll let you know."

"Thanks, Tor." We hung up.

I spent the evening and most of the night working on a surveillance team. I occasionally get calls when another warm, observant body is needed. Sometimes sitting for hours on end just waiting clears my thinking, but sometimes it just gives me a headache. I didn't even ask why we were tailing the person we were watching. The reasons usually don't make me feel better about myself. At six a.m., I stumbled home and to bed.

It was a little before one o'clock when I got up. I put on Bach's Brandenburg Concertos and brewed myself a pot of chicory coffee. Just as I raised the cup to my lips for my first sip, the phone rang.

"Hi, Micky. This is Alex. What are you and Cordelia doing a week from Thursday?"

"A week from Thursday? I don't know what I'm doing now, let alone then."

"Okay, I admit it. I'm sure that you had no idea, but Thursday next is my birthday. Just between you and me, is Joanne planning anything?"

"No, not that I know of," I lied. "She hasn't mentioned a thing to me."

"Oh…well—can you hold for a minute. I've got someone on another line."

I held, fortunately with no music in the background to clash with Bach. I had gotten several meaningful gulps of coffee before I became unheld.

"I'm sorry, but Ms. Sayers is on a long-distance call. Can I help you?" It was Barbara Selby. She is Alex's administrative assistant.

"Hi, Barbara, this is Micky."

"Micky, hi." Her voice relaxed from formal office mode. "How are you?"

"Fine. Surviving the usual chaos that surrounds me. Did Patrick and Cissy survive my babysitting?"

"They're fine. Well...Patrick is okay. Cissy...she hasn't slept very well the last few nights. It seems to be getting worse."

"Any idea why?"

"No, not really. She won't talk to me. Did she...when you were here...did she say anything, do anything that might give you a hint as to what's bothering her?"

"No, nothing that I could see," I admitted.

"I'm starting to get worried about her. I'm beginning to feel like a horrible mother. What have I done? Not done? Not seen?"

"Can I make a suggestion?"

"Sure, anything."

"I know someone, a therapist, who works with kids. It might help to have Cissy talk to her."

"Do you think?" Barbara said, then asked, "Who is she?"

"A friend of Cordelia's."

"That makes me feel better. Have you talked to her about Cissy?"

"Well, sort of. I just mentioned her, no names—"

"It's okay," Barbara interrupted. "Makes it easier, in fact. Did she say anything?"

"She needs to meet you, get your permission and all that."

"All right," Barbara agreed. "I can probably make a five thirty appointment, but not before that. Will you go with us? I'm...well, therapists are for crazy people, that's what I've always been told. Just hold my hand and tell me I'm doing the right thing."

"Of course I'll go with you. Do you want me to arrange the appointment?" I offered.

"I hate to use you as a go-between..."

"It's not a problem."

"Thanks, Micky. Any afternoon but Wednesday is okay. I appreciate your help."

"I hope it helps Cissy."

"Oh, God, yes, I hope it helps her," Barbara said, then, "My, we've talked for a bit. Alex is off her line. Do you want to speak to her?"

"If she has anything else to say to me." Barbara put me back on hold.

"So you don't know if Joanne is planning anything?" Alex came back on the line.

"She hasn't mentioned a thing to me." Don't lay it on too thick, I cautioned myself. "I'll talk to Cordelia. She might know something."

"You're a pal. I appreciate this."

Appreciated by all the right women for all the wrong reasons, I thought to myself as I dialed Joanne's number.

"Alex contacted me," I told Joanne. "She's worried that you've forgotten her birthday. Can I make a suggestion?"

"Can I stop you?"

"No," I rejoined, then continued, "You can't get away with pretending to ignore Alex's birthday at this point. Suggest a quiet dinner for the two of you. On birthday afternoon, you call and tell her a major crisis has occurred and you can't get away to pick her up. Pawn her off on Cordelia."

"Cordelia's too honest. She'll give it away."

"Cordelia, too, will have a crisis at work and be unable to escort Alex. At which point Alex gets dumped with me."

"And you could sell snake oil to oily snakes."

"Thanks. I think. And I, feigning a nefarious P.I. errand, take her to your posh restaurant."

"It's bizarre enough that it might work." Joanne left it at that. I thought it was a fairly nifty plan myself.

Calling Lindsey McNeil was my next task. Of course, I didn't speak to her. Amanda Jackson and I ended up doing the scheduling pas de deux. Lindsey had a cancellation Thursday at six p.m. After that I was tired of phone calls and decided to take a walk. But the damn thing rang just as I was trying to guess whether it was cool enough to wear a jacket.

"Hello," I answered brusquely.

"Micky, hi. Have I caught you at a bad time?" It was Cordelia.

"No, not really. I was just going to take a walk to clear my head. I feel like I've been on the phone all day."

"Then I won't keep you long. I just talked to Joanne. She told me your idea. I think it's great."

"It was nothing," I replied, the soul of modesty.

"Anyway," she continued, "my last appointment just canceled, and

I'm about to leave to check on a few patients in the hospital. How about dinner tonight? I'd love to see you."

"Sounds good to me. I'll cook," I said firmly. She had paid for dinner last time, and with the expense of Alex's birthday looming, I didn't want to let any more debts mount.

"All right. My place?"

"Your place. I'll run by the grocery while you're at the hospital. Say an hour, hour and a half?"

"See you then."

Since an invitation to spend the night had been implied with dinner, I began grabbing a few overnight necessities and throwing them into a duffel bag. I was down to my toothbrush when the phone rang again.

Hoping that it wasn't Cordelia calling to cancel our plans, I picked it up. I got what I wanted; it wasn't Cordelia.

"Micky, Joey called again."

"What did he want this time, Karen?" I asked, my impatience barely under control. I glanced at my watch. She had two minutes to get to her point and then I would cut her off.

"To see me. Alone. He says it won't be safe for you to go along."

"He what? He threatened you?"

"Not really. He made it sound friendly, like he was concerned. He said his friend, the owner of the bar, doesn't like you. That it wouldn't be safe for him to see you."

"You're not meeting at the Sans Pareil Club?"

"No, some other place. Over in Algiers. I told him I can't find my way around the West Bank, that I'd get lost the second I got off the bridge…"

"Wait, one point at a time," I interjected to halt Karen's scattered thoughts. "Did he say who this guy was and why he didn't like me?"

"He didn't give a name—I asked, really, I did. He said you had seduced his friend's girlfriend and that his friend hated your guts."

"That's not likely," I said. It was, however, possible. "Where is this place?"

"Over in Algiers, like I said. He said it's in walking distance of the ferry. He said it's just a quiet neighborhood bar."

"It doesn't matter if it's the neighborhood police station. You didn't agree to meet him, did you?"

"No, I didn't. He hung up before I really got a chance to say no. Just 'I'll see you,' and, then, boom, he was gone."

"When is this meeting supposed to take place?"

"Thursday at eight. He said he was tired of meeting on my territory and that it was my turn to go to him."

"Do you have any big, mean friends who can stay with you on Thursday?"

"Would you?" she asked, then added, "I'll pay you whatever you want."

Cissy's appointment was at six. I assumed that it was for a fifty-minute hour, but I wasn't sure. I didn't want to guarantee Karen that I'd be at her place at the expense of cutting Cissy short.

"I couldn't get there much before eight, and I can't promise even that for sure."

"That's okay. He won't know I'm not going to show up until eight thirty or so."

"Unless someone's watching your place."

"Oh." Karen was clearly discomfited by the thought.

"Karen, at this point, you really should consider going to the police," I told her. "Whatever Joey and his pals are up to, it's definitely illegal, not just irregular."

"I don't want to do that."

"You're in deep. I don't know if I can get you out."

"The police will only make things worse. I know that," Karen said vehemently.

"How?"

"All I need is to be charged with a felony and my trust funds are gone. Money's the only protection I have. Would you be helping me if I weren't paying you?" she demanded bluntly.

The question caught me off guard. "Probably not," I answered, angry at her for trapping me. "But remember, money got you into this to begin with. If you didn't belong to a snotty uptown club and if you didn't want to make even more money on top of the pile you've already got and if you weren't so greedy that you didn't ask the right questions in the beginning, you wouldn't be—"

"I don't need a lecture from you," she cut me off. "And I'm not going to the police. Not yet. I can't prove anything. That might be the most dangerous thing for me to do."

"All right," I relented. I had to ask myself if my wanting Karen in NOPD's in-tray was because I thought it was really the best place for her to be or because I wanted to hand her over so she could be someone else's problem. "I'll get you a couple of bodyguards for Thursday until I can get there," I told her. "In the meantime, vary your routine, keep people around you, lock everything securely. Be careful until this blows over."

"I guess," she answered unhappily, then to forestall what would have been my retort, "I know, I know, I will, I'll be very careful."

"And, Karen, if we get the evidence?"

"I'll go to the police."

"Right. See you tomorrow." I hung up.

And then I grabbed my toothbrush, stuffed it into my duffel bag, and hurried out the door before the phone could ring again.

CHAPTER 13

It wasn't until I started my car that I realized I hadn't brought my set of keys to Cordelia's apartment. I had meant to. Well, not tonight, I thought. I still needed to hit a grocery store. Since Cordelia was expecting me even as I shifted into second, I settled on a close, but iffy, one. Then on fish rather than chicken with a run by a good seafood place on St. Claude, not very far out of the way.

After getting the fish, I hit the grocery store. Some fresh vegetables, rice, and lemons were all I needed. I repeated my list as a mantra, eschewing the fight for the few remaining grocery carts. The asparagus looked good. I realized that I didn't know if Cordelia liked asparagus or not. A cart banged into my hip. The store was crowded with just-out-of-work grocery buyers. I grabbed the asparagus, then picked up the rest of my list.

Zigzagging around many paused carts got me to the least clogged checkout line. I glanced at my watch, seeing late become later as the cashier waited for the harried manager to approve a check. My turn to fork over my money arrived. Almost there, I told myself as I swerved through the confusion and muddle of the checkout counters.

The strong light of late afternoon had dimmed to twilight blue. The precision and clarity of the day was lost, the possibilities of the night encroached—violence, love, traces of dark and light that entice and repel. Night is always ambiguous.

His shadow fell across my hands as I put the groceries in my trunk. I should have seen him, known he was here, the lack of warning unnerved me as much as his physical presence.

"Michele, long time, no see, hey?"

Hannah Arendt is right, I thought as I looked at him, his suit rumpled, the shirt tight across the beginnings of a beer gut. Evil is banal.

"Mama wondered why you didn't come 'round last Christmas. You know how she is about family."

"I didn't know I was family," I answered.

"'Course you're family. How can you doubt it?"

Because you did everything you could to make me feel unwanted, an outsider, a bastard. But if I said that, he would deny it, tell me I was making it up. Of course, I was family—don't all families have a little girl somewhere to be toyed with late at night when no one is watching?

"I'm in real estate now, you know. Doing some commercial property down here."

He stood next to my car door, barring my way.

"Well, good luck with it," I said perfunctorily. "I'm late, I've got to go."

"Got a date?" He didn't move. "A new girlfriend?" The night wasn't dense enough to hide his leer.

"That's none of your business."

"Now, don't be like that, Mick. I'm not like Mama, screeching about perversion. You want to do it with girls, that's okay by me."

"Let me get to my car."

"Must be a hot-looking woman for you to be in such a hurry."

"Let me get into my car," I repeated.

"I got me a new girlfriend. You should meet her sometime. She loves sex. I bet she'd like to do it with a woman. Might be you could give her a few pointers."

"Move away from my car door. I'm in a hurry."

"Why, sure, Michele, but you got to say the magic word."

I didn't reply, instead I crossed my arms and looked away from him.

"C'mon, now, what's the magic word?"

"Fuck you, asshole."

"'Please,'" he chortled, having gotten a reaction out of me. "The word is 'please.' Didn't you learn no manners growing up out in that bayou?"

Hate or fear, it didn't matter which, as long as he still had some power over me. Little increments of control, standing at my car door, barring my way, telling me we were part of a happy family, daring me to deny it. If I say "please," he'll have to move away. But if I say "please," I'll be admitting that it is his game, with his rules.

"Bayard, you shit, leave me the fuck alone." I spun from him, walked to the other side of my car, opened the passenger door, and clambered over the stick shift to get into the driver's seat.

Bayard tapped at my window, but I ignored him and started the car. Self-interest is his middle name; he'll get out of the way, I thought as I slammed the car into reverse and pulled out, cutting off another car nosing through the parking lot.

"Fucking asshole, fucking, fucking asshole," I muttered as I raced out of the supermarket lot.

"Get out of my fucking way," I snarled at the sluggish traffic, running a yellow light, then pulling an illegal U-turn. Don't give him the power, I thought as I forced myself to slow down. Getting a ticket is not going to make anything any better.

I found a parking spot near Cordelia's building, but just sat in my car for a few minutes, until I finally glanced at my watch. It was now a little past seven.

It's past and gone. You may never see him again, I told myself. With that I grabbed my fish and groceries, locked my car, and pushed Cordelia's buzzer.

She was on the phone and waved to me as I entered. "I really don't see the need for an aggressive course in an eighty-four-year-old woman," she told her caller.

I bent down, kissed her on the cheek, and headed for the kitchen. As I unloaded the groceries, I eavesdropped shamelessly on her phone call.

"It's not a matter of…" Then a pause, until she finally broke in, "The answer is no. If it helps at all, it won't be much, and, most likely, it will make her miserable." A shorter pause. "I may be. You can discuss it with Nolan in the morning if you want." She hung up.

I busied myself putting the rice on to steam. Cordelia came into the kitchen.

"What a pain," she said, a reference to the phone call, I hoped.

I turned from my steaming rice, put my arms around her, and kissed her. It was the least I could do, particularly if she didn't like asparagus.

"That makes up for annoying young residents," she said as we finally broke off. "Do you think I'm an 'old woman'?"

"Maturity and wisdom, yes."

"I doubt that's what he meant. More like plodding and staid."

"His girlfriend told him to wash it before she'd touch it; you're three inches taller than he is; and he can't stand taking orders from strong, intelligent women," I replied.

"One of the things I like most about you is your astute mind," Cordelia answered. "What's for dinner?"

"Red snapper, rice—do you eat asparagus?"

"Yeah, I like asparagus."

"Good, I wasn't sure. And strawberries for dessert."

"Sounds great. How about a salad? I've got some tomatoes that have to be eaten."

"Okay by me, I like tomatoes," I told her as I cut up a lemon.

Cordelia went to her refrigerator and started pulling out salad things. "How was your day?" she asked, then continued, "Cucumbers, lettuce, bell peppers, and mushrooms. Any of those you can't stand?"

"They're all fine. As was my day." That wasn't quite true, but sometimes the truth isn't worth the effort. "How was yours?"

"Actually, pretty good. My last patient even called to cancel instead of just not showing up. And now I'm getting dinner cooked for me in the comfort of my own home."

"I'm just a slave to love."

"My very own love slave. I think I like that. Any chance dinner can wait?" she asked, looking directly at me.

"Fresh red snapper? The rice is already on. Aren't you hungry?"

"Very hungry," she said, putting her arms around me. Then she started kissing my neck just below my jawline in a very sensitive area.

"My hands are fishy," I said to explain my not returning her embrace.

"Hands can be washed and the rice can be replaced," Cordelia rationally replied.

Her phone rang. "Damn," Cordelia said as she let go of me. "I'll make this quick." Her "Hello" was not friendly and welcoming. She immediately amended, "Oh, hi, Mom, I thought it was someone else."

They exchanged a few pleasantries. I was referred to as "having dinner with a friend," then it seemed Cordelia's mother was going on about other family members, officially Cordelia's stepsisters and brothers. Her mother had not remarried until after Cordelia was out of medical school. She lived in Connecticut with her new husband while Cordelia struggled through her residency here in New Orleans. Cordelia was, at that point, involved with a woman, and, other than a few obligatory appearances, she maintained her distance from her mother's new family.

The process of coming out to them was still very much ongoing and had been somewhat hindered by a stepbrother telling homophobic jokes and a stepsister who considered it her personal responsibility to fix up Cordelia with eligible men whenever she visited. However, her mother knew that Cordelia was a lesbian and, after the initial shock, had been supportive. I had always sensed in the way Cordelia spoke of her mother that there was a deep bond between them. And, I realized as I heard Cordelia's joyful laugh through the open kitchen archway, I envied her that connection.

My mother, real mother, pregnant at sixteen, had left when I was five. If she did love me, she hadn't loved me enough to remain in the bayous taking care of me. She could have at least waited until I was in school, I thought angrily. Then when I was ten, my father, the man who raised me as his daughter, had been killed, and I had been sent off to live with my Aunt Greta and Uncle Claude in that ugly house in Metairie. Uncle Claude had been inconsequential, leaving anything to do with the kids to Aunt Greta. Aunt Greta believed in God, the Church, and Discipline. She was not a woman who dealt well with the grief and anger of a child. To Aunt Greta, I wasn't her child, I wasn't anyone's legitimate child (despite my father, Uncle Claude's brother, having actually married my mother), and she saw no reason to pretend I was.

I don't want to think about them, I told myself as I slapped the red snapper over in its pan, rummaging through possible spices to use. Particularly the encounter with Bayard that this dinner had cost me. How do you make hatred go away? How do you keep it from wrenching bits and pieces of your life from you even after what happened is long gone, only a memory from your past?

Someone came from behind and put his arms around me, encasing me with his embrace. I spun away violently, spilling spice across the counter.

Cordelia looked at me, shock and surprise in her eyes.

It's only Cordelia, I told myself. Not…not who it would have been in Aunt Greta's kitchen.

"Micky. Are you okay?" she asked.

"Yeah. Sure. You scared me. I didn't hear you."

"I'm sorry. I didn't mean to…" She took a step toward me.

"This is a mess, let me clean it up." I turned from her, getting a sponge from the sink to wipe off the counter. I didn't want to be touched right now, and I didn't know how to tell Cordelia that.

"How's your mom?" I asked as I wiped the counter.

Cordelia leaned against the refrigerator, sensing that I needed distance. "Oh, pretty good. My stepsister Emily had twins a few days ago. She was telling me about that."

I put the sponge back in the sink, then rinsed off my hands. "Boys, girls, or both?" I asked as I began squeezing lemon onto the fish.

"Two girls, identical twins, identical sets of lungs from what Mom says."

I put the fish in the oven, then checked on the rice.

"Can I help with anything?" Cordelia asked.

"Finish up the salad, maybe, while I deal with the asparagus."

Cordelia nodded, pulling out a cutting board and knife. As she cut things for the salad, she went into detail about Emily and her twins, more to fill the silence than for any other reason.

During dinner we talked of mundane things—the weather, or what didn't directly concern us, Danny's and Elly's latest home improvement, Alex's birthday party.

It was only after dinner, over the slow sipping of coffee that Cordelia reached out, took my hand, and said, "Micky, do you want to talk?"

"Maybe I should go," I replied.

"If that's what you want." Cordelia didn't let go of my hand.

"Oh, I don't know." Then finally, "I ran into my cousin today."

"The one who molested you?" Cordelia asked evenly.

"Yeah, him," was my brusque reply. "I don't feel like having sex tonight, I really don't."

"We don't have to."

"Then I'd better go."

"You don't need to go. No rule says we have to make love when you stay here."

"We're just supposed to get in bed together and not do it?"

"Micky, you can always say no, at any time, for any reason."

"That's a nice thought," I said, taking my hand away. "Let me try that some night after we've gotten hot and horny."

"We'll stop. I would never want to have sex with someone who doesn't want it."

"It's not always that easy to stop. Sometimes cunts have a mind of their own."

"I didn't do it," Cordelia answered. "I didn't molest you, and I didn't turn my back and pretend that nothing was going on. You can be angry at me, but I'm not the one who deserves it."

"So what should I do, get a gun and blow his face off?"

"Would that solve everything?"

"I don't know…I don't know if it would solve anything," I slowly replied.

"Why don't you stay? I would hope there is more to our relationship than sex. Sometimes…it's nice to just be with someone."

"If that someone isn't in a foul temper and liable to lash out at any and everybody."

"I think I've had enough therapy not to take this kind of anger personally."

"Some of us can't afford one-hundred-and-fifty-dollar-an-hour shrinks."

Cordelia sighed, then ran her hand through her hair. "You don't have to see a therapist if you don't want to; if you do, there are many that charge less than a hundred and fifty an hour; and if you did want to see someone who charged that much, I'd be glad—"

"I don't want your money," I cut her off.

"I know," Cordelia sighed again. "But I do wish you would stop feeling that the only way to prove that you're not with me for my money is to rebel against it."

"Maybe I should go. I don't think my temper is getting any better."

"You're welcome to stay, you can even sleep on the couch if you like."

"Too lumpy," I said as I stood up. "I'm sorry I'm in such a bad mood."

"Thanks for dinner," Cordelia said as she also got up. "It was very good."

I stood indecisively a few feet from her door. Part of me wanted to bolt, fly out the door and run into exhaustion and oblivion. Another part wanted to stay here and be held, like a cat on a lap, with no expectations or demands beyond touch and warmth.

"Can I do anything to help?" Cordelia asked.

I just shook my head slightly, and mumbled, "No, nothing. I'll be okay. I should just go home and get some sleep. I'll be okay."

For a moment Cordelia looked like she wanted to say something, but she didn't, just nodded her head. Then, still saying nothing, she gave me a gentle good-night hug.

I put my arms around her and laid my head on her shoulder. Suddenly I wanted to stay. But I felt too awkward and vulnerable to ask.

She held me for a long time, as if waiting for something from me. But I made one of those bargains with myself that I knew you should never make. If she asked me to stay one more time, I would. If she didn't, I would go. That way, I didn't have to actively decide, or risk, anything and the responsibility was, in some way, Cordelia's.

Finally something interrupted our embrace, the chime of a clock, a shout in the street, I wasn't sure what broke the moment.

"Will you be okay?" Cordelia asked.

"Yeah, I'll be fine."

"Are…?" she started to say, then changed it to, "Call me sometime?"

"Sure, in the next day or so." I kissed her quickly on the cheek, then turned and walked out her door, suddenly angry at her for not asking me to stay one more time.

It was only after I'd gotten into my car and was out of the Quarter that I remembered that rejection was a two-way street. Why did I think Cordelia was immune to it if it terrified me? Why would she offer again something I'd repeatedly rejected?

I was angry and alone, and I had backed myself into this corner. After I got home, I lay in bed, letting useless thoughts churn through my brain, until, with the soft light of dawn coming through my window, I fell into a restless sleep.

Chapter 14

Despite my restless night, the alarm clock showed no mercy. I counterattacked, slapping it off several times, until my brain awoke enough to remember all the things I had to do today. I was still groggy even in the shower, leaning against the wall in lethargy while the water poured over me. It was only on the second cup of quickly gulped coffee that I began to feel alert.

First on my agenda was to arrange some babysitting for Karen. I decided to indulge myself and hire the best people for the job without worrying about Karen's level of comfort.

Muffy and Tiffany Security, Inc. The two women who ran it were not, of course, named Muffy and Tiffany. They had met as Navy M.P.s, got caught in the same witch-hunt, and were thrown out together. How romantic. Since it is hard to get a good job with "queer" typed on your discharge papers (the Pentagon was into outing before outing was in), Sara and Lucinda had gone into business for themselves. The Muffy and Tiffany moniker emerged from a Bacchanalian Mardi Gras party.

Lucinda was slight and quiet, someone you didn't notice until it was too late. She claimed to have a bit of every race on the planet in her background. Sara was tall and wide and as dark as the darkest night. People, particularly white people, were afraid to mess with her; she fit all the stereotypes too well. Yet, in her spare time, she was a horticulturist, growing rare orchids, spoke perfect French, and wrote villanelles as meditation.

Two dark-skinned women, one of them a big butch, would be perfect for Karen, I thought as I dialed their number. More importantly, if anything did happen, I knew that no one could handle it better than Sara and Lucinda.

They were available as they did a lot of bar jobs, so their working day didn't start until ten in the evening or so. Taking an early evening job would be "sunlighting" for them, as Sara said.

After that I started a list that I knew was going to be hard to complete—the men who had enough access to Cissy to abuse her. Teachers, Little League coaches, Barbara's boyfriend Ted, relatives, and the like. Barbara would have most of the answers, but it would mean asking her some very uncomfortable questions. I think the real reason that those responsible deny it is because if no one is at fault, then the taint of guilt becomes dispersed, spread to the innocent and guilty alike. Was it you? Or you? Or you? Until all of us carry little pieces of guilt like some insidious dust caught on our pant leg.

I spent a long time just staring at that piece of paper as if some act of will could tell me what I needed to know. Finally the low angle of the sun reminded me of the hour and the duties that lay ahead of me. I quickly packed up and locked my office, then headed uptown to meet Barbara and Cissy.

I got there first, for which I was glad. This was strange territory for Barbara and Cissy, and I was the one who had brought them here. Lindsey's red Jaguar was in the parking lot, as was Amanda Jackson's car and two others. I got out and leaned against a fender to wait for Barbara and Cissy. A moment later Barbara pulled into the driveway.

"Hi, how are you?" I said as she got out of the car.

"Fine. Nervous." Barbara glanced quickly over at Cissy, who was shutting the passenger door.

"It'll be okay. You're doing the right thing," I told her.

"I know. I know that. I just wish…that circumstances didn't compel me to do the right thing."

Cissy was waiting for us on her side of the car. She seemed subdued and wary. I wondered what Barbara had told her. I led the way into the waiting room.

"Good afternoon," Amanda Jackson greeted us. "You must be Cissy. Hello, Cissy," Amanda gave her a special welcome.

Cissy nodded in response.

"Ms. Selby, could you please fill this out?" Amanda gave Barbara the usual paperwork, then she continued to Cissy, "Would you like to meet the fish? It's important to be properly introduced."

With that Cissy noticed the fish tank. She took a few steps toward it, as if unsure how much permission she had in this strange, new place. Amanda came beside her, then put her hand on Cissy's shoulder and led her to the fish.

"That big silver one is Calliope. The one in the corner, with black and gold stripes, that's Clio."

"Who's that?" Cissy asked, her finger pointing at a blue streak.

"That's Erato. She's one of my favorites."

"How do you know it's a she?"

"Not too many he's have babies." Amanda pointed to some small blue specks weaving in and out of one of the plants.

I sat and watched Amanda tell Cissy about the fish, explaining what kind they were, where they were from along with other assorted fish lore.

Barbara had just looked up from her paperwork when a soft chime sounded. "Ms. Selby, Cissy," Amanda said, "please come with me." She led them back into Lindsey's office.

I sat and waited. I picked through a few magazines, but nothing seemed interesting. Amanda sat behind the reception desk, working on her computer. I thought of talking to her, questioning her about Lindsey (Does a doctor named Cordelia James call here? Did they ever sleep together?) but I knew she wouldn't or couldn't answer the questions I wanted answered. Also, I felt the need for stillness, to listen as if secrets being breached had a sound.

Finally I remembered something I needed to do before Barbara came out. "I'm paying for this," I said as I approached the reception area.

"I know," Amanda answered as she finished entering some data on the computer. "The initial consultation is free. If Dr. McNeil decides to take on Cissy as a patient, then you can start paying."

A door opened down the hallway and Barbara came out. "She wanted to talk to Cissy alone for a little bit," Barbara offered as explanation. She sat down on one of the straight-backed chairs, clutching her purse as if at some inquisition. In a way, she was. We were the failures. I resented Lindsey in there with Cissy, probing the dark secrets that she wouldn't tell me. Whatever resentment I felt, I knew it was nothing compared to the hell Barbara was in.

A clock ticked somewhere, the beat of slow seconds. Finally the door down the hallway opened again and Cissy came out. Lindsey, leaning heavily on her cane, followed her, as if even the short distance from her office to the waiting room was too fraught with danger to let a young girl walk alone.

"Can I talk to you, Ms. Selby?" Lindsey asked. She glanced briefly at me, but that was all.

Cissy headed for the fish, staring at their quickly flitting shapes as if pushing aside some ugly reality that she had been forced to confront.

And I knew then that it would not be easy. It would not be kind or gentle. Lindsey would produce no magic; answers, if they came, would be slow and anguished. From resenting Lindsey, I now wondered how she could pick at wounds until they bled fresh, clear blood. Even that couldn't guarantee that the wounds would heal without hideous scars.

I knelt beside Cissy. "I think I like the blue one the best. Which one do you like?"

"The little babies," she answered.

The children, I thought. "They are a very pretty blue."

The door to Lindsey's office opened again, and she and Barbara came down the hallway into the reception area. Barbara seemed less shaken.

"Let's see if we can find a regular time for Cissy to come in," Lindsey said.

The best we could do was Wednesday afternoons at four. I offered to give Cissy a ride from school and then home. Barbara protested, mentioning buses, but I insisted and she didn't protest further. I knew Barbara didn't really want Cissy on a bus, and that driving Cissy to and from her appointments was a way for me to keep directly involved.

A girl, maybe fifteen, came into the waiting room. She was by herself, no parent or guardian. She looked down at her shoes, away from us, as if ashamed of her aloneness in the face of three obviously connected strangers. I hoped, for her sake, that this was an aberration, that someone, someone who cared, would return for her.

"Thank you, Dr. McNeil," Barbara said, and took Cissy's hand.

Lindsey nodded to Barbara, then said, "I'll be with you in a minute," to the girl. She caught my eye for a moment, but beyond a direct acknowledgment of my being here, her look revealed nothing. She went back down the hallway to her office.

I followed Barbara and Cissy out the door. A bicycle was locked to the stair railing. The girl had ridden the bicycle here and she would ride it back in the dark when she was finished. I suddenly felt as if I lived in a savage world, where even small kindnesses are rare.

"Thanks for coming with us, Micky. I know it was boring for you," Barbara said as she unlocked her car to let Cissy in first.

"No problem. I'm glad I could do something." We walked to the driver's side.

"If you should change your mind about taking Cissy…"

"I won't."

"Okay. Thanks." She opened her door and got in.

I watched as she drove away. Only then did I get in my car. I glanced once more at the bicycle on my way out, then turned onto Prytania and headed for Karen's Garden District home.

Her house was actually the least pretentious on the block, more of a summer cottage (a fancy one) than the opulent mansions that made this part of town famous. The house was a pale blue with shutters and trim a deep cobalt. A generous porch covered the front of the house. Perfect for sipping mint juleps on, I thought. The second story had a screened-in porch. I noticed several pieces of white wicker furniture up there.

I crossed the porch and rang Karen's bell.

"Who is it?" Lucinda asked through the closed door.

"If you were watching this place properly, you'd know who it is."

"Well, I knew you looked like Micky Knight," she said as she opened the door. "And now I know you talk like Micky Knight. But are you really Micky Knight?"

"Who knows?" I said as I entered. "I certainly don't."

Lucinda did a quick scan of the street, then shut the door. "Spoken like the real Micky the K. It'll have to do."

"How's it going?"

"Fine. Karen and Sara are having a grand time in the kitchen, playing French chef, including the language."

I had expected to find Karen cowering in the corner, not palling around in the kitchen with Sara. Lucinda gave me her famous strange-things-happen shrug and led me to them.

"Micky, hi," Karen said when she saw me, trying to rub flour off her nose, but only succeeding in getting more on it. Definitely not how I had pictured Karen.

"Bon soir, Michele," Sara greeted me. *"Comment ça va?"*

Foreign language has never been my strong point. I had picked up some Spanish in high school and some German in college, but it was laborious, and I had never reached fluency. The older I got, the more I regretted it, but that didn't mean I liked being reminded of my lack. Particularly by Karen, with her expense-paid summers in France with Mama.

If you can't beat them at their own game, play another one. I switched from language to business. "Has Joey called? Anything happened?"

"No, nothing," Sara answered.

"No, he hasn't called," Karen seconded her.

"Why don't you and Luce bar the door and guard the way, while Karen and I finish here in the kitchen?" Sara suggested.

"Sara thinks we'll make her soufflé fall." Lucinda again shrugged and led the way out of the kitchen. I followed. Karen and Sara began prattling in French.

"Is that obnoxious, or am I just getting old?" I asked as we returned to the front room.

"Both." Lucinda pulled the drapery back slightly and scanned the street. "How long do we wait?"

I glanced at my watch. It was seven thirty. "She's supposed to meet him at eight. I guess until after dinner."

"Sounds good to me." Lucinda let go of the curtain and sat down. She picked up a book she had been reading, but every few minutes put it down again to glance down the street.

I alternated between pacing and sitting. At just before eight, Lucinda did rounds, going upstairs to check all the rooms, the same downstairs, and into the yard. She returned just in time for Karen's announcement of dinner.

Sara and Karen had certainly amused themselves in the cooking arena. We started out with oysters Rockefeller; the main course was barbecued stuffed shrimp followed with bananas Foster for dessert. A few dirty looks from Lucinda and myself did get Sara and Karen to stop speaking their Parisian French.

I couldn't help glancing at my watch. By eight thirty Joey must have realized that Karen was not going to show up. I wondered how much of this was game playing or if he really thought he could make Karen go to the West bank. My best guess was that he was just trying to see how far he could push us.

Nine o'clock came and went, and we cleared away the supper dishes.

At nine fifteen the phone rang. For a moment nobody did anything, as if the ringing phone demanded a momentous decision. Then Karen started to reach for it, but I stopped her and picked it up.

"Hello," I said in a neutral voice, then for a brief moment wondered what I'd do if it turned out to be Cordelia. It wasn't.

"Karen," a man's voice replied. I thought it was Joey, but I couldn't be positive.

"Who is this?" I asked.

"Karen, darling, you're late," he mocked.

"I'm not Karen. Who is this?"

"You're not?" His tone was still languid, unhurried as if he had plenty of time to play his game. "Who are you?"

"You're wasting my time, Joey. What do you want?"

"Micky, is that you? Miss Micky Knight, little Karen's favorite watchdog. Rowf rowf."

I held my temper. He was trying to goad me, and I had to find out his limits without giving him mine. "You're still wasting my time. What is it you want?"

"You know, what I really want is to watch you and Karen do it. I want to watch you go between her legs and lick..."

I held the phone away from my ear so I wouldn't have to listen to his voice. Karen, when she understood what he was saying, started to make a sound, but I cut her off with a motion of my hand. I put the receiver down, muffling Joey's spew, and then stood up and paced a few steps away. It was a game and timing was everything. Finally his voice stopped and he waited for my reply. And he waited.

I held another beat, then picked up the phone.

"Sorry, Joey, my tampon was bleeding over and I could feel blood running down my legs. I had to pull it out, it was covered with big, dripping clots. What were you saying?"

For a moment there was silence on his end, then he snarled, "What the fuck do you want, Knight?" His languid, unhurried tone was gone.

"A meeting at our time, on our territory."

"Yeah? You're at Karen's. What the fuck's gonna stop me from coming over there now? You think you're that butch a chick?"

"No," I said calmly. "That's why I've got a couple of ex-Navy M.P.s here. They'd love to rip out a little white-boy throat like yours."

"Fuckin' cunt," he muttered, just clear enough for me to hear. I let him get away with it. I'd won the battle and that was all that really mattered.

"We'll meet at the Sans Pareil Club," I said, looking at Karen to get her agreement.

"Soon," Joey added.

"Tomorrow at eight," I replied, again getting confirmation from Karen. "Joey? No games, no shit. You'll gain very little by making me your enemy and you might lose a lot."

Joey grunted what I hoped was compliance, then said, "I'll see you tomorrow." The line went dead. I put the receiver down.

"You want Luce to stay, Mick?" Sara asked.

"No, it'll be okay."

"You sure?"

"I let him get away with calling me a cunt. That should salve his ego enough to keep him away from here."

"If you need us, you call," Lucinda said. "We're working that new bar on Rampart tonight. Be there until four or five. Home after that."

"Thanks, I will."

"We'll check the yard one more time, then be on our way," Sara said as she and Lucinda put on their jackets and headed for the door.

I let them out, checking the street as I did. It was possible that Joey was calling from a pay phone a few blocks away. I watched as Sara and Lucinda disappeared around the side of the house, then waited at the front window until they reappeared and Lucinda flashed me an all-clear sign.

"You could go to a hotel," I said, turning to Karen. "It might be safer."

"Do you really think he'll do anything?"

"No, I doubt it, but there is the chance."

"I'd like to stay."

I nodded. "You do have a burglar alarm, don't you? Is it on?"

Karen showed me her alarm and how to work it. The rich havens of the Garden District are close by some less than gentle areas of the city. These upper crust houses tend to have the latest in security devices. Karen's was no exception. If Joey really wanted to get in he could, but it wouldn't be easy and it would be noisy. He didn't seem the type who would do the grunt labor required. Joey was a bully and a show-off. He liked driving his Porsche and hanging out at the Sans Pareil Club.

"You can go to bed, if you want," I told Karen after we'd finished making sure the house was secure. "I doubt we'll see Joey until tomorrow night."

"What about you?"

"I'll stay up. I'd much rather overestimate him than underestimate him."

"Can I fix you some coffee or anything? Espresso?"

"You would have an espresso machine."

"And a cappuccino machine. My daddy gave them both to me on my twenty-first birthday." She paused for a moment, then continued, "So that whenever he came to visit, I could make him cappuccino and espresso, because by that point he'd divorced his second wife and he didn't have anyone to make it for him."

I started to sympathize with Karen, but instead I rebelled. "No one gave me anything for my twenty-first birthday. I went out and got drunk by myself." That wasn't quite true, Danny had sent me a card and I didn't end up alone, although I couldn't recall the name of the woman I slept with that night.

"I'm sorry," Karen said, adding ruefully, "Would you like an espresso or cappuccino machine?"

"No, no thanks. Maybe some coffee. Hold the machine."

Karen went into the kitchen to make it. I looked out the front window, checking the street again. Nothing. A few minutes later Karen returned with my coffee, neatly arranged on a tray with sugar and milk.

"Can I get you anything else?"

"Thanks, no. This is fine. Good night, Karen."

"Good night, Micky." She turned to go, then stopped and turned back. "Look, I'm sorry about those things Joey said. I…I saw the look on your face. I didn't want…"

"It's okay, Karen. He was trying to make us feel ugly and embarrassed." Karen was wearing no makeup tonight, and the strain and worry of the last few hours had wiped off her veneer of assurance and sophistication. I had thought she was around my age, but now I realized she was in her mid-twenties. For a moment I did feel sorry for her. Poor little rich girl. All she had were the things money could buy. "Try to sleep," I said gently. "Don't let him get to you."

"Okay. Thanks, Micky." She headed up the stairs to bed.

I turned off the lights, leaving only one on in the small sitting room off the front room. I went back into the darkened front room and sat next to the window. From there, I could see out onto the street without being easily seen. I had brought my gun, although I don't really like guns and would prefer to do without them. But if it came down to it, a gun was one thing that Joey would understand.

It was tedious watching the street. Particularly since the smart money was on Joey downing some Dixies at his local bar. I got up every once in a while and walked around, listening to the different sounds of the house, wind in the trees, the sighing of settling boards. I heard nothing beyond the ordinary whispers of the night.

In the early morning, with only the first hints of sunlight in the sky, I heard Karen come downstairs. She turned to go to the room with the light in it.

"I'm here," I said, not wishing to startle her.

"I couldn't sleep very well," she said as she squinted to see me in the dim light.

"If Joey was going to do anything, he would have done it."

"Aren't you tired? Have you been up all night?"

"I'm used to it," I replied. "You can go back to bed, if you want."

"No, I'd just and toss and turn."

"What are your plans for today?"

"My plans?"

"Yeah, where are you going, what are you doing? It might be better for you not to hang around here by yourself."

"What am I doing today?" Karen repeated, running her hand through her hair. "Oh, I guess the usual, shopping in the morning, lunch with some friends, maybe the gym to workout or sit in the sauna, meet some people for drinks or dinner."

"That's how you usually spend your day?" I asked.

"It varies. Some days I don't go shopping, some days I get my hair done."

"I'm so glad you keep busy with such vital activities."

"That's not fair. You did ask."

"Not fair? There are kids starving ten blocks away and you talk about not fair?"

"I don't have to justify myself to you."

"No, you don't. But someday, Karen, you're going to have justify yourself to yourself."

"Easy for you to say, isn't it? If I hadn't taken a wrong turn to Queerville, I'd be married to some socially acceptable man by now. I'm the perfect wife—I cook, I smile, I dress well. Everything a man could want."

"Yes, but what do you want?"

"What do I want?" Karen paused and looked out the window. "I don't know. No one ever told me I could want something," she said with a small, regretful smile.

It passed quickly, a moment of terror in her eyes. Risk and loss and pain were impossibly foreign to her. But Karen would have to find her own way. Or not. I changed the subject.

"I'll wait around until you're ready to go out, then I'm going home to sleep."

Karen went back upstairs to shower and dress. When she came down again, I told her to wait while I made one last check around the house.

"I'll see you tonight?" Karen asked as she got into her car.

"Yes, you'll see me. Call if anything suspicious happens."

I watched as she drove away, making sure no one followed her. I took my last look at Karen's elegant and expensive house, picture perfect. It looked as if it was waiting for someone to live in it. I got into my car and drove home.

CHAPTER 15

Before I went to sleep, I phoned Cordelia. I called the clinic because I knew my chance of actually reaching her during the busy morning hours was slight.

"Hi, Micky, how are you?" she said when she came on the line.

"Uh, fine," I stammered out. "Well, actually tired. I've been working all night."

"Nothing dangerous, I hope."

"No, just routine," I lied. Then there was a pause. I had called her, so I filled it. "Anyway, I'm just calling to tell you I'll also be working tonight."

"Oh, okay. How about tomorrow?"

"Tomorrow?"

"Do you want to get together?"

"Well…yeah, sure," I answered. Tomorrow was Saturday, I remembered. "But I don't want to go jogging. I'll probably crash during the day."

"That's okay. How about the evening? Maybe dinner?"

"Uh, yeah, something like that. I guess meet at your place?"

"Seven o'clock?"

I mumbled an affirmative.

"I'll see you then." I could hear several people talking in the background and a baby screaming from a not very far distance. Busy was reclaiming Cordelia.

I both wanted and didn't want to see Cordelia. It was only after she confirmed her desire to be with me, that I realized how afraid I had been that she might be reluctant or ambivalent about it. And, although I still had a voice somewhere in my head saying, "Get out now, before you really get hurt," I was happy and relieved that we were getting together tomorrow night.

I turned down my phone, closed the shades, and went to bed.

I awoke around four in the afternoon. It took me a few minutes to orient myself to the late hour of the day. I was meeting Karen at her place around seven. After a leisurely shower, I made a pot of coffee and drank a few cups to wake myself up. I didn't start dressing until a little after six. I still had Torbin's black dress that I had used last time. It would do, I wasn't trying to impress anyone with my varied wardrobe.

The same could not be said for Karen. I arrived at her house to find her wearing an expensive black suit of raw silk. She could smile and she could dress.

Several of her friends were over, having drinks on the veranda. Karen introduced me, but I didn't pay much attention because these weren't people I wanted to know. A closeted doctor, some closeted lawyers, well dressed, proud of themselves for their comfortable lives. While Karen finished powdering her nose, I listened to a man who owned a business explain why he couldn't come out to his employees.

Karen returned, her nose looking no different. Her friends gulped down the remains of their drinks as they prepared to head off to other parties and other drinks. Then the vultures flew away, and Karen and I headed uptown to the Sans Pareil Club.

"Nice bunch of friends you have there," I commented.

"You think so?" Karen continued, "They're not friends. They're the kind of people money can buy. I thought I'd purchase a few so I wouldn't have to be by myself today."

I nodded, then said, "I'm glad you noticed."

"Why?"

"Because if you really thought those were your friends, there'd be no hope for you."

We turned into the gates of the San Pareil Club. The grounds were an immaculate green, something off a touched-up postcard. I was still impressed by the smoothness of the doormen and parking valets. They opened the car doors at precisely the right moment, just as you were ready to get out, with no fumbling or delay as there usually is when someone else does something you're accustomed to doing.

The maître d' led us to the back booth where we had been before. A waiter instantly appeared and asked, "The usual?" At Karen's nod, he glided away. When he reappeared with a white wine for Karen and club soda for me, I had a vision of drill maître d's grilling the waiters on drink orders ("No, no, it was club soda with a twist of lime, not lemon. For that you have to bus tables for a week").

"So," Karen asked as she sipped her wine, "what are you going to do?"

"Tell Joey to leave you alone."

"Do you think he'll do that?"

I nodded, then added, "I'm not asking for your money back."

Karen took another swallow of wine and said, "That's a lot of money."

"So? Economize. Buy a few less friends."

Karen glared at me, but didn't reply. She put down her wineglass and got a cigarette out of her purse. She lit it, making no attempt to keep the smoke out of my face. For the moment, I ignored it.

She blew another cloud of smoke in my direction, and, still getting no reaction, went on the attack. "Don't give me your goddamn holier-than-thou shit. I know your reputation. Every bar dyke in town has a story about you. Is there any lesbo trash in this city that you haven't slept with? 'Slept' isn't the right word, is it? A few minutes in the backseat, a drunken roll in the park. At least I've never broken off an affair by telling someone that I was too drunk to remember sleeping with them."

"That's enough, Karen." That was my past, it was over, and I didn't want her throwing it in my face.

"I'm goddamn-well-not perfect, but I'm not dirt beneath your feet. You may be sipping club soda now, but there isn't a drug I've tried that you haven't used and I know you've been in a lot more sexual positions than I ever have or will be."

"That is enough, Karen."

"Do you still like to be tied up? Still like taking it up…"

I grabbed her wrist, roughly twisting her arm onto the table. I took her cigarette and stabbed it out in the ashtray. "I told you that that was enough. I'm not going to have rumors and gossip thrown in my face like you own them."

"Just rumors and gossip?" Karen shot back. "Then a lot of women are telling lies about you, Micky. They think you had sex with them. That you got drunk or high with them. I've been asking about you and I always get the same answer."

I twisted her arm hard enough to hurt her, anger spilling beyond my control. "Don't fuck with me, Karen. Get it out of your empty little, rich girl head that you know anything about me. Anything at all. If you say anything else to anybody, I will make you regret it."

"You're hurting me," Karen gasped.

I wanted to hurt her. I wanted to lash out, and Karen was an easy target.

"Don't, please don't," she whimpered as my hand tightened around her wrist. "I'm sorry."

Suddenly I let her go. I had been out of control, following my anger. I wanted my past to let go of me. I didn't like Karen reminding me of how hard a task that would be.

Karen stared at me from across the table, clutching the hand I had twisted as if protecting it. I knew I should apologize, give some reassurance that I wasn't going to hurt her, but I didn't, leaving her fear in place. And the power that fear gave me.

"Ms. Holloway, Ms. Knight."

"Francois." Karen turned to him, hiding her wrist under the table as if it were something to be ashamed of. For me, it was.

"Mr. Colombé asks that you join him."

"Well…" Karen shot me a quick glance.

"At your convenience." Francois was too astute not to notice the charged air. I hoped he wasn't astute enough to notice what the air was charged with.

"Thank Anthony and tell him…we will be along shortly."

Francois bowed and disappeared.

"Cigarette smoke bothers me," I said. It was as close as I could come to an apology.

"I can make excuses for you later," Karen said in reference to her accepting Colombé's invitation for both of us.

I shrugged noncommittally, wondering how interesting it might be to meet Anthony Colombé.

"Karen, Micky." Joey arrived at our table.

Karen started to get up. I took a slow sip of club soda, before I put it down and stood up to go with Joey. I wanted to be in control. We would do things at my pace. I followed behind Joey and Karen, lingering a bit, slowing them down. They were turned and waiting for me when I entered the room.

"Shall we sit?" I said after I had shut the door.

"No, thanks, I'll stand," Joey said.

I sat down, arranging my dress, keeping control of the pace. Karen, following my lead, also sat.

"So, you want your money back?" Joey asked, trying to take the initiative from me.

"No. Who said anything about money?"

"Whadda you mean?" Joey's Ninth Ward accent was peeking out.

"It's simple. You want money, Karen wants peace and quiet. We're going to make a deal."

"What if I don't like your deal?" Joey retorted. He wasn't happy with my setting the terms.

"Then you don't like it," I said calmly. "The deal is that you keep the money. No strings, free and clear. The trade is that you let Karen go, no strings, free and clear. You don't call her, you don't see her, you don't take Sunday afternoon drives in her neighborhood."

"And if I don't take your deal, Knight? Where's your muscle?"

"I prefer not to deal in threats. I think we're both aware that we could make life uncomfortable for each other."

"You're talking to the air, Knight."

"Yeah, that's possible. Maybe my ex-M.P. friends will never find your skinny little ass. And maybe Anthony's not going to listen to Karen when she says you're causing her problems. And the cops might have better things to do than figure out what you're up to."

"You're scaring me," was his final piss in the wind, because he then said, "But I tell you what, I'm a gentleman. I don't go where I'm not wanted. Karen wants to end our relationship, it's over. How's that?"

"Almost. But, Joey, this relationship isn't just over, it never existed."

"Whatever you want. Now if you'll excuse me, ladies, who I never met before, I've got to get going." And he was out the door, slamming it behind him, his coiled impatience finally let loose.

"'Whom,'" I corrected after him.

"What?" Karen said.

"'Whom I've never met before.' I was just correcting his grammar."

"Do you really think he'll leave me alone?"

"I think so. Unless he gets desperate for something you have. Or something he thinks you have."

"Should I go to the police?"

I thought for a moment before replying. What Joey was involved in wasn't legal and it wasn't pretty. But Karen had very little to give the police and what little she did have was only enough to wake a sleeping monster, not behead it. "No, not as long as he keeps his part of the bargain. You're better off out of it."

"Thanks, Micky. I was afraid...I thought you might abandon me."

"Next time you get yourself into a mess like this, you can get yourself out."

"I don't plan on there being a next time."

I shrugged and forewent pointing out that she hadn't planned on this time either.

"Well, I guess I need to put in an appearance with Anthony," Karen said. She got up, checked herself in the mirror, hesitated, then turned to me. "About those things I said earlier—"

I cut her off. "You don't know anything about me. That's all there is to say."

"Okay," she said very softly, chastened. She turned from me for one last look in the mirror, but nothing had changed outwardly. Then she opened the door, letting me go first.

When we returned to our table, Francois appeared.

"Ms. Holloway, Mr. Colombé is in the Blue Room. Ms. Knight, will you join us?"

Karen looked at me, as if in apprehension of whatever answer I might make.

"Yes, of course, I'd be delighted," I answered coolly.

He nodded and led us up the stairs. Surreptitious glances followed us as we ascended, the select of the select. The stairs led to an inner balcony overlooking the main floor of the club. At the far end of the balcony was a heavy oak door with ornate brass handles. Francois ushered us through the door into a room that resembled a very rich man's library. Oak-panelled walls led into a series of bookshelves, all stocked with expensive leather-bound books. Brass wall sconces gave off a soft, amber glow. A number of paintings, all original from the look of them, were illuminated by lights hidden in the ceiling. I recognized an Audubon, a Walter Anderson, and, as the centerpiece of the room, a Picasso from his Blue Period. At the far end of the room was a huge fireplace, a picture-perfect fire blazing. Leather chairs and couches were placed at comfortable intervals throughout the room.

I recognized a number of the people in the room. The rich and powerful. A major Hollywood actor, in town for the shooting of his latest movie, was holding court in one corner. Many of the men were there with women not their wives. It was a parade of the young and the beautiful flattering the old and the powerful.

At the far end, next to the fireplace, the most beautiful surrounded the most powerful. Anthony Colombé sat in a rich black leather chair, a throne really, on a pedestal that offered him an overview of the room. He took a final puff on his expansive cigar, then handed its remains to a young, handsome man at his side. The young man took it as if it was an honor and privilege to handle Colombé's chewed cigar butts.

Karen and I made our way across the room to stand at his outer circle. Francois hovered discreetly, all of us waiting until it was convenient for him to notice us.

"What does he do?" I asked, turning to Francois, meaning how did he earn his money.

"I'm sorry, Miss Knight, I don't really know." He spoke with a slow, sad smile as if admitting he had the soul of a servant. I noticed that he called me "Miss" not "Ms." Colombé's preferred form of address held sway here.

"Karen, how are you?" I heard Colombé say, holding out his hands as if he were some potentate at his castle. I almost expected her to kiss his ring. Instead she took his hands, then leaned forward to give him a kiss. I suppressed a shudder as their lips touched. He was in his seventies, skin freckled with age spots, his lips thin and dry.

"Anthony," Karen murmured, "it's so good to see you again."

"Introduce me to your friend," he directed, although I knew he already knew who I was.

Karen did and he held out his hands to me just as he had to her. It would be foolish to needlessly antagonize this man, so I gave him my hands, but made no motion to lean in and kiss him. He didn't seem to expect it, however, instead holding me at arm's length and appraising me. I held his gaze. His eyes, beneath the glasses and wrinkled folds, were sharp and bright, like a gleaming blade.

"I've heard a lot about you," he said.

"Not the truth, I hope," I replied. While I didn't want to antagonize him, I didn't intend to be obsequious either.

"Some of it true, I suspect. I hear you lead an interesting life."

"Isn't that a Chinese curse, 'May you lead an interesting life'?"

He chuckled dryly, squeezed my hands, then let them go. "Do make yourself comfortable. If there's anything you need, let Francois know." He turned his attention to someone else. I was a plaything and I had amused him for a bit. I stepped away, back into the outer fringes of the circle.

I hovered nearby long enough to be polite, then I wandered around a bit, got a glass of mineral water, and listened to the conversations around me.

The rich are not different from you and me, they just have the money to buy the comfort most of us can only wish for. I didn't feel enlightened and privileged as if I had been let into some sanctified world; rather, it seemed as if these people were diminished, blinded by what their money could buy to the point that they had forgotten that there are things that money can't buy.

I found Francois and asked him, "Have I been here long enough?"

"You wish to leave? Is there no…amusement that appeals to you?"

"I don't wish to offend…anyone." We spoke in the code that was part of the game. I looked around the room, the young and beautiful bodies I was being offered. Vintage wines, pure drugs. "But no, there's nothing that appeals to me."

Karen was in the inner circle, seated next to Colombé. They seemed content in their mutual usury—he pretending he was a man with conventional sexual desires, potent enough to attract a beautiful young woman; she pretending that she had access to real power. I couldn't think of anything to say to Karen; even good-bye seemed pointless.

"Allow me to get you a car," Francois offered. We left through the solid oak doors.

"What would happen if I just hoofed it out of here and caught the trolley? Would you be shot at dawn?" I asked as we descended the stairs.

"No, madam, the firing squad was disbanded several years ago," he answered smoothly. "However," and for a moment he let down his servant's mask, "it would make my life easier if you play by the rules."

"I have no reason to make trouble," I granted.

Francois led me out to the veranda, signaling one of the doormen to get a car. "Good, I hope it remains so."

So do I, I thought as I got into the car. This time it was a modern limo driven by a silent man.

The case of the Blond Bitch is closed, I thought as the car sped noiselessly through the late night traffic. "Closed" was a better word than "ended." Joey and whoever he was working for were still doing what they were doing. Karen was still looking for money to buy her happiness. The rich and powerful people of the Sans Pareil Club were still beyond the law. All this case was, was closed.

My silent chauffeur dropped me off at my place, waiting while I fumbled with the keys to get into my apartment. Then the car purred away into the night.

I hiked up the stairs, uncomfortable and off balance in my high heels. There were no messages on my answering machine, not that I expected any. I kicked off the heels, pulled off the dress, and unhooked my bra. I was tired of these uncomfortable clothes. I looked around my apartment for a moment.

Then I picked up the phone. I dialed Karen's number. "Why did Colombé want to meet me? What have you told him?" I left on her answering machine. She would get my message whenever she got home from the club.

Somehow I couldn't stop asking questions.

I hung up Torbin's dress, turned out the lights, and went to bed.

CHAPTER 16

Rain had arrived in the night, a rumbling lightning storm that had Hepplewhite cowering under the covers. Her flicking tail and the boom of thunder were very efficient at disturbing my sleep. Consequently, when I awoke again, it was late afternoon. I lay in bed for a bit, the grogginess of mixed-up hours and interrupted sleep slow to let go of me.

Finally, forcing myself out of bed, I went to the kitchen to start coffee. With the assurance of a brewed pot awaiting me, I forced myself through a shower.

With another cup of coffee in hand, I checked my answering machine. The first message was from Karen, answering my questions from last night. “I never mentioned you to Anthony. I don’t know how he knew who you were.” Not a very illuminating answer.

The next message was from Cordelia. “Hi, Micky. I hope your night went okay. My day’s been hell here. I’ll tell you about it tonight. Is it okay if we just order in? I don’t think I’m up to either going out or cooking. If that’s not okay, give me a call.”

I was in the Quarter at a few minutes past seven. On impulse, I made a detour to a flower shop over on Chartres. I didn’t dwell on the fact that it was Karen’s money buying Cordelia flowers.

At her doorstep, I realized that I had again not brought the keys she had given me. I had envisioned sneaking into her apartment and presenting her the flowers with a flourish, but instead I rang her buzzer. She was waiting with the door open as I came up the stairs.

I awkwardly thrust the flowers at her. “Here, just call me a hopeless romantic,” I said. “Or a hopeless something.”

The flowers between us, Cordelia took them. “Thank you, Micky, they’re beautiful,” she said as she went to the kitchen to find a vase.

I stayed in the living room, suddenly feeling awkward and foolish. Flowers were hopelessly romantic. Cordelia returned with them in a vase.

"What happened to the blue pottery one?" I asked.

"Nothing. It's just that Rook has discovered how tasty some flowers can be. I don't want her to pull it over and break it." Rook was her cat, a rambunctious one-year-old.

"Of course. Save it for some special occasion."

"Lindsey gave it to me. I'd hate to have it broken."

"How long do we have to be together before you use things old friends gave you for me?" I snapped, suddenly jealous.

"Micky, that's not fair," Cordelia flared back. "I'd put the damn flowers in the blue vase if I thought it would convince you that I love you, but it's just one more hoop for me to jump through."

I started to ask her about Lindsey, but realized that I was picking at scabs, scratching and irritating them.

"Can we call a truce?" Cordelia asked. "Do I get a hug? I've had one of those days when I really need one."

"Of course you get a hug," I said. I crossed the room to her, somewhat chastened by her having to ask for something that used to be assumed.

She held me gently at first, then her arms tightened about me as if she needed to be touched with no trace of hesitation or doubt. I returned her embrace, wanting very much for our touching to overcome the chasm that seemed ready to open between us.

Finally, she let me go. "Okay, I'm ready to tell you about my day. But first I think I'm going to get a cup of tea."

"Let me," I offered. "Sit down, take off your shoes and enjoy one of the benefits of having a lover." I didn't add, *Since you've been putting up with some of the drawbacks*. I went into the kitchen and put on the water.

With the tea bags in hot water, and a little milk in Cordelia's, I brought them out.

"Sit beside me?" she asked, still not willing to take closeness for granted.

I sat next to her, taking her hand between both of mine. "Now tell me about your day."

"My first patient was a man in his twenties. His mother brought him in. He wanted an HIV test." She paused.

"Did you give him one?"

"No. He didn't need an HIV test. Oh, he'll get one. But I didn't see any point in drawing blood when he's going to go to Charity and get his blood taken there, too. He had AIDS. I didn't tell him that. Or his mother.

You can't diagnose AIDS in a fifteen-minute physical exam. But…he was emaciated, had thrush, problems walking, problems breathing, probably PCP. Twenty-eight years old with the face of an old man. Sometimes you know.

"I sent him to the emergency room at Charity. He probably has a few months left, at best. He's seen a doctor three times in his entire life. Once when he was two years old and had a raging fever, once when he was fifteen and got shot in the leg on his way to school, and now. Poverty kills people. Sometimes I think it's that simple."

Cordelia paused again, then put her arm around me as if seeking warmth.

"Then another mother came in," she continued, "with another child. But this time the mother was seventeen years old, barely beyond a child herself. Her three-year-old daughter was bleeding vaginally and rectally."

I shuddered beneath Cordelia's embrace, warmth a fragile and fleeting thing.

"She had the kind of cuts and bruises that don't come from a fall. A broken rib, a throat infection that's probably gonorrhea."

"Three years old? Only three years old?" I cried out, unable to sit still as I pulled away from her. Relaxing in a comforting embrace didn't seem possible.

"The mother, the seventeen-year-old, admitted to using crack. The man she lives with, not the girl's father, didn't want her to take the child to see us. Somehow the mother had enough maternal instinct to realize her baby needed to see a doctor. She snuck away from him to bring her in. She told me she wants to get off crack, but she's having difficulty getting into a treatment program because she's pregnant again."

Cordelia was quiet for a moment, then spoke softly, "I had to turn her in. I couldn't let the child go back into that home. They arrested the mother, of course. The child got sent to Charity to be sewn together, and then she'll be sent off to foster homes. The police haven't found the boyfriend yet. I don't feel like much of a hero or savior," Cordelia finished.

I didn't answer. I slowly leaned back into her embrace. Warm and alive and not in immediate pain seemed to be all that I could offer her.

"Of course, that backed up all the rest of my patients. Then I had to go to the police and give a statement. God, it's been a long day."

"What can I do?" I asked.

"Nothing. Not a damn thing. 'All the king's horses and all the king's men…'" She trailed off.

Can't put broken lives together again, I thought as I tightened my arms around her. We sat that way, silently, for a while.

"Have you had anything to eat lately?" I asked at last, wanting to get back to the small things, the ones I could do something about.

"No, I don't guess I have. Not since breakfast."

"Let me see what I can find in the kitchen," I said, starting to get up.

"You're not my cook." It came out as a reprimand. Cordelia added in a softer voice, "Why don't we just order something?"

"Well, then, order whatever you want. I don't have much money."

"Look, Micky, I'm not comfortable with you serving me. You're always the one who cooks or goes to the grocery store. Sometimes you even do my laundry."

"And I'm not comfortable with you spending money on me."

"Money's just paper. Time is the equalizer. We all have only twenty-four hours a day. Money's not the same. Some people have a lot, some very little. Luck, that's all."

"What about hard work and the American dream?" We were heading for an argument. I could see it coming, but I could see no way to stop it, like a stone falling off a ledge, no way to push it back.

"Sure, some people have money because they've worked hard. But there are some people who've worked just as hard and have nothing, not even the bare necessities. My money doesn't equal your time. I don't care to pretend that it does."

I watched Cordelia as she spoke. She believed what she said, but if I gave in to her wishes, then the power became hers and I would have to trust that she would not use it.

"I should just take your money and get over it?" I retorted.

Cordelia massaged her forehead for a moment, then replied, "Yes, why not?"

"Because I'm not that kind of person and, if I were, you wouldn't be with me," I shot back.

"I'm not talking about buying your soul. Or a house, or car, or even a goddamned jacket. I'm talking about spending somewhere in the vicinity of ten dollars on buying us a pizza or po-boy. It's not worth the kind of argument we're having."

"It's not the amount, it's the idea. As long as it's your money, it buys what you want. I'll never have…"

"Control? Is that what's bothering you?"

"If you were in my position, wouldn't it bother you?"

Cordelia was at least honest enough to reply, "Yes, I suppose it would. Where does that leave us?"

"Let me see if I can find something quick and simple to fix and, if not, you can order out?" I turned to go to the kitchen.

"All right," Cordelia replied. "But let me help."

I turned and led the way to the kitchen.

"And," Cordelia said from behind me, "I promise not to sneak up on you."

"What the fuck is that supposed to mean?" I shouted, wheeling on her. As I lost control, I realized how fragile it had been in the first place.

"Micky," Cordelia said, halting abruptly at my anger, holding in the archway to the kitchen. "I think we need to talk about this."

"Don't sneak up behind someone. That's common courtesy. That's all there is to it."

"Your reaction when I tried to put my arms around you had nothing to do with manners. I'm not a shrink and I don't play games well."

"I'm not playing. This is my fucking life that you think should be open to you at will. What if I don't think we need to talk about this?"

"What do you intend to do? Keep repressing your anger and letting it spew out in all directions when you can't keep it in any longer?"

"I thought you said you weren't a shrink."

"I can see what's obvious. And you're obviously very touchy and angry about—"

"I said I don't want to talk about it. What the fucking hell do I have to do to get that through your head?" I snarled at her, my voice ugly and threatening.

For a moment, Cordelia was taken aback, but then she said, "Can't you see it's gone beyond whether you want to talk about it or not? It doesn't have to be me—"

"Maybe your friend Lindsey?" I cut in.

"Maybe," Cordelia replied evenly. "Or someone else. I won't be ambushed by this kind of anger. It's not me. At least have the courage to fight those who deserve it."

"I guess I'm leaving, then," I said, brushing past her. She didn't try to stop me.

"Micky," Cordelia called out as I reached the door. "I do love you."

"What's love got to do with any of this?" I mocked.

"Not much. But it's the only weapon I have."

"I just need to…be alone. I'll call you sometime." But I wasn't sure if I meant it.

"Good night, Micky."

"Goodbye," I replied, then closed the door behind me.

I quickly hurried down the stairs and out of the courtyard, feeling ragged and torn, unwilling to have her voice leave another mark on me.

The courage to fight those who deserve it, Cordelia had said. I didn't know if I could stop myself from being angry, but maybe I could take that energy and fury and aim it—the young girl Cordelia had treated today, Cissy with her nameless monsters, the others who hadn't walked so directly into my life. I began to believe in evil, the monstrosity that can see nothing beyond its desires. It turns or devours the needs and hungers of others, so that a brief sexual spurt becomes more important than the damaged trust and terror of a child. That was evil. I would fight it as best I could.

CHAPTER 17

Sunday was a day of laundry, dishes, mopping, a major grocery run, all those mundane things that kept me occupied. Body and mind, at least. I knew my soul was elsewhere. In the evening I finally gave in to what I knew was turning into an obsession and started the list of men with access to Cissy. And women, I reluctantly admitted. I couldn't blind myself to that possibility. I remembered Warren Kessler and wondered if I could ask him about Cissy's teachers. Then I wondered if I should put him on the list. I scribbled his name at the bottom, then, because I liked the man, put two question marks next to it. I sat and stared at the list for a long time, but no possibility greater than the others appeared.

Finally, I flipped the page and started another list, a chronology of the events in Karen's case. Colombé nagged at me. Was it just idle curiosity that prompted him to invite me into his inner sanctum, a fly to his wanton boy, toyed with for sport? Was Joey what he seemed—a small-to-medium-time grafter who somehow had squeezed through the doors of the Sans Pareil Club? Or had Colombé invited him in? And, if so, why? Did Joey procure sexual playthings for Colombé as Torbin's less-than-reliable source had hinted at?

I looked at my jumble of questions scratched across the page and realized that not only did I not have any answers to them, I had no way of getting answers. And if I did get answers, they would cost me a lot. I closed the notebook. For a moment, I considered tearing out the last page, but I left it.

Monday turned into a bureaucracy day. My friend Ralph had been a bartender until the day his persistent cough had turned into something worse. The bout of pneumonia had left him weak and unable to work. I was taking him to the food stamp office. I'd offered and he'd accepted, but I suspected that he was afraid to be alone in this strange, new world of poverty and that he didn't want his still-healthy friends to see him pale and emaciated, asexual. I was a woman, a lesbian. He'd never have sex with me, never wanted to have sex with me. I would never look at him and see a man I'd once desired.

The food stamp people were basically kind. Maybe they figured that by the time you reached their office, life had already humiliated you enough. I remained with Ralph for a while. We talked of nothing important, local scandals, the weather, movies, until he was tired. After wishing him good night, I left. It was only seven thirty in the evening.

I drove around for a bit, trying to decide what to do. Finally, I ended up at the lakefront, sitting on the breakwater watching the glint of distant lights on the waves. I knew I should call Cordelia, but my demons were back, and I wasn't sure how to make them leave, or even how to prevent them from hurting someone I cared about. I deliberately stayed at the lake until it was too late for her to call me.

The next morning no bureaucracies awaited me. Tomorrow you take Cissy to see Lindsey, I told myself. If that doesn't change anything, then you get to ask Barbara those uncomfortable questions. I reviewed the chronology to remind myself that there was indeed motion and direction in what I was doing.

The phone rang, interrupting my thoughts. "Hello?" I answered.

"Micky. Hi." It was Cordelia, her voice subdued, tentative.

"Hi, how are you?" Then, without giving her a chance to answer, "I meant to call you. I've just been real busy."

"That's okay. I understand."

Did she, I wondered? Or was it one of those polite lies? And did she understand my being busy or did she understand my lying about planning to call her?

"Actually, I'm calling about Alex's party," Cordelia continued. "It's this Thursday."

"I haven't forgotten it," I said somewhat defensively. I hadn't been paying much attention to it either, though.

"I didn't think you had. Are you still willing to have Alex foisted off on you?"

"Yeah, sure," I agreed, then, not to seem too abrupt, "Alex gets off around five?"

"Usually. You can plan to pick her up around then."

"Okay." Then there was an awkward pause, the concrete details taken care of.

"And Micky?" Cordelia said, breaking the silence, "You don't have to go with me if you don't want to. You're Alex's friend, too. I know she'd like you to be there, even if we're not..." She trailed off.

There is was, out in the open. "Do you want to go with me?" I turned the question back to her. "Or would you prefer not to?"

"I would…I would prefer to go with you. If you don't want to… Let's be honest. It will be easier in the long run."

Some absurd part of me wanted to ask why is honestly easier? "I guess…I've got some things to work out. But I would like to go with you."

"Okay. Good. Good, I'd like that," Cordelia replied, the tension in her voice easing. "So, I'll see you on Thursday, dragging a confused Alex with you. I'll call you then. Millie's poked her head in twice now, so I'd better get back to work."

We said a hurried good-bye and she was gone.

On Wednesday, I got to Cissy's school early. It was raining, and I knew parking would be complicated by overprotective parents wanting to make sure their little Johnny or Susie didn't melt. I sat in my car watching the rain drip down the windshield, trying to be practical and realistic. There would be no miracles today, no dramatic changes, and I would have to ask Barbara all those difficult questions.

I spotted Cissy. I wondered if she would remember that I was picking her up today. After a moment of uncertainty, she saw me and ran toward my car, her raincoat only half fastened against the downpour. I opened the car door as she got near, letting her jump in out of the rain.

"Hi, how are you?" I greeted her.

"Okay. Wet, I guess," she answered, brushing back a strand of dripping hair.

"So, how was school today?" I asked as I pulled out. "Anything interesting happen?"

"Fine. Nope," were her succinct answers.

"Do you know where we're going?" I asked.

"To see that lady."

"Dr. McNeil?"

"Yeah, her."

"Do you like her?"

"She's okay, I guess."

I couldn't really watch her to get an idea of what she wasn't saying. Too much of my attention was demanded by driving in the rain; the streets were starting to flood. Was she angry at me for arranging this, for sending her to see Lindsey? Had I become just another adult not to be trusted? Or were her demons so powerful that nothing could get in?

I turned into Lindsey's driveway.

"Why don't you go ahead and get out here?" I suggested when the car was as close as it was going to get to the porch.

Cissy nodded and ran to its shelter. I parked the car, rummaging around in the backseat until I found the least broken umbrella of the ones accumulated back there. Even with an umbrella, I was soaked from my knees down before I got to the porch.

The door opened; a mother and daughter came out. The mother was protected by a fashionable trench coat, an umbrella with her initial on it, and perfectly fitting, feminine rain boots. Her daughter had gone a long way down the road of adolescent rebellion. She was probably sixteen, her hair a buzz cut, an ear pierced in three places; her blue jeans were torn, she wore black boots, and, what was causing her mother the most consternation of all, a sweatshirt that read, "Amazon U." with a double women symbol below it.

Elegant mother did not look comfortable with strangers seeing her dyke daughter. She hurried the girl past us, then pointedly looked at the contrast of my dark hair and eyes and Cissy's blondness and blue eyes. Her superiority established, she turned away. Her daughter cruised me, a look I didn't dare return.

I led the way into the waiting room.

"Hello, Cissy. Hi, Micky," Amanda greeted us.

"Hi," Cissy answered shyly. She headed for the fish tank, ignoring us. Amanda turned back to her computer, and I sat down, letting Cissy have the fish tank all to herself.

In a few minutes I heard the chime followed by Amanda saying, "Why don't you come this way, Cissy?"

Cissy obediently followed her down the hallway to Lindsey's office.

Amanda came back to the reception area, then called to me, "You can pay us this time. We prefer that you pay by month," she explained, "but you can do it by session."

"How long have you worked for Dr. McNeil?" I asked, wondering how much information I could get out of Amanda Jackson as I wrote a check for the month.

"Around six months, since she opened her practice," she answered as she took my check.

"How is she as a boss?"

"I have no complaints about Dr. McNeil," she answered. *And if I did, I wouldn't tell you*, was her unspoken message.

I sat back down and picked up a magazine, leaving Amanda to her computer. It would be another forty-five minutes before Cissy returned.

I had skimmed through just about every magazine in the waiting room before I heard Lindsey's door open again. Cissy came out, her face still closed and unreadable. I wondered if she had opened up for Lindsey. If she had, there was no outward sign. Lindsey followed behind her. She nodded at me, then put her hand on Cissy's shoulder, clearly the beginnings of a tentative connection between them.

"I like your fishes," Cissy said.

"They are pretty colorful fish, aren't they?" Lindsey answered her.

"Uh-huh. I like the little blue ones best."

"You know what," Lindsey said, talking only to her, "so do I."

Cissy smiled for her, then turned and went to the aquarium to look at her favorite fish one more time.

Lindsey turned to me and asked, "Are you taking her home?"

"If the flooded streets let me."

She nodded, as if this was important information, then said softly so that neither Cissy nor Amanda could hear, "I'm going to be here until six or so. There's something I'd..."

Amanda, who had just answered the phone, called to me, "Micky, I have Barbara Selby on the line. She's still at the office and wants to know if you can drop Cissy off there."

"Tell her that's fine," I said.

The door opened and Lindsey's next client came in.

"Six," I said quietly to Lindsey. She nodded, then headed back to her office.

"Come on, kiddo," I called to Cissy, "time to make like a duck."

She waved good-bye to the fish, I waved good-bye to Amanda, then we were out the door. I paused on the porch to stuff Cissy into her raincoat, then we dashed to my car, my semi-dry pants legs getting wet again.

"We're going to your mom's office," I explained to Cissy.

"I know, I heard you," she replied, letting me know I'd said a stupid adult thing.

I had to pay attention to driving; the road was half flooded and a traffic light up ahead didn't seem to be working. Cars were either inching through the flooded streets or playing kamikaze, assuming if they went fast enough, we'd get out of their way.

Somewhere beyond this mess, Cissy asked, "Do you think my mom would let me have some fish?"

"For dinner or as pets?"

"For pets, silly, like Dr. McNeil has."

"Probably, they're pretty easy to take care of."

"Did you ever have fish pets?"

"No, but a…a cousin of mine did." Bayard had kept fish.

"What kinds did your cousin have?"

"I don't really remember. Nowhere near as pretty as what Dr. McNeil has. I don't think he really liked fish." When he decided he didn't want them anymore, he'd taken bleach and poured it in the water. I remembered him calling me over to watch the fish die.

Barbara was waiting just inside the lobby of her building. I stopped in front. Barbara waved and Cissy opened the door to bound out to her.

"Thanks for doing this," Barbara called to me as she gathered Cissy safely under the overhang.

I gave Barbara a wave to let her know it really was okay, then pulled out before my stopped car became a target for a moving car. It was still raining heavily.

I headed back uptown. Between the still-pouring deluge and threading through stalled cars and flooded streets, I didn't get back to Lindsey's office until almost six thirty. Her car was still in the lot. I didn't even bother with my dilapidated umbrella, instead just dashing from my car to the porch. Wet was inevitable, fighting it would just take time and effort. I tried the door, but it was locked. The dim streetlight wasn't much help in locating the buzzer, but I finally found it.

It took a minute or two before I heard her footsteps and cane crossing to the door.

"It's Micky. Micky Knight," I called through the door.

"A wet Micky Knight, I see," she said as she stood aside to let me in.

"You're here by yourself?"

"Yes, why shouldn't I be?" She was leaning heavily on her cane.

"Well, it's a mess out there. Your parking lot's a swamp."

"So?" Lindsey countered.

"How could you be sure I was coming back?"

"I wasn't. Believe it or not, I can make it across the parking lot, even in a drenching rain. It may not be easy or pretty, but I can do it."

"I didn't mean to—" I started, taken aback at her sudden passion.

Lindsey cut me off. "The only things I don't do are the ones I cannot do. If there's someone around to help or a shortcut, I'll take it, but I won't have my life ruled by imagined limits."

"I'm sorry," I said, abashed at my clumsiness.

"It's okay. Overly helpful people are a sore spot with me."

"Was Cordelia overly helpful?" I asked, taking a shot in the dark.

"No," Lindsey replied, "she was not. Why do you ask?"

"Curious."

"Well, I have something for you to be curious about," Lindsey said, turning to lead the way to her office.

I followed her. She motioned me to a chair, then slowly lowered herself into hers. After putting her cane aside, she opened her drawer and took out a matchbook. She handed it to me. On the cover of the matchbook was the name of a bar. Not one I'd ever heard of. I looked expectantly at Lindsey.

"Sometimes what someone doesn't tell you is the most potent signal of all," she said.

"What's that have to do with this?" I asked, holding up the matchbook.

"How does a matchbook like that get in a little girl's pocket?"

"She got it from her parents, found it on a street corner, a playmate's father goes there or mother works there. Any number of ways," I replied.

"True. Cissy spent the entire hour we were talking with her hand in her pocket, playing with that matchbook as if it were a talisman. When I finally asked her about it, her whole demeanor changed. She became reclusive, as if hiding something. She seemed torn between not wanting to give it to me and feeling compelled to let me see it."

"So you think it's significant?"

"I think Cissy has found a way to tell us something without violating whatever taboo she's constrained by."

I looked again at the matchbook. "Heart of Desire" was scripted in gold on a black background. Some of the gold lettering had begun to chip.

"Any guesses?" I asked Lindsey.

"No, not really. The matchbook was the only thing Cissy revealed that might be relevant."

"Why not tell Barbara?"

"Cissy asked me not to. After she showed me the matchbook, on her own initiative, she said, 'Don't tell my mom.' Then I asked if I could 'show'—I changed the verb from 'tell' to 'show'—show it to you. She replied, 'I guess.'"

"So where does that leave us?"

"You're a detective. Here's a clue. Go investigate."

"I'll do my best. But…" There could be so many different things this matchbook was meant to tell us. Sorting out the right one could be difficult, if not impossible. Was it the bar? Someone who smoked? Collected matches? Something that made sense to Cissy, but I couldn't see?

"I know," Lindsey said quietly. "It's not a lot to go on. And what it may mean to Cissy might be impossible to find out unless she tells us."

"Will she tell us?"

Lindsey shrugged. "I hope so. But, honestly, I'm not sure. I don't think it will be any time soon."

I nodded somberly, then put the matchbook in my jacket pocket.

"I need to be getting home," Lindsey said. "Will you give me a hand, or would you prefer to watch me fall on my face in the mud?"

"I'll give you a hand. Let's save the face in the mud for some other time."

Lindsey got ready to leave, moving papers off her desk, locking a file cabinet. I listened to the rain on the roof.

"Let's go," Lindsey said, reaching for her cane. She stood up slowly, grimacing for a second as she caught her balance.

I thought of reaching out to help steady her, but she hadn't asked.

"I'm not taking my briefcase," Lindsey announced. "I know I'm not going to do any work at home and the rain will just ruin it." She motioned for me to lead the way out, as she followed behind, turning off lights as she went.

At the outer door, when she saw only her umbrella in the stand, she looked at me and said, "Where's your rain gear? You'll get wet."

"My umbrella is down to one spoke and less useful than running quickly."

Lindsey handed me her umbrella to hold while she turned off the lights, then locked the door.

"I like big umbrellas," she commented as I opened it up. Lindsey linked her arm through mine, then asked, "Do you mind?"

"No, of course not." I wondered if she was asking merely to be polite or if she had noticed my tension at the unexpected close physical contact.

We made our way down the porch stairs.

"I would only mind if you tripped and pulled me down into the mud," I said, the silence growing too dense.

"So you'll just let me fall on my face with no attempt to prevent it?"

"On a clear day I'd do anything for you. But it's not a clear day."

"Anything? I'll have to wait for the sun to shine." Then Lindsey added, "Does Cordelia know you flirt with other women?"

"I wasn't flirting."

"In other words, she wouldn't approve."

"We've never really discussed it. But I really wasn't flirting."

Lindsey stumbled, leaning heavily against my arm to catch herself.

"And even if you were," Lindsey said as she caught her breath, "I wouldn't tell her. Where are my keys?" We were at her car. She fumbled for a minute, muttering, "I hope I didn't leave them in my briefcase," before she pulled a set of keys from her jacket pocket. She let go of my arm to open her car door.

I held the umbrella over her as she got in.

"I could drive you to your car," Lindsey offered, only half jokingly.

"That's okay. I'll run."

"Good luck. I'll see you next week."

For a moment I forgot what "next week" meant. "Right. If the matchbook turns up anything, I'll let you know." With that, I hurried to my car. I got pretty wet before I slammed the rain out. I noticed that Lindsey headed uptown when she turned onto the street.

Instead of pulling out, I turned on the overhead light and took the matchbook out of my pocket. I hadn't really examined it carefully in Lindsey's office.

On the back was the picture of a woman, her blond hair denoted by the chipping gold. She was smiling and her skirt was swirling, the crude graphics of the matchbook rendering what was supposed to be sexy and inviting, instead ludicrous and cartoonish.

I flipped open the matches. None had been used. On the inside was a phone number and address, then in big, bold letters, "At the corner of Law and Desire." I carefully put the matchbook back in my pocket. Law and Desire. What a treacherous intersection that could be. I turned onto the street, driving through the rain.

CHAPTER 18

I drove a few blocks before pulling under a street lamp to find my rather crumpled New Orleans map. Uptown was obliterated by a large coffee stain and some all-too-hurried folding. But Desire and Law weren't uptown streets. I noticed, as I traced that map with my fingers, that the intersection wasn't a very good place to be. Did I really want to go there on an ugly rainy night? After a moment or two of debate, I decided that a downpour and darkness might be my allies, giving me cover and disguise that sunshine or people on the street would strip away.

On the map, Law was an unbroken line, but I knew some of the area it traversed was intersected by rail lines and canals. I couldn't trust Law Street to get me there, I would have to take Desire. I pulled out, leaving the tree-lined elegance of Prytania Street for a very different world. On the way there, I made a quick stop at my apartment, changing into a baggy sweatshirt, and adding a jacket a size too big on top of it. The less definitely female I looked, the better.

Then I got back into my car and found Desire, following it into a dark night. Street signs were missing or illegible. Poverty doesn't mean danger, nor does different skin color. Sometimes the worst treachery is from those most like you. I've been in poor neighborhoods that felt much safer to me than rich ones. The streets I was driving on were poor; this was an area that Karen Holloway and her uptown friends, even if they lived their entire lives in New Orleans, would never come near.

I reached where Law Street crossed Desire. Heart of Desire sat on one corner, a tawdry whore of a bar. The entire building had been painted black, with the doors and windows, glass panes included, blood red. Colored floodlights illuminated the entrance, but the colors seemed random, the reds a jarring orange-red next to the purple-red of the trim. A green light hit part of the doorway, turning it a mud brown. The caricature of the woman on the matchbook was reproduced on the door. But the hands of the artist had been unsure, her crude smile transformed into a sinister leer.

I continued through the intersection. Ahcad of mc Dcsire Street ended, running into the Florida Canal. On the other side of the canal loomed the Desire Projects, an ill-conceived, half-abandoned housing project. I went around the block, parking next to Heart of Desire on Law Street. This was not a kind and gentle place; even the air felt thick and oppressive, as if hope wasn't something that was lost, but something that had never existed.

I glanced at myself in the rearview mirror. New Orleans is a cabal of people and colors. Legally, I'm white (Louisiana considers such things important), but my skin is just dark enough to keep it from being a sure thing. This bar and this neighborhood was the kind of place where a strange white girl would be very noticeable. The first rule of detecting is don't stand out, unless, there's some advantage to it, not the case here. In sunlight, or even on a clear night, you'd never make it, I thought, looking at my image, but a rainy weeknight might be possible. It was time to see what was inside the bar.

I got out of my car and locked it, turning up my jacket collar. I was getting wet, but wet was just another alteration of my appearance. Passing under the sickly green light, I entered the bar. No one was at the door to stop or even look at me. The entrance way was cluttered with cigarette machines and pay phones. One of the phones dangled uselessly; the other was occupied by a man wearing dark glasses who paid no attention to me. The lighting was dim; some corners could have held dead bodies or orgies, and I would have never known. The entryway opened into a large rectangular room. At the end closest to the door was a bar. It was painted red and black, the top of the bar black, a very forgiving color. A few bar stools, most of them with ripped covers, circled the bar.

Mismatched tables lined the wall of the room. At the far end was something that might be politely referred to as a stage, really just a raised plywood platform, one corner of the skirting gone, showing the understructure. It was lit with another of those ugly red lights. The center of the room was bare. It could have been a dance floor, but nobody was dancing and my feet were walking on rough concrete.

I sauntered up to the bar, trying to act as if I knew what I was doing. "Draft," I said to the bartender. He gave me a bored nod, then took a glass that was not next to godliness if that was where cleanliness got you, and poured me a beer. "Seventy-five cents," he said. He didn't seem at all bothered with strange, androgynous creatures in his bar.

I handed him a dollar. He gave me a napkin for my generous tip. I wandered over to one of the unoccupied tables, using my napkin for a surreptitious wipe of the seat. Then I sat down, letting my eyes become accustomed to the light.

One of the first things I noticed was that the outside of the building was much larger than the interior. The obvious guess was prostitution, little warrens of rooms in the back and upstairs. As my eyes adjusted, I spotted several women who lent evidence to that theory. Their skirts were too short, the heels too high, and the makeup too visible, even in this light, for me to believe that they were just hardworking gals out to have a few brews and relax. The next interesting thing I observed was that this was a mixed group of prostitutes, black, white, even one that looked Asian. Equal opportunity prostitution.

I noticed that the bar patrons were a heterogeneous group, too. I saw a number of white men as I glanced around the room, a few of them in suits that wouldn't look out of place in a bank. The presence of these incongruous patrons ruled out this being what it looked like, a neighborhood dive. This bar had something with city-wide appeal. To a gutter mind like mine, drugs and sex about summed up the possibilities.

The music did one of those awkward and jarring shifts from background trash to attention-must-be-paid. A few more red lights spotted the stage. Show time.

A woman clad in something red and sequined wiggled out. Her dancing wasn't top notch, but her breasts were larger than average and that, I suspected, was her selling point. (My gutter mind at work again.)

She gyrated across the stage to the music, every once in a while stopping in a pose of clichéd provocativeness. After several boring minutes of this, she finally started stripping. Some of the tables nearest the stage began to show interest. A few hoots and hollers accompanied the slow removal of her top. She took her time, evidently aware of what her main attraction was. One strap came down to almost reveal the breast, then was flung back over her shoulder. Her fans paid close attention. They didn't want to miss that exact moment when her nipple was revealed. Legally, it would have to be a pasty, but I doubted that such legal niceties applied here.

I was more intent watching the audience. To see people in those unguarded moments when they believe that they are the ones who are watching, not the ones being watched. A man in a corner was massaging his crotch in an obvious fashion. One of the prostitutes walked over to him. I couldn't tell if it was a slow night and she was trying to drum up business or if it was just company policy that no one got any freebies and it was her turn to enforce it. After a few minutes she got up and walked away; his hands remained on the table.

A couple of the women were serving drinks to tables too engrossed in the show to leave for the bar. I watched one of them, flirting and laughing as she placed the drinks on the table, playfully shaking off the hands that roved. But when she had turned her back to them, she gave them the finger. Several of her friends burst into laughter at her small defiance until another male customer, attracted to their laughter, joined them. I couldn't hear the words, but they were blowing him off, just too politely for him to notice. He was laughing at what he thought was their joke, but they were laughing at him and, the more he thought he was included, the more they laughed at him. Then he made an offer to the blondest one and the laughter stopped. He still had the power to buy what he wanted. The blond got up, leaving the other women behind. She led him to a door in the wall. For a moment, there was a square of harsh yellow light as they entered, then the door shut, black in a black wall.

A loud chorus of grunts and yells told me that the nipples had finally appeared. I glanced back at the stage; yep, pure flesh—unpastied, illegal nipples.

One of the prostitutes was headed in my direction. I thought she was the best looking of them, but she was black and evidently not as desirable as a blond white woman. She smiled at me. She probably assumes I'm a man, I thought.

"Hi, how you doin'?" she asked as she sat down at my table.

"Fine," I answered, wondering how soon my voice would give me away.

"Never seen you here before."

"Never been here before."

She gave me a bit of an odd look, as if she knew something wasn't quite right, but she wasn't sure what it was and, even if she figured it out, it wasn't her place to comment. I was a paying customer and the customer is always right.

"You interested?" she asked.

I shook my head.

"I do girls," she said, catching me off balance.

"Good guess," I commented.

"Matter of fact, I prefer girls."

"Slow night?"

She chuckled dryly, then said, "A bit. But I do like girls enough to take you where you want to go."

"I'm not going in that direction tonight."

She nodded, then looked at me shrewdly and asked, "So why you here?"

I countered with, "What's the real story here? Those white boy bankers aren't coming here for a few beers and a girl."

"You a cop?"

"No, I'm not."

"Dick?"

This time I just shrugged.

"You got that look about you. A dyke dick. What you want here, anyway?"

"I found a matchbook advertising this bar in a real odd place. I got curious."

"Curiosity kills cat."

"I'm a dyke, not a cat, remember?"

"Still got a pussy somewhere, honey." She stood up. "You be careful around here."

Noise from the crowd escalated. The stripper was down to her G-string, and the men ringing the stage were clamoring for it to come off.

"Can you answer a few questions?" I asked her.

"Over the limit, boo. I've sat here too long just talking. Just talking can get a girl into a lot of trouble."

"If I come back, who should I ask for?"

"Camille. Ask for Camille." She walked away, heading for the next table.

I had ten dollars in my pocket and I knew that wouldn't buy much here. The man at the next table got up and went with her through the dark door in the dark wall. If I had to, I would buy some of Camille's time and ask her some questions.

The stage show was reaching its climax, pun intended. Most of the men within a thirty-foot radius of the stage were shouting for her to take it all off.

I watched her struts and juts dispassionately. I know I'm supposed to be attracted to women, but none of this appealed to me. I wondered if some of the appeal for the cheering men, fully clothed on the sidelines watching, wasn't the power of their money to buy this show of big tits. The power imbalance that attracted them, repelled me.

Of course, why is selling your body for sex any worse than working in a numbing factory job or having to smile every time you answered the phone or said hello? Does one force you to give up a greater part of your soul than the other? Or was it just the idea of having sex with a nameless, ultimately faceless man that repelled me?

I've slept with a lot of women, but even at its crudest, it was sex traded for sex. Then, with a growing shame, I realized the lines had not always been so clear and defined. A good meal, a place to stay, clothes, or a loan; sometimes the exchange was not just the equality of desire. If I had desperately needed money and a woman had offered me some, I suspected there were times I would have taken it. If I did ask Camille some questions, maybe I should ask her that one.

Several men in the back rows were standing up, blocking my view of all but the stripper's head and ample breasts. A loud and raucous chorus of cheers told me she had taken it all off. That, of course, is even more illegal than bare breasts, but that seemed of concern to no one. There was a brief moment of whistles and shouts, then the men sat back down to their beers, the background music replaced the stage blare, and only the one red light remained on.

The stripper, her act over, picked up her G-string and other pieces of her costume as she made her way offstage. What little glamour and animation she had had was gone. Instead she walked with a tired wobble, a drop of sweat sliding down her back into the crack of her butt. As she turned to edge between the curtain and the wall, I saw what the men had been cheering for. Her pubic hair was entirely shaved, she looked utterly naked, the intimate fleshy contours of her vulva visible even at this distance. I found the sight very disconcerting. Why this show of flesh? Was it just pandering to the myth that women grew no coarse body hair? A pretense of innocence, a woman before sin and sexual knowledge? A young girl? My god, a young girl, I thought, the most powerless woman there can be.

I looked at the beer in front of me, suddenly wanting something to wash my dry throat with. But it hadn't looked appetizing when it was cold, and it wasn't even cool now. I didn't want to call attention to myself by going to the bar and ordering a club soda.

I heard a scrape and a thud. A man pulled up a chair at my table and sat down.

"Enjoying the sights?" he gruffly asked me.

"As much as you are," I retorted. He must have just come in, because I hadn't noticed him before and I would have noticed him. Tim O'Connor was a police detective with whom I had crossed paths before, and it had not been joy all around. I've seen him command a room, diverting all attention to himself, but tonight he appeared nondescript, a middle-aged man, a little tired, a little gray, the kind of man who was looking for pieces of a shallow youth because it was better than a shallow middle-age. But I was close enough to see his eyes and I knew better than to believe that façade. He was my height, barely, with a slightly droopy mustache, and a mostly full head of gray hair that still showed a few streaks of the brown it had been. He wasn't exactly who I wanted to run into here.

"What are you doing here, Miss Knight?" he demanded.

"Aw, Tim, old buddy, after all we've been through, why don't you call me Micky?"

"I don't have time to play games. You can tell me what you're doing here, and now. Or I'll have you picked up tomorrow and taken down to the station."

"I'm conducting an investigation," I responded.

"An investigation of what?"

"Client confidentiality."

O'Connor gave me a look that clearly showed he was not pleased with my answer. "I got news for you. You're out of here now."

"Aw, Tim, I promise not to tell your wife I ran into you here."

That was an even less pleasing answer. "Listen, Knight, and you listen good. I've got something going down here, and, if you step into it, not one of your big-shot friends are going to be of much help to you. Ever."

I said, "What are you working on? We might—"

"We're not," he cut me off. "What I'm working on is off-limits. Get out now."

"And if I don't?" I challenged.

"I'll have you arrested for everything I possibly can."

"Don't you think arresting me might blow your cover?"

That answer was even farther down on the pleasing list. "You could spend the next week sitting in my office answering questions. If you so much as forget to signal a lane change, you'll have a ticket. Get my drift?"

The only replies I could think of would only get me into more trouble. O'Connor and I just stared at each other for a moment. Finally, I decided to play his game. "Look, the reason I'm here is…"

"Get out of here. Now. Be at the station tomorrow at two. Tell me then." With that, he got up and walked away.

It was past my bedtime anyway. I would talk to O'Connor tomorrow. I wondered if he would find it odd that a young girl would have a matchbook advertising this place in her pocket. Oh, yeah, real likely.

My friend, the rain, was still visiting in torrents, the thirty feet to my car a drenching distance. I hadn't found anything that would tell me how the matchbook had gotten into Cissy's pocket. It didn't seem likely that she had come in, bellied up to the bar, asked for a glass of milk, and taken a book of matches.

It was time to go home. I was wet and cold, and I didn't have the energy or concentration to think about the things I needed to think about. I started my car and drove away from the darkened streets.

Chapter 19

The rain had not left by morning, merely gone offstage for a bit. The sky remained dark and potent. Time felt ambiguous with the sun so completely obscured. I had to glance first at my alarm clock, electric and subject to power outages, then my wristwatch to be sure of the time.

After a scrubbing shower and brewing a pot of coffee, I sat down at my desk. Usually, I make case notes every day, a rough scribble meant for no one but myself. It can contain everything from the prosaic (what I did that day) to hunches and stray thoughts, right-brain scattershot. Sometimes it's useful, most often not. From those notes, I culled my progress reports and case files that I passed on to the client. I hadn't really been keeping case notes for my investigation of Cissy's behavior. Patrick, ostensibly whom I was working for, was a bit of an irregular client, not to mention that, as a minor, I doubted he could legally enter into a contract with me. Aside from the legal aspect, there were a lot of things about this case that I couldn't just jot down and hand to a twelve-year-old boy.

I forced myself to do the work I had been neglecting, expanding on the few sketchy notes I had made, writing a complete log of what I'd done and where I'd been. After that I sat staring at the paper for several minutes, until I finally told myself, don't censor, just write. I had no hunches, so I had none to write down, that left the passing marginalia.

The first thing I scribbled was, "Lindsey and Cordelia—lovers?" then I scratched it out. Their past had no bearing on this case. Then I wrote it back in, as illegibly as I could. Lindsey had a bearing on the case and her past was part of who she was. If my present lover had been a lover of hers, I needed to at least acknowledge it. Then I wrote, "Pulled away from Cordelia as if she were someone else." I scratched it out. That didn't fit in with this case.

I made lists of names, drawing lines to show their connections. As a final thought, I added O'Connor, putting a question mark next to his name instead of a line. I looked at my handiwork, but nothing emerged from the hodgepodge of names and events.

I put aside my pen and notepad and got up to feed Hepplewhite. She didn't like it. Nothing was going to be easy today. I had a sneaking suspicion that seeing O'Connor at two o'clock would not change the tenor of the day.

Since it was likely that I would spend some time with O'Connor, I needed to wear clothes that would fit in with Alex's party. I had almost forgotten about it. As everyone else would be coming from work, I decided on professional woman drag, a sober gray suit, a white shirt, and sensible black pumps, the heels low enough so that I wouldn't be taller than O'Connor.

I presented myself at the appointed hour, but O'Connor was nowhere around. A not very precise "I suppose he'll be back sometime" was the only information I was offered.

I waited an hour. I couldn't decide whether he'd forgotten me or just gotten busy. I finally veered toward busy, as being forgotten isn't a very flattering feeling, and why let unpleasantness intrude into your life if it doesn't have to? An additional inquiry into O'Connor's whereabouts gained me no additional information.

I left him a note. A polite, "I was here" note without the "where the fuck were you?" postscript that I contemplated. So, at a quarter past three, I was standing beside my car, wondering what to do next. Going home wasn't very useful. I would just be leaving again to pick up Alex.

Then I decided to see what the Heart of Desire looked like in the daylight. Just a quick drive by before I picked up Alex for her party. I headed back downtown. The light of day dispelled the dense and threatening shadows from the night before. The peeling paint, and leaning porches were clearly visible. Even though it was only afternoon, there were clumps of men standing on the sidewalks, paper bags covering the malt liquor or cheap wine in their hands. Did I really think I was so different from them, that if I led their lives, that my best respite wouldn't be some drink or drug to obliterate these streets?

I've been what passes for poor, eating crackers and raisins once for four days, because that was all I had, and no money to buy anything else. My car is old, my apartment cheap, and in a neighborhood that has its own share of poverty and despair.

But I'd never been hungry as a child, my parents so powerless that they couldn't even feed their children. I've never watched a world of new cars and large houses on TV that I knew I could never enter, never even visit.

I could, if I wanted to, take my fancy college degree and go earn money. Go to law school, medical school. Even if I didn't take those avenues to money and so-called success, I had a map of how to get there.

I glanced again at the passing men standing on corners. Did any of them, even the youngest, think it possible to be a doctor or lawyer? Not an idle thought or a fierce struggle, but a reality, like it was for the sons and daughters of the middle class? I wondered what my life would be like if the only possibilities I'd ever seen were the ones Aunt Greta had cast my way.

Heart of Desire came into view. As I had the night before, I turned onto Law Street. A car suddenly roared around me, pulled in front of me, and then stopped abruptly. I jammed on my brakes to avoid hitting it. It was a black Porsche with a familiar license plate. He remained stopped long enough to let me know he'd recognized me, then slowly and deliberately, inviting me to follow him, pulled over to the side of the road.

At first I was angry. I had told Joey I didn't want to see him again. No, I had told him Karen didn't want to see him, although not seeing me again was implied, I would have thought. Then curiosity hit. What was smooth-talking Joey Boudreaux doing in this neighborhood? New Orleans is just a small enough city that it could be coincidence. But I had a hunch that Joey was on the illegal side of whatever O'Connor was tangled up with. And if I could find out enough about who was involved to find a name that intersected with Cissy's life, I might blow this case open. Admittedly a series of jumps, but I finally had a direction and some possibilities. I pulled behind Joey's car. I was prudent enough to let him get out first, before I opened my door and stepped onto the cracked sidewalk.

"I know you're not the uptown girl Karen is, but I didn't think this was the kind of place you'd hang around," Joey greeted me. "I saw you last night," he added, "leaving here."

"What's it to you?" I answered, taken aback at having been seen.

"What's a nice girl like you doing in a neighborhood like this?"

"Trust me, I'm not nice," I retorted.

He leered for show, then said, "So, are you naughty?"

"Not in any way you'd appreciate."

Joey nodded slowly. He'd been putting on a show so my rejection barely pricked his ego. "How's Karen these days?"

"I wouldn't know," I said coldly.

"You're not…friends?"

"I did what she paid me to do. No, we're not friends."

"Money's the ticket?" he asked.

"The only ticket that gets you anywhere." Discussing morality and good and evil didn't seem the way to impress Joey.

"It seems we think alike. Good thing I ran into you."

"Yeah? Why's that?" He clearly wanted me to ask, so I did.

"Want to earn a little extra money?"

"Doing what?"

"Using your talents to the fullest."

"Not an answer."

He changed his tactics. "Making some good money. I'm overbooked at the moment. I need an assistant."

"Back to my original question, doing what?"

"Making some connections. Getting person A to person B."

"Is this legal?"

"As legal as two girls together," he answered.

"And what crime against nature would I be committing?" In Louisiana, sodomy, oral sex, and all that fun stuff—covered under the heading "crimes against nature"—is a felony.

"I have a client who has, uh, unusual tastes. Your job is to arrange for the right person to meet his needs."

"You mean pimp?"

"I wouldn't call it that."

"No mere 'pimping' allowed in the Sans Pareil Club?"

Joey shot me a look, then recovered, "I am impressed, Ms. Knight. I didn't think that was something Karen would know." Then he added, "Or dare to tell anyone."

"Karen didn't know. Or, if she does, she didn't tell me. I have other sources."

Joey shrugged. "So you understand the nature of the business."

"To a degree. What I don't understand is why you'd turn over keeping someone like Anthony Colombé happy. Displeasing him must have its consequences."

"I'm not turning it over. This is just temporary. I have a major conflict in the next few days. I just need a little help to keep both my masters happy. Of course, if it works out, sometime in the future…" He trailed off invitingly.

"Your other job must be something big. For you to blow off Colombé."

"I'm not blowing him off. He'll be taken care of. That's what I'm working out now." But Joey couldn't help bragging, "But, yeah, the other job is big. It could be really big. It could mean old Joey B. never working for nobody again."

I let the bad grammar go. "How big?" I asked.

"Too big to talk about," was his answer.

"You sound like you're talking about olives—large, jumbo, and huge."

"Hey, it's a train that's going places. No one says you got to ride it."

"Why are you offering me a ticket?" I countered.

"Why not?"

I gave Joey a look that said, "Bullshit."

He continued, "'Cause I need help. You've got the talent to help me. You're pretty butch for a girl."

I started to make a caustic comment and be on my way, but I stopped myself. If Joey, however obliquely, held the key to Cissy's terror, I had to follow it up. "Oh, I am, huh?" was my ever-so-polite reply.

"Yeah. You're not working for Karen anymore, are you?"

"No, I'm not."

"So you want to help me for a little bit?"

"What about this 'big' thing?" I wasn't really interested in Colombé.

"That's my deal. I just need you to help with Colombé," Joey said.

"But is it big enough that you might need help?"

Joey gave me an appraising look before answering slowly, "Yeah, yeah, it might be that big. Come on, let's see how you work out on this gig."

"What's the deal?"

"Tonight I take you through the ropes. We split half and half. Then you cover the next few nights for me. You get it all. I won't even take a cut."

"How kind of you."

"Hey, the first month I did this I had to split fifty/fifty with the old guy. He did shit, I did all the work."

"You're all heart, Joey."

"I sure am. Follow me," he said, turning to his car.

I started to ask him again what he was doing in the neighborhood, but didn't. If I played it right, that would come in time. Joey wanted to show off, but he wasn't sure yet that I was the person he could show off to. I had to convince him that I was. I got into my car and followed him. He led me to a gas station on Claiborne, near the I-10 ramp. He pulled up next to a pay phone. I stopped behind him.

"Always use a different phone," he said as we both got out. "You got to learn where a bunch of them are." He strode over to the phone, punching in a number before I could get close enough to see it. I stood near him to overhear the conversation. His end of it was, "Yeah," and "Uh-huh," repeated several times. Very enlightening.

When Joey hung up, he turned to me and said, "Tonight he wants to watch a tall, dark, handsome man fuck a young, blond dude. We get to arrange it." With that, Joey got back into his car.

I followed him again, this time to Rampart Street, finding semi-legal parking places next to Armstrong Park. Rampart is one of the boundaries of the Quarter. It openly exhibits the decadence that Bourbon Street only hints at. Tourists don't wander down Rampart; only those who know what they want come here.

"So what do we do now?" I asked as I caught up to Joey. "Just ask some guys if they want to make some money?"

"Naw, that's how you get busted. You use your brains and your contacts." We crossed the street and he led me into one of the bars that crowded this part of Rampart.

As we entered, Joey did a quick scan of the place. Evidently he didn't see who he was looking for as he headed for a table and sat down.

"I need to make a phone call," I said. I didn't sit with him, but instead headed to the pay phone next to the bar.

"What's the number?" Joey asked as he picked up the phone before I could get to it. He had followed me.

I reluctantly gave him the number to Cordelia's clinic.

"Who do you want to talk to?" he asked as he punched in the number.

"Cordelia. Cordelia James."

Joey nodded, as he waited for the phone to be answered, then I heard him ask for her. There was a pause, he looked at me and said, "Dr. James? Is she your girlfriend?"

"A friend." I didn't want to give him that. "We were going out to a birthday dinner for another friend tonight. She needs to know I'm not going to meet her."

"She's not around, so you can tell them that." Joey handed the phone to me, but he stayed close enough to hear everything I said.

"Hi, this is Micky."

"Micky, what's going on?" It was Elly.

"Something important has come up. I can't make Alex's party."

"But you're supposed to pick her up."

"I know, but I'm not going to be able to do that."

"What's so important? Are you okay?"

"Yeah, I'm fine. I can't explain right now. Just tell Cordelia, and everyone else, that I'm very sorry."

"All right, I'll tell her," Elly said shortly. Her disapproval was evident. "Is there someplace she can call you?"

"No, I'm not at home."

"I'll let her know you called." Elly hung up.

I held on to the phone a moment more, listening to the disconnected buzz. I wanted to leave Joey and his sordid job behind, to go and laugh and party with them. What was more important, playing my hunches or my commitment to my friends? But if I walked away now, I might never get another chance to find out what Joey was involved in, what had led us both to the intersection of Law and Desire.

I said, "Goodbye," for Joey's benefit and put the phone back down. I wondered if Cordelia and I would still be lovers after tonight.

Around forty-five minutes later, the man Joey had been looking for came in. He was nondescript, looking like an accountant who would never make it past lower middle management. Joey introduced him as Mr. Smith. They went over a list of bodies, looks, price, preferences. Joey shook his head as each description went by.

"Let's go," Joey finally said, and we left Mr. Smith in the bar.

The next place netted us a blond boy who sounded promising until we met him. He was on something heavy-duty and his hair was matted and greasy. Joey shook his head and we left there, too. At the next bar, Joey couldn't find his connection.

"When does Colombé want them by?" I asked as we headed into the Quarter.

"Soon," was Joey's reply. He had started out buoyant and expansive, enjoying his role as mentor, but as the evening wore on and he couldn't meet Colombé's demands, he became tense and nervous. It seemed that he really wanted to impress me, to prove that he was slick and successful. That seemed important to Joey.

It was getting chilly and there was a fine drizzling mist in the air. It was not a pleasant night to be out hunting flesh. Walking with Joey, dressed in my gray suit and sensible pumps, pimping for Anthony Colombé, felt a bit surreal. Any minute I expected a director to yell, "Cut, we need a rewrite on this scene." Instead, what broke through my thoughts was Joey calling out, "Houston, my man, whcrc y'at?"

Houston, half hidden in the shadows, was a large black man wearing a massive collection of gold chains and an expensive leather jacket.

"Depends, Joey, depends on where you want me to be." Houston spoke with a perfect Oxford accent. He gazed at me questioningly. This man looked very intelligent, not good or bad as some intelligences are evil and others kind, but intelligent in a startlingly neutral way.

Joey seemed oblivious to the question Houston was directing at me. "I'm looking for some boys. I need a performance tonight."

Houston flicked his eyes over Joey, a bare acknowledgment that he had said anything. "I only do girls. You know that" was his dismissal.

"Oh, well, gotta try," Joey shrugged and turned to walk away.

"What do you suggest?" I asked Houston.

He was too neutral to offer, but if asked he might reply.

"For the right person, the right price, anything is possible."

Joey turned back to stare at our exchange.

"Who do you work for?" Houston asked.

"I can't tell you," Joey said.

"Anthony Colombé," I answered.

Houston nodded, then spoke to a woman standing in the shadows behind him. "Sheila, show Joey what you have." With a motion of his head, he instructed Joey to follow Sheila into the renovated slave quarters behind us. They would take care of the business details. I didn't follow, neither did Houston.

"Why are you with him?" he asked me.

"He has something I want."

Houston nodded as if he knew about wanting. "Anthony Colombé is not a man to be taken on lightly."

"I don't intend to take on Colombé. Unless I have to."

He nodded slowly, then asked, "Why?"

"A long story."

"One simple reason."

"A friend, a young girl that I know is having nightmares. No young girl should sleep in terror."

"No, no child should sleep in terror." In his stark words I caught a glimpse of what underlay the savage neutrality. Then it was back in place.

Joey and Sheila reappeared. Joey was again in high spirits. "We're on our way. Thanks, Houston, Sheila."

Houston nodded, then turned away. I followed Joey back toward our cars.

"I've got an address," Joey said as we walked along. "There'll be some guys waiting for us there. If they fit the picture, we rack 'em up, drop 'em off, and call it an evening."

"What if they don't fit the picture?"

"They will. I've got a feeling about this one."

I did, too.

"Okay if we take my car?" Joey asked. "It'll be easier."

"Sure." I've learned to trust my instincts and they told me Joey wasn't a threat. There wasn't anything sexual going on, and at the moment, I was a solution to a problem Joey had. More than that, what he really wanted from me was a reflection of himself the way he wanted to be, smooth, successful, and important.

"You want to drive?" he asked, handing me the keys. "Stick with me and someday soon you'll have your own Porsche."

I took the keys and didn't tell Joey that, even if I had the money, I wouldn't spend it on this kind of car. I had a moment's qualm at leaving my car parked on Rampart, but I noticed a Mercedes parked in front of it and hoped that no self-respecting thief would pass over a late-model German car for a very out-of-date Datsun. And if they did, I could just stick with Joey and get a new car out of it.

Joey rattled off an address as I scanned the unfamiliar controls. Then, with the hope that he had comprehensive insurance, I pulled out and headed for the street number he gave me. It was only a few blocks away, a building with balconies and old world charm. These were high-class hustlers we were picking up.

I double-parked in front, waiting while Joey knocked on the door. He said something very brief to the person who opened it; a moment later, two young men came out. One was very handsome in a dark, masculine way—square-jawed, heavy-lidded with black, sensual eyes. The other was blond, boyish, with an upturned nose, and wide smile that made me think he couldn't be more than nineteen until I noticed his eyes. They put him in the mid-to-late twenties. Old enough to know what he was doing, I told myself. They climbed into the backseat, staring openly at me. Whether they didn't like women in general or whether they were just uncomfortable with a woman witnessing their prostitution, I couldn't tell.

Blond Boy tapped me on the shoulder, "Hey, honey, you want me to drive this thing?"

I didn't answer. Instead, after a quick check of the traffic, I pulled out, pushed the car into third gear in half a block and did a squealing U-turn that slammed the backseat boys into each other.

Joey grinned at me, held securely in place by his seat belt. By putting me down, Blond Boy was ridiculing Joey's choice of me. I did realize that his attempted insult was nervous tension, flailing back at that macho thing that "real men" aren't bottoms. Everyone in the car knew he was going to be fucked by another man. Much as I disliked being a part of this, I didn't feel sorry for him. Some of it may have been bad luck or ill fate, but he had made some choices that had brought him here.

"The Club?" I asked Joey, as I roared, like all good New Orleans drivers, through a yellow light.

"That's the place," he answered.

"Where are we going?" Blond Boy asked.

"You'll find out," Joey replied.

"Well, at least it's good money," he said. "All I can say is that dick of yours is going to be wrapped in ten rubbers." However, it wasn't all he could say. Blond Boy kept up a monologue about how he was only doing this for the money and that this was going to be his ticket to L.A. He might have been in his late twenties, but his dreams and fears were still those of a teenaged boy. His companion grunted and "yeah-ed" in the right places, only once saying anything, answering Blond Boy's direct question about what kind of condoms he had with him. "Maxi, of course, everything else is too small," was Dark and Handsome's modest reply.

I turned into the gates of the Sans Pareil Club. Instead of going to the front, Joey pointed to a drive branching off from the main one. The white slave entrance, no doubt. I followed it as it wound around behind the Club to a large and luxurious garage, pausing while Joey hit a remote to open the doors. As I drove in, the doors slid shut behind us. Just as I cut the motor, Francois opened the door.

"Good, you're here," he said. For just a split second, he was surprised when he saw me, then he covered it as if nothing had happened.

"We're not too late, are we?" Joey called as he swung out of the car. The triumph in his voice indicated he knew the answer.

"Of course not," Francois answered smoothly, giving me a bare nod of acknowledgment. "You're just in time." Behind Francois, I noticed two of Colombé's elegant and tuxedoed muscle men. "If you gentlemen will follow me?" Francois continued, motioning Blond Boy and his friend in. "I'll be with you in a moment," Francois said to us as he shut the door behind him.

"So, is this the usual deal?" I asked.

"Pretty much. I always come to the door. Francois always opens it."

I started to ask how Francois knew just when we arrived, but then I noticed several video cameras stationed around the garage. I waved at the one focused on us to let them be aware that I knew I was on candid camera.

The door opened and Francois reappeared. "Mr. Boudreaux, Ms. Knight," Francois said, "Mr. Colombé is very pleased with your work. In addition to your usual, he is offering a five-hundred-dollar bonus."

"I won't argue," Joey said, taking the money. Cash, I noticed.

"Mr. Colombé has an additional favor to ask of you. One of his guests has a special request. Can you obtain it?" Francois handed Joey a small piece of paper.

"Sure, no problem," Joey answered as he read whatever was on the paper.

"This should take care of it, your fee and the cost." Francois handed Joey another bundle of money.

"It should," Joey replied. "See you in a bit," then to me, "I'll drive this time." He walked over to the driver's side.

"It's good to see you again, Ms. Knight," Francois said to me, as if saying, "See, you, too, can be a servant."

I gave him a bare nod, then turned and walked around the car.

"Half and half," Joey said as I got in.

I nodded. I hadn't been thinking about the money. He handed me seven hundred and fifty dollars. I stuffed it in my pocket.

"How much will they make?" I asked, referring to Blond Boy and his friend.

"It depends," Joey answered, as he turned the car around, "on what they're willing to do." The Porsche nosed its way onto the drive. "I almost had a wreck here. You just don't expect any other cars. I nearly front-ended a Rolls."

"How much for the basic package?"

"How basic?"

"One round of relatively safe anal sex."

"With rubbers? Fifty cents. Without, a quick butt-fuck'll get them a couple hundred each."

Joey pulled out of the gates of the Sans Pareil Club.

"Colombé's not going to let them use condoms?" I demanded.

"Naw, it takes all the fun out of it."

"Those are lives he's playing with."

"He has enough money to be God," Joey calmly answered.

"He has enough money to buy desperate people," I replied angrily. "Shouldn't we have told them before we left them off?"

Joey just shrugged.

"Shouldn't they have had the choice?" I demanded.

"If they don't like it, they can walk out. Colombé might even give them bus fare home."

"How generous, how fucking generous." I slumped back in my seat.

"For seven-fifty, I don't worry about the other guy's problem," was Joey's philosophical solution.

"Yeah, I guess." I had that queasy feeling of having slammed into something that I couldn't change, I could only live with the consequences.

"I gotta pick up some coke. You can come with me, and I'll show you the ropes. Or if you want, I can just tell you what to do in case it comes up."

I didn't particularly want to go with Joey, but I managed to push aside my remorse long enough to ask, "Where's the place?"

"You know it. You were there last night."

"Yeah, I'll go with you." Remorse would have to wait until tomorrow. Tonight I was going to a place where a few more of my questions might be answered, the bar at the corner of Law and Desire.

CHAPTER 20

"Why this particular place?" I asked Joey as we headed downtown.

"Real good blow. The man never cuts it."

"How nice. Quality control among thieves."

"Gotta get them repeat customers back."

I glanced at my watch. It was a little past twelve-thirty. I wondered if Alex's birthday party was still going on. Why the hell wasn't I there? Instead I was picking up drugs and pimping unsafe sex. Then I remembered Houston's words, "No child should sleep in terror."

"So, what's your story, Joey? How'd you get into this?"

"The usual shit. I didn't do too good in high school."

English in particular, but I kept that to myself.

Joey continued, "I did a few years in the Navy, but I hated it, up early in the morning, people yelling at you all the time, wasn't for me. So I got out, drifted around, got shit jobs, warehouses, loading trucks, that kind of stuff. People always saying, 'Old Joey Boudreaux ain't never gonna make nothin' of himself.' Hell, you should of seen the looks on their faces when I drove up to my folk's place in this car. Gold rings and money in my wallet. Took my mom and dad, pissant brother, his wife, and all their stupid kids out to the best restaurant in Lake Charles, my old hometown."

"Boudreaux your real name?"

"Yeah, why not?"

"Some guys in your line of work have a lot of names."

"I'm making my wad and then I'm getting out of here."

"What will you do?"

"I'm going to open a Porsche dealership back in Lake Charles. I'll get a new one every year. I'm good with cars, good with people, all I need is the money to pull it off."

"Why Lake Charles?" I wondered if I should suggest to Joey that he might be safer retiring in some place like Nome, Alaska.

"'Cause all those guys who made fun of me in high school will come to me to buy their cars. Or hope someday that they might be able to."

"How'd you get to work for Colombé?"

"I met the dude that was doing this before me. He was slipping, too much of the blow, needed some help. He slipped a bit too far and I got it. Here we are," he said as he pulled up next to Heart of Desire.

When I had been here last night, it had been earlier in the evening. With the later hour, more people were here, more cars on the street, a clump of men outside the door.

"Stay close to me," Joey instructed as we got out of the car.

A man stationed next to the door nodded at Joey, then at me when Joey indicated we were together. The entrance was crowded, all the pay phones in use, two men leaning against the cigarette machine engaged in a heated argument, one man trying to edge between them to get cigarettes. Joey and I threaded our way between them as we made our way to the main area.

A woman, naked except for a feather boa drooped around her neck, was walking off stage. We had just missed the show. Joey led the way to an empty table against the wall, out of the light from both the bar and the stage.

"Do you want me to get you something?" I asked Joey. I wanted to prowl around and look at the faces hidden in the half-shadows of this bar.

"Naw. Don't be queer. It's queer for a girl to get a guy drinks. They'll bring it."

I sat, scanning the room. Again, it was an odd mix of people, white, black, a few Asians. Most of them were men. I didn't see any of the working girls. They were probably busy behind closed doors.

A waitress, who looked too young to be working here, came up to our table. "Can I get you something?"

"A beer and?" Joey looked questioningly at me.

"A beer."

She nodded and headed back to the bar.

"So, do you come here often?" I asked Joey, wincing at the cliché. "How did you find this joint?"

"This place has a rep. Anything you want. Too far out of the way for the cops to mess with."

I didn't bother to correct Joey. I wouldn't be sorry to see this club busted wide open. If Joey went with it, well, you play this game, you take your chances.

The waitress returned with our beers. Joey peeled off a ten, handed it to her, then asked, "Has Hugo been around lately?"

"Maybe. I'll ask." She took the ten.

"Is Hugo your connection?"

"The usual one. But asking for Hugo always gets you someone." Joey drained his beer in one long swallow.

I left mine on the table. "You think his name really is Hugo?"

"You know, I got no idea. Maybe it's Melvin or Fred and he thought Hugo would be better." Joey laughed at his joke.

All I managed was a weak smile. I was getting tired.

"You don't want your beer?"

"This stuff is pig piss."

Joey laughed, then reached over, took my pig piss beer and drained it. "Can't let good beer go to waste," he explained as he wiped his mouth with the back of his hand.

The Hugo du jour sat down at our table, a perfect man for the shadows, dark enough to be black, light enough to be white, neither old nor young.

"So, who's your friend?" Hugo asked.

"Micky. She works with me. She might be coming around sometimes," was Joey's reply.

Hugo nodded, then got down to business. "The usual?"

"The usual."

"Follow me," Hugo said.

He led us behind the shadowed door in the dark wall. There wasn't much to see in the hallway beyond it, a few closed doors and walls in need of paint. At the end of the hallway, Hugo opened one of the doors and ushered us into a small office. It had a battered metal desk, beige paint showing more than one layer of grime, the banality behind the evil; this could have been any office in any run-down factory.

Hugo sat down behind the desk, Joey opposite him. I remained standing, the only other chair had an overflowing ashtray perched on the seat. Hugo took out a set of keys, selected one, then opened the top desk drawer. He took out a mirror and razor blade, poured some white powder on the mirror and proceeded to cut a few lines of cocaine. He offered a line to Joey. I watched Joey snort it and wondered how many laws I would be breaking tonight.

Hugo did a line, then offered it to me.

"No, thanks," I declined. "Coke makes me drink and I'm trying to cut down." It wasn't the best excuse, but it seemed to work for Hugo. He finished off the cocaine.

"Good stuff," Joey offered.

"The best in town. Smooth and easy."

"But a good rush. It goes everywhere."

Tired of harsh nose candy? Try new lite coke, the kinder, gentler drug, with all the full-bodied charge and paranoia you expect from real coke. Joey slapped some money down and Hugo produced a fair amount of his expensive white powder.

Hugo then led us back to the main part of the bar. We exchanged a few minor pleasantries, and he melted back among the shadowed people.

"You want to hang around? Watch the show?" Joey asked.

"No, not particularly. Do you?"

"I thought you liked that kind of stuff."

It took me a moment to realize what Joey meant by "that stuff." He was pushing me, testing my limits. I didn't want to play games, so I just let my anger reply. Sometimes anger from a woman is the most unexpected answer. "You mean watching some dolled-up, fake woman walking around naked pretending to be sexy? I've never gotten off on the illusion of sex. Maybe you can answer some questions that have been bothering me. Why do you guys like having sex with someone who wouldn't do it if you didn't pay her? Why do you like looking at pictures of women you'll never have? Or watching some bimbo at a distance take her clothes off? What do you get out of it?"

"You're asking the wrong guy. I don't know why these guys are here. Either they're stupid, they got too much money, or they're too kinked up to do it with a real person."

"Or all three."

"Yeah, sometimes all three," Joey laughed. "Yeah, you gotta keep your eyes open, see what people want, what they'll pay for."

"What about the damages? Bad drugs, bad sex, people get hurt, killed."

"That happens anyway. Someone's going to make money. It might as well be me. The damage'll happen anyway."

I shrugged. "Let's get out of here."

As I started to turn, a large man ran into me, grabbing my arm with his hand.

"Aren't you tired of this boy yet? Why don't you spend some time with me, honey?"

"Get your fucking hands off me," was my polite answer. But I would be spending some time with him. My only consolation was that he couldn't arrest me on the spot or he'd blow his cover.

"Hey, Pops. Hands off the merchandise," Joey said.

O'Connor let go of me, then said, "She ain't worth what you're paying for her," before he stalked off.

"Let's get out of here," I said. I headed for the door without waiting for Joey. A few propositions were mumbled as I pushed through the entrance. I ignored them.

Joey caught up with me at his car. "I could've handled that old geezer."

"Can the macho show. I'm not interested. And, Joey, if it gets down to it, I know where to kick."

Joey shrugged and unlocked the car. I let him drive, figuring his coke-induced energy wasn't any more dangerous than my long day's lethargy.

The late-night streetlights became a blur as we drove uptown to the Sans Pareil Club. I sat in the car and watched Joey and Francois interact their brief exchange, a few words, a quick transfer of drugs, nothing noticeable enough to ripple the polished façade of the Sans Pareil Club.

Joey was still jazzed up as we drove back to my car. He rattled on about growing up in Lake Charles, being called "Slow Joe" by his older brother. I tried to listen, but it was the same sad story, not-quite-good enough, not-quite-loved enough. Joey wasn't a very good storyteller. "But I'm going to show them. I'm really going to show them," were his final words as he let me out at my car. He handed me his beeper so that Colombé could summon me whenever he wished. I wondered what would happen if I forgot to turn it on.

Joey, gentleman that he was, or perhaps realist, waited while I fumbled with my keys and got into my car. Only when I was safely locked into its tin can interior did he take off.

On impulse, I turned off Rampart into the Quarter to drive by Cordelia's apartment. But there were no lights on, nothing suggested I would be welcome. Some part of me very much wanted to talk to her. I wanted her advice and conscience. Was I doing the right thing, was I going too far? But I didn't know if I could explain what was driving me, or whether I had already gone far beyond her boundaries. I wanted to verify that there were brakes on my obsession. I wasn't sure if I had any anymore. I kept on driving, heading downtown to my apartment. It would be morning soon, and I was very tired.

I threw off my clothes, that damned uncomfortable gray suit, a reminder of my abandoned plans for the evening. The light on my answering machine was, not surprisingly, blinking. I flopped down in the chair next to it and hit the play button.

"If you're dead or seriously injured, you have an excuse. If not, you're shit, Mick," was Joanne's message.

"If it's a really good excuse, wait a couple of days before you call me. If it's not a good excuse, wait a year," was Danny's.

O'Connor had called twice. Both messages were versions of, "Eleven o'clock at the station. At eleven-oh-five I send the squad car after you."

The one person who had not called was Cordelia. Anger, even fury, would have been more welcome than her silence.

I went to the bathroom, stood under the shower for a few minutes to wash the sweat and smoke off of me, then, wet hair and all, went to bed.

Chapter 21

The ringing of the phone jarred me out of sleep. I mumbled a half-awake hello.

"So you are alive." It was Joanne. She hung up on me.

I glanced at my clock. Only eight thirty. I fell back asleep, only to be re-awakened an hour later by my alarm clock. I finally forced myself up; it was not in my best interest to keep O'Connor waiting. I showered and dressed in a hurry.

Leaving my car in the most legal-looking parking space I could find, I went into the police station. This time when I stated who I was and asked to see O'Connor, I was told to go right back to his cubicle. He brusquely motioned me to sit down while he finished filling out paperwork.

It was several minutes before he looked up at me, then he merely said, "Explain."

I tossed the matchbook Lindsey had gotten from Cissy onto his desk. He picked it up and looked at it, then looked at me.

"How does that get into the pocket of a nine-year-old girl?" I asked.

"You tell me."

I shrugged, then stared at the matches O'Connor had put back down on his desk, trying to think of what I could and couldn't reveal. "A young girl I know—her behavior changes, she becomes afraid of things. The only clue I have are those matches."

O'Connor nodded slowly, tiredly, then asked, "Who's the girl?"

I shook my head. Then, to blunt my refusal, said, "She won't tell you anything. She won't say anything to her mother or me or even a shrink she's seeing. Dragging her down here to talk to you won't help."

O'Connor nodded, seemingly satisfied with my answer. "How'd you hook up with Joey Boudreaux?"

"How do you know who he is?"

"Answer my question first."

"A client was involved in a deal with him. It was somewhat irregular and she felt she needed my assistance in getting out."

"Something illcgal?"

"Probably. But my client won't talk, neither will Joey, and I don't have any proof."

O'Connor shrugged this time. These weren't the fish he was after, so he would probably let it go.

"I was driving by Heart of Desire," I continued. "I saw Joey there. I got curious." I ended my story there.

"Tell me exactly where and what you did with Joey last night. Every inch." O'Connor leaned forward, his eyes drilling me as he waited for an answer.

I sat for a moment before finally replying, "I need to talk to a lawyer first."

O'Connor grunted, then slowly sat back in his chair, staring at me the entire time.

"How deep are you?" he asked. "Over your head?"

"I haven't lost sight of land." That was a hope more than an answer.

O'Connor gave me a long, appraising look before he finally said, "Good. Don't lose sight of land. You've got your foot in a door I haven't even found yet. You work with me, you stay legal. You don't, you might drown."

"Can you get me that kind of deal?"

"For this I can. I can clear it by this afternoon."

"What's this?"

O'Connor reached into his desk and took out a black binder. He handed it to me.

Balancing it on my lap, I opened it. I didn't know what to expect, and it took me a moment to realize what I was seeing. I slammed the binder shut. Then I took a deep breath and, prepared this time, opened the cover again. I quickly looked through the pictures, glancing hurriedly at just the faces.

"She's not in here," I said, closing the binder against those young faces with their false smiles.

"Your friend with the matches in her pocket?" O'Connor asked.

"She's not there," I repeated.

"Not yet."

I put the black binder back on O'Connor's desk, a faint unsettled queasiness rolling in my stomach.

"You okay?" O'Connor asked me.

"Yeah, sure," I mumbled. "Didn't eat breakfast."

"You want something? Coffee? Donut?"

"No, no thanks." Neither sounded like they would do my stomach any good.

"You don't have to do this. Say good-bye to Joey, stay out of my way, and you're out."

"I want to do this."

"You sure?"

"How many more girls are going to get their pictures taken, or worse, while you try to find the door I've got my foot in?"

O'Connor nodded slowly. "We haven't got a lot. Copies of these pictures have shown up in places as far away as Miami and New York. NYPD iced some of the distributors and they pointed back this way. Someone's working out of Heart's. It could be a lone operator selling it, it might be just another distribution point, or it could be more."

"How's Joey involved?"

O'Connor shrugged. "Don't know. He's got a few arrests, no convictions. Soft stuff. May have been a pimp, but nothing solid. He might be involved, he might know someone involved."

"In other words, reel him in and see what we've caught."

"We want the head of this snake. A few years back, it was coming out of Philly. Cops up there got his tail once, but it's grown back. I don't want that to happen here."

"Can you tell me anything else?"

"Concrete? Not much. We could bust the small fish, but that's all."

"All right, I'll work Joey."

"Think about it. Go home and get some sleep and think about it. You'll be real far out. Your best protection will be how hard it is to trace you back to the cops."

I nodded.

"It might get messy and it might get dangerous. Two of the little girls from Philadelphia disappeared. No one believes they're alive."

"All the more reason to get them, don't you think?"

"Yeah, I think. But I still want you to go home and sit around for a couple of hours before you say yes or no. Call me later this afternoon. Use a pay phone. I'll get something official so you can stay out of trouble."

I stood to go. "I'll call you this afternoon, but I'll do it."

O'Connor nodded, then added, "You'll be safer if you stay away from your friends, Sergeant Ranson and Danielle Clayton. A cop and an assistant DA might concern the wrong people." The last time our paths had crossed,

I had made it a point to let O'Connor know who my friends were. It hadn't made much of a difference to him.

I shrugged. "I don't think that will be a problem." Not after last night, it wouldn't.

I walked out of the police station, the queasy feeling still roiling my stomach. Those pictures were slick, professional. It was the intimation I had glimpsed behind the makeup and camera angles, that disturbed me. The faces of the men were never seen, only the girls were fully exposed to the camera. Some staring at it with a frightening coyness that would have been out of place in a twenty-one-year old; others seemed placid, compliant, as if it were the only coin they knew to trade, and no one had ever told them how to say no or struggle. And, finally, there were the faces of those who had fought back and lost, the look of the vanquished whose will has been taken from them.

What O'Connor had hinted at, but not directly said, was that pictures of Cissy existed. I reached my car, bracing myself against it, waiting for a dry heave to pass.

Could I do this, I wondered. It was unlikely I would get to the head of the snake without passing more of these pictures, and perhaps the young girls themselves. Could I just walk by that and pretend it didn't sicken me?

It would cost me a lot to will myself into the kind of monster who moved easily in that world. Just looking at those pictures brought up a pounding anger. *Can I hold it and direct it, or will I lash out at whoever is within reach?* If I wanted to attempt to salvage my relationship with Cordelia, I would have to do it now. But this case could take weeks or months, and the distraction and resonances of working through the rough areas of love and sex would be impossible in the face of it.

I got into my car. But whatever the cost, it would cost me more to walk away.

I frittered away the afternoon, starting several things that I had neither the concentration nor patience to finish. I put off calling O'Connor, delayed making the irrevocable commitment. Finally, the afternoon was slipping out of the workday into early evening. I drove to a drugstore with a pay phone in the parking lot. I called O'Connor.

"You still sure?" he asked.

"Yeah, I'm still sure."

"Okay, take it easy, don't push. Drop a few hints that you're real poor and would do anything for money."

"How do I reach you if I need to?"

"I'll give you three numbers. Home, work, and beeper. I'll keep the beeper with me at all times, I'll sleep with it, I'll take a crap with it, and when I take my wife out on our anniversary dinner, I'll have it."

"How many years?" I asked.

"Next Tuesday, it'll be twenty-three."

"Congratulations." I couldn't even make three months.

"I'll be wearing the beeper. Call if you need. My wife's used to it. We got married right after I got out of the police academy." Then O'Connor admonished me to, "Memorize them," as he gave me the phone numbers. He continued, "This is the part I hate—if something happens to you, who do I contact?"

I thought for a moment. Legally it would probably be Aunt Greta, but she was the last person I'd want involved. "I guess my cousin, Torbin Robedeaux."

"Does he have medical power of attorney?"

"No. Actually, Danny, Danielle Clayton, does." It was something she had talked me into a few years ago. Being a lawyer made Danny aware of how important these things are, particularly for gay people who are estranged from their so-called family. And Danny, whom I'd known since college, and, more importantly, whom I trusted to do the right thing, was the logical choice to hold my medical power of attorney.

"All right," O'Connor said. "I know how to get in contact with her."

"We were friends in college," I added. "Only two kids from New Orleans there." It was one thing for me to be out of the closet, but Danny had to work with a lot of people who didn't like blacks, didn't like women, and would hate a black lesbian.

"She's good at what she does," was O'Connor's only comment. "I don't want to use that information. But I do want to get those creeps. I got three daughters. I don't ever want anyone messing with them."

"We'll get him. You can't want him any more than I do."

"Why? What pushes you?"

"I used to be a little girl," I answered, stepping into the intimacy of fighting a common enemy and the danger involved. I immediately pulled back—it wasn't a real connection and I couldn't trust it. "And we queers always get blamed for this shit. I'm sick of it."

"Just be careful out there, Ms. Knight. If it gets to you, you're not doing us or yourself any good."

"I know," I answered impatiently. "I've thought about that."

"Don't forget it. Call me if you've got something or you want out. Maybe check in once a week. Got that?"

"I've got it."

"Good luck." He hung up.

I stood for a moment, still holding the phone. The light was easing into twilight, the early darkness of winter encroaching. I put down the phone. *Thinking will only get you in trouble. Don't think. Just do what you have to do.* Thinking about Cordelia would hurt too much, and, as for what I would be doing, I couldn't afford the anger, it might rip me apart. I suddenly felt very lonely, unconnected, adrift from the world. It would occur to me to think, "But ya are, Blanche, ya are."

O'Connor had told me to wait, be patient. I spent the whole weekend reading. I didn't think about Cordelia. And I didn't think about the pictures O'Connor had shown me in his office.

CHAPTER 22

Monday afternoon Joey called. "So, anything happen?" he asked.

"Nothing." Remembering my cover, I added, "I didn't make one damn cent."

"That's too bad. I think Francois said something about being out of town. Anyway, I need to get that beeper from you. You free anytime this evening?"

"Pick a time."

"Eight-ish, that bar on Bourbon Street we went to."

Around seven thirty, I threw on my best black T-shirt and a jean jacket, and headed for the Quarter to meet Joey. I hadn't really intended to drive down Cordelia's street, but I found myself there. I passed her apartment. A light was on, but I didn't see her or her car in the lot. Half a block further on, a red Jaguar was parked on the street. That was awfully goddamn quick, I thought as a bolt of jealousy streaked through me.

Then I realized it wasn't Lindsey's car. The license plate was from Texas. A car behind me honked. In a childish display of temper, I made an obscene gesture.

Fortunately, the Monday French Quarter parking gods are more benevolent than those of other nights, allowing me to find a spot without too much trouble. Joey wasn't at the bar yet, so I ordered a club soda, found an out-of-the-way table, and settled myself in.

Joey showed up some ten minutes later. "Sorry nothing worked out," he said as he approached with an easy smile.

"Sometimes you get lucky, sometimes you don't." I shrugged.

He sat down. "But now you know how to do it, maybe something else will come up."

"I hope so. I could use the bucks."

"Whadda you drinking? Can I buy you one?"

"Sure. Club soda."

"I think I can cover that." Joey headed over to the bar to get our drinks. He seemed in a good mood, not in a hurry to finish up things. I wanted to ask about his other business, but it was too early to push. He returned with my club soda and a beer for himself.

"Can I ask a nosy question?" I asked.

Joey shrugged a "maybe."

"What are you into? Boys? Girls? Nuns? Dalmatians?"

"What's your interest? I didn't think I was your type."

"You're not. You know what I like. I'm curious about what you like."

"You really want to know? Built blonds. California hair."

"Boys or girls?"

"Seventy/thirty girls, boys. Sunshine hair with a great bod, big tits, big muscles does it for me. So you're not my type either."

I nodded. I was glad to have that settled. I didn't care to be Joey's type.

"Like Karen," Joey continued. "She wasn't bad looking. She your flavor of girl?"

I shook my head. "I like them dark and smart."

"A good thing. You send the blonds my way, and I'll send the eggheads to you. That way we won't get into any fights over it."

"Cheers," I said, lifting my glass. Joey clinked his beer against mine.

"So, I might have some work for you," he said casually.

"Yeah? What?"

"Tell me what you won't do for money."

"I wouldn't fuck any of the Republicans in Congress. Even the women."

Joey barked out a laugh. "Anything else?"

"Murder one. I think I'd like to stay away from that."

"Sex stuff? Leather? Bondage? Videos of that? Any problem?"

"People ought to be able to do what they want to do. I don't have a problem with that." I stopped myself from adding, as long as it involves consenting adults.

"What about real kinky stuff? Sicko things? Animals, stuff like that?"

"The doggy didn't consent? I'm supposed to give a shit about that? I prefer people in my bed, but, hey, whatever gets you through the night."

Joey nodded again, then said, "Yeah, maybe we can work something out." He drained his beer. "Look, I'll call you. Maybe tomorrow night, around midnight. You doing anything?"

"No, midnight's not a problem," I answered. "But how much do I make, and do I get it in cash?"

"Enough," Joey replied. "And it's always in cash." He stood up, and I handed him the beeper. "Okay, I'll give you a call if something happens."

"Thanks. I could use the money."

"See ya 'round."

I watched Joey walk out of the bar. The fish had taken the bait. But look what usually happens to bait. I didn't drive by Cordelia's apartment on my way out of the Quarter.

The next day, I considered calling O'Connor to let him know what was going on and where my notes were, but I finally decided against it. I would let Joey play himself out a little more. Besides, I was torn between wanting to trust O'Connor and rely on him and resisting the reality, that I, as it was now, had no choice in the matter. I was also embarrassed that I had almost admitted to him that I had been sexually abused.

Joey didn't call until after midnight. "So, Mick, can you drive a truck?"

"How big a truck?"

"Small rental truck. Piece of cake."

"Piece of steel, but I can handle it."

"Good. I'll come by and pick you up. Be ready in fifteen minutes."

"Where are we going?" I asked, after telling him where I lived.

"I'll tell you when I get there."

I didn't push. "Okay. I'll be waiting downstairs."

Joey hung up.

I tried to think what I might need on this unknown jaunt. My gun wouldn't be very friendly, might even make these guys think I didn't like them. Finally, I settled on the usual—a lighter, a small pocket knife, and some aspirin. Detecting can often give one a headache. After one last quick run to the bathroom, I went downstairs to wait for Joey. He arrived a few minutes later.

"So what's the deal?" I asked after I had settled myself in and buckled up.

"Nothin' unusual. You get in the truck, you drive it."

"Drive it where?"

"Remember that bar on Desire? We work out of there. You can get anything you want at that place."

"Drugs, sex, porn—sin for sale. One-stop shopping, what a great marketing concept."

"Gotta keep the customers happy," Joey said. I don't think he caught my sarcasm.

"Who's 'we'?"

"The usual gang. Lenny guards the door. Zeke is my contact. A few other guys. I don't even know their names."

"But who gives you orders?"

"Why do you want to know?"

"Knowledge is power, Joey. If I'm involved in this shit, I want as much power as I can get."

"So why should I tell you? 'Knowledge is power.' I got it, you don't."

"Can't hurt to ask."

Joey grinned. "Sure can't. Keep asking and maybe someday I'll tell you."

"How'd you get involved?"

"Same way as you. Someone asked me if I wanted to do some work."

"What happened to him?"

"He moved on," Joey paused for a second, then decided to elaborate. "He had a record. He…uh…got too emotionally involved in the work, if you know what I mean."

"A dangerous habit."

"It's a business, just a business. You gotta keep your eye on the green stuff."

"Yeah, you sure do." We were heading out to New Orleans East, taking old Highway 90. I was beginning to wonder if we weren't on the back road to Mississippi, when Joey turned off. He took a few more turns, two of which he almost screeched past before pulling over. We were in the middle of the block.

"The truck's just around the corner," Joey instructed me. "Parked in the back of the lot at Joey's Diner. I liked the name," he added. "Tell the dude at the counter that you're here to pick up the truck for Rob. He'll give you the keys."

"What if he doesn't?"

"He will. They'd never think a girl could steal a truck. Besides, they're expecting someone."

"Okay. So I meet you at Heart of Desire?"

"That's the story."

I got out of the car. Joey drove past, gave me a quick little wave, and was gone. He was testing me, but all I had to do to get a passing grade was drive the truck to the Heart of Desire. It occurred to me that the main danger was being arrested. Through the good graces of Detective O'Connor I didn't have to worry about that.

I entered Joey's Diner. This was not a busy hour, and there were maybe five people in the place. I was the only woman.

"Hi," I said to the counterman, who was giving me a somewhat odd look. "I'm here to get Rob's truck."

"Yeah?" he asked, making no move to get the keys. "Where's Rob?"

"He's sick."

"Yeah? What's wrong with him?"

"A toothache," I prevaricated, then realizing more than that was required, embellished, "His wisdom teeth are impacted and they've gotten infected. He had a root canal today, and he's going to have two more. He's got wads of cotton in his mouth and a couple of do-not-drive pain pills in his system." That ought to do it.

"Yeah? That's too bad." No wonder he had so few customers, if the preceding was any demonstration of his conversational skills.

"So can I have the keys?" I asked.

He reached for the keys, picked them up, and held them as he asked, "Yeah, sure. So what'd you say your name was?"

The obvious reply, "I didn't," wasn't the one that would get me the truck keys. "Esmeralda de Ville," I answered, giving my subconscious free rein in name picking. "My friends call me Essie."

"Well, Essie, I hope Rob feels better real soon." He handed me the keys.

The counterman and most of his customers stared at me as I left. I had to hand it to Joey, this was a really smooth and slick operation, with our tracks well covered. Those guys had the same chance of forgetting my appearance there as Joey's Diner had of serving nouvelle cuisine. With my audience still very interested in my every move, I got in the truck and started it. I was tired of performing for them, so instead of taking time to check over the truck, I shifted into what I hoped was reverse. After doing a quick turn around in the parking lot, aided by the lack of other cars, I clunked the truck into first and got onto the road, leaving Joey's Diner behind.

The truck was not an easy crate to drive. It was a dirty white with a few sprays of graffiti, nothing resembling identification anywhere on it. Far from the curious stares of the diner crowd, I pulled over. There was nothing in the glove compartment, not even registration or proof of insurance. I hoped O'Connor's pull extended to the traffic courts. The back of the truck was padlocked and the only key the counterman had given me was the ignition key. It was possible that I was being checked out, someone could be following me. Stopping to look for registration might be reasonable; stopping to open the back would be suspicious.

When I got to Heart's, I saw Joey's Porsche parked in an alley behind the bar. I took that as a hint and pulled in behind it. No watchful video cameras seemed about to alert someone that I was here, so I went to look for a loading door. I had to run an obstacle course of broken beer bottles, used crack vials, and day-old condoms to get to the only thing that looked promising. I was about to knock when the door opened and a rather large, unfriendly man demanded, "What are you doing here?"

"I'm looking for Joey," I replied, hoping that this was the equivalent of "Open sesame" around here.

"Who's lookin'?" Mr. Unfriendly asked.

"Micky Knight."

The door slammed shut in my face. Mr. Unfriendly was not a well-trained butler.

A few minutes later, the door reopened. Joey, two other men, and Mr. Unfriendly trooped out.

"That was pretty quick," Joey told me.

"I hate to go under the speed limit in strange trucks with no registration and no insurance. Keeps me on the road too long."

"You stupid bitch," Mr. Unfriendly opined. "That's how to get stopped."

"She was making a joke," Joey corrected him. "Our Miss Knight's a funny lady."

"And law-abiding, too. I even had my seat belt on," I added.

Mr. Unfriendly grunted in reply.

"Let's get this thing unloaded," one of the other men said.

"Right," Joey seconded him. "Why don't we pull the truck up to the door?" Not waiting for an answer, he instructed, "Mick, let me have the truck keys."

I handed him the singular truck key.

"Here, Lenny," Joey said, handing the key to Mr. Unfriendly. "Turn the truck around and back it up to the door." Joey then handed me the keys to his car. "You get to move mine. Pull it in behind the truck once he's parked."

I took the keys, gave Joey a mock salute, and got into his car to wait for Mr. Unfriendly to move the truck. He made a few awkward gear shifts on his way out. After I had moved Joey's car to a safe vantage point on the street, I watched Mr. Unfriendly try to back the truck up the alley and had the pleasure of watching someone who has just annoyed me make a fool of himself. A few shouts and curses, some damage to the transmission, and one badly mangled garbage can later, the truck was parked within loading distance of the back door.

I pulled back into the alley. I made sure there was not enough room for another car to park behind Joey's and block us in.

By the time I rejoined them, they had opened the back of the truck. Inside were a number of cardboard boxes. They were all taped shut, with nothing written on any of them.

"She gonna help?" Mr. Unfriendly demanded of Joey.

For an answer, I hopped into the truck, hefted one of the boxes, turned to him, and said, "Catch." I half-handed, half-tossed the box at him. He bobbled it, letting it slip almost to his knees before he caught it and righted himself.

"Take it inside," the other man with a speaking part said.

His silent partner took a box from me and followed Mr. Unfriendly into the bar.

"Where you puttin' them, Zeke?" Joey asked him.

"The small storage room, next to the office."

Joey nodded, seemingly satisfied.

I continued unloading the truck, moving the boxes to the edge of the truck bed, where they could be easily grabbed. These were heavy boxes. My best guess was paper, books, something tightly packed in them. I counted the boxes as I moved them. There were forty of them. This was not some small-time shipment.

Joey's contribution to the unloading was to move some of the boxes out of the truck and put them next to the door. Zeke mentioned his bad back at least three times and contented himself with occasionally going inside to "check on things."

Moving the boxes was hot and hard work. I couldn't stand up fully in the truck, so I had to carry them hunched over. After the first few boxes, I was sweating heavily. But I had something to prove, so I didn't stop. I even helped carry in a few boxes after I had unloaded them all from the truck. It made Mr. Unfriendly seem glad to see me.

"Good work, boys," Zeke said as the last box was chucked into the storage room. "And girl," he added for me.

Mr. Unfriendly, Mr. Silent, and I just caught our collective breath.

"You guys want some brews?" Zeke generously offered. "Come in the office. I got some in the fridge."

We trooped behind him to the dingy office. Mr. Silent took his beer and flopped down on the floor. Mr. Unfriendly took his, then stationed himself in the hallway, next to the door, a guard of dubious value. I moved a stack of newspapers and sat on top of a file cabinet. I used my beer to cool my forehead. Zeke and Joey took the two usable seats in the room.

"So, when does this move out?" Zeke asked Joey.

"Soon. I haven't gotten the word yet."

Zeke nodded, his question seemed a formality. "So, how'd you know this little lady could drive a truck?" he asked, presumably to keep the conversation from flagging as well as to display his enlightened view of sexual equality.

Joey gave him a laid-back grin and said, "She's a dyke. All dykes can drive trucks. Didn't you know that?"

This got me a look from both Mr. Silent and Mr. Unfriendly.

"What's the matter? You don't like men, honey?" Zeke asked me.

I held my temper. Joey was playing with me, testing my limits. "I like men. I even love some men. I just get real bored with them when they take their clothes off."

"That so?" Zeke asked, looking me over. "You oughtta come up to my place sometime."

"Why? You got a good-looking daughter?" I replied.

Zeke didn't like my answer, but Joey guffawed and even Mr. Silent snickered. Zeke was probably in his fifties, short, his balding head shiny with sweat.

"No wonder you're doing this kind of shit," Zeke retorted. His implication was clear. Whatever was in those boxes was about sex and it wasn't missionary position.

"It's late. We'd better get going," Joey said. But he didn't hurry; he was still enjoying Zeke's discomfort.

"No harm meant," Zeke said to Joey, keeping his "eyes on the prize," so to speak. Joey wasn't the top dog, that was clear, but he was the connection to the top dog.

Joey nodded, then said, "You want another beer, Mick?"

I shook my head. I hadn't touched the one I had.

"You want something else?" Zeke asked me. I was the assistant to the top dog's connection.

"No, I'm fine," I answered politely.

"Well, you come by any time you want. Any friend of Joey's is a friend of mine."

I merely smiled at his generous offer.

"I'll call you in a few days," Joey told Zeke as he stood up.

I slid off the file cabinet. Zeke, proper gentleman that he was, also stood up. I stepped over Mr. Silent, who didn't budge an inch. As I passed by Mr. Unfriendly, I handed him my untouched beer. "Here, you look like you need this more than I do." He almost smiled at me. I had made a new friend.

Joey said good-bye to Zeke, then joined me in the hallway.

"Did you count the boxes?" he asked.

"No," I lied.

Joey headed for the storeroom. I followed and watched while he counted boxes.

"Thirty-nine," he said. "That's not right. Goddamn, they shorted me one."

"Why don't we both count?" I suggested.

Joey started on one side and I started on the other. Several piles of boxes that had been stacked haphazardly, making it hard to count. I clambered between the boxes to get close enough to see what I was doing. One pile had a dangerous lean to it. I could see why Mr. Unfriendly and Mr. Silent hadn't done too well on the competitive career track of unloading trucks and had been forced into a life of crime.

"Those guys are assholes," Joey commented as he noticed the off-kilter stack.

The leaning tower of boxes began to fall over. I was able to catch the stack and keep it from going all the way down. Joey joined me, moving the boxes to a safer location while I held the weight. The bottom box had split open.

"So, what's in there?" I asked, able to see nothing clearly through the damaged box.

"You really want to know?"

"Like I said, 'Knowledge is power.'"

Joey shrugged and picked up the box. "Some of this stuff is fucked anyway," he said as he opened it up. "Karen's money paid for this," he added.

No emotions, play his game, I cautioned myself. It wasn't neatly bound, like the one in O'Connor's office. A cheap paper cover, now torn, was the only barrier hiding these pictures. I shrugged as Joey handed it to me, feigning a nonchalance and disinterest I didn't feel.

"This is where the money is," Joey obviously felt some need for explanation. "Cheap-shit pictures. Guys pay big bucks for them."

"Cheap labor, too," I commented. *Keep him talking, find out as much as you can.*

"Yeah," Joey gave a nervous laugh, "Yeah, you're right."

"Where do you get this stuff?"

"You get a camera, you take a picture."

"You?"

"Not me. Some other people."

"Here?"

"Around here. I try to keep away from that part of it."

"Why?"

"Hard to spend the money when you're in jail. I don't take pictures or do any of that shit, so why hang around and risk it?"

"Makes sense to me." I shrugged. "Can I have this?"

Joey looked at me, trying to figure out why I wanted pictures of men having sex with children.

"Revenge," I explained. "This could be real embarrassing if it were found in somebody's desk."

"Hey, good idea. I never thought of that." Then after a moment more, he added, "But can you hold off for a few weeks? I can't have this turning up some place weird when it's supposed to be sitting here in a box."

"Sure, no problem. Revenge is best when it's least expected." I had to resist skimming through the pictures to look for Cissy. If I found her, Joey might not survive it. "So, let's count these boxes."

We counted, or Joey counted and I pretended to count.

"Forty," he said when he finished. "Is that what you got?"

"Forty, it is."

"With one box damaged. Let's get out of here."

I couldn't agree more. I tightly rolled up the porn magazine, holding it in my fist like a weapon. I wondered what a good shrink, seeing my body language, would think. I followed Joey out, waiting as he padlocked the door. At the far end of the hallway, one of the prostitutes was leading a man upstairs. Neither of them looked at us. No one else was in the hall. We left, using the back alley door.

"You know, you forgot one thing," Joey said, turning to me. We were alone in the dark alley.

"Yeah? What's that?" I tensed, ready for a fight, wondering if he had a gun.

"You forgot to ask just how much you get paid."

"So how much do I get paid?" I asked, keeping the relief out of my voice. "And when? I need some bucks."

"You should always ask that, you know."

"Next time I will. But let's be real, I need the money too much to squabble over what you'll pay me. You were fair on the Colombé deal;

you'll be fair here. And if you want to screw me, you'll screw me no matter what you say up front."

"Ain't that the truth. Anyway, you get half-a-K for tonight's work," Joey answered. "I'll get it to you in a few days."

We got into Joey's car, and he pulled out of the alley onto the street. He didn't take Desire, cutting over to Louisa instead. For a while Joey elaborated on all the reasons I should buy the same kind of car he had. I listened politely for a bit, giving him a chance to justify his choice until I judged it wouldn't be impolite to change the subject on him.

"How'd you get Karen involved?" I asked.

"She had money, I had a place to spend it."

"Just like that, huh? What made her spend the money on you?"

"Charm, good looks." Joey reflected for a moment. "Probably being at the Sans Pareil. She didn't know I was a poor boy from Lake Charles. You get in a place like that and say 'surefire money maker,' and their eyes just glisten. Rich people always want more money. I was in the right place, and I made money for Karen. She didn't ask too many questions."

"Why'd you have to get the compromising picture?"

"Hey, every business deal has to have insurance. That was mine. It came in handy. It got Karen to roll over a few more times after she wanted to pull out. Besides that, if I hadn't leaned on Karen a bit, she wouldn't have called you and we never would've met."

"An odd spin of fortune's wheel."

"Yeah, something like that." Joey didn't seem to quite know what to make of my metaphor. "Don't worry about Karen. She's got enough money to go around."

I started to say it wasn't her money but her mortal soul that I was worried about, but Joey wouldn't understand and I was beyond explaining it.

"When do I get paid?" There, that should be prosaic enough for Joey.

"After I get paid. I'll call you sometime during the day. We'll arrange something."

"I may be in and out," I hedged. I didn't want Joey to think I'd sit at home waiting for his call. "But you can leave a message on my machine." I got out of the car.

"See you, then." He pulled away.

Still tightly clutching the magazine, I let myself in, trudging up the three flights to my apartment. It was almost dawn. Alone, on my home ground, I realized how wearing the pretense had been. I was reluctant to look at the pictures, to see the images, let alone what I might find there. Finally, I forced myself to sit down and open the tattered cover.

I quickly skimmed the magazine again, looking only at the faces of the young girls, trying to blot out all the other details. They were all girls. It was hard to be sure of their ages under the makeup and costumes they were wearing, but I guessed that the youngest was perhaps six, the oldest no more than twelve. They were all made to look like the "perfect" middle-class little girl—no glasses, color added to give them rosy cheeks, one Asian-American, the rest white.

But some of them could have been cut out of cardboard for all the emotion they allowed their faces to show. Others had eyes that were haunted, trapped animals in a cage. Who suffered the most, those who tore their emotions into little pieces like so much trash no one wanted them to have, or those who felt and showed the full brunt of how powerless they were? I closed the magazine. I didn't want to know these girls. Even behind the makeup, the façade of fantasy, their personalities showed, anger in one, bewilderment in another.

I didn't find Cissy. But something nagged at me, as if there was an image in there that I had seen before. I thought of leaving it until morning, but I knew sleep wouldn't be possible while the phantom thought hovered just out of reach. I forced myself to look at the pictures again, one by one.

At last I found it, the face that had seemed familiar. I hadn't caught it at first, because I had never expected to see her here. I had only seen the autopsy photos. In this picture, she stared at the camera, her expression caught on the cusp of fear and longing, a girl who wanted to trust and believe in the kindness of others, but who knew it wasn't always there.

I stared for a moment at the picture, wondering if Judy Douglas had ever decided on fear or trust. Then I began to wonder if it really was an accident that caused Judy Douglas to trip and fall. Or had she been running from monsters so embedded in her mind and memory that, even when she was alone, she couldn't escape them?

CHAPTER 23

What little sleep I did get was restless, my dreams disturbing. Cissy's face replaced that of Judy Douglas as she lay on the autopsy table, then, as a young girl of ten or eleven, my own. But when I lay there, I wasn't dead, merely immobile, unable to talk or do anything. I heard voices and saw movement in my peripheral vision. I knew someone was coming for me. I awoke from the same dream several times.

With the light of dawn, the dreams finally left me and I slept. I didn't wake until a little before two in the afternoon. Distracted as I was when I went to bed, I had forgotten to set my alarm clock. Today was Wednesday and I was supposed to be at Cissy's school in an hour to pick her up for her appointment with Lindsey. I jumped out of bed, debated about skipping a shower, but decided that last night's miasmas had to be washed off. I took my hurried version, not even waiting for the water to warm up before jumping in. It was a ruthlessly efficient way of fully waking myself up.

I paused long enough for a cup of coffee. My hair was still wet, and, given the overcast drizzle, probably would remain damp for the foreseeable future.

I got to the school just as the bell was letting out classes for the day. There was just an illegal sliver of parking, but Cissy was outside waiting. She had no problem noticing my beat-up, lime green Datsun amid the sleek and polished sedans.

"Hi, how are you?" I asked as she got in.

"Okay, I guess." She seemed a bit down.

"What did you do in school today?" I swerved around a van that was parked even more illegally than I had been.

"Nothin' much. Mr. Elmo yelled at us."

"What does he yell at you for?"

"Not me. He yells at other kids. I'm always a good girl," Cissy added with emphasis.

Traffic ground to a halt. There was an accident at the intersection ahead that people were inching through. Cissy didn't seem inclined to talk, so we drove in silence. She didn't even seem interested in looking at the wreck as we drove by.

Cissy finally broke the silence by asking, "Do you think Dr. McNeil will let me go to the bathroom?"

"Yes, I'm sure she will," I answered, taken by surprise at her question. "Just a few more minutes and we'll be there." Then I added, "Why shouldn't she let you go to the bathroom?"

"I dunno. Some grownups don't."

"Who hasn't let you go to the bathroom?"

"I dunno. Nobody."

"Some teacher?" I probed.

"No, nobody." Again, we drove in silence.

I turned into the driveway of Lindsey's office.

"We're here," I announced, stating the obvious, then asked, "Do you like Dr. McNeil?"

"She's okay. I like her fish."

The wreck and the rain had made us late.

"Hello," Amanda greeted us, for the moment distracted by something on her computer screen.

Cissy headed over to the fish, not returning Amanda's greeting. I said hello, then sat down in one of the waiting room chairs.

After only a moment Amanda said, "There, that's finished." She turned away from her computer. "Want to go back? The doc's ready," she said to Cissy.

Still watching the fish, Cissy nodded her head, then slowly turned away from the tank and started to follow Amanda.

"Can I go to the restroom?" Cissy abruptly asked as she passed in front of me. I wasn't sure if she was asking me or Amanda. Or asking Amanda in front of me so I would back her up with my previously given yes.

"Of course you can," Amanda answered. "It's right this way." She led Cissy down the hall past Lindsey's office.

I settled back in my chair for the fifty-minute wait. Instead of coming back to the reception area, Amanda ducked into Lindsey's office to chat with her. I picked up a magazine to read.

Several minutes later my attention was caught by Amanda tapping on the bathroom door, asking, "Are you okay in there?" I couldn't hear

Cissy's reply. It seemed to satisfy Amanda, who leaned in Lindsey's door to continue talking to her.

I went back to skimming through the magazine, not paying much attention to it. I did notice that when Amanda went back to tap on the bathroom door, Lindsey appeared in the hallway, hovering near her office door.

"Cissy, can I come in?" Amanda asked, then slowly opened the door. After a moment or two she stuck her head out and motioned Lindsey in.

I put the magazine down and stood up, taking a couple of steps toward the bathroom. But I didn't go any further. Whatever was wrong, Lindsey and Amanda were much better qualified to handle it than I was. I would be just another person invading what Cissy was trying to keep behind closed doors.

It was several minutes before Amanda emerged from the bathroom. Lindsey didn't come out.

"Do you know how to reach Mrs. Selby?" she asked, heading purposefully behind the reception desk.

I tried to remember Barbara's work number, but my mind blanked.

"Never mind, I can pull it up," Amanda answered as she sat down at the computer.

"What's wrong?" I asked.

Amanda ignored me as she hit the computer keys to bring up Barbara's name.

"What's wrong?" I repeated.

"Let me call Mrs. Selby first," she said.

I almost reached over the reception desk and grabbed her wrist. Amanda, sensing my intensity, paused for a moment and said, "She's okay. She appears to be bleeding vaginally."

"What?" I exclaimed, feeling a chill place grow inside me.

"She's okay," Amanda repeated, then dialed Barbara's number. She spoke very briefly, just asking her to come by, that there was something that Dr. McNeil wanted to discuss.

"What happened?" I demanded as soon as Amanda put the phone down.

"The urination may have irritated the area or perhaps wiping. There's not much blood, just some spotting."

"How do you know it's not her period?"

"It's possible," Amanda replied, but her tone and body language added, *It's not very likely*.

"What do we do now?"

"Lindsey's going to talk to her, make sure she's okay. We'll wait for Mrs. Selby and see what she wants to do."

"Can I talk to her?" I asked, starting to head down the hallway.

Amanda reached across the reception desk and grabbed my arm to stop me. "Lindsey's very good at this. Let her handle it."

Amanda was right. My anger and outrage wouldn't help Cissy. I turned away from the hallway.

"Should we call the police?" I asked.

"That's up to Mrs. Selby."

"What if it's someone she knows? Someone she'll believe over her daughter?"

"We'll cross that bridge when we come to it," Amanda calmly replied. "You might go walk around the block a few times if it would make you feel better," she suggested.

I shook my head and settled for pacing around the waiting room. The nightmare had become real. Part of me was in the shock that comes when you see what is going to happen and how powerless you are to stop it. That alternated with a deep fury that I was afraid to directly look at—it had no control and no mercy. I finally managed to hold these warring emotions in abeyance, forcing myself into a façade of calmness.

It took Barbara about half an hour to get to Lindsey's office. The door opening startled me. I was standing at the tank watching the fish flit back and forth.

"Hi, Micky," she said, a nervous catch in her voice.

I started to return her greeting, but Amanda said, "Hello, Mrs. Selby, please come this way."

Barbara cast me a quick look, but I wasn't invited and I remained at the fish tank. Amanda led her down the hallway into Lindsey's office. Lindsey, holding Cissy's hand, came out of the bathroom and went into the office. Cissy's face was pale, her eyes downcast. Amanda followed, closing the door behind them. I was left by myself in the waiting room. I tried to sit, but couldn't, instead falling into an agitated pacing, covering the waiting room in long strides. I sat down once or twice, but immediately got up to resume my pacing.

Finally the door to Lindsey's office opened. Amanda came out first, followed by Barbara holding Cissy's hand, whose eyes remained downcast. Lindsey was behind them. Her cane, Cissy's lowered eyes, the grim set of Barbara's lips, were all talismans of how often we're bent and battered by acts of fate or will that can never be undone.

"Look, Ms. Selby, if you want…" Lindsey was saying.

Barbara cut her off with, "I appreciate what you're trying to do, but it's my decision. I have a lot of things I need to think about."

Lindsey tried again, "If I can help—"

Barbara again cut her off. "I'll let you know. I need to take Cissy home now."

"I understand, I—"

Barbara turned on her. "Do you? Do you understand?" Her voice was agitated, a wavering edge of anger in it. "How can you?"

"I'm sorry," Lindsey said slowly, calmly, allowing herself to be the lightning rod for Barbara's anger.

"This is my daughter, not yours," Barbara lashed out at her.

"I'm very sorry," Lindsey repeated with the same quiet calmness.

Barbara started to say something else, but didn't, staring instead at Lindsey as if this were a dream she might wake from any minute.

I finally broke the silence by asking, "Is she okay?"

Barbara, Lindsey, and Amanda all looked at me. It was Cissy who answered, "Yeah, I'm okay. I'll be okay."

"I know you will," I told her, more because she needed to hear it than from any belief that it was true.

Barbara turned from Lindsey to look at me, holding tightly to Cissy's hand, as if any of us might be the enemy. "Why didn't you notice?" she demanded of me.

Why hadn't I protected Cissy was her real question. I shook my head helplessly.

Barbara looked around the room. "I don't really know any of you. I only have your word…" She looked at me.

"Ms. Selby," Lindsey said, "I'd be glad to show you my credentials, give you references."

"I know," Barbara said, but she still looked at me. "I have a lot of things to think about. Right now, I just need to take Cissy home."

She brushed past me, taking Cissy with her.

"If there's anything I can do…" I said.

Barbara didn't answer. Cissy turned back to look at me, then Barbara pulled her through the door and they were gone.

For a moment there was silence, then Amanda said, "Shoot the messenger. She'd do better to take it out on the person who did that to her daughter."

"She's angry," Lindsey replied. "And we don't know who did it." Then she added softly, "We may never know. What does a mother do with that kind of anger?"

The front door opened and Lindsey's next patient came in.

Lindsey shook her head, as if clearing it, then went back to her office. Amanda returned to the reception area.

I didn't move. I had no idea what to do next. Amanda greeted the newcomers, her face a polite, official mask.

Finally I said, "Ask Lindsey to call me." Then I left.

I got into my car and headed straight home. I was hoping Lindsey would call, and I wanted to be there when she did.

It was almost eight o'clock when she called. "Sorry it took me so long to get back to you. Can we meet?" she asked.

"Yeah, I guess," I replied, wondering what she couldn't say over the phone.

"Good, I've got to get out of this office and I'm starving." We decided on a Japanese restaurant that was equally inconvenient for both of us and said good-bye.

The rain was still pouring down, messing up traffic and driving the already not-very-stable New Orleans denizens to new heights of vehicular insanity. A Volkswagen and a Mack truck played chicken at a broken stoplight.

When I got to the restaurant, there were only a few parking spaces, the close, convenient handicapped place, and several in the far corner, beyond a few lake-sized puddles. With a sigh, I drove to the far corner.

I stood under the restaurant awning for a few minutes, trying to dry off. Lindsey pulled in, taking the convenient spot.

"Hi," she said as she got out. "You look wet."

I nodded. I was wet. She took my arm to walk up the stairs. The women who run the restaurant settled us into a corner, with me next to a heating vent. With any luck, I'd be dry before I had to go out and get wet again.

After we ordered, Lindsey said without preamble, "There's not much I can really tell you. Sessions are confidential, and without Barbara Selby's permission, I can't reveal anything."

"Okay," I replied. I felt like saying, "Then I can't tell you anything either." But Lindsey was right. She was tired by the sound of her voice. and I needed her help.

"I have a few things for you, but they can't go beyond this table," I said.

"What do you have?"

"I traced the matchbook. Real seedy place over by the Desire Project."

"Shit," Lindsey interjected. "How did something like that get in Cissy's pocket?"

"That I don't know. Yet. This bar is the kind of place where you can get anything you want. Anything," I added for emphasis.

"Like children?" Lindsey asked grimly.

"Pictures, at the very least."

"Photos or drawings?"

"Photos."

"Real kids?" she asked.

"Yeah."

Lindsey was silent for a moment, then said, "If they've got to have it, why can't they draw fucking pictures?"

Since it wasn't a question she expected an answer to, I continued, "Cissy's picture wasn't there. But a classmate of hers was." I explained to Lindsey about Judy Douglas.

When I finished, she asked, "So what does that tell us?"

"A young girl has a matchbook from a bar that sells kiddie porn. That tells me a lot."

"But Judy Douglas wasn't murdered. She was killed in a senseless accident. No link there."

"Someone took a picture of her. Now Cissy's been molested." I made it a statement so Lindsey couldn't hide it behind confidentiality.

"Yeah, probably."

"I'm not stupid," I said angrily. "She was bleeding vaginally. What the hell else does that mean?"

"Estimates vary, but between twenty-five and fifty percent of all girls are molested. On my cynical days I think it might be even higher than that. Certainly there is a possibility that Cissy is a victim of the same pornographer that got Judy Douglas. But there's also the very real chance that it's just common everyday sexual abuse—father, brother, uncle, teacher, preacher, friendly neighbor, practically always a man, rarely a woman, but it does happen."

"Is Barbara going to the police?"

"I don't know. I don't think so."

"Why?" I demanded.

Lindsey sighed, as if weighing what to reveal. "All the police can do is arrest someone. So far there's nobody to arrest. What's gained by putting Cissy through the trauma? Even if she reveals who did it, what happens if it's her word against his?"

"If she doesn't testify, he walks, if she does..."

"She gets raked over the coals by his attorney," Lindsey finished for me.

I knew she was right. Law and justice aren't the same thing. "Is she okay? How badly hurt is she?"

Lindsey paused again, then said, "I don't know if I should be telling you this. Well, I shouldn't actually." Nonetheless she continued, "It appears that there's not much physical harm. I did a fairly superficial exam. There was some abrasion on the outer lips, cracked skin that was causing the bleeding. The inner lips and vaginal opening showed signs of irritation, appearing red and swollen. I only did an external examination. There were no bruises or evidence of tearing or distention of the vaginal opening."

"No penetration?"

"Was she raped by an adult male? No, probably not. But…'penetration' can consist of many things." Lindsey sighed again and added, "The reality is that a defense attorney could argue that all this was caused by 'avid masturbation.' And with no suspect…" Lindsey trailed off.

"But you think she's being sexually abused?"

"Did you ever masturbate to the point that you abraded yourself?" Lindsey asked sarcastically. "I doubt Cissy did this to herself. And she is terrified of something."

"Where does that leave us?"

"You probably won't like this, but now that Barbara Selby's aware, the molester may find Cissy a not very safe target and disappear into the woodwork. That's the best of what's likely to happen."

"To go molest some other child."

"Probably."

Lindsey was right. I didn't like it. "I have a hard time letting it go at that."

"Believe it or not, so do I. Find out who it is and find the evidence that can stop him without destroying his victims."

"Is that possible?" I asked sarcastically.

"Or drop it and get on with your life."

"I can't do that."

"Well, call me if you need to talk," Lindsey said.

"Yeah, thanks. Or if I find out anything," I added, not wanting this to be a one-way street.

"That, too."

Our food arrived, sushi for Lindsey, chicken teriyaki for me. For several minutes, we ate in silence.

Then Lindsey asked, "Will I see you Friday night?"

"Friday night?"

"The roast, toast, and crawfish boil for Karol Escapade in honor of the magic he's done with benefits for PWAs, and for Nurse Claire for her work in early intervention. I know Cordelia's going to be there since she sold me the tickets."

"Uh…no. I'm not going to be there."

"Oh," Lindsey retreated, realizing she had stumbled into something. "Is Cordelia going by herself?"

"I don't know," I said shortly. I didn't want to be reminded of Cordelia.

"Not something you want to talk about?" Lindsey probed.

"You got it."

"An argument or a breakup?"

"You going to give me a bill for this?" I retorted.

"No, you're not a client," Lindsey mildly replied. "People's deep, dark secrets always interest me. The words 'I don't want to talk about it' always perk up my interest."

"This isn't a deep, dark secret. Cordelia and I are no longer seeing each other. There, is your interest sated?"

"Not quite, a few more gory details. You were only going together for a few months, weren't you?"

"If that."

"Quick breakup."

"Some things aren't meant to be."

"I'm sorry."

"Things happen. Time to move on."

"If that's how you feel."

"It is. 'Monogamy is a synonym for monotony.'"

"I'm a psychiatrist. Don't protest too much. I'll heap all sorts of Freudian symbolism into it."

"Then I won't protest at all. I'll take the expedient exit and silently eat. That way you won't have anything to analyze."

And with that, we finished our dinner in silence. But it was a dense quiet, with a tension between Lindsey and myself.

As we paid our check, she broke it, "If I promise not to analyze, will you promise to call and let me know what's going on?"

"Yeah, I'll do that."

"Okay. And, Micky? If it's a brick wall, don't bang your head against it."

"I'll try not to."

"Will you help me to my car?" she asked as she slowly stood up.

"Of course."

Lindsey took my arm, causing a few people to glance at us, at two women touching, which gave having her arm linked through mine more intimacy than it really had.

I held her umbrella over us as we left the safety of the awning and stepped into the rain. Lindsey found her keys and unlocked her car. Then she turned to me and put her arms around me. For a moment, she held me, then let go.

"Good night, Micky. I want to hear from you." She got into her car.

"Good night, Lindsey." I handed her the umbrella, then hurriedly dashed for my own car. By the time I got into it and had enough water out of my eyes to see, she was gone. Driving in the rain was distracting. But it wasn't enough of a distraction to keep me from thinking about abused children.

CHAPTER 24

The sun was finally shining, although I wasn't in much of a mood to appreciate it.

I again thought about calling O'Connor, but knew it wouldn't be prudent to use my phone nor the height of wisdom to walk out of my building and use the phone on the corner. I also wanted at talk to Barbara. All the major items on today's agenda were things that I would prefer to avoid. I kept busy until the only chores left to me were the truly repugnant instead of the merely odious.

By this time it was five thirty, and Barbara should be home from work. The sun was setting as I got there, the short days of winter approaching. I sat in my car for a moment or two trying to think of what I wanted to say, to ask. I looked up to see Barbara coming across the lawn. I got out of the car to meet her.

"Hi," I said.

"Hello," she answered, wary but not hostile. She didn't appear surprised to see me.

"How's Cissy?"

"She's okay. She's watching TV." Barbara crossed her arms across her chest, a barricade to my concern. "I'd prefer you didn't see her."

"I don't need to see her. I really just wanted to find out how she's doing. See if there's anything I can do. Maybe this weekend…"

Barbara didn't say anything for a moment, her arms still held tightly across her chest. She looked away from me before she spoke. "I mean not see Cissy…for a while."

"'For a while'?" I stupidly echoed.

She still avoided looking at me. "I just think Cissy needs to be with her family for a while, that's all."

"A week? A month? Six months?" I took a step toward Barbara, but she took a step away.

For a moment Barbara's eyes met mine, then she looked away. "I need to protect Cissy. I've seen some of the people you hang around with, men who wear dresses, women in motorcycle jackets. I don't know them or what they—"

"They're not child abusers," I cut her off. "I didn't think you would fall for those ugly—"

"Micky!" Barbara cried. "I can't afford an experiment in liberalism. This is my daughter. My daughter has been hurt."

"Pandering to ugly myths and stereotypes won't help her," I shot back.

"This is my daughter," Barbara repeated fiercely. "I don't care what I have to do to protect her. I can't afford to be fair and just and open-minded. Not if she gets hurt."

"You might hurt her even more," I replied. "Because if the only place you look is at the queer part of town, you'll miss the real child molesters. The teachers, the ministers, the nice neighbor, a relative, a boyfriend," I added pointedly. "That's where they really hide, behind their façade of normality and kindness."

Barbara shook her head. "It doesn't change my mind. Cissy sees no one but family."

"What about your boyfriend, Ted?" I demanded. "Does he have a criminal record? Any idea? Or does protecting your daughter only extend to getting rid of queers?"

Barbara glared at me before saying, "I think you'd better leave."

"If you really want to protect Cissy, you're going to have to ask yourself a lot of difficult questions. You may like the answers even less. But it's the only way—"

"I know all this," Barbara cut me off. "I'll do what I have to do."

A car pulled into her driveway. A stocky man in his late forties got out. "Barb," he called, "what's going on?"

"It's okay, Ted," she answered. To me, she said quietly, "You'd better go now."

I spun on my heel, angry at her. Then I turned back and said as gently as I could, "If you need my help, you know my number. Call me anytime."

Barbara seemed surprised by my offer. I turned away again and got into my car without looking back. Before I drove away, I jotted down the make, model, and license number of Ted's car. It couldn't hurt to check him out.

After a few blocks, I saw a convenience store and pulled in. I got a soda, then hit the pay phone in the back to call O'Connor. In a brief, and, considering the less than secure corner I was in, cryptic version, I told him of my truck-driving adventure.

"I got a new magazine with some interesting stuff in it," I said, as a customer drifted down the aisle. O'Connor tried to ask several questions, but I couldn't really answer them. Finally, we decided to chance a meeting. Monday was the earliest we could arrange.

"But be sure and call me if anything happens," O'Connor ended with. "Anything."

I left the convenience store and headed back to my place.

I had just walked in and hadn't even decided which direction to go, bathroom or kitchen, when the phone rang.

"Hey, Mick, I owe you some money." It was Joey. "You interested?"

"More than interested. Just about desperate," I told him. Desperate women get invited places sanguine women don't.

"So, I'm hungry. How about the lakefront? You in the mood for seafood?"

"Sounds good. Do you want to meet in the 'mixed' parking lot?" I asked. "You know, the one that several restaurants use."

"Okay, I think I know what you mean. How'll we find each other?"

"We have distinctive cars, remember?"

Joey snorted out a laugh, and said, "Yeah, we sure do. But I'm glad my car doesn't have the distinction yours does." He laughed again.

"If I keep working for you maybe I can change that. See you there in half an hour?"

"Twenty minutes. I'm starving," he amended.

I agreed and hung up. I made a quick run to the bathroom, brushed my hair, and headed back out the door.

It took me twenty-two minutes to get to the west end of the lakefront where a number of seafood restaurants are located. Joey was leaning against his Porsche, waiting for me.

We haggled for a minute over which restaurant to go to, finally deciding with the flip of a coin. My choice, which I knew to be a better restaurant, won.

The maître d', assuming us to be a boring straight couple, spoke to Joey and, after seating us, gave him the wine list. *Beware of your assumptions*, I wanted to tell the maître d', a woman, no less. *This man sells child pornography for a living*. Sometimes it's the small things, the ones you don't notice until they're directly in front of you. The maître d' deferring to Joey and ignoring me, as if it were not only common but acceptable. I wondered what she did with two women diners.

The waiter came and took our drink orders, Joey getting his usual beer and a club soda for me. When the waiter returned with our drinks, Joey ordered the fried seafood platter. I opted for stuffed flounder.

After the waiter was out of earshot, Joey leaned forward and said, "So how much do you think that little jaunt of yours was worth?"

"Oh, I'd guess half a mil," I replied.

Joey chuckled softly. "How about half-a-K?"

"Sounds good to me."

He handed me some money. I quickly glanced at it. It appeared to be several hundred dollar bills, some fifties, and a few smaller bills. It looked like five hundred. I stuffed the money in my pocket, not wanting to sit in a restaurant and count out that kind of money on the table.

"Thanks, I needed that," I said.

"There's more to be earned."

"Yeah?" I tried to sound interested.

"Yeah. This is just the start. This next one's big and there's a lot of money in it."

"So where do I fit in?"

"Where do you want to fit in?"

"Near the money."

"Good. Because that's where I'll be. You help me, you'll stay next to the money." Joey sat back and took a sip of his beer. He continued, "You know, at first, I didn't think a girl could do it. Even a queer girl. But then I sat and thought about it. You were pretty tough fronting for Karen. And I thought maybe a girl might be better than a guy."

I didn't interrupt Joey and tell him that this "girl" was a woman. My anger gave way to the rational argument that the more preconceived notions I left in place, the less likely that he would ever see who I truly was and what I was really doing.

"So I thought," Joey was still going, "no one will suspect a girl."

Of course not, sometimes they don't even see us.

"If you and I are together, they won't look at us like two guys and what are we up to. But a guy and a girl, hey, it's a date. No one expects a girl to be involved in something like this, so it throws them off guard, they got to scramble for how to react. So I figure, hey, this is it. You're on the road, Joey. You got the gig and you got the angle to take it all the way. So, Mick, you stick with me, and we'll both have trouble deciding which Porsche to drive today."

"Guess I'd better stick with you, then," I answered. Part of me felt contempt, but that was leavened by realizing that Joey was offering me what mattered most to him in the world. He believed he was giving me so great a gift that no one could turn it down. For this to work, I would have to play into Joey's world, pretend to the point that I actually lived my role and take what he offered to betray him with it.

The waiter brought our dinner.

After a few minutes of eating, Joey surprised me by asking, "You like Zeke?"

"Zeke?"

"Yeah, Zeke. Ol' bad-back Zeke."

"A fine fellow. Almost man enough to make me go straight."

Joey snorted. "Yeah, that's about what I thought. You know the trick to this game is always keep moving, never stay in the same place."

"What's that got to do with Zeke?"

"Zeke don't know that. He's gotten real comfortable at Heart's. Thinks everything's gonna stay the same. Money always comin' in and not much work involved." Joey continued, "At first we needed Zeke a lot. We still need him now, but not so much. Soon we won't need him at all."

"I'm not a murderer."

"Naw, nothing like that." Joey waved away the thought with his hand. "Zeke takes a bad fall. What if the cops found a couple of them boxes piled up in Zeke's office? Zeke thinks nothing's gonna change. He'll sign off on the next shipment, his name all over everything. Zeke'll go down and we'll be gone. With no evidence, who'll believe him?"

"You'll have to run his files to get everything out."

"That's where you come in."

"I figured." I was going to get to do Joey's dirty work.

"Piece of cake," Joey assured me. "Late Monday, early Tuesday is the dead time. One rag-ass bartender and the working girls. Walk in, walk out. Zeke's sloppy, he's got everything thrown in one big file."

"It's still breaking and entering."

"It's money. You'll get paid for what you do."

If I stole the file, it would be one more thing to turn it over to O'Connor. I nodded.

"Good. You haul another load. Just like you did. Zeke does the paper shit. And then he finds out how quickly things can change."

"Who gives the order?"

"I do," Joey said.

"But who gives you the order?"

Joey gave me a sardonic grin, as if he didn't like being reminded that he wasn't really the one in charge. "What do you care?" he tossed off. "You work for me."

"'Knowledge is power,'" I reminded him.

"And I got it and you don't."

I shrugged and half-smiled, letting Joey know that this was a game and he had won this hand. But, as I smiled, I thought, and you, too, Joey, will learn how quickly things change. Even a plea bargain wouldn't be kind to Joey.

Dinner was slow and drawn out. Joey talked of all the things that money could buy. "Cars in different colors, like women buy friggin' shoes. And a box at the Dome. I'll throw a big party every Saints game."

At some point, as he had still another beer and the plates were cleared away, I asked, "And then what? Once you have that, then what?"

Joey laughed off my question. "Maybe I'll get rich enough to buy the Saints. But only if they're winning." Then he added, "I want to be as rich as Anthony Colombé. Watch people jump when I raise my eyebrow."

There are richer men than Colombé. But I didn't say that to Joey, just nodded my head, a pretense of agreement.

It was almost eleven thirty when I said good-bye to Joey in the parking lot. He reminded me to keep Monday free.

I drove along the lake, the lights from the Lake Pontchartrain Causeway bright and unmoving in a night that had become cool and clear. One boat crossed the water, its running lights skimming toward the Causeway, using the shimmering lamps to steer by. For a moment, I longed for something as clear and unmovable as a beacon atop a concrete pillar. But I had no guidance other than what I could discern, my biases and blind spots making that a dim and shadowy path. I turned off the lakefront and headed home.

When I got there, my answering machine was blinking. I ran the tape back, hoping it was Cordelia. And feeling a sharp sting of disappointment when a male voice began talking.

What did Cordelia mean when she said, "I love you," I wondered angrily. Dropping me when I was no longer convenient or easy? Anger held me for a minute or two more, then I had a vision of her playing back her answering machine, hoping to hear my voice. I almost picked up the phone to call her, but the late hour prevented it. And the slow realization that I couldn't see what happened next. Did she want me to call so we could be lovers again, or did she want the clear-cut finality of telling me it was over? Indecision and uncertainty returned. Maybe I would call her tomorrow. But the thought was more a wish than a resolve to actually do it.

I hadn't even heard the message that had played through. I rewound the tape and this time listened to the male voice. "Hello, Ms. Knight…I'm not good with these machines. Anyway, this is Warren Kessler. I've got some things that I'd like with talk to you about." He left his home number, saying that he would be up to around eleven, and then two different work numbers. I jotted down the numbers and erased the tape.

Then I took a long, scrubbing shower. Somehow the dinner with Joey made me feel a need to cleanse myself, as if I could wash off some of his greed and corruption. Or my duplicity.

Chapter 25

Last night's chill had remained in the air, making crawling from under my covers difficult. The sky was gray, not the gray of rain, but the herald of changing weather, changing seasons.

I ran a hot bath, letting the steamy air fill the bathroom. After last night's shower, I didn't really need a bath, but I was cold and the hot water was inviting. And maybe I could wash off a little more of my sense of betrayal.

After the bath, a big mug of coffee was next. Fortified by heat and caffeine, I was ready to face the day. I dialed the first work number Warren Kessler had given me. I got a secretary who sounded as if she were surrounded by attacking Visigoths. I realized that she probably was—schoolchildren out for lunch (or was it recess? My memory of school-day schedules had been blurred by adult reality). After three transfers and as many holds, I was connected to Warren Kessler.

"Hi, this is Micky Knight, returning your call," I greeted him.

"Hi, thanks. Listen, it's a zoo here, but I'd like to get together and talk to you. Any chance you might be able to come by this afternoon?"

"There's a chance. What time would be good?"

"It's mayhem until the kids are gone. How about my office at four thirty?"

"All right, I'll see you then." Phones were ringing in the background and voices were clamoring for attention. Zoo, indeed. We hung up.

The rational part of my brain wondered what Warren Kessler wanted to talk to me about. The irrational part wondered why Cordelia hadn't called. And why I was so terrified of calling her.

I left a little before four, going out of my way to avoid the CBD and the beginning of rush hour. Without children and parents waiting for them, the school had a quiet, expectant air. The hallway, designed for the crush of bodies between classes, was somber, its promise unfulfilled by my solitary footsteps.

Growing up in bayou country, I had gone to a small school built of clapboard and weathered shingles. It wasn't until after the death of my father and coming to live with Aunt Greta and Uncle Claude in Metairie that I had gone to a school like this one. Despite the large number of children, I never felt that I fit in with them. I was angry at my father's death, angry at having to live within the restricted confines of Aunt Greta's arbitrary rules. Those were the days when children weren't beaten and incest was a word none of us knew.

I stood for a moment in the hallway, wondering which way to turn. I saw no one to ask where Warren Kessler's office was. As I stood there, I realized that one of the most profound things that had separated me from those sunny middle-class Metairie children with their comfortable lives was that I was having sex with my cousin. That festering secret built a wall, a boundary about me that I was simply unable to breach. Keeping secrets, powerful, destructive secrets, requires distance and denial, emotions choked and deeply buried, until knowing yourself, your wants and needs, becomes impossible.

For years I had repeated to myself that it hadn't been so bad. I hadn't really been hurt, there was no physical damage, as if the only real pain is the kind that bleeds so much that it can't be hidden.

Alone in this empty hallway, I was a metaphor for the way I felt during those years, aloof and apart. Only now could I realize how deeply the damage had gone. What if I hadn't felt tainted? What if I hadn't seen myself as a child seductress, with guilt and shame my constant companions, twisted into believing that if the secret came out, the fault would cling to me? I didn't make friends, because I always felt I was only a few fragile inches from losing them. If they only knew…

How many of those skewed childhood lessons still haunted me today? That I was fighting my past, I knew. What I was only now realizing was how often I lost to it.

"Can I help you?" A man in baggy overalls carrying a custodian's broom was coming down the hall.

"I'm looking for the principal's office."

"Here to see the principal, huh?" he asked, no hint of humor in his voice. "Down to the end of the hallway, take a right. Can't miss it." He continued down the hallway.

I headed in the direction he had indicated. For a moment, the sound of our footsteps mingled, then his faded into the distance and mine alone echoed.

When I was fifteen, a high school sophomore, another girl, a senior, had seduced me. After I got over my initial shock, I discovered both the power and release of sex. Misty was head cheerleader, a popular senior, and she wanted something from me. Desire became a powerful connection between us. Misty would wait until I got off from my job at a burger place. The head cheerleader waiting for a skinny, dark bayou girl. It was a heady experience. Then, in the car her parents had given her, we would drive somewhere quiet and still, and eagerly fumble with each other's clothes, both afraid of discovery, too shy and awkward to fully undress. Our hands would travel to the forbidden places. Our secret became delicious, whole and powerful, a hidden desire that we each gave permission for the other to explore. It became something that only we possessed.

Misty was, like a proper cheerleader, dating the captain of the football team, Ned. But Ned, too, had a secret. He and his best friend Brian were lovers. The four of us, with our shared secrets, gave me a power and closeness I had never known before. It was the first time since my father's death that I felt I belonged somewhere. Finding out at fifteen that I was a pervert, a queer, was one of the best things that ever happened to me.

Two secrets ruled my life. One was destructive, held only by myself and someone who simply used me; the other bound me closely to three people and gave me the profound freedom that would shape my life. The knife always has a double edge.

Misty and I occasionally talked of love, but there was no path, no way to protect those youthful embers. I couldn't wear her class ring, go openly on dates with her, even hold hands in the movies. Fear of discovery was constant.

The school year ended, she graduated. We made no promises to each other. Then she was gone, off to college on the West Coast. I was left with a secret I could share with no one during those long school days. But I had learned of the bars in the French Quarter, and I was tall enough to get in. Sex is what connected me to Misty, and sex is what connected me to the women I met in those bars.

I came to the right turn in the hallway.

What conjunction of secrets had led me to connecting only through sex? Bayard, teaching me that caring and trust had no currency, that the only value I had was what I could offer physically. Add to that foundation the twilight world of bars and alcohol, an arena so small and confined for women to meet other women in. Sexuality and sex, hidden for so long in so many ways, became the focal point. Having sex isn't that big a sin when you're already queer.

I was finally, in fits and starts, beginning to get beyond those early lessons to a place where touching was a way to show love and caring and concern, wasn't a replacement for them. Uncharted land is the most terrifying place to go. If I wanted a reason for not being able to call Cordelia, that was it.

But I wasn't here to remember my past or solve the problems of my future. I knocked on the door to the principal's office.

"Come in," Warren Kessler called out. He had a large office, stacks of books and papers everywhere. Children's drawings lined one wall. "Welcome to my chaos," Kessler greeted me. He stood up, extending his hand.

"Chaos and I are well acquainted," I answered, taking his hand. His grasp was warm, lasting just long enough to be friendly.

"Why did I suspect that?" he bantered as we sat down.

"Male intuition," I replied, then said, "So, what can I do for you, Mr. Kessler?"

"Please, call me Warren. I'm not sure. Just…there are some things that have been nagging at me, and I thought you might be the one to help."

"How so?"

"You were worried about Cissy Selby?"

I nodded and he continued.

"I think something is going on here, at the school."

"What makes you think that?"

"I don't really know. Little things, a change in attitude, a child who suddenly doesn't smile anymore."

"Have you considered going to the police?"

"I haven't got anything a cop would listen to. Just an uneasy feeling."

Again I nodded. Warren was probably right. Intuition, male or female, wasn't something cops put much stock in.

He continued, "So, basically, what I want is to hire you, have you nose around a bit and see if you can find anything."

"What do you think I might find that you can't?"

"What do you mean?"

"You know your teachers, your students. I'm a strange face. How many questions can I ask?"

Warren slowly nodded, then gave me a rueful smile. "Maybe I have a television view of private detectives. I guess reality's a bit less clear-cut."

"Just a bit," I answered his smile. "Maybe you should get a teacher you trust, have her or him help you. It's hard for an outsider to come in and ask questions, particularly the kind of questions I would have to ask."

I knew I couldn't take the job. I had so many layers wrapped around myself that I couldn't trust unveiling a piece here, a sliver there. *A dead student of yours has her picture in a porno magazine*. How could I reveal that to him? Did I tell him I was working for Joey? Could I risk my cover with O'Connor? Investigating the school might turn up something or it might not. Despite both Cissy and Judy Douglas, there was no guarantee that this school had anything to do with them. Nor was there any guarantee that they were even linked. Too many children were sexually molested by too many people for me to risk making those kinds of assumptions.

At the same time I knew I would have to put him off, I was touched by Warren's concern. I wanted him to keep looking at his school and the children who came here.

"Yeah, that might be an idea," he slowly replied. "It's…just, well, I've seen this before."

I gave him a questioning look.

"I used to be an assistant principal at a school in Camden, New Jersey. There was this ring, a ring of men who sold children."

"How did you know?"

"The cops eventually busted them. Got most, but not all of the bastards. But I remember the feeling at the school, the atmosphere, as if the air was full of…" He groped for the words.

"Of secrets. Guilty secrets," I supplied.

"Yes, that's it exactly. It wasn't a thing, or a fact, or an incident, just a feeling. I'm starting to get the same feeling now, and I don't like it."

"What do you think's happening here? Another conspiracy of child abusers?"

"I guess that's my gut feeling, yeah."

"Do you think Cissy's caught in their web?" I asked.

"It's a possibility. What do you think?"

"What about the usual places?"

"Which usual places?"

"A father, brother…cousin, uncle. Not rings and evil plots."

"But those evil rings do exist. I've seen one."

"They do," I answered. "But don't ignore the common places. That's where most of the damage is done."

"You've been there, haven't you?" Warren unexpectedly asked me.

I looked away from him, the question touching emotions that had surfaced only minutes ago in the hallway. I didn't want them reaching me.

"It's okay. I know, I've been there, too," he said gently.

"You?" I asked, again able to look at him.

"It's not something I talk about, at least not very much. But, yes, white, middle-class, American boy, it happened to me."

"I'm sorry." It seemed the only reply to make.

He shrugged. "I survived. I guess it taught me it really can happen to anyone."

I wanted to ask him, *Does it still make trust a pitted and treacherous path? Does every act of kindness make you wonder what someone wants from you?* But all I said was, "Yes, it happened to me, too."

"I'm sorry."

And like he had, I shrugged.

"It was my uncle," Warren said, answering a question I would not dare to ask. "I was around eight or nine. He was the Boy Scout type, camping and all that stuff. My parents liked him because he would take us kids away for a weekend. Four boys. I was the youngest. So it happened that my three older brothers got one tent and Uncle Bert and I got the smaller pup tent. One morning I woke up and he had an erection. I was curious, so I looked. He caught me looking. I confronted him about it several years ago, and he claimed that, because I looked at his penis, it meant I wanted to do it. I tried to tell him that it was just a young boy's curiosity, but he couldn't hear it. Nothing I could say would make him see it wasn't like that." Warren shook his head at the memory.

"Did you really think he'd admit, 'Yeah, you're right, I took you to the woods, put you in my tent, and, the first chance I got, took advantage of you'?"

Warren let out a small laugh. "I guess I did expect something like that. He was wrong, so wrong, and I thought, of course, it's obvious, anyone can see that."

"Were you sorry you confronted him with it?"

"No, not at all. It made me see what kind of a person he really is. What a sad life you have when you live within a lie. When I think of him now, I just feel sorry for him."

"I'm glad you've gotten to that point."

"You haven't?"

"Not yet," I answered quickly. "I'm working on it. It was a cousin…I lived with his family at the time." But that was all I could say.

"How old where you?" he asked gently.

"Uh…around ten, I guess."

"How long did it go on?"

I looked at the floor for several moments before I finally answered, "For a while. I lived there…I couldn't get away from him." Then I said, "I'd prefer to talk about something else."

"I hope you get to a place where it's okay," he replied.

"Yeah, me, too." I knew I owed Warren my story, he had given me his. But my story didn't have his happy ending, or any ending at all, and the shadows were still too deep for me to venture easily into them. I changed the subject. "It does appear that Cissy is being molested. By whom or where is up in the air."

"Any suspects?"

"Her mother has a new boyfriend." I couldn't help but wonder if he didn't have something to do with Barbara's banning me from seeing Cissy.

"Are you worried about Cissy?"

"I've known her, and her family, for a while."

Warren nodded, as if that were a better answer than it really was. Then he asked, "Do you suppose anyone can do anything? Given the right reason?"

"I suppose. Given the right reason." I thought of how far I was going—had gone—to protect Cissy.

"Could you?" he asked.

"Yes, I guess I could," I answered. "I probably…have."

"I've always wondered about that," Warren said.

"That's only my answer."

He nodded again, as if it were the answer he wanted, then asked, "Are you sure you don't want to help me track down the villains?"

"I'm sorry, I can't." I shook my head. "Let me know what happens. I'll be glad to look over your shoulder and offer advice."

"Be careful, I might take you up on it."

"I'm always careful about what I offer."

We were interrupted by a knock on the door. Without waiting for a response, the custodian entered. "Sorry to bother you, Mr. Kessler. We got a leak in one of the second-floor bathrooms and it's making a mess."

Warren sighed and said to me, "Thanks, Micky, for coming by."

"You're more than welcome," I said, standing up. "Call me again if you need to." I left him to the custodian and the plumbing problems.

As I walked into the chill of late afternoon, I wondered if I should have told him what had happened to me. Maybe I needed clear space and time, not the worrisome arena I was now in, a world cluttered with pretense for Joey, worry about Cissy and the pain of losing Cordelia. Maybe in a few weeks, or months, when this was all over, it would be time to fight my own ghosts.

I spent most of the weekend at my apartment. No one called me, and I called no one.

CHAPTER 26

The chill of autumn had settled in. Monday was gray and overcast, the high humidity of a city between a river and a lake and the cool air combining to create a biting wind. I had started down my stairs, but the cold air in the stairwell caused me to reconsider. I went back upstairs, put on a heavier jacket, and, a real concession to winter, a scarf. With it wrapped tightly around my neck, I again descended the stairs, on my way to see O'Connor.

Since bounding into a cop shop might cause suspicion should the wrong person catch me at it, we had agreed to meet at a coffee shop up on Magazine Street. It was not a place either of us ever went to.

I left my apartment an hour early. Part of it was caution, but part of it was that I wanted to be about and moving, as if motion could dispel the cold and gloom of the day. I decided on the bus, several buses actually; my car was a lime green beacon to anyone looking for me. One bus took me to Canal Street, the sometimes grand, sometimes gaudy dividing line between the French Quarter and what is now the CBD. When Louisiana was newly sold to America, the French left stranded in New Orleans did not take kindly to their American cousins. The new settlers, not welcomed in the French Quarter, took up residence on the uptown side of Canal Street. It is not for nothing that the medians in New Orleans are known as neutral grounds. The Americans wouldn't even use the street names from the French—for example, Royal Street becomes St. Charles Avenue.

Canal is broad, supposedly the widest street in the world. Three lanes of traffic on either side of a neutral ground, median, if you prefer, that is wide enough to have two bus lanes (streetcars a generation ago) plus pedestrian room. It is impressive to see that space filled on Mardi Gras, but the real effect of all that width is to keep one's foot light on the gas pedal when the light turns green. Savvy New Orleans drivers know that it is a Crescent City tradition to gun for yellow lights. On streets as wide as

Canal, a light that is yellow when one starts to drive across is solidly red before one gets to the other side.

I stood on Canal Street, watching a few near misses, tourists who were unfamiliar with the idiosyncrasies of Big Easy drivers, the ubiquitous drunks. Twenty-four-hour bars and alcohol sold in everything from drugstores to gas stations doesn't improve driving conditions here. After loitering long enough to make sure no one was following me, or, at least, if I was being followed it had to be by two, if not three, people, I caught a bus uptown.

I let the bus travel several blocks beyond the coffee shop before getting off. I meandered my way back, stopping to look in the windows of the antique shops. A deep cobalt glass bottle caught my attention. It was probably an old medicine bottle of some sort. Cordelia would love it, I thought. She had a small collection of them on her mantel. I started for the door of the shop before I realized that I probably wouldn't be seeing her anytime soon, let alone giving her a gift.

I continued walking down the street. When I got to the coffee shop, O'Connor wasn't there yet. It wasn't very crowded, only a few late lunches and two solo coffee drinkers. I ordered expensive Jamaican coffee, hoping the luxury of it might prove to be a distraction. I didn't want to think about a blue bottle I would never give to Cordelia.

Shortly after my coffee arrived, O'Connor appeared. He was dressed casually, almost as if he was a tourist doing the trendy junque shops of Magazine Street.

"Where's your car?" he asked.

"Too lime green. I bussed it."

"No one can follow a city bus. So, what do you have?"

"I can't show it to you here, we'd probably get arrested," I said as I took the porno magazine out of my knapsack. It was in a paper bag wrapped in a plastic bag. I handed it to O'Connor.

"Is your client in here?" he asked.

"No, but a classmate of hers is." O'Connor raised his eyebrows, and I continued, "A dead classmate." He raised his eyebrows even further. I explained about Judy Douglas as best I could, who she was and how she died, without revealing Cissy's identity.

"I'll double-check her autopsy report. This is getting awfully messy," O'Connor commented.

"It gets messier. My client has pretty definitely been molested. A doctor uncovered some physical evidence."

"You think it's linked to this other girl?"

"It's possible. Of course, two girls being molested out of a class of several hundred has to be connected, doesn't it?" I added sarcastically.

"You know, and I know, that if only two kids out of that class are being abused, it's a miracle."

"Yeah," I grimly agreed. "But my client knew the dead girl, although not very well, and she's afraid the same thing could happen to her."

"I don't gather she gave any indication of who might have abused her?"

"No, none."

"Did she and this other girl ever go anywhere together, do anything that might link them?"

"I don't know. Her mother gave Judy Douglas a ride home from school once or twice."

"A field trip with a certain teacher, belonging to the same Girl Scout troop, anything like that?"

"Not that I know of."

"Any chance you can ask?"

"Not really," I slowly replied.

O'Connor didn't ask a question, he just waited for me to elaborate.

"Her mother is…upset," I continued. "And doesn't want her to see anyone outside the family."

"Including you?"

"Especially me." The bitter reply escaped before I thought about whether or not I wanted to reveal this to O'Connor.

"Why's that?"

I shrugged. He let the silence hang. I guess it bothered me too much to remain quiet. "All us queers molest children. Come on, Tim, old buddy, you're a good Catholic family man, surely you know that. Her mother decided she didn't want a perverted, baby-snatching lesbo around her snookums."

O'Connor remained stoic under my attack. "You're upset about this, aren't you?"

"Upset? Why should I be upset?" I acerbically shot back.

Again, O'Connor didn't reply, leaving the silence for me to fill.

"Just because a woman I thought was a friend of mine accuses me of, at best, consorting with someone who would molest her daughter. And, at worst, being… Why should that upset me?"

"Because it's a very ugly thing to be accused of," O'Connor stated. "For what it's worth, I think I'm pretty good at reading people. You could be a murderer. I can see you angry enough to pull the trigger. But an adult having sex with a child, that requires being slimy and underhanded. It's not your style. You might tangle with giants, but I can't see you fooling with kids."

"Thanks, I think. I guess if it comes down to it I'd rather be a murderer than a child abuser."

"Don't ever repeat this from me, but some people deserve to be murdered. No kid deserves to be abused."

I nodded slowly, but made no other reply.

O'Connor got back to business. "Any chance her mom will change her mind soon?"

"I doubt it. I'll probably have a better chance of catching her molester, at least, Judy Douglas's, by hanging out with Joey."

"Yeah, you're probably right." Then he corrected me. "We'll have a better chance of catching the slimewads. You're not a solo act."

"Yes, sir, Mr. O'Connor," I replied. "I'm doing another job for Joey tonight." I told him how Joey wanted me to set up Zeke and steal everything but what incriminated him. "So if you hear about a B&E at Heart of Desire, come bail me out," I finished.

"Try not to get caught. The cops aren't your main worry."

"Trust me, I know that." After that there wasn't much else to say, at least not about Joey and scared children and obscene pictures of them. I took a sip of my coffee. "Do you have kids?" I asked O'Connor.

"Three girls. One boy. Gina, my oldest, she wants every brass ring there is. She's twenty-two and starting a double-degree program, law and MBA. She's always giving me and Em advice about money. Sometimes I take a look at her and wonder where this kid came from.

"Maria's my second. Nothing like Gina. She wants to be a cop the way I wanted to be a cop when I was her age. She's getting her criminal justice degree, works out every day, and she gives me advice about what I should do. 'Dad, you heard about the latest in DNA fingerprinting?' Part of me thinks it's great and part of me goes, wait a minute, I'm not supposed to be teaching my daughter how to take out a perp. She doesn't seem to have time to date guys."

"Girls?" For some reason, I was determined to push it today.

O'Connor looked at me. "I know what you're thinking and...and who knows? Maybe. She's just eighteen. Did you know when you were eighteen?"

"I knew."

"It'll be hard for her to be a cop if she is."

"There's that."

"How'd you tell your parents?"

"My parents are dead." My father was, my mother might as well be.

"I'm sorry."

"Don't worry, my coming out didn't kill them."

"Glad to hear it. If any one of my kids kills me, it'll be Robby, my boy. He pulls every knuckleheaded stunt a teenager can. Leaves a beer can in the car, *Playboy* magazines under his bed. Not only is he too stupid not to do stuff like this, but he's too stupid not to get caught at it. He has a different girl every week, and the skirt's always a little tighter and the lipstick a little redder." O'Connor shook his head.

"If it's just beer and *Playboy*, he's not doing too badly."

"No, I guess not. Some fifteen-year-olds are on heroin." He sighed.

"I'll make a deal with you. If I see any of your daughters around the gay girl hangouts, I won't call you up and say, 'Hey, Tim, I saw your daughter down at the lesbo bar sucking up Dixie longnecks with a couple of biker gals.' I promise not to do that. Even if I do see them."

"Did I tell you I could also see you as a murder victim? Particularly when you run your mouth off like that?"

"That's been brought to my attention before," I replied, then prompted him, "I thought you had three daughters?"

"Yeah, I do. Deidre's eleven. She's…special. You want to meet her?" he suddenly asked. "Em's got a teachers' meeting today, so I get chauffeuring duties."

We got up, fishing in our pockets for tip change and then headed out of the coffee shop.

"Could I get you to play a hunch for me?" I asked as we crossed the street to O'Connor's car.

"Yeah? What do you need?"

"A license plate check. A car I saw around my client. I'd like to run it through."

O'Connor opened his car and we got in. I handed him a piece of paper with Ted's tag number on it.

"I guess I can do that," O'Connor said as he put the piece of paper in his jacket pocket.

"Thanks. Sometimes you have to try your hunches."

"No matter how many dead ends you run into," O'Connor commented sardonically.

We drove for a while in silence. O'Connor had his police radio turned on, its rasp a constant background drone. He pulled in front of a large house. Several children were waiting out front. I could hear the sound of others playing in the background. I could see some of the kids in the back, running and playing. They looked young, preschool. O'Connor crossed the yard to the front door.

Suddenly, one of the children broke away and screamed, "Daddy!" She ran with an awkward choppy gait. Then I noticed she had braces on her legs. O'Connor swept her up in his arms. He swung her around and then eased her down while he talked to a woman at the door. His daughter had her arms wrapped around his waist as if she was extravagantly happy to be with him. Then, taking her in hand, he led her to the car. She wore thick, heavy glasses, the kind that, on a child of eleven, labeled her as other, something wrong.

"Deidre, this is a friend of mine," O'Connor introduced us. "Her name is Micky Knight."

"Hello, Deidre," I said.

"Hi," she said very briefly, before ducking her head shyly. Then in her choppy run, she sped around the car and got in the passenger side.

I climbed into the backseat.

"But maybe your friend should sit here." Her features clouded, suddenly unsure if she'd done the right thing.

"It's okay. I like the backseat," I reassured her. Deidre probably spent a lot of her time being out of place, different, with its taint of inferior.

"How was school today?" O'Connor asked her.

Her reply was disjointed, jumping from subject to subject. Some of her words slurred, as if pronouncing were a constant struggle. I wondered why O'Connor wanted me along for this, what he wanted to prove.

"I got to stop by the station for a little bit. Do you mind?" O'Connor asked me.

"No, no problem."

"I don't want to take the evidence you gave me home."

As we pulled into the precinct parking lot, O'Connor turned to me and said, "I got about a half hour of paperwork, most of it yours."

I shrugged. Babysitting duty, that was my reason for being here.

"Deidre, pumpkin, Daddy's got to do some work. So you and Miss Micky are going to go play for a while. Is that okay?"

"Okay, Daddy," she replied.

Miss Micky? There are disadvantages to being an adult. We all got out of the car. O'Connor opened the trunk and took out a big, brightly colored ball.

"We got a little patch of ground back here that passes for a yard," he said as he led us through a passageway between buildings. He was right, it was just a patch with some anemic grass on it and one picnic bench that had seen better days. O'Connor left us there.

I glanced at my watch, then at Deidre. She was standing motionless, as if her animation had left when her father had. I tossed the ball in the air, then asked, "So, do you want to be the pitcher or the catcher?"

She smiled at me, but didn't seem to understand the question.

"I'll throw the ball to you," I motioned throwing, "and you toss it back. Okay?"

She nodded and held out her arms. I tossed the ball gently to her. She tried to catch it, but it slipped through her hands and hit her in the stomach. Deidre thought that this was funny and giggled. She ran for the ball, kicking it out of her reach several times before she finally got it. Using both arms, she gave it a wild throw in the air that I had to scramble to catch. She laughed, a loud, open-throated laugh, as if playing catch in this dingy yard was the most fun she could imagine having.

We continued throwing the ball back and forth, with pretty much the same results. I found myself starting to laugh with her. If she thought it funny when she dropped the ball or threw it straight up in the air, then I could find it funny, too. At first, I had concentrated on doing correct "adult" throws, then I realized it didn't matter. Instead I started tossing the ball overhand, underhand, between my legs, bounced it off my head, all way off target, but fun as hell.

Finally, we both collapsed on the bench, having tossed the ball every possible way. Deidre leaned into me and wrapped her arms around my waist, avoiding her imperfect words to tell me that laughing with her had made me her friend. I put my arms around her shoulders and hugged her back.

Then I tensed. What would it look like, a lesbian alone with a young girl in a secluded yard? All the things that Barbara Selby had implied about me jumbled in my mind. Why didn't O'Connor come back when we were playing ball, impeccably innocent? Now Deidre's head was on my lap, one arm resting across my thigh.

I realized that O'Connor was not a stupid man. And I knew why he had asked me along to meet his daughter, his special, trusting daughter. It was to leave me alone in this secluded space with her, to make up for Barbara's mistrust and accusations.

A few minutes later I heard O'Connor's footsteps in the alley. Deidre and I were still sitting on the bench, her head in my lap, and I was telling her the story of the tortoise and the hare. O'Connor sat at the end of the bench, listening quietly until I had finished.

"You ready to go?" he asked us.

I nodded.

Deidre stood up and said, "I'm like the tortoise, Daddy, slow, but I get there."

As we went back through the alley, I said to O'Connor, "Thank you."

"For what?" He brushed it off.

"Trusting me."

"With four kids I'm always looking for good babysitters."

"Still…" For a moment, I thought I might cry. I felt a tremendous relief, guilt washed away as the dirt it was.

"Hey," O'Connor responded. He awkwardly put his hand on my shoulder.

"Better find out my rates first," I said, quickly wiping my eyes. "I consider kids a dangerous duty."

I had O'Connor drop me a few blocks from my place. It was a little after five. I promised Deidre that I would come over sometime and play ball with her. We were still working on the Miss Micky part, though.

Chapter 27

Joey didn't call until after nine o'clock. "You ready for some fun?" he asked. "This time the truck's over in Kenner, near the airport. Gotta keep changing. Never the same place twice."

"I guess. You going to drive me out there?"

"Naw. You get to take the bus."

"To Kenner?" Kenner was beyond Metairie, the suburb of a suburb. "I'd have to take five or six buses. I won't get there until tomorrow."

"Relax. I'm jerking you. I'll be over in about half an hour to pick you up. We'll go over the rest of the stuff on the way out."

"See you in a little bit," I said. I remembered to get both my jacket and scarf when he rang the buzzer. I had no faith in the truck's heating system.

"Another night of fun and games," Joey said as he shoved the car door open for me.

I got down to business. "So when does the ceiling fall on Zeke's head?"

"Probably the weekend. He's always there Fridays and Saturdays. So tonight you do the same thing, just drive the truck to the Heart."

Joey zoomed up the entrance to I-10, flaunting the speed of his car by merging in front of several cars. I was glad I had my seat belt buckled.

"Yeah," he said. "Except this time, I'm gonna get called away. Mr. Colombé needs me. So you gotta handle it yourself. You got any problems with that?"

"No. Should I?"

"No, you shouldn't. Get Zeke to sign off that he received that stuff."

"Zeke's not going to sign anything that says he's received forty boxes of kiddie porn. No one's that stupid."

"Naw, not even Zeke. It says boxes of packing material, something like that. But you see, one box is gonna tear. You attach that torn part to the paper Zeke signs."

"And the cops find that box and, bingo, Zeke's linked to it."

"That's the game plan. Make sure it works."

"Who calls the cops?"

"We got an impeccable source. None of us grubby underworld types. It's all on the up-and-up, except for where you let your fingers do the walking tonight." Joey roared down the interstate, the speed limit a meaningless restriction.

"And when do we become expendable?" I wondered aloud.

"We don't," Joey retorted. "You and me, we change, we adapt. We're survivors."

"Isn't that a quote from Tyrannosaurus Rex?" I asked sardonically.

"Who?" Joey wasn't up on extinct creatures.

"A Roman emperor of the Ming dynasty."

"Yeah, something like that," Joey replied, totally unfazed. "We change, we adapt, we survive. I like that."

"In Latin, it's 'Adaptulus, changiorum, et non splatus.'" It was a foolish thing to do. If Joey found out that I was mocking him, it would make my life difficult. It also meant that I was being lazy, making assumptions. I didn't know that Joey didn't know Latin. He might have been an altar boy at an earlier age. My next assumption could be wrong and it could be dangerous.

Joey swerved across two lanes to take the Veterans Memorial Boulevard exit. His driving almost said, "You may know Latin, but I'm driving a Porsche."

Don't play games and don't make waves, Micky, the stakes are too high.

Veterans Boulevard is mile after mile of commercial strip. Every chain, every fast food joint is located somewhere on this concrete stretch. I found the miles of neon and bright lights distracting and confusing. Joey, however, seemed to know where he was going.

"How much do I get paid for this, anyway?" I probed, to keep Joey talking. A silent Joey would reveal nothing.

"So, now you ask."

"You told me to ask, so I'm asking."

"You a gambler?"

"Not unless I have to be."

"How about a percentage?"

"How big a percentage and of what?"

"Percentage of what goes down. You take the risks, you get the rewards."

"What percent?"

"Two percent."

"Gross or net?"

"Gross or net what? What accounting school did you go to? You think we pay taxes?"

"There are expenses," I replied, then decided it was in my best interest to be agreeable. "All right, I'll go for two percent."

"Now you're talking my lingo," Joey said as he took a sharp turn off Veterans. I couldn't catch the street sign.

After a few blocks we came to a construction site, some new subdivision. Parked amid the lumber and brick was the truck.

"Who drives it here, anyway?" I asked.

"The guy that prints this shit. All he knows is that he drives this truck somewhere and leaves it. So he don't know where it goes and who gets it. The photographer just takes it to the printer. That's all he knows. If they go down, we don't go with them."

"A comforting thought."

"So you got it straight?" Joey asked as he handed me the keys.

"Dump this stuff, get Zeke to sign for it, rip a box, attach a piece to the sheet with his signature, get the rest of the paperwork out, go home and relax."

"That's the ticket. Have a fun ride."

"Thanks," I said as I got out.

Joey took off without waiting for me to find my way across the construction site to the truck. There are better places to be than dark lots in Kenner.

Damn, I realized as I got in the truck, I didn't have a way to get from the Heart of Desire back to my place. Getting a cab to go to that neighborhood would be an iffy proposition. Maybe I would be taking a bus tonight after all.

I decided to stay on Veterans rather than cutting over to I-10. Its slow speeds and stoplights were more fitted to the truck's abilities than the fast lanes of the interstate. Also, Zeke wasn't a patient man. I wanted him waiting to leave by the time I got there. An extra half hour of transit time would have him tapping his toe waiting for me.

He was standing at the door in the alley as I pulled in. Mr. Unfriendly and Mr. Silent flanked him. "Where have you been?" he demanded as I hopped out of the cab. I had backed into the alley, saving Mr. Unfriendly the wear on his ego.

"Traffic's a mess. Some wreck somewhere." Being New Orleans, that had to be true. "It wouldn't do for me to get a ticket, now, would it?"

"Where's Joey?"

"He got called away."

"You handling this?"

"Yeah. You have a problem with that?" I looked directly at him, took a step to get close enough to invade his space and to make it clear that I was a few inches taller. Nothing like a little psychological advantage.

"Naw. If it's okay with Joey, it's okay with me."

"Let's unload this." I strode away from Zeke to the back of the truck and undid the padlock. The quick way to take charge is simply to give the orders. I shoved up the door of the truck and jumped in. "That same storeroom okay?" I called to Zeke.

"Yeah, yeah, sure."

I started handing boxes out to Mr. Unfriendly and Mr. Silent.

"I used to unload trucks like this all by myself," Zeke started. "That was before I injured my back. It's a hell of a thing to get old. Here, let me get that door for you." He held open the back door as Mr. Unfriendly and Mr. Silent carried boxes into the building.

I decided not to tell Zeke that unloading a truck like this all by himself was probably why he had a bad back. No, no, I wanted Zeke to like me and trust me enough to let me wander around the bar after he left.

"So how'd you end up here?" I asked him as I hefted another box to the lip of the truck.

"Whadda you mean, how'd I end up here?" Zeke looked suspiciously at me.

"I mean, you seem pretty important. How'd you get from unloading trucks to running this joint?"

It's amazing how quickly flattery will open a small mind. Zeke let go of the door and came over to lean against the truck. "Well, now, it took me a while to work my way up here." Zeke started telling me has life story. We had the truck halfway unloaded before we got out of his childhood. Mr. Unfriendly and Mr. Silent kept up a steady pace, not wanting to linger in the vicinity and hear what were obviously reruns for them. I only half listened, nodding and uh-huhing when it seemed needed. We were down to the last boxes before we got anywhere near the time I was interested in.

"How'd you meet Joey," I interjected when he took a breath.

"He just started hangin' around here. I don't really remember," was

Zeke's ever so helpful answer. He then went on to give me a list of his woes, how winter made his back really hurt, in summer he might help, but winter, forget it, how hard it was to run this place, "And the girls, they're impossible. They get someone, they take 'em upstairs, they fuck 'em. That's it. It shouldn't be hard. But no, 'Zeke, I don't feel good. Zeke, that guy smells. Zeke, I need more nose candy.' It's always something."

"It's hard when you're a manager," I commented. Oh, the trials and tribulations of being a pimp. If Zeke was complaining to me about his problems with the "girls" it meant he had gotten over my being a woman. It also meant he was incredibly stupid.

I handed the last box to Mr. Unfriendly, then hopped out of the truck. Zeke led the way back into the building. Mr. Silent followed me, closing the door on the cool night.

"Summers it's too hot," he muttered. "It's too damn hot for him to unload a truck." Then Mr. Silent was silent again.

We went into Zeke's office. I took the chair that Joey had sat in before, leaving the henchmen to fend for themselves. Mr. Silent opted again for the floor, while Mr. Unfriendly stood in the doorway, obviously trying to work his way up the career ladder.

"You want to sign this?" I asked Zeke, taking an invoice out of my jacket.

"Let me look at it." He took the invoice from me. Look is all he did, he couldn't have read it before he signed it. "Safe sex instruction guides, what'll you guys think of next," he chuckled as he handed the invoice back to me. Then he said, "Joey usually signs on the bottom line." He handed me a pen.

How nice of you to mention that to me, Joey, I thought as I took the pen.

"Since I'm acting in his stead, why don't I just sign his name and initial it?" I suggested. It was somewhat irrational, but I didn't want to put my name on any of this.

"Sure," Zeke agreed with a shrug.

I wrote Joey's name in, then scribbled my initials as illegibly as possible. I gave the carbon to Zeke and kept the top copy for myself. He opened up a file cabinet and shoved the invoice into a file folder. At least it appeared that Joey was right about Zeke being sloppy and putting everything into one file.

"I'd love to stay and chat, but I gotta get out of here," he said as he stood up.

"Mind if I hang around and get a beer?"

"Naw, not at all. Monday's half-price night."

I smiled at his generosity. "Can I leave the truck where it is?"

"You want one of the boys to take it?"

"It's no problem." It's my ride home.

"Just don't leave it here too long."

"A beer or two and I'm gone," I promised Zeke.

"Okay, boys," Zeke said as he led the way out of his office. "We call it a night." To me he asked, "You goin' out the back door?"

"Yeah, probably better not to be seen on the street."

"Just be sure you throw the bolt when you leave." Zeke turned and locked his office.

Damn. It didn't look like the world's greatest lock, but busting down Zeke's door wasn't the subtle approach I had in mind.

We walked a few feet down the hall. Zeke stopped in front of a dusty barracuda—mounted, not live. He put his office key into the barracuda's mouth. Obviously, Zeke wasn't expecting an inside job.

"I should probably count the boxes again," I said as I stopped outside the storeroom.

"You want one of the girls to get you a beer?" Zeke, ever the gracious host, offered.

"That'd be great." It might give me a chance to ask some questions without the bartender or whoever keeping track of how long they lingered with me.

"Which one do you like?" Zeke's lips had a salacious twitch to them.

"To get a beer? It doesn't matter."

"You want one of them?" Zeke had to push it, to play his little game. "I've got some good girls here, they'll do anything I tell them."

"Out of my price range," I said shortly, to end this conversation.

"On the house. Which one you want?"

Mr. Unfriendly and Mr. Silent had both paused in their exit to watch this little drama. I looked at Zeke, his pudgy face glistening and decided it was time to stop being polite. Too often men attack women because they think we won't fight back. Zeke had no control over me and I could afford to expend some rage at him.

"You do it with them?" I inquired.

"Yeah, yeah. It's a perk of the job." His twitching lips widened into a lascivious grin.

"You really mean you use whores for sex? That mechanical, fake orgasm stuff turns you on?" I stared at him. "I've got several girlfriends.

They love it when—I guess you can't do that with your bad back. I guess that's a good reason to see a hooker, if you can't do the real stuff."

Zeke turned a color that an interior decorator friend of mine called aubergine. He spun on his heel, muttered, "Fuckin' dyke," and headed for the door. He turned back for a moment and sputtered, "You tell Joey to call me. I got something to say to him." He turned back, again muttered, "Fuckin' dyke," and slammed out the door.

Mr. Unfriendly, mindful of his career climb, followed his boss. Mr. Silent chuckled, then let out an "Asshole," clearly intended for Zeke and ambled out of the building.

I went in the storeroom, just in case Zeke decided to return for another round. I really did count the boxes. This time there were fifty boxes of "safe sex instructions." A growing business. I put on a pair of gloves and picked a sacrificial box to open. I forced myself to do a quick glance through the magazine. Cissy's picture wasn't there. I didn't recognize any of the other girls. It gave me a small, false sense of relief. Not knowing just meant I didn't know the exact damage that had been done. The same anxious, begging eyes stared at me from those photos.

I tore part of the box flap off. Then I got a magazine and tore part of it to correspond with the torn box. *Okay, Zeke, you and Joey just think this is a game to earn money. Let's play for some real stakes, not "just" the lives of little girls.*

No one was in the hallway. I quickly stuck my hand into the barracuda's mouth (what a metaphor) and grabbed the key to Zeke's office. After opening his door, I went back in the storage room and got the damaged box. I carried the whole thing into Zeke's office. By moving and shifting a few junk piles, I found a place for the box, then covered it back up with the junk. Zeke would never notice it, but the police would be sure to find it.

I opened his file cabinet. I rifled through all his files, before taking the one Joey had instructed me to get. I stapled the torn porno magazine and box piece to the invoice he had signed tonight. That was all I put back into the file folder. Nothing else looked interesting and the cigarette stench in this office was giving me a headache.

I slipped back out of the door. Camille was standing in the hallway.

"Where's Zeke?" she asked warily.

"He's gone," I said calmly. It wouldn't do to act as if I didn't have a right to be here.

"For good or just the day?"

"Just the day, I'm afraid."

"He know you're in his office?"

"No," I admitted. I wouldn't make Zeke's mistake of underestimating Camille. If I lied, all she'd need to do is mention it to Zeke tomorrow and I'd be caught out.

"You a dick?" she asked.

I couldn't help myself from looking down at my crotch before answering, "No."

"I know you don't have one. What's your game?"

"I'm private," I admitted.

"What's in those boxes?" she asked, with a nod of her head at the storeroom.

"You don't want to know."

"There's a lot of things I 'don't want to know' around here."

"Like what?"

"Like why should I tell you?"

"If I were you I'd be sick over the weekend."

She slowly nodded, then asked, "If you're private, how do you know?"

"I have my sources."

She nodded again, then said, "Come on back this way. Standing in the hall's not a good place to be talking."

I quickly locked Zeke's door and put the key back in its hiding place, then followed Camille to the end of the hallway and up rickety backstairs.

"Here we are, hooker heaven," she said, ushering me into a small room. There were a few pieces of second- and third-hand furniture, an old couch, a wooden packing crate for a coffee table. A radio in one corner was tuned to a jazz station. And, incongruously, hung up on one wall were several pictures drawn by children.

Camille caught me staring at them. "I got two kids. Welfare didn't put nothing but beans and rice on the table and I could never get shoes to fit them. That wasn't a life."

"This is?" I couldn't help but ask.

Camille gave me a get-rid-of-your-middle-class assumptions look and said, "To get by, yeah. I know I've got only a few more years 'til my looks are going to need a real dark room. Or I end up on Tulane Avenue. So I'm careful with my money, I don't party when I leave here. I go home, get my kids ready for school. I got my GED last year, and now I'm taking a college course, business. And in a year or two, Betsy and me are going to start a dressmaking business. Welfare wouldn't put me on that road, wouldn't even give me a map. They just give you so much, so you never have enough."

"Why this dump?"

"It's not so bad. Zeke's too stupid to really rip us off. Plus the johns got to come in the bar first. They decide to play rough or not pay, they got to go back out the bar. They only get far enough to regret it. So what are you doing here, Miss Private Eye?"

"Seeking answers. Who makes what's in those boxes."

Camille nodded, then asked, "It got to do with kids?"

"Why do you ask?" I kept my voice as neutral as I could.

"What's an eight-year-old, blue-eyed, blond-haired white girl doing at a place like this? Now, I got two kids, so I show their pictures and Audrey shows her kids, and Hugo shows his, so I know all the kids that might have any business here. That kid didn't belong."

"How long ago was that?"

"'Bout a week."

Another woman slipped in through the door. She looked at me, then at Camille.

"This is Betsy," Camille introduced us. "You got a name?"

"Micky," I replied. "Hello, Betsy."

Betsy nodded at me.

"Me, Betsy, Audrey, and Gloria fixed up this little room. No one comes here but us," Camille informed me.

"Hurricanes," I said.

"Hell, yes," Camille responded. "Might as well use a hurricane for a hooker name."

Audrey, Betsy, Camille, and Gloria were all names of hurricanes. New Orleans, a city built on a swamp, is prime fodder for a storm. Betsy, in the early sixties, had done serious damage. Camille, several years later, had veered east, slamming into the Mississippi Gulf Coast. It was the most powerful hurricane to ever hit the continental United States, with winds of over two hundred miles an hour.

She added, "Some have caught on, but none as quick as you."

"Zeke still hasn't figured it out," Betsy put in.

"Tell Micky about last Wednesday night," Camille instructed Betsy.

That the request came from Camille was enough for Betsy. She began, "There were three little girls here. They were tarted up in frilly dresses and patent leather shoes. You know, not kid clothes, but adult clothes for kids. They had makeup on, red lips, and eye shadow. Zeke yelled at me to get out of the hall. Later he first told me I didn't see them, then that they were a bunch of lost school kids and not to worry about it."

"Right," snorted Camille. "In a whorehouse at three in the morning."

"Anything else?" I asked.

"One of the other girls claims some dude offered her big bucks to do a shoot with young girls. But she's on too many things to trust what she says. Is that why you're here? Those kids?" Camille asked.

"That's why I'm here."

She and Betsy looked at each other, then Camille said, "What we do is one thing, but messing with kids is sick. If we can, we'll help you."

"Can you call me if any more children show up here?"

"Can't promise, but can try," Camille agreed.

"We can't exactly say, 'Yo, bro, take it out, I got to make a phone call,'" Betsy said. "If Gloria's here, she's got a portable phone. If not, we have to use the one in the hall."

"You gotta bust us on Saturday night?" Camille asked. "We might get more if you waited."

"It's not me. Or the cops. Whoever's running this thing has gotten tired of Zeke. They're setting him up and dropping him hard."

Camille shook her head, "Like a snake shedding its skin."

I gave both Betsy and Camille my phone number. Then, with Camille running interference, we headed back downstairs.

"Look, thanks for your help," I said as I stopped at the storeroom. I opened the door and pointed at one of the boxes, "I've got to get some evidence."

Camille nodded, then looked at the file of Zeke's I was still holding under my arm. "You want to make a copy of that?"

"Yeah." I had planned to stop at a twenty-four-hour copy shop on my way home.

Camille smiled at me. I grabbed a porno magazine, then locked the storeroom. Camille led me to a little alcove next to Zeke's office. She turned on the light, and lo, and behold, a copy machine was before me.

"For some reason, I just like this idea," Camille said as she turned the machine on.

So did I. Camille stood watch while I made the copies.

"This is the most fun I've had all week," she said as I turned the machine off.

She walked me to the back door. "You take care of those kids," she said. Then kissed me on the cheek before walking away.

I let myself out the door, remembering to turn the lock in the handle as Zeke had instructed me to do. Be a good guest and your hosts will invite you back.

It was cold outside. I hopped into the truck to get out of the wind. I started to drive out, then stopped. Zeke's file, the copy of it and the porn magazine were laying next to me on the seat. I took the copy and the magazine and stuffed them into my jacket, zipping it up so they were concealed. I wasn't supposed to have them and I was uneasy about leaving them in plain sight. For all I knew, Joey was waiting for me just around the corner. Besides that, it's warmer, I told myself as I edged the truck out to the street. Only the scant traffic of the early morning hours was around.

I made good time back to my neighborhood. This truck was becoming like a second car to me. I parked it about half a block away, in front of a warehouse. That way it wouldn't look like the truck was connected to me, and more importantly, it wouldn't block any resident from parking in front of her house.

Just as I got out of the cab, Joey's Porsche roared up beside me.

"What took you so long?" he asked through his open window.

"I got to hear Zeke's life story."

"Did you get the file?"

"Yeah, I got it." I handed it to him.

"Good," he said, tossing it in his backseat, careless of the disarray of paper. "Did you get him to sign the invoice?"

"Yes, I did. You could have warned me that you usually sign it, too."

"Sorry, I forgot about that."

Like hell you did.

"So what'd you do?" Joey had to ask me. "Smart girl like you should be able to figure a way out of it."

"I signed your name."

"You what?" Joey demanded, his easy manner disappearing.

"Relax, I slipped a page over the carbon. Your name's only on the original."

"Shit, you had me goin' for a second. Come on, we gotta move the truck."

"We?"

"Yeah, get in. Just follow me."

"I've got to go to the bathroom."

"There's a john where we're going."

"With a supply of tampons?"

"Oh, shit, you girls and your fuckin' periods."

"I'll be right back," I said. I trotted around Joey's car and went into my building. I did not want to be carrying that copy and pilfered magazine on who knows what jaunt Joey was taking us on. I ran up the stairs, as if speed could some safety. Pulling things out of a desk drawer, I shoved the evidence in, then piled various papers on top of it. I went to the bathroom and got a couple of tampons, just in case Joey wanted proof.

Joey had pulled in front of the truck and was impatiently waiting for me. I waved that I was here and ready to go, then jumped in the cab and started the truck. Joey roared off. I let him pull away. I decided that if Joey wanted me to follow him, we'd do it at truck speed, I wasn't going to try to make this jalopy behave like a Porsche.

He was waiting for me at the next light. "Hey, hurry up," he yelled.

"This is a truck with the shocks of an ox-drawn cart. You'd have to take it downhill on Mt. Everest to get it to go over fifty-five. Be real," I shouted back.

Joey continued leading, but at a more sedate pace this time. We ended up in some beat-up trailer park in Chalmette, a town just east of New Orleans, where the famous battle of New Orleans was actually fought.

I handed the keys to Joey as I got out of the truck. He crossed to one of the trailers, rapped on the door, and when it was opened, he handed the keys to a person I couldn't see through the barely cracked door. If either of them said anything I couldn't hear it.

"Shit, what a day," Joey said as we both got into his car. "Colombé wants every friggin' perversion under the sun, two men, two girls, threesome, you name it. Then"—he almost said a name, but stopped himself—"the guy running this stuff wants to move things up. Gotta go by the weekend, not next weekend. So a lot of things are fucked up." Joey turned a tight U out of the trailer park, his anxiety showing in his driving.

"How so?" I asked.

"Well, I've been doing some side deals. The money's out and it's not back in again."

"You borrowed money from people who don't like to lend money," I stated.

"Yeah, something like that. Now I need fifty grand in the next few days to pull through. Nothin's gonna break by then."

"Like fifty boxes instead of forty?" I suddenly asked.

"Yeah. I put in an extra ten. I get the whole take. But it doesn't go out until Wednesday. No way it'll be back by Friday."

"What else do you have going?"

"What do you mean?"

"You want me to help, you level with me."

"Okay. Hugo and I got a coke deal. I skimmed a little money from Colombé. And…a lot from someone else. It'll be back in a week."

Joey, you stupid shit, I thought. You're a pussycat biting a tiger's tail. "You ever considered going to the police?"

"What?! You crazy?"

"Maybe. But you might be safer there than anywhere else. Go state's evidence, finger Colombé and this other guy and you might walk."

"Walk where? With what? I just need to hold on a little longer and I'll be clear. I'm gonna make a killing in the next week or so. I just need to get there. What about Karen? Can you lean on her?"

"She paid me to get you away from her," I reminded him.

"So you go. Old times' sake. Or better, just show her what her money paid for. I bet she'd pay fifty grand to keep that a secret."

"Maybe. She'd have to have it liquid. What happens if you don't get it?"

"I don't know. I can't think about that. Look, you gonna try Karen?"

"Yeah, I'll try Karen. But that money's going to buy me something."

"What?" Joey asked warily.

"Everything you know. Every name, every place, every inch of the deal. 'Knowledge is power.' I want it."

"You get the money, yeah, sure."

I reached in the backseat, took an invoice with Joey's signature on it, and put it in my jacket pocket. "Insurance," I said. "You don't hold up your end of the deal, and you and Zeke can be cell mates."

"Hey, no problem. A deal's a deal."

"The real reason, Joey, for honor among thieves is that dishonor costs too much. Don't push people when they don't have limits."

"No double cross, okay? I get the money, you get what you want."

I didn't reply. It looked like this was another lesson life would have to teach Joey.

"Can you have it by Thursday?"

"I'll try," I answered shortly.

"Try hard, try real hard." That was how Joey said good night.

I slowly climbed the stairs to my apartment. Joey, and his desire for money, had caused a lot of complications. I knew, even if Joey didn't, that the fifty thousand was not likely to return. I wondered if I could get O'Connor to mark the bills. Maybe that way we could trace some of it. The easy thing to do might be to let Karen in on my cover. But then Karen wasn't exactly someone I would trust with a secret like that.

Oh, hell, what a fucking mess, I thought as I threw off my clothes and got into bed.

Chapter 28

I had set my alarm clock for an early hour. I was tense and in need of action. Again, I decided I couldn't risk calling O'Connor from here. I couldn't even risk calling Karen. If Joey's double-dealing was discovered, he was dead meat no matter how quickly he paid the money back. I took a quick shower, poured some coffee into a traveling mug, and hit the road.

I headed to the lakefront; early on a cold weekday morning there shouldn't be too much traffic around. I found a pay phone and pulled in. First, I called O'Connor. I had to use his beeper to reach him. I gave him a quick rundown of last night's events.

"So he promised you the whole kit and caboodle if you get him the money?" was O'Connor's comment.

"He promised it."

"Can this client of yours give you that kind of money?"

I hadn't revealed Karen's name. I didn't want to unless I had to. She had been a client, but also some gut instinct told me that if Karen got hauled in by the police, one of the first people she would call would be Cordelia. Her fluff friends were useful for window dressing, but they wouldn't hang around if it wasn't a good time.

"I think so," I answered O'Connor. "I'm not going to tell her what's really happening. As far as she'll know, I'm just hitting her up for Joey."

"That makes you seem a bad guy."

"What she doesn't know can't hurt me. It would help if I thought I could get most of the money back."

"I'll see what I can arrange. Maybe I can get marked money and we do an exchange."

"Whatever. Joey wants it by Thursday. Is that possible?"

"I'll do what I can. But, Micky, if it gets much hotter, bail out. If Joey slips up, he's going to have a lot of people mad at him and they might not like his friends either."

"Too bad I can't advertise that I'm not his friend."

"But you're not their friend either," O'Connor pointed out. Then he said, "I ran that license number you asked me to."

"And?" I hate suspense.

"Ted Pollard. One DWI four years ago. Moved here from New Jersey six years ago. Occupation is listed as basketball coach at McDonogh Number 44 School."

That was Cissy's school.

"This mean anything to you?" O'Connor demanded of my silence.

"I don't know. Maybe," I answered. "Let me go play with Joey."

"Just be careful." With that we hung up.

I had some questions to ask about Ted. Maybe if Warren had been checking on him, he could answer them.

Next I called Karen. I woke her up. "I need to talk to you," I told her.

"What?" she said, still blurry.

"I'll be over in half an hour. It will be useful if you're awake, coherent, and have gotten rid of whatever trick you picked up last night."

"I'm sleeping alone," Karen huffed.

"Good, then you only have to deal with awake and coherent. See you." That should set the tone for our conversation. I headed back to my car.

I took a long meandering drive to Karen's house, throwing in several U-turns just in case I was being followed. I made sure at least forty-five minutes had passed before I pulled up in front of her house. I wanted Karen both ready and a little tense from waiting. Action, bad guy, take one. I got out of my car, crossed the yard to her door, and leaned on the buzzer. I let it shrill long enough to be annoying.

Karen opened the door. "Micky, hi. Come in."

She was dressed in blue jeans and a sweatshirt, no makeup. She actually looked more attractive than I'd seen her in a long time. Maybe because she didn't look devious.

"Do you have coffee?" I asked, heading back toward her kitchen.

Karen followed me. "Yes, I just made somc."

I took a coffee cup from her cupboard and poured myself some coffee.

"Do you want milk or sugar or anything?"

"No, this is fine." I sat down at her kitchen table, then motioned for her to sit opposite me.

She did, then after a moment of silence, asked, "So, Micky, what do you want?"

Her tone, the way she was leaning to me, all let me know that Karen wanted me. It gave me power over her. It's only money and she'll get most of it back, I told myself. But she wants something from me I'll never give her and I'm going to use her want to get what I need.

"You know the money you lent Joey? I found out what he used it for."

"Yes?" Karen said slowly.

I tossed the porno magazine across the table at her. She opened it and looked, an expression of growing revulsion as she flipped by each picture, until finally she slammed it shut and pushed it away.

"Those are children!" she exclaimed. "I never knew...I wouldn't have..."

"You never knew because you never asked. It was your greed and your willful blindness that allowed them to get going. They don't need you anymore because they're making enough money on their own now."

"Oh, my God," she let out, stunned into silence.

I shoved the pictures back at her. "Why don't you count the number of little girls in there? Really find out what your money bought?"

"Those pictures are...sickening," Karen gasped. "I can't look at them."

"Why not, Karen? There's a big profit here. It's a great place to invest your money," I taunted her.

"Damn you!" Karen stood up. "If I had known..." She strode across the kitchen, agitated. It seemed as if something had finally gotten to Karen Holloway. "Can we go to the police?" she suddenly asked me.

I hadn't expected that. Karen was not supposed to do the right thing. "No," I told her. "What proof do you have?"

"But we can't...can't just let this go on."

"I might be able to get the evidence."

"Really? How?"

I answered that with a shrug, then said, "But I'm not going to risk my butt for nothing, so you can wipe all the shit off of yours."

"What do you mean?"

"Fifty thousand by Thursday. For that, I won't tell anyone how you made your money, and I'll see if I can get something that keeps both of us out of it. That's what you want, isn't it?"

"It's what I'd prefer," Karen said slowly. "But I don't know if I can get the money..."

"What happened to the seventy in cash Joey gave you?" I cut in. "Don't tell me you just waltzed up to the bank and deposited it."

"Well, no, but I don't have that kind of money sitting around here."

"By Thursday or it's no deal."

"What do you need the money for so soon?"

"What did you need the money for so badly that you hooked up with Joey and forgot to ask questions?" I yelled at her. I knew I needed to keep her on the defensive and not asking questions. But I wasn't doing just that. My anger was coming out, flaring because I could get away with directing it at Karen. I didn't like myself for it, but I didn't stop. "Maybe I'm goddamned tired of driving a car that's falling apart and barely paying my rent every month."

"Francois suggested it, Joey, I mean. I wanted money of my own, not just doled out to me from a trust fund. How was I supposed to suspect that something like this was going on at the Sans Pareil?" But Karen didn't want me to answer that question and she quickly changed the topic. "If you want a car, I can buy you a car. Or a place to live. I'd do that for you."

"If I slept with you."

"No," she answered too quickly.

"You'd always want me to."

Karen was honest enough not to deny it. "I'll try to get the money," she said. "Let's make this a business deal. Let me hire you to get what it takes to stop them. Right now, this feels too much like…like…"

"Blackmail," I supplied.

Karen didn't acknowledge the word. "I want to know what's going on, what you find out. Even what you don't find out. Is it a deal?"

"If you get the money," I agreed.

"I'll get it."

I turned to go.

"Don't hate me," Karen called after me. She was starting to cry.

If I had the time and space to be a decent person, I would have put my arms around her, and said, "I don't hate you. You've done something stupid and foolish. People have gotten hurt. That can't be undone. Don't repeat your mistakes. That's the only way you'll ever atone for them." But now wasn't the time and I wasn't the person to do it, with my anger still dangerously near the surface. I merely said, "I don't hate you," and left her crying.

Oh, yes, we are a good guy, fighting for truth, beauty, and the American way, I thought as I got in my car and started it. I went and got some packing material, and wrapped the porno magazine and the copied file. I sent it certified delivery to O'Connor. It was safer than risking dropping it off at the police station. I wondered if I was committing a felony by sending obscene material through the mail.

After that I went back to my apartment. Now the game was to wait. I thought about calling Joey, but I figured letting him stew a bit longer would be good for his soul.

At some point I realized I was tired. Late nights and early mornings will do that to you. Since it's just as easy to wait while asleep as awake, I lay down to take a long nap.

The phone woke me. It was late afternoon. I listened to my answering machine take the call. If it was really important I could jump up and catch the phone. Like Cordelia. The thought caused me to sit up in bed.

But the voice that came over the machine was not hers. "Hi, Micky, this is Amanda Jackson. I just realized that we have Cissy scheduled for tomorrow. Have you had any contact with her mother? Do you know if she's going to be there? Since you've already paid for it, we'll keep the slot open. Bye."

Being reminded of both Cissy and Cordelia wasn't the most pleasant of wake ups.

I briefly considered calling up Barbara Selby and saying, "I am too caught up in this. I have to know how Cissy is." But I had enough sense to know that that emotional edge would push Barbara away, or worse, she would hear guilt or blame in my voice.

I also thought about calling Cordelia and demanding essentially the same thing, that we had a connection I couldn't easily break or ignore. But as she was obviously resisting any urge to call me, I might as well return the favor.

I got up and headed to the bathroom. After dressing and feeding Hepplewhite, I started looking through my kitchen to find something to feed myself.

The phone rang.

"Hey, Mick, what's happenin'?" It was Joey. "So, did you get to Karen?"

"I talked to her."

"Yeah, and?"

"She says she'll try to get the money by Thursday."

"Hey, you're great." Wasn't I ever? Joey continued, "You think she can do it?"

"I think so."

"Great, wow, that's just great." Relief was rampant in Joey's voice. "I knew I was right when I picked you."

"How about a little from your end of the deal?"

"Like what?"

"Who runs this thing?"

"What are you going to do with that if I tell you?"

"I'm going to know it, that's what. Are you backing out of our deal?"

"No, no, nothing like that. But look, this thing's a friggin' octopus. I don't even think I got it figured out."

"We'll work on it. Just tell me who gives you the orders."

"Francois."

"Francois? Not Colombé?"

"It gets messy. Yeah, Francois, I think. He kites money from Colombé. But maybe it's just a setup to keep Colombé's hands clean. Francois pointed Karen out to me, told me how much money to get and all that."

"But if it's Colombé, he has plenty of money. No reason for him to fool with Karen."

"Maybe it's just part of his game. But what I can't figure is Francois calls me up and says, yes, do this, then later, no, don't do it, like he's on the end of someone's string."

"You have any ideas?"

"Not yet. But Francois and me are gonna have a talk. You call me Thursday when you get the money." Joey hung up.

Let's hope my phone's not tapped. Joey should have thought of that, as deep in as he was. It was hard to contemplate Francois, with his servant's soul, as running this whole thing. Did that take us back to Colombé? I had assumed that his perversions were of the adult variety. Had they paled, were children now the last thrill left to him? I shuddered at the thought of his wrinkled hands fondling a young girl. But why make a business out of it? More money on top of the massive amount he already had? Or was it just another game for him to play? Or was one of his chess pieces merely a player in someone else's game?

Chapter 29

The next day, the chill still held. I couldn't shake the nervous anxiety I felt, as if all this was careening at a speed I could barely control. It wasn't just Joey, but my whole life. Was I incapable of really connecting with someone? I used to think I was a good person, not perfect, but basically decent. But why had Barbara been so willing to throw me out, like trash beside her child? Or Cordelia. We had been lovers and now we weren't. I had no idea how to get back there. Or maybe I was just too terrified to try.

It didn't do anything for my self-worth to find a small article in the *Times-Picayune*'s Metro section. Clinic Breaks New Ground was the headline. Work was scheduled to begin on the new building for Cordelia's clinic. The ground had been broken yesterday. There was a picture of the mayor holding a shovel and beside him Emma Auerbach, co-chair of the board of directors. Just in back of her was Cordelia. And though they weren't named, behind her I recognized Danny, Joanne, Alex, and Elly. I scrutinized other faces, wondering if any of them were Cordelia's new lover. Maybe she hasn't taken a lover yet. She doesn't jump from bed to bed like I do. Like I did, I reminded myself. Sex used to be how I connected to people. It let me think I was being intimate without directly confronting the responsibilities of loving another person.

I turned the page and read the rest of the paper. I didn't let myself glance back at the picture. After I finished the paper, I threw it in the trash. Then I turned around, pulled it out again, and clipped the article. Cordelia would probably appreciate an extra copy. Maybe someday I would get the chance to give it to her. I put it in my desk drawer, next to the keys to her apartment. At some point I had to give them back.

I sat at my desk, with my checkbook in front of me. I told myself I was balancing it, but I was just staring at the numbers without seeing them. Finally, conceding that even if I did manage to accomplish anything, it would be hard to trust the accuracy of my figures, I closed my checkbook. I looked over letters that I should answer but left them in a heap for another day. Then I looked in my datebook, just to be sure I wasn't missing a crucial appointment. Circled for this afternoon was Cissy's appointment with Lindsey. I started to pick up the phone to say we wouldn't be there, but then I wondered if Lindsey would talk to me. I had already paid for the time.

I was surprised at how relieved I was at the thought of talking to her. Then an ambivalence crept into that relief. What if she does tell me I've gone too far? Suddenly, a wall of rejection loomed in front of me—my mother leaving when I was five; my father's death when I was ten; the daily rejections of living with Aunt Greta and Uncle Claude; Bayard's rejection of everything I offered except sexual favors; Misty, Ned, and Brian all going off to college and leaving me with two more years of high school. Lovers I'd had and discarded before they ever had a chance to reject me.

I've felt like an outsider for a long time, sometimes with my nose pressed to the glass, desperately wanting in; at other times, reveling in my outcast status, taking it as my definition. In a large part, it's why I became a private detective. I tried the respectable route, putting on a dress, going to a so-called good job, a bank, no less, Monday through Friday nine to five. But I didn't want to count my success in memos, reports, and if someone else earned a profit from my forty hours a week. One Friday afternoon I told my boss, "I'm leaving." "You don't have to tell me that," he said. "Yes, I do. I'm not coming back." And I didn't. I did odd jobs, bartending, waiting tables. One day I saw an ad for a security guard, night shift. I worked there for almost a year, never in the common hours, so I was usually by myself. On one job I ended up working with a private detective. He called a few weeks later and hired me as his assistant. We worked together well until he asked me out. When I told him I was gay, he said it didn't matter, but it did. Several months later, I went solo, back to my comfortable role of outcast, rejected again.

But Lindsey will probably point out to me, if she doesn't point out that I'm wallowing in self-pity, that these weren't all rejections. Some were losses, like my father's death and my friends leaving. And, although I had lost contact with Misty and Brian, Ned and I had become friends. When he'd come east to go to law school, we'd ended up rooming together during my senior year in college. To this day we remain close. My cousin Torbin and I found each other because we had turned into the lavender sheep of the family.

My ambivalence seesawed back and forth until it was time to go. An upswing caught me and I left my apartment, got in my car, and headed uptown to Lindsey's office.

"Hello, Micky," Amanda greeted me. Seeing me alone, she added, "I gather Cissy's not going to be here today."

"No, she isn't."

"You could have phoned to tell us that," Amanda said agreeably.

"I could have. But I wanted to talk to Lindsey for a little bit and I knew she'd have some free time now."

"I'll tell her you're here," she replied, the expression on her face inscrutable. She went down the hallway to Lindsey's office.

I wanted Amanda to think that I had just dropped by to talk about Cissy, not that I wanted anything for myself. But maybe she was so used to the overlays people put on themselves, she could easily see through mine.

Lindsey came out of her office. To Amanda she said, "You can go if you want."

"Thanks. I have a few more things to enter on the computer. Then I'm gone."

"Come on back," Lindsey said to me.

"I'm sorry. Am I keeping you? I thought you had other patients."

"None scheduled today. But that's okay. I'd just be doing paperwork." Lindsey smiled at me, then took my arm for support as we walked down the hallway.

"If you're sure."

"I'd much rather talk to you than do paperwork." She let go of my arm to close her door. "Make yourself comfortable."

"Should I sit on the couch or a chair?"

"Whichever you prefer." She took my arm again, but left it to me to choose which way to lead.

"Only if you let me know the deep symbolic meaning of one over the other," I replied, her hand a warm point of contact. The simple touch felt good.

Lindsey laughed, then said, "Why don't we both sit on the couch?" After we got settled, she let go of my arm, and asked, "So, what's happening? What can I do for you?"

"How about solving all my problems?" There, that was a start.

"This afternoon?"

"Maybe just my most pressing ones."

"Such as?"

Not a coherent sentence came to me. Everything jumbled in a competing pile. Cordelia, Cissy, my investigation of child pornography, and what it was costing me, my own history of incest, I didn't know where to begin. "Hell, I don't want to bore you with my problems," I finally stumbled out.

Lindsey said, "I don't find you boring." Then she asked, "How's Cissy?"

"I don't know," I admitted. "Barbara decided she didn't want any queer trash hanging around her kid."

"She told you to stay away?"

"Yeah. Only family is safe. Including her new boyfriend."

"How does that make you feel?" Lindsey asked. She didn't even sound like a shrink saying it.

"Like shit. I'm not a child molester."

"Barbara Selby probably knows that."

"What do you mean? Why did she kick me out?"

"We don't know who did it, so she can't unleash her anger at him. You and I, particularly you, are the messengers. She blames us."

"If we're to blame, she's not." I added, "Do you think she'll ever stop blaming me?"

"That depends. If she's intelligent and honest, she'll work through it. Or if the real culprit is caught."

"If not?"

"Then not. It's something she has to work through."

"I think she will."

"Then she probably will. You know her better than I do. You're a good judge of character," Lindsey said, giving strength to my statement that Barbara would come around. Her easy confidence in me felt good.

"Thanks. Let's hope I'm right."

Lindsey gave me a quizzical smile on being thanked, but didn't question it. "Have you seen Cordelia lately?" she questioned.

"No, no, I haven't. Have you?"

"Yes, I saw her at that benefit last week."

"Oh," I said shortly.

"You sure you two are broken up?"

"Yes. You know how it is, you always want to make sure your ex-lover is with someone stupider and uglier than you."

Lindsey laughed. "Well, the woman she was with isn't as attractivc as you are. I didn't have a chance to talk with her long enough to find out how smart she is."

"That was quick." I hadn't really expected Cordelia to be going out with anyone.

"What?"

"Cordelia finding another lover."

"I don't know that they were lovers."

"Yet." Then in an attempt to be flip, "Well, that's unusual, Cordelia finding someone before I did."

"Why's that?"

"I am…" I looked for a polite way to say it.

"The more sexually experienced one in the relationship?" Lindsey suggested.

"To put it mildly."

"You've had a lot of lovers?"

"Yes."

"How many?"

"Enough to have shocked Cordelia," I replied, my mind still on her.

Lindsey chuckled. "That's not so hard to do. She has a naïve streak."

"Conservative," I amended. Then I asked the question that had been bothering me for so long. "Were you ever lovers?"

"Yes," Lindsey answered. "But it was a long time ago."

So Lindsey did sleep with women and she had slept with Cordelia.

"You sure you two are finished?" Lindsey must have heard something in my voice.

"Yes, I'm positive," I answered, my tone firm.

"Because if you weren't, I wouldn't do this." She took my face between her hands, looked into my eyes for a moment, and then kissed me. It was a long, lingering kiss, the tip of her tongue playing at my lips.

I didn't know what to do except respond. I had not expected this. I had come up with dozens of scenarios, but none of them had included Lindsey kissing me.

Being kissed felt good, the warmth of her hands on my cheeks nourishing. After Cordelia and the easy touching she offered, the absence of it felt stark and lonely. Maybe I didn't desperately want Cordelia back, maybe I just wanted someone to hold me.

"I think you're a very handsome woman," Lindsey said, breaking our kiss for the moment. Our lips were still almost touching. One of her hands traveled from my cheek, down inside my shirt, pausing on my collarbone, but promising other destinations. The other hand found its way into my hair. She again pulled me to her, her mouth opening and the play of her tongue more forceful.

I put my arms around her, aware for an instant of the difference in her size and shape. I had gotten used to holding Cordelia, tall and broad, her breasts full, stomach rounded. Lindsey was smaller, her shoulders not so wide, her waist perfectly trim.

Yet part of me was saying, *No, I don't want this*. At least not yet. There were things I wanted to talk about, to release from the rattling cage my brain had become. *Maybe afterward, she'll hold me and we'll talk.* This time I saw that bargain for what it was: I'll have sex with her, it feels good, why not? But more importantly, if we have sex, if she gets what she wants, it will connect us, and maybe I can get what I want. If I refuse the sex, I risk her rejection, that she won't listen to me, and then I won't even have her touching me.

Lindsey shifted, breaking our kiss long enough to lay me down on the couch, then began kissing me again, this time her tongue was deeply in my mouth. Her weight and warmth on top of me was a powerful reminder of how much I wanted to be held and made love with.

So what are you complaining about, I chided myself? Isn't this the therapy fantasy? To have a stunningly beautiful shrink take you on her couch? Wasn't I enjoying having Lindsey on top of me, kissing the hell out of me? Yes, of course. But it also scared me and made me wonder if this was all she wanted from me.

My hands kept moving, pressing her close to me, as if desire and the physical could banish my uneasy thoughts. Lindsey's hand slipped under my shirt, coming up from my waist. Her fingers encircled my breast, teasing and pushing it, until she suddenly sat up. She took off her blouse, laying it over the back of the couch, then her bra. She gently tugged my shirt up and over my shoulders, laying it on top of hers.

"That's much better," she said as she spread herself over me.

The full warmth of her breasts on mine was a contact so directly erotic that the physical did take over. It became a given that we were going to make love. Our kisses were sloppy, wet and open-mouthed. She sucked on my tongue, taking it into her mouth. My hips rose against hers, and my hand cupped her ass, pulling her into me.

"Yes, that's it," Lindsey murmured. Her lips moved down my throat to my breasts. She kissed them with the same fervor she had used on my lips, her tongue leaving long wet streaks, sucking on my nipples until they were full and very hard.

I had my hands in her hair, holding her to my breasts. She pulled away from me for a moment, holding herself up on one arm as she undid my pants.

My hips again arched as her fingers slid under the waistband of my underwear. She traced my outer lips, then moved her hand to my thigh, then back between my legs, her whole hand covering, pressing in on me. One finger slowly slid between my inner lips, teasing around my opening.

Then Lindsey took her hand away and said, "Take your pants off."

I raised my hips to accommodate her tugging them off. She pulled my pants down all the way to my ankles, then left them there.

"You, too?" I asked.

"Not yet. Spread your legs for me," Lindsey instructed. This time her fingers weren't teasing. One, then another, entered me, pushing deeply inside. At first she moved slowly, all the way out until just the bare tips of her fingers remained in me, then deeply in until she could go no further. Then she stopped, holding her fingers inside, and began kissing me again. Her tongue was in my mouth like her fingers were in my cunt. She began moving both her fingers and her tongue, playing inside me in two places. My hips began arching in answer to the probing of her fingers. Finally, I had to pull my mouth away from hers to let out a moan.

"I want to make you come," Lindsey whispered to me. "Should I keep fucking you? Should I go on your clit? Hard? Soft?"

"My clit," I breathed out. "Around it." Then I gasped as her fingers found where I wanted them to go.

Her head lay on my breast. I tightened my arms around her shoulders, letting myself fall completely into her touch, feeling her fingers as they thrust deeply into me, moaning after them as she withdrew, only to plunge in again. She quickly fell into my rhythms, riding the arch of my hip, playing with my clit, then off for a moment, until orgasm convulsed through me, wave after shuddering wave.

When my spasms subsided, we lay still. Off in the distance a horn honked, in the office the ticking of the clock, these seemed loud with our passion now stilled.

I looked down at Lindsey as she lay on my breasts, her hair tousled. I brushed a strand of it back into place and wondered, Is this a beginning? Will we hold each other again? And suddenly, I wanted a new and perfect starting place, where I didn't have to look back on my mistakes and false steps.

"Hey, your turn," I said softly as I ran my fingers through her hair.

"Um," Lindsey replied, slowly lifting her head. She kissed each of my breasts, then said, "I've forgotten how much fun it is to make love to a woman."

"Who do you usually make love to?" I questioned, with a feeling I wouldn't like the answer.

"I consider myself bi. It's been a few years since I've had sex with a woman, though."

"Oh."

"Does it bother you?"

"No." But it did, so I changed it to, "Well, maybe."

"Why?" Lindsey asked.

"I guess I've had too many so-called straight women dally with me, then run screaming back to their safe little heterosexual lives."

"You've been hurt by it?"

"If every bisexual woman admitted, 'Yeah, I've fucked a woman, too,' to someone other that the woman they've fucked, we'd have a revolution."

"You're probably right," Lindsey agreed. "We change the world one piece at a time. For what it's worth, I've tried to be honest about who I am, in more places than just the bedroom. I do have a few, dropped jaw, gaping mouth level shocks notched on my belt. More than anyone else I know."

"I guess it counts for something," I said. "But I've got you beat in the shock department."

"Yeah?"

"There are several dictionaries, in which if you look up self-righteous, you'll find the picture of my Aunt Greta."

"And you've shocked her at every family gathering?"

"From the time I was ten until I was eighteen, I lived with her and my Uncle Claude. On good weeks, I could shock her seven days out of seven." I wondered why I was bringing up Aunt Greta at a time like this.

"Must have been hard on you. How do you feel about her now?"

"You're in an awfully compromising position on your couch to turn into a shrink on me."

Lindsey laughed, then said, "That's true."

"Why don't you take off your pants and get on your back?"

"Okay," she said, hesitating before continuing, "But it's hard for me to be on bottom. And...perfect Lindsey ends at the waist." She stood up, and matter-of-factly took off her pants, watching my face for any emotion. Stepping out of them, she got tangled and lost her balance. I reached out to steady her.

"Thanks," Lindsey said, resting her hand on my shoulder, letting me look at her.

On one leg a scar ran from her hip almost to her calf. On her other leg there were several deep scars, the longest ending just above her knee.

Some of them were the jagged, tearing scars of an accident, others cleaner, precise man-made scars from operations.

"I'm sorry," I said.

"Don't be. I survived." It was a short, closed reply. Lindsey picked up her pants and threw them over a chair. "Lie down. Let me get on top of you."

"I could go down on you," I offered.

"Um, no," Lindsey said as she pushed me back down on the couch. "I haven't been very celibate lately. I'd prefer to stick to the safer stuff."

"Oh," I replied, nonplussed. Lindsey got on top of me. "Are you seeing someone?"

"Do you really want me to answer that question?"

"You just did," I retorted shortly. But she was lying on me, and I still wanted her.

"Does that change things?" Lindsey asked.

"Everything changes all the time," I muttered noncommittally.

"Do you want to stop?"

No, I didn't want to stop. I wanted to stay here, with her spread over me, her breasts meeting mine, where nothing mattered but touch and desire. But my reply was, "That hardly seems fair. I got mine, you don't get yours."

"Life isn't fair."

"How profound." Then I said, "No, we don't need to stop."

"Are you sure?"

"Let me make love to you," I offered. It was all I could think to offer, to keep her touching me.

"Thank you," she said and kissed me. She let up for a moment to say, "My legs don't work very well, but everything else down there is fine." She shifted again. "Sorry, I'm trying to get comfortable."

"Can you sit in my lap? Would that be a more comfortable position?"

"Yeah, I think so." Lindsey slid off me and I sat on the edge of the couch. She got back into my lap, sitting astride me. "I think this is okay. I'm not too heavy on you, am I?"

"No, you're fine. Relax, I can hold you."

"Hey, this is kind of fun," she said as she eased into me. "Bend your face up, I want to kiss you."

At first our kisses were gentle explorations as if some die had been cast that said, retreat, go back to the beginning, and start over again. Then we began deeply kissing. My hands ran down her hips, her thighs, as she played with my breasts. Gingerly, I brushed against one of the scars, letting my hand move down her thigh. Lindsey didn't flinch or move away. She almost seemed relieved that I didn't avoid part of her. I explored her legs, from her ankle, up to her calf, then her thighs and hips. I circled closer and closer and finally, I ran my hand between her legs, massaging her outer lips in against her clit. Lindsey gasped and broke away from our kiss. I moved my mouth to her breasts, running my tongue across an already hardened nipple.

"Yes, oh, yes," Lindsey murmured as my fingers found their way to her inner lips. She lifted one of her breasts, feeding it into my mouth. Her other hand was on the back of my neck, holding me to her.

I finally lifted my head and whispered, "What do you want? How do you want to come?"

"Give me everything," Lindsey gasped.

"Everything?" I offered.

She moaned in reply.

I reached one arm around her thigh, putting my hand between her legs from behind. I let two fingers circle the rim of her cunt, before I slowly went up her. I gave her a few deep strokes, then I moved my thumb to her ass. Lindsey shifted slightly, opening herself to me. I slowly worked into her ass, hearing her gasp, then feeling her open herself even more as I entered her. I let my other hand play around her clit. I fucked her in the ass and the cunt, until her juices were dripping down my hand onto my thighs. Then I went slowly in and out, taking her clit in my fingers, flicking directly against it. I did it slowly, making her thrust against me. I kept the rhythm unhurried and steady, feeling her get huge under my fingers.

As she came, she clutched me in a spasm, then let out a cry that slid into a low moan. Her hips rocked into my fingers, then away. I kept the pressure up and Lindsey came several times.

Finally, she leaned away from me, letting out a throaty laugh. "Let me catch my breath," she gasped.

I slowly took my fingers out of her cunt and ass. They made a wet, sticky sound. Lindsey shuddered at the movement. Then she kissed me deeply. I wrapped my arms around her waist, holding my slick hands away from her.

It was a moment of connection, perhaps not as shining and perfect as I had thought a few moments ago. But maybe there was a beginning here that could stretch into the future. I wondered if you could make love to a person without having, at least for an ephemeral moment, some primal connection that nothing else could offer.

Her intercom buzzed. "Lindsey?" Amanda said, "Peter called. He lost his keys and needs yours. He's on his way over here. I thought you should know."

"Okay, thank you." Lindsey said evenly. She disentangled herself from me and stood up. She took a box of tissues off her desk, grabbed several and put them between her legs, then offered the box to me.

Without a word, I took some, wiped my hands, then got several more for between my legs. Lindsey cleaned herself, then threw them in the trash can.

"Sorry for the rude interruption. I thought Amanda had left by now."

"Isn't it a good thing she didn't? Otherwise Peter might have shown up knocking on your office door," I replied sarcastically. "Or am I jumping to conclusions about Peter?"

Lindsey picked up her clothes, leaning heavily on the couch to balance herself. "Well, at the moment, we live together," she finally answered.

"Oh." I grabbed my clothes and pulled them on.

Lindsey hobbled to a chair and sat down before trying to put her pants on. I didn't offer to help. Her slowness in getting dressed prevented me from storming out. After watching her try and fail several times to get her bra fastened, I finally came over and did it for her.

"Does he help you get dressed, too?"

"Sometimes, if I ask."

"Does he know you like girls?"

"I've told him I'm bisexual."

"Does he know you do it on your office couch?"

"I don't tell him everything. I never gave him complete access to my life." She put on her blouse, then said, "I'm sorry that this happened. I know you're upset."

"Who's upset?" I retorted. "It was a quick, easy fuck. That's what you wanted, that's what you got. You're not the first married woman I've screwed."

"I'm not married."

"You just happen to be living with a man."

"I do, yes. I didn't mean to mislead you."

"But you just wanted sex with me."

"Is that such a bad thing to want? Can't we be sexual without having all sorts of baggage attached to it?"

"Maybe you can."

"And you can't?"

I let out a hollow laugh. "Yeah, I can. It's what I do best. Sex and nothing else. How asinine of me to want to change that."

Lindsey was dressed. I opened her office door and stalked out.

Amanda was still at the reception area, working on the computer. I shoved my hands into my jacket pocket as if I could hide where they'd been. Amanda was probably used to Lindsey's trysts here at the office.

"I hate computers," she said. "They never do what you want them to."

"Yeah, something like that. I'm late for an appointment," I muttered as I rushed through the waiting room.

"See you around," Amanda called after me.

I could feel the heat of a blush on my face. I hurried out the door and to my car. Not likely, not fucking likely, I thought.

I grabbed a napkin out of my glove compartment and wiped my hands again. Then I started my car and pulled out. The first thing I did was find a burger place where I washed my hands. I soaped them several times, scrubbing up to the elbows. After I finished in the bathroom, I stopped at the counter and got a soda, taking a deep gulp of it to wash the taste of her kisses out of my mouth.

Then I just got in my car and drove. I've slept with bisexual women before. I've even slept with married women, although it wasn't something I was comfortable doing. Sleeping with men didn't appeal to me, I felt no erotic charge with them. But that was me and my life and I didn't feel a need to impose it on anyone else.

Lindsey had wanted sex and I had wanted, if not love, at least a connection. She had gotten what she wanted and I hadn't. That was what made me so angry. We hadn't been equal and we hadn't been honest. At first, I blamed all the dishonesty on her, then I realized that I, too, hadn't been completely truthful. My dishonesty might have matched hers, my power didn't. We were on her ground, in her office, with her diplomas hanging on the wall. Lindsey wasn't insensitive or stupid. Her life was people's emotions and their troubles. She knew that I had recently broken up with my lover and that I had just been accused by a woman I had thought to be a close friend of being responsible for her daughter being sexually abused. Even I knew that my nonchalant answers weren't meant to fool anyone into believing I really didn't care, they were signals not to probe or ask questions, because, in truth, it still hurt too much to talk. If she couldn't, on some level, realize the turmoil I was in and how vulnerable it might make me, she shouldn't be charging money to listen to people.

Well, at least I'm not blaming myself this time, I thought. I guess that's progress.

I had driven out of the city. Only a faint glow remained in the western sky. The lonely stretch of road I was on opened into one of the small fishing villages that dotted the bayous. I was a good twenty to thirty miles beyond New Orleans.

My heart had been hurt, but not broken, at least not by Lindsey. I wondered what I would say to her if I ever saw her again. Did I even want to see her again? I remembered Warren Kessler and his story of confronting the uncle who had abused him. Suddenly, I wanted to see Lindsey McNeil again. I wanted her to know what she had done.

The dark country road slowly took me back to the lights of the city.

CHAPTER 30

Bright sunshine edged into my eyes, waking me up. The cool clouds with their threatening rain, had lifted. Today was the money exchange day.

Joey had left a few semi-panicky messages on my answering machine last night, reminding me (as if I needed it) of how important this money was and how much money we (*we, kemo sabe?*) could make. I had finally returned his calls and left him with the less than reassuring "I'll do what I can."

I took a long shower, then made a several-hours-of-waiting pot of coffee. After that, it was the ubiquitous daily chores while waiting for the phone to ring.

Karen didn't call until after four p.m.

"I have it," she said, her voice strained and tired. It sounded as if she had made a lot of phone calls to a lot of people and given a lot of made-up explanations.

"Where are you?"

"Out in Metairie. Can we meet at my place?"

"No," I said. I wanted to meet in an open public space. "Why don't we meet at the zoo parking lot? Far end of the row by the main entrance. I'll be there."

"The zoo. How appropriate," Karen answered dryly. "I'll be there." She hung up.

I called a cab, giving it the address of a corner grocery store a block away from my apartment. I had the taxi take me to a rental car place in the CBD. I didn't want to be driving my noticeable car, and I still had enough money in the bank to afford this.

The first car they offered me was a sporty red model that I turned down with a lame excuse, mumbling something about not liking red. The clerk ever so politely put the keys back and found a color more to my liking, unnoticeable navy blue. I only took the time to orient myself to the basic car functions, steering, gas, and gear shifts, and the lights, as it would be dark soon, before zooming uptown to meet Karen.

The rental car was fast and quiet and, unlike my car, had a radio that worked. Not wanting to leave Karen sitting in a parking lot with fifty thousand in cash, I sped up Magazine Street to the zoo. Even so, Karen was there, waiting for me.

The zoo was closing, the parking lot quickly emptying. There were several open spaces surrounding Karen's car, its red color turning to crimson in the setting sun. I pulled up next to her and stepped out of the car. Before she had the chance to do more than recognize me, I opened the passenger side of her car and got in.

"You got a new car?" She looked at it over my shoulder.

"Rental. Mine's still parked in front of my apartment."

"Oh," Karen said, then she asked, "Is this dangerous?"

I shrugged, then since she was fronting the money, answered, "No, not for you, it shouldn't be."

"I've got it," she stated. She pulled a briefcase from the backseat. "Banks don't like to give money out. Not in this amount. I could only get thirty thousand out of them."

"Damn," I said.

"I've got it all," Karen hastily continued. "I had to borrow the other twenty thousand from Cordelia—my cousin Cordelia."

"What did you tell her?" I asked, trying not to let my annoyance show. I didn't want Cordelia involved in this.

"God, I've told so many lies in the past few days." She paused for a moment, then said, "I told her I had a friend who was in trouble and needed the money. That I couldn't get to the cash until Monday. I even signed a note promising to pay her back as soon as I could. She wasn't happy, but she lent it to me."

"Did you mention my name?"

"I had to tell her who the friend was. I gave your name."

"Goddamn it!" I let out.

"I'm sorry," Karen stumbled. "I couldn't think of what else—"

"It's done now," I cut her off. "Did Cordelia say anything?"

"She just said okay, that she would do it. That's all. Not even the usual lecture about the kind of friends I have."

Cordelia. What the hell did she think of me now? I took the briefcase from her.

"Micky." She put her hand on my wrist. "Joey called me."

Damn him, I thought, wanting to explode, but holding it.

She continued, "He told me that if I didn't get the money that some bad things might happen to me. He said that you weren't going to protect me anymore. That you and he were partners." Karen looked at me for a moment, then away as if she was afraid to let accusation slip into her eyes.

"Joey shouldn't have called you," I said, mentally alternating between cursing him and trying to think of what I could tell Karen.

"Are you…working with him?" There was fear in her voice, her trust in me shaken.

"He thinks so."

"Let's go to the police, Micky," she said, a firmness underneath the catch in her voice.

"No, not yet."

"Why not?" she demanded. "He threatened me, he threatened Cordelia…"

"How'd he find out about her?" I interjected.

"I don't know. People know we're related. When you have money they pay attention to you," Karen spoke rapidly, her fear expanding. "He said he'd kill my cats, torture and kill my cats…oh, hell." She let out a wavering sob.

My brain churned. Should I tell Karen I was working for the police? What if Joey called her again and she let something slip? Would it put her in danger? I finally decided that I couldn't risk it. But I couldn't leave her sitting in fear and distrust. It might explode at any time in any direction. I could think of only one thing that would get her solidly back into my corner and keep her there. I put the briefcase down, then reached over and covered her hand with mine.

"Karen, please," I said, my voice gentle, "Please trust me just a little longer on this. If by Monday, I don't have what we need, we can go to the police." Her hand relaxed under mine, holding my wrist, no longer gripping it.

"But I'm scared. He scared me."

"I know. It'll be okay. Find someone to stay with for the next few days."

"My uptown friends? They'd smile and let him in if he threatened to wrinkle their linen jackets," she said acerbically.

"Stay with Cordelia. Tell her you're tired of your uptown friends."

"Reform? No parties, no drugs, no well-dressed shallow friends?"

"Your life?" I reminded her.

"My life, yes." Karen slid her hand down my wrist, twining her fingers with mine. "Do the right thing. It could be the latest kick. All right, I'll call Cordelia. She will probably be shocked if she believes me." Karen let out a small laugh. "You know, I used to think she was boring and out of it. But right now, you and she are the only people I feel I can really trust." She tightened her grip on my hand.

"I've got to get going," I said.

"Okay," she said, looking away from me. That wasn't the reply she wanted. "Will you be all right?"

"Me? I know what I'm doing. I'll be fine." I hoped I was right.

"Will I," she hesitated for a moment, "see you again?" Her other hand moved up my wrist, her fingers exploring under my cuff, an intimate gesture.

"Uh…probably," I answered slowly.

"For fifty thousand you should do better than that. At least lie better," Karen said, stung at my implicit rejection. "Can I at least tell Cordelia what's really going on?"

I was, I told myself, in some fashion, protecting her, protecting myself, letting some young girls keep their childhood, and for those who already had theirs stolen, offering, if not justice, at least the retribution of the law. "No, not yet. I will see you someday," I answered. Then I put my other hand on the nape of her neck, pulled her to me and kissed her. I held it for a moment, then released her and got out of the car.

"Good-bye, Micky. Please be careful," Karen called after me.

I smiled at her, letting her read into that whatever she wanted, then got into my car. I headed back to the CBD, to one of those tall anonymous buildings. There were still people in the building, dressed in their professional drag. I was somewhat out of place in my jeans, sweater, and beat-up leather jacket. Not to mention a briefcase with fifty thousand in cash. I got off the elevator at the seventh floor. A security guard stopped me. I gave her my name. She disappeared for a few minutes, then came back and led me through the locked doors and down a long hallway.

I didn't knock on the door, I just walked in. They were expecting me. Inside the office were O'Connor and three other men I didn't know. On a polished wooden table in front of them was fifty thousand in marked bills.

O'Connor introduced me as I handed him the briefcase. He passed it to one of the other men who opened it. The three men, as if choreographed, took the money from the briefcase and began counting it. No one spoke, the only sound was the whish of the bills. As they each finished their pile, they jotted down the amount, then passed their stack to the next counter.

Each of the men counted all three piles. Then they added their numbers up and, still silent, passed their sheets to the man who looked to be the oldest of them. He glanced across the sheets, scanning the numbers.

He finally said, "Fifty thousand."

I felt like I had passed some major test.

"Of course," he continued, "we can't match denomination for denomination since we didn't know the composition of your amount until now."

It took me a moment to translate that into "We won't have the exact number of twenties, fifties, and hundreds as you do." I said, "It doesn't matter. There's no way for the people who receive the money to know what we started out with."

The older gentleman nodded portentously, as if I were answering a matter of great importance. "Then you may take the marked denominations." He said it as a preacher might say, "Now you may kiss the bride."

Trying to prove I was a worthy suitor to his marked bills, I carefully placed the money into the briefcase. "Thank you, gentleman," I said, snapping the briefcase shut.

The older man nodded his benediction to me, his younger versions copied his motion.

"I'll walk you to the elevator," O'Connor said.

I didn't ask O'Connor who these men were or what bank they worked for. Time felt like a closing vise on me. Joey had made a serious mistake by threatening Karen. I had to get the money to him before he made other serious mistakes. I had no guarantee that Karen wouldn't tell Cordelia everything, at least what she knew. And most pressing of all, the children.

"Joey's getting desperate," I told O'Connor as we walked down the long hallway.

"That might be good. His desperation could be to our advantage."

"Not if he makes stupid mistakes."

"If it's dangerous, Micky, get out," O'Connor told me.

I hit the elevator button. "So far it's contained. I caught his one big stupid mistake."

"Can you be sure?"

I shrugged.

O'Connor shook his head. "It's too risky. I'm pulling you out."

"No!" The elevator arrived. I got on.

O'Connor followed me. "Getting yourself killed won't solve anything."

"So what are we supposed to do?" I demanded The elevator door hissed shut. "Let faceless men keep sticking things in little girls' vaginas? Let them take pictures of it?" I stabbed the first floor control. "What if you saw pictures of a young girl in leg braces? Would you pull me out then?"

O'Connor's head jerked just a fraction. For a moment he was silent, then he said, "If I thought anyone would hurt my kid that way, I'd kill them. I'd want to. That's a father speaking. But I'm not a father right now, I'm a cop. That's who's telling you to pull out."

"Give me few more days. If it doesn't break by Monday, I'm out."

O'Connor slowly nodded. The elevator came to a stop, its doors sliding open.

I slipped out and held the door for a moment. "Francois Brunette," I told O'Connor. "He gives Joey the go. But I don't know who gives him the orders." I let the elevator door shut. O'Connor would ride back up to finish whatever business he had to with the money priest and his acolytes.

I got back in my rental car and drove a few blocks until I spotted a pay phone. I called Joey.

"Mick," he cut into my hello. "You got it?"

"Yeah, I've got it," I assured him.

"Shit, I've been sweating bullets, no, make that bombs."

"Where do you want to meet?" I broke into his relief.

"Right, yeah. Where y'at? Why don't we meet at your place?"

"No, on the street. It's safer." I didn't want Joey in my apartment.

"How about Rampart near that bar?"

"On Rampart with fifty in cash?"

"No, I guess that's not the best place."

Joey wasn't being terribly resourceful. I decided to set the rules. "Elysian Fields. Between Chartres and Royal. Park on the downtown side. I'll be there." I hung up on him.

Below the French Quarter is a part of the city called the Faubourg Marigny. Elysian Fields bisects it. It is a broad, open street, with enough traffic zooming by to give you the protection of a constant stream of people without their intrusive curiosity.

I didn't park on the block I specified to Joey. He didn't need to know the kind of car I was driving. I crossed the street heading to our meeting place, looking carefully around me. I didn't want any of Joey's stupid mistakes creeping up on me. Not to mention your good old everyday mugging.

I didn't think I'd have to wait very long for Joey. I was right. I heard the distinctive roar of his black Porsche even before I could pick out its headlights. He squealed a U at Chartres to get to my side of the street, doing a less than perfect job of parking right next to me.

I sauntered over to his car and spoke through the passenger window. "In a hurry, Joey?" I didn't give him the briefcase.

He kept his eyes on it, as a cat watches a bird. "Yeah, shit, my neck's burning, I got so many people breathing on it. What took you so long?"

"I ran into a problem. Karen almost didn't give me the money."

"She didn't? That bitch."

"She almost didn't give me the money because you called her up and threatened her," I said in a deadly calm voice.

"Look, I was only trying to egg the deal on…I figured this is a new thing for you, you might need the muscle."

"I wasn't muscling Karen, I was sweet-talking her. You almost queered the deal by threatening her."

"Hey, I'm sorry."

"You shouldn't have done that, Joey."

"You're right, I shouldn't have." I had the briefcase, Joey was being very agreeable.

"I want you to stay away from Karen and her cousin and her cats. Don't ever threaten them again."

Joey heard the rigid edge of anger in my voice. "Look, I'm sorry, okay? I didn't mean nothin'. It was just words, I wasn't ever going to really hurt her."

"You already hurt her. You called her up, you scared her and you threatened her pets and her family. If you think words don't hurt, I'll tell every bar on Rampart Street that your dick never gets harder than a jellyfish and you measure it in fractions of an inch."

"Hey!" Joey yelled. But I still had the briefcase, so he calmed down. "Okay, okay, I get your point. Look, I admit it, I fucked up, okay? Okay?"

"Don't ever do it again," I finished. I still wanted to shout, "Don't you ever threaten Cordelia James!" But if I reacted like that, it would tell Joey something he didn't know.

I opened the door of his car and got in. I put the briefcase between my knees. "Let's go for a little ride. If you tell me what I want to know when I get out of the car, I'll leave the briefcase," I told Joey.

"Mick, I ain't got much time."

"Talk fast." I took a small notepad and pen from my jacket pocket. "I want to know what you know. That way, if you fuck with me again, I can run this without you. The photographer, the printer. Names, please."

Joey began sputtering out the list, all the little cogs in this big, ugly machine. "And that's all I know. Don't ask, I don't got their friggin' addresses," he finally finished up.

"What about Francois? Who does he dance to?"

"I don't know. I really don't know. But I'm working on it. This weekend's a go. By Monday, you and me'll both know."

"Okay. Why don't you take me to that bookstore on Frenchmen?"

"Sure, no problem." Joey, secure that the briefcase was his, was getting his confidence back. "We're still partners, right?"

"As long as you don't pull any more stunts on me."

"Hey, no way. Well, partner, we're taking a little trip on Saturday and when we come back we're going to be very, very rich."

"Where are we going?"

"Somewhere, does it matter?"

"Got to know how to pack."

"I'll call you on Saturday morning. Some things still aren't worked out."

"Such as?"

"Payment for a few things," Joey said, with a pointed look at the briefcase.

"Call me Saturday," I replied. We were at the bookstore.

"You know, Mick, you got brains and you got balls. We stick together, we'll make big bucks. I'm sorry about double-guessing you with Karen, okay? It's just I got used to leading with you following. But that's not the way it is anymore. Sometimes you lead, and I'll follow. I'll sure keep my paws out of your business." It was Joey's way of apologizing.

"Sure, Joey." I smiled at him, another fake smile for him to read what he wanted into. "As long as we understand each other. I'll hear from you on Saturday." I got out of the car.

Joey took off, ever so eager to pay his debts. So, Saturday was it, the big day. Zeke got busted and the operation reached its peak. But this time there would be a different ending. And by Monday, one way or another, it would all be over.

I went into the bookstore, but all I could find were trashy lesbian romances. The last thing I wanted to read about was someone else's happy, if fictional, love affair, and books I had already read. I got some grade A, high-level gossip from Alan, the bookstore owner and then headed back home.

I don't like waiting, but that was all I could do at the moment. Time still felt like a vise closing in on me.

Chapter 31

The next morning I was still waiting. I had not slept well, tension invaded my dreams. I tried to sleep late, but couldn't. Finally conceding that my tossing and turning wasn't helping anything, I had gotten up.

The phone was a tantalizing object. I thought about calling Barbara, demanding to know how Cissy was. Then I thought of calling Cordelia. Sometimes it went as far as her telling me she still loved me, but that was a fantasy too intangible to hold on to. I could call Lindsey and confront her. Or Karen to tell her I was sorry I misled her with that kiss, but I needed the money. I considered phoning Joey, finding out what he was doing, preventing him from making any more stupid mistakes. I even considered calling O'Connor just to connect with somebody. About an hour ago I had legibly copied last night's scrawled names from Joey and mailed them to him, several different versions in several different envelopes. It would serve no purpose to call him and repeat that. I wanted to call Danny and Joanne, but after my disappearing act on Alex's birthday, it would take more that just a phone call to make amends. And, after that, there was only the weather and the time.

I finally broke down and called Karen. Her machine answered. It gave a standard message, then added, "I can also be reached at…" and I recognized the number as Cordelia's. I wouldn't be calling Karen there.

Beforc the phone became too demanding a temptation, I decided to get away from it. I got in the nondescript rental car and drove. But even speed and motion and controlling a powerful machine didn't dispel my tension. I paid little attention to where I was going, a turn, another turn, a new street, whichever way seemed easiest.

The sun was low in the sky, the early evening approaching, and I realized that I was on a familiar block. Was it just chance that I came this way? The traffic opened up, making the left turn easy. I took it as an omen and pulled in, parking next to Lindsey's red car. Amanda's car was the only other one in the lot. It was just a little past five o'clock.

I got out of my car. I thought for a moment of hiding inside it, but if I was going to do this, timidity was of no use. I leaned against Lindsey's car so that she had to see me.

The warmth of the day followed the setting sun. I zipped up my jacket, then thrust my hands back in its pockets. Maybe Amanda and Lindsey were comparing notes. How many conquests this week?

I heard the door opening, then the sound of their voices, words robbed of meaning by the grinding of a passing truck. They rounded the corner of the building, Amanda carrying Lindsey's briefcase. Lindsey saw me first. She had years of experience at not reacting; the emotion that flitted across her face was too brief for me to discern whether it was surprise or anger or fear. Or just curiosity.

"Hello, Micky," she said evenly.

Amanda looked from me quickly back to Lindsey. Her emotions were easier to read, she was both curious and wary. Crazy and desperate people had camped on Lindsey's doorstep before. She didn't know whether or not I was one of them. "Hi, Micky," her greeting was more guarded.

"Hello, Amanda. Lindsey." I watched Lindsey, trying to get a sense of what she was feeling. Then, I told myself, don't worry about her feelings. "Can I talk to you for a moment?" I asked, looking at Lindsey. It was barely a question.

"Of course," she replied, her voice maintaining its practiced calm.

"Do you want me to stay?" Amanda offered, with another quick glance between the two of us.

"No, there's no need. Have a good weekend," Lindsey told her.

Amanda handed Lindsey her briefcase, then got in her car and drove off. I remained silent the entire time. Lindsey waited for a cue from me.

I crossed my arms over my chest, a barricade of sorts. "I need a shrink's advice," was my opening. "How do you say no when someone's making a sexual advance that you're not sure you want?"

"Is that what this is about?" Lindsey asked calmly. She set her briefcase down.

"I happened to be in the neighborhood. Or maybe it was just my subconscious."

"I didn't mean to mislead you…"

"No, you just omitted a few pertinent details, like living with someone."

"You're right. I'm sorry," Lindsey admitted.

"Why?" I demanded.

"I thought if I told you, we wouldn't make love."

"We didn't make love. We had sex," I shot back. "A quick fuck on your office couch, remember? Does Amanda know?"

"Good Lord, I hope not." Lindsey did seem taken aback at the thought.

"Does she suspect?" I pushed.

"Amanda's not stupid," Lindsey slowly acknowledged. "She knows Peter and I aren't on the happily-ever-after track. That I don't believe in monogamy." Lindsey sighed, then added, "She probably suspects."

"So that's your excuse to sleep around? Your live-in doesn't understand you?"

"I don't need an excuse to 'sleep around.' I like sex, having sex. I try to be honest and up front about my desires. I don't think love and sexual fidelity are the same thing. We substitute one for the other because we can measure one. You sleep with one person or you don't. Love can't be reduced to anything that simple and easy."

"How oh-so-fucking liberal of you."

"There are a lot of things I can't do anymore," Lindsey rejoined, the measured calmness gone from her voice. "I won't ever ski again, or hike anything that isn't short and tame. I can't even just spend a day walking around, exploring new neighborhoods on foot. But I can still have sex, still enjoy it as much as I ever did. I'm not going to give that up just to pay obeisance to someone else's morality."

"Oh, yes, the I-have-noble-reasons-for-fucking-as-many-people-as-I-can school of philosophy."

"What's the issue here, Micky? That my sexual life doesn't toe a monogamous line? Or that I had sex with you?"

"What's the difference?"

"The difference is that I have the right to live my life. I don't have to agree with you or reflect your choices. Until I involve you. Then we have to reach some sort of understanding. Do you believe I took advantage of you?"

"You're not stupid, Lindsey," I shot back. "We were in your office, your territory. I'd just been all but accused of being a child molester, recently broken off the most serious relationship I've had in my life, been working on a case that involves children being molested and having to relive… And watching the hell they go through," I covered. "I thought it might be nice to talk to somebody about a few of these things. I got sex instead. Maybe you don't consider that taking advantage of someone."

"I don't guess I thought…" she slowly let out.

"Deny it, Lindsey. Tell me how unfortunate it is that I'm so deluded."

"That's what I'm supposed to do?"

"Doesn't everybody?" I retorted acidly. I wondered what redemption I would get from this. Or would I just have more lies added to those I already had to crawl over?

For a long time Lindsey didn't answer. I didn't think she would, but finally she said, "No, not everybody. Truth can be harsh, but lies haunt you. You're right, I wanted you, so I nipped and tucked reality until it reflected my desire. I'm very sorry."

I had not expected Lindsey to apologize. I had no response for this. The only reply I made was, "Yeah, well…" Then I shrugged.

"You've been sexually abused, haven't you?" Lindsey asked gently.

This time I just shrugged.

She continued, "I don't want to repeat old patterns, particularly destructive ones. And, yes, I knew that, saw it. A lot of your involvement with Cissy had overtones of you saving her from something no one had saved you from. Is that a fairly accurate guess?"

I shrugged again, then managed to utter, "Does it really matter?"

"Of course it does," she replied. "Do you mind if I lean?" She waited for my quick nod before coming over to rest against the car. We were close, but not touching, as if she wanted to give me space without putting distance between us. "I realize that you're not comfortable talking about this. I won't push it. You may never feel comfortable with me. That makes me regret that I didn't pay more attention to what you needed and less attention to what I wanted."

"I'll be okay," I mumbled.

"Yes, you are okay and you will be okay," Lindsey said. "That's the amazing thing about people, the damage they can survive and still be decent and kind. As you are."

"Thanks."

"I am very sorry," she said, looking directly at me. "If there's anything I can do to make up for it…"

"Careful, I may think of something."

"I hope you do. I hate living with guilt."

"Can I ask one question?" Lindsey nodded, so I continued, "Were Peter's lost keys planned or accidental?"

"He may have planned it, but I didn't. To be honest, I'd considered seducing you for a while. I hadn't planned our adventure on the couch. Carpe diem is a favorite saying of mine. If we hadn't been interrupted, I would have suggested dinner—to explain a few things—and I wanted to spend the night with you."

"That makes me feel less used. Can I ask another question? If it's so over with you and Peter, why don't you just move out?"

"Because I own the house," Lindsey replied with a wry laugh. "Peter moved in with me. He thinks we can work it out. But unless he decides to make peace with my making the money and not being monogamous, I don't see this relationship being saved."

"I'm sorry."

"Why? I'm actually looking forward to the time alone."

"Still, you didn't start living with him in the hope it would end."

"Is that a comment on your relationship or mine?" Lindsey asked.

"Touché. No wonder they pay you the big shrink bucks."

"Good avoidance technique. But I'm not going to let you get away with it. Did you break up with her or did she break up with you?"

"Neither," I admitted. "I was supposed to go with her to her best friend's birthday and I stood her up at the last minute. I had to, something came up on the case, but…we haven't spoken since."

"What do you want?" Lindsey asked gently.

"I don't know…I guess for things to be okay…like they were with us."

"You want to get back together with her?"

"Yes, I guess I do," I answered softly, afraid to voice the desire for fear the words would turn into faint smoke on the wind.

"If it was over, Cordelia would tell you. I know from experience."

"What happened between you and her?"

"You really want the whole sordid experience?"

"Consider it payback."

Lindsey snorted, then said, "Okay. On one condition. Can we sit in my car and get out of the wind?"

After we were settled, Lindsey turned in her seat until she was facing me. "I first met Cordelia when we were both residents. She was fresh out of medical school, on her first rotation. I was three years ahead of her. I saw her in passing. Cordelia was even more shy then than she is now. I ended up working with her and another intern for a few hours one night. She was useful, he wasn't, but that was about it.

"An enclosed place like a hospital sometimes seems like four walls and a gossip mill. One night one of those awful cases came into the emergency room. A fourteen-year-old-girl, pregnant. Her family was in total denial, they'd written it off as weight gain. She probably didn't know enough about sex to know she'd done anything to get pregnant. No prenatal, nothing. It was a breech birth, the baby wasn't coming out, the girl had been in labor for hours. She was bleeding. By the time she got to the emergency room, she had lost a lot of blood and was in shock. She didn't survive and the baby strangled in the umbilical cord. Within an hour of their arrival at the hospital, they were both dead."

"My God," I said.

"Yeah," Lindsey answered, then continued, "Her family, mother, father, some uncles and aunts, were all in the waiting area. The attending doc decides he needs to take a woman with him. Cordelia's the only female doctor around. When they get in sight of the family, he suddenly cuts out, leaving Cordelia. He didn't have a great reputation, but this was pretty high-handed, even for him.

"Cordelia, with no chance to prepare, told the family that their daughter was dead, she had been pregnant, and that the baby was dead, too. There was quite a scene. From all reports, Cordelia handled it well, certainly better than the other doctor would have, but the family was pretty upset. A couple of versions of the story had the father taking a swing at her. In any case, it was a mess.

"After I heard about it, I decided to go find Cordelia and see if she was okay. I finally located her in one of the crash rooms, a hole in the wall with some beds in it for the residents to crash during their overnight calls. By the time I got there, she had curled up in a fetal position.

"Words just seemed useless, so I crawled into bed with her. I held her and she cried. Then, it just seemed the right thing to do, I made love to her. I didn't even think about the fact that we were both women. Worrying about sexual orientation seemed insignificant. She needed someone to touch her."

Lindsey paused for a moment, then said, "I did the right thing. To this day, I believe that." She sighed, then continued, "But people can't always be noble and virtuous, at least, I can't. Things went back as they were, our lovemaking confined to that one special need and time. I should have left it there, but I didn't.

"Several weeks later, Friday, I had the weekend off, and I ran into Cordelia leaving at the same time. I asked her to dinner and we went out. After that, I suggested dancing and took her to one of the gay bars on Bourbon Street. We danced for a while, this was before my accident. I was in a devil-may-care, randy mood, drinking steadily and I didn't want to go home alone. At the next slow dance, we stayed on the dance floor, and

I let my hands rove to places that weren't platonic. The song ended and I maneuvered Cordelia into a dark corner and got even more explicit.

"Then we stumbled back to her place, she lived on Dumaine Street, and we made love all night." Lindsey paused in her narration, looking away from me into the night.

"So that's how you became lovers? You were bored and Cordelia was available."

"I'm not proud of it. I was Lindsey, the golden girl. I had a big career in front of me. A shy woman three years behind me didn't fit into my plans."

"You had your fun, you dumped her," I interjected.

"We saw each other a few more times," Lindsey explained, "but I stopped returning Cordelia's phone calls, deluding myself that I was letting her down gently, when I was just avoiding being fair with her.

"I know," Lindsey responded to my look of disgust. "It wasn't the right thing to do. We saw each other occasionally at the hospital and we were polite. I was busy, I was co-writing a couple of papers, flying off to conferences, doing all the things a golden girl does.

"I began working with a noted doctor from Harvard visiting down here. Our intellectual passion turned into something else. At Mardi Gras, some of his distinguished colleagues came down to visit him."

"Of course," I snorted. "Men are so much more acceptable."

Lindsey shrugged and continued, "We went to a party and we drank a lot. Then we went to another party and drank more, and left that party with drinks in our hands to go to another party. We got in the car. My lover was driving. I ended up in the backseat, half passed out. I vaguely recall driving up Canal Street, the blur of those bright lights.

"I remember that split second of panic, instant fear—I never saw the other car, but someone did, and his terror became palpable. Then there was the scream of metal on metal, and, when that stopped, the scream of pain and shock from those trapped in the twisted metal. I just remember that nightmare vision, everything broken and out of place and blood everywhere.

"Then a few scattered memories, being pulled out of the car, the intense pain, the bright lights of the emergency room and thinking it so bizarre that I should be a patient. The next few days were a blur, pain and numbness that never balanced into any rest, and a creeping fear that something was terribly, terribly wrong.

"My lover had walked away from the accident with only a few

scrapes and bruises. I never saw him again. He quickly disappeared behind a barricade of lawyers.

"Two of the passengers of the other car, a mother and her son, were killed. The father and a daughter survived, although they were seriously injured.

"I wasn't very golden anymore. I was crippled and I deserved it, an arrogant drunk who killed a child. It didn't seem likely that I would be a doctor, let alone an important doctor." Lindsey was silent for a moment.

I said nothing. I didn't think Lindsey deserved the accident, but that was a road she had to walk.

Finally, she turned back to me, and continued, "The first time Cordelia came and visited me, I thought she was just being polite. A lot of people made quick, little runs by my room, then disappeared. But she came back. One night, when I was in pain and the on-call doctor was one who preferred me screaming to risking addiction to a narcotic, she stayed with me. Just holding my hand, until she finally convinced the doctor to increase my dosage.

"And once, when I felt sorry for myself and demanded of her, 'Don't you think I deserve this?' she answered, 'No, you've done nothing that deserves this.' I will always carry guilt for my part in the accident, but Cordelia's simple statement took me away from what I couldn't change, and into the future.

"Cordelia was the one who took me home from the hospital, and, when I balked at physical therapy, she pushed me. I couldn't walk. I refused to even try. One night, I sat in my wheelchair and moaned and wailed in my despair. Cordelia listened for a while, then she told me I was too much of a coward to try to walk.

"First, I was shocked that she would dare say that to me, then I was furious. I decided I would prove to her I couldn't walk. I heaved myself out of the wheelchair and stumbled no more than an inch or two before I fell. Cordelia caught me and said, 'See, it's a start.' She came almost every day. At times, she wold infuriate me, telling me I was weak and couldn't do it when I would complain. I'd get angry again and I'd walk. It took weeks, but I could finally walk across the room. Then she opened a door and backed into my bedroom to make me go even further.

"Finally, she had to back up until she was beside my bed. When I made it to her, I pushed her back across my bed and fell on top of her. She started to protest, but I took her face in my hands and said, 'No. I love you.' We made love. It was terrifying and it was wildly passionate. I didn't know what my body would do, if it would work. Cordelia was the only person I could possibly trust on that journey. When it was still there, when I knew I could give and receive pleasure, it was as if some dam had burst, some torrent of physical need.

"I kept her in bed for hours, we made love over and over again. I left bruises on her thighs and arms. She stayed the night, even though she had to get up early the next morning"

I felt a surge of jealousy. I knew I wasn't Cordelia's first lover, but that wasn't the same thing as hearing Lindsey describe this.

"After that night," Lindsey said, "I wanted to have everything I could have. To accept no limits except for the utterly implacable ones. I learned to drive again. Cordelia helped me. I knew I was safe with her, that she would get me home. But often, she would come through the door and we would make love, sometimes there on the floor.

"Finally, I was strong enough to finish my residency. That's when things began to change. Cordelia and I were still at the same hospital. Perhaps no one would have fired us on the spot, but it was clear, at that time, in that place, that being queer wasn't good for your career.

"We pretended to be just friends. We didn't ask to change our schedules to be together. She ate lunch with her friends and I with mine. Since people assumed we were heterosexual, we heard the comments. Cordelia was warned, 'The nurses are all dykes on the fifth floor. Don't go into a room with any of them if the patient's comatose.' The horrible jokes about AIDS were starting. We couldn't live together. Having the same address would be a dead giveaway. For two women.

"Cordelia and I hid that we were lovers. Little daily lies, a denial that permeated everything we did. A nice romantic dinner in some cozy restaurant? What if someone saw us? Grocery shopping? Do you know how intimate two women pushing one grocery cart is? If her car was in the shop, she couldn't take mine. What if someone saw Cordelia James driving Lindsey McNeil's car? Almost every day, in some way we had to deny we loved each other.

"And, bit by bit, Lindsey, the golden girl, came back, tarnished, with a limp. But I was co-writing papers, giving presentations, and people were paying attention to me.

"I was coming to the point where I had to make a career choice. New Orleans is not known for its psychiatric training. My ex-boyfriend's guilt pulled a few strings. I was offered a coveted position in New York. Cordelia didn't ask me to say no; she knew how much I wanted it." Lindsey was silent for a moment.

"So you moved to New York?" I prompted.

"Yes, I moved to New York. I was terribly busy, terribly lonely, and I missed Cordelia terribly. One night the loneliness got to me. I went out for a drink with coworkers. One of the men made it clear he was interested in me. After a few drinks, I figured one little roll in the hay wasn't going to hurt.

"Of course, Cordelia called and he picked up the phone."

"I thought you didn't believe in monogamy."

"I don't. But I had promised Cordelia not to sleep around on her. I cared enough to want to keep that promise. We talked. I wanted us to work out. She tried to find a residency in New York, but the only offer she got was a year away and she'd virtually have to start over again.

"I think if we'd gotten just the modicum of support that even the most wildly inappropriate straight couple gets, we might still be together. Love can have such odd requirements," Lindsey mused.

She continued, "I got an offer to go to Europe. But it would have meant leaving six months after Cordelia moved to New York. We let it go. She stayed in New Orleans and I accepted Europe.

"One day she wrote, 'Lindsey, I'm tired of being a shadow in your life. We've only seen each other a few weeks out of the last two years. I don't know who you are anymore. Let's not hold on to the past when there's no future in it.' After that she stopped writing me, I stopped writing her. I became involved with a French doctor, a woman. We had a grand, passionate affair that ended only when I returned to the States some two years later.

"On some days I think I owe Cordelia my life. It took me almost a year after I got back to America to find the courage to look her up."

"Do you think you might ever get back together again?"

"No, we've changed. I knew Cordelia as a scared young resident, now she's the director of her own clinic. We weren't there for each other as we changed and grew, we lost that connection, being part of the dailiness of each other's lives. Sometimes the only thing you can do is let the past go." Finally Lindsey was silent.

"I don't think I'd like you as a rival."

"I'll take that as a compliment."

"I meant it as one. Thank you for telling me this."

"You're welcome. Besides, it gave me a chance to give you my version before Cordelia can tell it her way. I must have had terribly pious Catholics somewhere in my background, I find I rather enjoy confessing my sins."

"I was raised as a Catholic. I hate confessing my sins."

"Probably because you and the Church don't agree on what sinning is. To love another person, to hold them, and touch them, is not a sin."

"No, it's not."

"Now I must confess one more. Desire. I still want you. I don't think that's appropriate under the circumstances, but that doesn't change it. So please get out of my car, before I do something inappropriate."

"Thanks for the warning," I said. I started to get out.

"Damn, I was hoping you'd say what the hell and stay around."

"It's the time and the place. Sex…isn't free and easy for me right now."

"I know. You have the right to say no. Don't ever let anyone take that away from you. I hope we can be friends."

"There are always possibilities." I leaned over and hugged her. I didn't trust myself to kiss her—that might keep me in the car. "Thanks for the offer, Lindsey. It does feel nice to be wanted."

"Take care, Micky. I mean that."

"I know." I gently shut the door of her car, then got into my car. I glanced at her one last time as she drove away.

Chapter 32

The phone woke me up. "Hello," I mumbled, sleep slurring my voice. I glanced at my clock—it was just after six a.m.

"Is this Michele Knight?" a woman's voice asked.

"Who is this?"

"Is this Michele Knight?" she repeated.

"Yeah, this is Micky," I responded. "Who is this?"

"Camille, the hurricane, you remember?" Her voice had an edge in it. Sounds of traffic were in the background.

"Of course I remember. What's happened?"

"Betsy's gone. She's not at the house, not where she hangs. I thought maybe Heart of Desire, though I warned her to stay away this weekend. I drove by, the place is locked up, barricaded, the police have been there. I can't find her."

"Could she have gone away? Out of town?"

"Not without calling me. She knows I would worry. Harm has come to her." Camille made it a statement.

"Do you think it's because she saw the children?"

"Yes. There could be other reasons. But I think that's it."

"What can I do?"

"Women who sell their sex die easily, our lives are low cost. A short paragraph in the paper for another woman gone. Don't let her disappear into silence."

"I'll try not to."

"Make sure the police don't forget about her. Perhaps they cannot find justice for her, but I want them to look."

"No, I can't promise justice, but I won't let the police put her on a dusty shelf and forget her."

"That's all I ask," she said softly. "Your sources, have they told you of the raid?"

"No, not yet," I admitted.

"Word on the street says it was three a.m. That Zeke was in his office with a new girl at his knees when they found him. They say he wasn't even given time to find his pants, that he was booked in his dirty underwear."

"Justice of a sort, don't you think?"

"Yes, I think. A little justice may be all we ever get."

"Where can I reach you?"

"You can't. I think it best that I move quickly. I probably will go some place else soon. But I'll call you to find out about Betsy."

"Do you have her real name? Address? It'll help if I can give that to the cops."

"Lia Gautier. She is exactly five-three, weighs—weighed one hundred and four pounds. She had a butterfly tattoo on her left inner thigh." There was just the slightest tear as her voice slipped into past tense. She gave me Betsy's address and then Betsy's mother's address. "I will call you someday." Camille hung up.

I slowly replaced the receiver. Camille was probably right. Betsy had seen the children. Even someone like Zeke had to know what kind of jail that would get him. It all made a sickening sort of sense. Men who would abuse children for money, would murder a prostitute to protect that money.

I was jolted by Camille's phone call. I couldn't go back to sleep.

I went to my case notes, jotting down this latest information. I reread them, searching for a pattern. But the only image I saw was of a snake shedding its once useful skin, now to be sloughed off and left behind. A prostitute killed, Zeke and his henchmen in jail, silenced by the damning evidence against them. Soon it would be Joey's turn, and then mine. The vise was tightening.

All I could do was wait for Joey to call. The hours stretched into oceans of tension. I was tired, but I didn't dare take a nap. I doubted that I could sleep anyway.

Finally, around five o'clock in the afternoon, the phone rang.

"Yes?" I grabbed it on the first ring.

"Hey, Mick." It was Joey. He seemed easy and confident. "So what's up?"

"The usual boring shit. What's going on?"

"Old Zeke got caught with his pants down. For real," Joey snickered.

I pretended I hadn't heard that from Camille and let Joey tell me about Zeke's arrest. I let him gloat for a bit before asking, "So what's going on with us? What happened to the trip you mentioned?"

"It's all set. Don't pack, don't act like you're goin' anywhere. We'll get stuff on the way, if we need."

"Come on, Joey, what kind of trip is this? Car, plane, bus? A little info among partners."

"A boat trip. A scenic cruise. It's a specialty version of the love boat. I'm in charge of it. You get to help me."

"Where is this boat? Where's it start?"

"I'll take you there, don't worry."

"Are there going to be kids on this boat?" I asked, trying to keep my voice neutral.

"That's what we're charging the money for," was Joey's cavalier answer.

"Where do these kids come from?" Neutral slipped away.

"Hey, don't get sentimental on me. Parents throw away kids every day. At least we feed 'em well."

"And if we get caught?"

"Who's going to catch us? The perverts who diddle little girls? No one'll believe the kids. Besides, this is the money. You take the risk, you make the bucks."

"What do we do at the end of the cruise? Throw the kids overboard? Do we make the final leg a snuff cruise? Pay extra and you can kill the kid you molest?"

"Since when did you get a conscience? Did you think they were using midgets for those pictures we've been peddling? You're in kinda deep to be backing out now."

Just a little longer, Micky, I told myself. Keep playing the game a little longer. Don't make Joey suspect you. "Sorry," I said, glad I was on the telephone. Joey couldn't see how tightly held my fists were. "I guess I'm a little nervous. These seem like awfully high stakes. But I guess that's how we get rich, right?"

"You got it."

"Is Francois still giving the orders?"

"That wimp? He never gave an order in his life. If he wants to shit he has to ask what color brown it should be. He was a middleman, he just passed things on. I'm tired of dealing with flunkies, so now I get the deal from the top dog himself."

"Who is?"

"I'm leaving in just a minute to meet him. I'll get the final stuff from him."

"You don't know who he is?" I persisted.

"Half an hour, the guy in the blue T-shirt. That's all I know. Then you and I are gonna meet. How about seven?"

"All right. Where?"

"The Heart of Desire. For old times' sake."

"They just raided it."

"I know. No one'll be there. And no one will expect anyone to be there. I gotta get going. I'll see you there, okay?"

"Yeah. See you there." He hung up.

I decided it was time to start carrying my gun. I threw a few things that I might find useful, like a flashlight, batteries, a lighter, and some tampons, into my knapsack.

I needed to call O'Connor. But even a pay phone seemed too risky—I didn't want anyone watching me. I got in the rented car and headed over to the gay and lesbian bookstore on Frenchmen. Its doors and windows were plastered with enough posters that nobody could see in. John was behind the counter. He said okay when I asked to use the phone, and just shrugged when I asked if he would stand at the door and keep watch while I made my call. A perfect gentleman, he even went outside the door, shutting it behind him.

I gave O'Connor a quick rundown of what Joey had told me. It was Saturday evening and this store wouldn't stay empty for too long. "Can you follow me?" I asked.

"In your green car? Sure, any rookie can handle it."

"I'm not in my car," I snapped. Tension and the press of time stretched my anger to a thin line. "It's rented, a navy Ford Taurus. Shit, I don't know the license number."

"What if we pick you up at Desire when you meet Joey?"

"Yeah, whatever. Keep in mind I might leave with him. He drives a black Porsche, vanity plate. Eat or be eaten. That's what it spells out."

"Okay. We'll keep you followed."

"One more thing." I heard John, outside talking to some potential customers. "Lia Gautier. She was a prostitute who saw some kids at the Heart of Desire. She's disappeared." I gave O'Connor the information Camille had passed on to me.

The customers came in the store. "I've got to go," I told O'Connor. "Don't lose me." I hung up, then thanked John on my way out.

"I hope you solve it," he called after me.

I glanced at my watch. It was a little past six. I wanted to make sure O'Connor had as much time as possible to set up the tail. I told myself that I wouldn't head for the meeting until a quarter to seven. That should give them time to get in place.

I walked down Frenchmen to Decatur, and from there cut over to the French Market. I tried to act like a tourist and browse, but I couldn't pay attention to anything I tried to look at. Finally, at twenty to seven, I gave up and strode back the car.

I tried to drive slowly, but my impatience made it hard. I wondered about the kids, were they already there? Was it only girls? So far, I'd only seen pictures of girls. Was Cissy one of them? No, she wasn't a throw-away child. Barbara would protect her. As she had protected her against me. Cissy probably wasn't even involved in this. Most likely she had been molested by an uncle, or Barbara's boyfriend, the usual places. It was only coincidence that led me to her and to this thing at the same time.

It will be over soon, I calmed myself. Joey will take you to this boat. The cops will move in. It will be over.

I took Elysian Fields to Law Street. But Law was a truncated and tortuous road, abruptly running into embankments and railroad yards. I had to backtrack and find another way. I hoped that it wasn't a metaphor.

In the dark of an autumn night, the unlit building that used to be the Heart of Desire became a black monolith. Even the tacky red lights would have been welcome instead of this dim shape. With only the headlights of the car to guide me, I nosed into the alley behind the building. Joey's Porsche was parked there.

When I cut my lights, all illumination disappeared. I quickly dug in my knapsack for my flashlight. I decided I liked the feel of my gun under my arm and left it there.

Trying to be discreet about using my flashlight, I made my way to the back door. Joey had left it ajar.

I closed it behind me, so the beam from my flashlight wouldn't be seen outside.

"Joey?" I called softly. I got no answer. Damn him, he could be anywhere in this cavern. I took a few more steps down the hall before calling out again. Still no answer.

The doors and stairs of the hallway were shadowy and sinister in the beam of my flashlight, the black very deep beyond its feeble glow. As I played it down the hallway, it caught a macabre sight: the mounted barracuda had been cut open, its stuffing hanging out like exposed entrails. It had probably been searched for drugs or other paraphernalia.

I assumed Joey was going to play a joke on me, jump from behind some door as I neared it. I made my way down the hallway to Zeke's office. It had been left in disarray. Papers were strewn everywhere, the file cabinets still hung open. The incriminating file was gone, of course, as was the box of pornographic magazines from where I had hidden it. And, most barbaric of all, crumpled under the desk was a pair of wadded-up men's pants. I poked them with my toe. I wondered if they were really Zeke's pants or just part of Joey's bizarre prank.

I backed out of the office into the hall. I started to call out Joey's name again, but I thought I heard a sound. I snapped off my light, listening intently in the dark. Several minutes passed and I heard nothing. Joey obviously had more patience than I had given him credit for.

Then I heard a soft, indistinct noise that I couldn't place. I kept my light off and inched down the hallway in the direction of the sound.

Again I paused, listening. I didn't care to be surprised in the dark by anyone. If this was a joke, it wasn't funny anymore. In the pitch black of this windowless hallway, my attention focused on listening, I heard nothing. No soft scrape of a shoe, no held breath slowly let out. As I stood in the hall, I had two distinct feelings, that I was definitely alone in the building and that something was very wrong.

Where the hell was Joey, I wondered. His car was in the alley. Was he somewhere in the neighborhood, running an errand, making a phone call, perhaps? Maybe Joey's double-dealing had been discovered. He could have been followed to the alley and never made it into the building.

The thought and the cold and the dark caused me to shudder. Then I remembered I had a couple of cops tailing me. All I had to do was walk out to the street and wave and I'd have some big men with guns surrounding me. Or petite women with guns, it didn't matter.

I heard it again, that indistinct sound. It was muffled as if a closed door was between us. The storeroom? I slowly crept down the hall until my hand found the edge of the door. I slid my fingers down until they were on the doorknob. Then I stepped away, my arm at an awkward angle. Slowly I turned the handle, alert for any sound in the room. Nothing. I opened the door an inch. Still nothing.

Then I kicked the door open, slamming it into the storeroom. I jumped back into the hall, in case anyone shot at the door.

Nothing happened. Once the crash and bang I had created died down, there was no sound, nothing. But somehow I didn't quite feel I was alone in the building anymore.

I reached inside the door, groping for the light switch. Initially I hadn't wanted to turn the lights on because the building was supposed to be empty and a light coming on was a sure sign that it wasn't. But now the dark felt too dense and I would do anything to cut through it. I threw the switch, the soft click amplified in the dark. The electricity had been cut off. I pulled my gun, although I kept my finger off the trigger. The dark had already spooked me enough. I didn't want to do something stupid.

I turned my flashlight back on and quickly swept it around the storage room. The arc of light showed an empty room, the floor littered with some broken beer bottles, the discarded trash from a fast food outlet, and a few cardboard boxes.

Then I noticed in the middle of the room a box with an envelope on it. Out of the careless chaos, it seemed deliberate. I walked to it. On the envelope was my name, strung together with crude, cut-out letters.

I reached for the envelope, then I heard that soft indistinct sound. It was very close.

I looked up and swung the flashlight around the room at eye level. The dirty walls stared back at me. I flashed the light up to the ceiling. Water had damaged it, the rotting tiles exposed rough wooden beams.

An incongruously bright yellow nylon rope was knotted to one of the bare beams. Joey hung at the end of it, his feet over six feet from the floor, as if his killer was trying to prove how strong and powerful he was. I barely recognized him. Someone had killed Joey and they had done it recently.

The indistinct sound I had heard was the soft dripping of his bowels, let loose at the moment of death.

I tightened my grip on my gun, my finger curling around the trigger. Whoever had done this had planned it, the hanging in this place at this time, the box with an envelope addressed to me left on it. I picked it up without thinking. The cops would probably prefer that I left everything alone. But it had my name on it—it was a clue in a game I had to win.

I looked again at Joey. Death had not been kind to him. His face was covered with blood and snot, his open eyes an alien stare blotted with hemorrhages caused by the rope around his neck. I slowly backed out of the room, save for the envelope, leaving everything as it was for the police to search through. They would be the ones to cut Joey down.

I quickly flashed my light up and down the hallway to make sure no one was there. As far as I could see, it was empty.

It was time to go introduce myself to my police escort. I headed for the alley door, pausing for a moment to put my gun back in its holster. Joey's rictus stare had shaken me. I needed to be more calm and in control than I was to be walking around with a gun in my hand. Only on TV cop shows is the gun in the right place at the right time.

Just before I went out into the alley, I stuffed the envelope inside my jacket. I intended to read it before I handed it over to the police. I would tell them the shock of finding Joey's body made me forget it.

I opened the door. Standing beside it was a very large man. Given that he wore three earrings and had his nose pierced, I didn't think he was a cop.

"Michele Knight?" he asked, his voice a rumbling bass.

Seeing no point in denying the obvious, I said, "Yes."

"I have been sent to be your escort. Would you please follow me?"

"Escort to where?" I didn't move.

"To the boat, of course." He started to go.

"Ahh…what about Joey?" I asked.

"I was only told to get you. I only do what I'm told." He smiled at me. I couldn't tell whether it was a friendly smile or the smile of a wolf at the sight of a lamb. This man was probably close to seven feet tall with the build of a sumo wrestler. It crossed my mind that he had killed Joey.

"My name is Algernon," he rumbled as he headed further back into the alley. "I'm leading you the back way so we will not be seen coming from this place. A wise move, don't you think?"

"Who would see us?" I inquired as I stumbled away from my car, Joey's car, and the police tail.

"I don't ask questions. I was told to find you here and take you to a certain location. I was paid well to do it."

At the end of the alley was a tall wooden fence. There were loose boards at the far end of it. Algernon shoved it open wide enough for us to get through. Gentleman that he was, he held the boards for me while I wiggled through, then he followed. We were in a garbage run, a place where the buildings leave their trash.

"Do you have a gun?" Algernon asked.

"Uh…no." I wasn't in a position to pull it on him. I'd be dead before I got my hand into my jacket. But hope springs eternal.

"What's a nice girl like you doing in a place like this without a gun?" Algernon chided me. "I have a few with me," he continued. "I can let you have an inexpensive revolver I obtained from a young man who didn't show me the proper respect. If you wish something more reliable I have a Smith and Wesson .38 and a Browning 9mm that we could work out something on. I also highly recommend the SIG-Sauer 9mm, but I don't care to part with mine."

"I lied, I have a gun," I admitted.

"Good idea. What kind?"

"Colt .45."

"Too big for most women, but you look strong enough to handle it."

"Who sent you?" I asked.

"A contact of mine passed this on to me. I do not reveal his name and he does not reveal mine."

My best guess was that there were two possibilities, the one I liked least was that Algernon had been sent to kill me. The other was that he really was sent to escort me to the boat. I couldn't read what was in the envelope if I was dead.

As we picked our way through the garbage I causally asked, "Can I see the Browning?"

Algernon was wearing a black leather trench coat. He reached inside and took out the gun, then handed it to me.

"Is it loaded?" I asked.

"It would be foolish to pull a gun that is not loaded. And equally foolish to carry a gun you cannot use."

I checked the gun. It was loaded. I suddenly turned and pointed it at Algernon. He stopped and merely looked at me.

"I just have a few questions," I said. "Have you been sent to kill me?"

"If I wished to kill you, would I hand you a loaded gun?"

"Probably not. But since it's my life, I need a better answer than a probably."

"No. I have not been hired to kill you. I do not kill without a reason. And my reason cannot be only money. Because then money rules everything. I was poor for too long to give it that kind of power.

"Last week, I killed a man. I was not paid to do so. He laughed as two of his little thugs beat and robbed an old woman. They beat her to steal nothing more than change from her food stamps. He dealt crack and he ran that block with no more remorse than a slave master would show to his slaves. He thought he would die young. He did. For his thugs, I merely broke their knees, now they will walk slower than the old women." He looked directly at me and said, "Until you pulled the gun on me, I had no reason to wish to harm you."

"My goal is for neither of us to get hurt."

"Good. Then we share the same goals. You may keep the gun if you prefer, but it would be a step toward our mutual goal if you would not point it so directly at me."

I lowered the gun slightly. I knew what O'Connor would want me to do. Tell Algernon thanks, but no thanks, and hightail it back to the street where my police tail was supposed to be. My only other choice was to go to the boat without any backup or anyone who even knew where I was.

If I didn't get to the boat, it would sail off with no one to stop it. The kids would be abused and dumped. I lowered the gun. "Let's go. We don't want to keep them waiting." I started to hand the gun back to him.

"Keep it until the end of the ride. It's my gesture of trust."

I followed him out to a quiet back street. There were a few people on the corner, but no one was near us.

"Here," he said, indicating a black, vintage Cadillac. "I will have to ask that you sit in back on the floor. My instructions are that you are not to be seen leaving this neighborhood."

I did as I was told, climbing into the backseat and getting on the floor.

"Lie down and pull the blanket over you. That way no one can look in at a stoplight and see that you are there. Certain people, like the police, would ask very awkward questions if you were seen like that."

The blanket was really a deep navy flannel sheet. I covered myself with it as Algernon had instructed and was glad to notice that it was clean. The car started and Algernon drove away. I wondered how long it would take my police escort to realize that I wasn't coming out of the building.

After a few blocks I cheated and pulled the blanket off of my head. But from my angle all I could see through the windows of the car was the dark night sky and an occasional streetlight. Frustrated with that, I took the envelope out and opened it. It contained several smaller envelopes and a word-processed letter to me. I could only read it in sections, when the street lights gave enough illumination to see by.

> Dear Micky,
>
> Congratulations on your recent promotion. As I'm sure you've noticed, Joey is no longer up to the job.
>
> You're going to take a boat ride, and at the end of it you will be a very rich woman. There should be an envelope with your name on it and the first installment. The other envelopes are to pay your crew. You will be traveling along the Gulf Coast, with stops in Biloxi, down the Florida coast and on to the Caribbean. You will get further instructions on the boat.
>
> There will be a crew of eight. They are all experienced seamen, each with only a few flaws that make them unable to get commercial work. Quince, the captain, assures me that he can control them. Keep watch, though, most of them are drunks if they get the chance. There are convicted pedophiles, so keep them away from the merchandise. (Unless it suits your purpose not to.)

> You will be in charge of the passengers and the four stewards who serve them. (To be picked up in Biloxi where you get your first passengers.) Whatever problems arise, you get to decide how to handle them. Make sure the passengers get what they've been promised. Exactly how that's done is up to you.
>
> In the alley you will meet your escort to the boat. That way no one can follow you or recognize your car.
>
> Happy cruising!

The letter wasn't signed. It didn't sound like Francois, but who knows what he had hidden in him. It was easier to believe Colombé wrote (dictated?) the letter. Cheerful callousness seemed to be his style. I stuffed the letter and smaller envelopes back into the bigger one and tucked it away in my jacket.

"Where are we going?" I chanced asking Algernon.

"To the boat," he replied. "My instructions are by miles and turns. It lists no destination or place."

"But just between friends, which direction are we headed?"

He laughed, then said, "Between friends, we are in Chalmette and will probably go a ways beyond it before we get to wherever it is we're going."

Now that I had gotten that hard-won information, there wasn't much to do with it. My plan of action was to get on the boat, ride it to Biloxi, figure out some way to get the kids safe, then call the police. And maybe I could find something that would tell me who had written that letter.

The steady ride of the car began to lull me into drowsiness. I fought it, telling myself that I needed to be awake and thinking. It would be better if I could get a message to O'Connor. It might take a while to convince the Biloxi police that something this bizarre was actually true. But Algernon was not a man who would let me stop and call the cops.

It might work out for the best anyway. Get on the boat, check it out, get as much evidence as I could, and make sure the kids were safe before I brought in the police. Maybe there'd be a radio I could use on the ship.

Suddenly the car stopped and Algernon said, "You're here."

I tossed off the blanket and sat up. We seemed to be in the middle of nowhere. It was a dark road and I could only see trees on either side of it.

"Here?" I questioned, not seeing anything that looked like a "here" to me.

"There is a path in the woods. It will take you where you need to go," Algernon explained.

"Here's your gun back." I handed him the Browning.

"Thank you." He smiled. "I wish you luck and success. As you well know, they are not always the same thing."

There was nothing for me to do but get out of the car, wave goodbye to Algernon, and watch him leave. As his car lights disappeared, the darkness became complete. There were no stars, no moon on this night. I had hoped to be able to move without my flashlight, but that wasn't possible.

I switched it on and found the path into the dark woods.

CHAPTER 33

The path was a narrow footpath. The beam of my flashlight revealed that the overgrowth had been recently trampled down. About fifty yards into the woods, I heard men's voices. I paused to listen. I couldn't catch what they were saying. Probably my crew.

Another twenty yards and I could see a faint light in the distance. It was the wavering light of a lantern or powerful flashlight, perhaps several of them. I came to a clearing that revealed a tumbledown shack. Flickering lights shone from several windows and the men's voices were a rumbling undertone. Pausing for a moment, I prepared myself to be a vicious, money-hungry bitch. I had to be cool and enough in control to walk off the boat in the next port and get the police. I thought about knocking on the cabin door, but decided that if I was in charge, I had the right to enter. I opened the door and walked into a kitchen with a rusted sink, a stove that didn't look like it had cooked anything in years, and a place where an icebox had been.

One man, drinking a beer and sitting in a chair that was leaning precariously, was the only occupant in this room. His chair almost went all the way back when I came in. He wasn't able to right himself without dropping his beer.

The thump of the beer brought another man to the inner door. A little taller than me, he had the wiry thinness of someone who does physical labor. His hair was a brown that had seen too much harsh sunlight and sea salt. It hadn't been cut lately; scraggly ends hung over his collar. His dark eyes were hidden in weathered creases. Years of hard drinking and smoking had aged him. "Who are you?" he demanded of me.

"Who are you?" I returned, then added, "Is Quince here?"

"Who's askin'?"

"Micky Knight."

"You're a girl?!" he exclaimed, obviously not at all prepared for my gender.

"Yeah, I'm a woman. What's your name?"

"Uh…Vern," he stammered out, still unable to get over my not being a man.

I took one of the pay packets out and waved it in Vern's face. Then I said, "I don't pay sexist assholes. You want your money, you'd better deal with me."

"Yes, sir…I mean, ma'am." He didn't like it, but he reached for the envelope. I kept it out of his grasp.

The other man, who may have been strong and sure like Vern was thirty years ago, was more concerned with salvaging his lost beer than paying attention to us.

"Good. Where's Quince?" I asked Vern.

"Uh…this way." He led me into the main room.

The flickering lamplight gave the room a hellish appearance. A large group of men sat around a table, gulping cheap beer. A stunned silence took over when I entered. Off to one side I saw a young girl, but that corner of the room was hidden behind the open door.

"Where's Joey?" an older man I guessed to be Quince growled out. He was tall and stocky; several days growth of beard covered his face and he wore a grimy captain's cap. He had the eyes of a man who only understood power.

"He got hung up," I replied without thinking. I ignored my unfortunate choice of words and continued, "He'll meet us in Biloxi." I might be able to use that as my excuse to get off the boat.

"So you're Micky? I'll be damned," Quince said, shaking his head.

"You're Quince?" I asked, not mentioning that he probably would be damned.

He nodded his head. Vern shut the door behind me. I purposefully didn't look into the shadowed corner where the young girls were.

"Are we ready to go?" I asked.

"You got the money?" Quince responded.

I pulled the pay envelopes out to join the one I had waved in front of Vern.

Then from the corner where the children were, a voice called out, "Micky?"

I slowly turned to look at Karen, not wanting to give anything away in my response to her. No, I thought, why the hell aren't you with Cordelia.

She was a blond shadow in that dark corner, surrounded by several young girls.

"What's she doing here?"

"Tying up loose ends." Quince shrugged.

Then I saw Cordelia sitting on the floor behind Karen. She was staring at me.

"Micky? What…?" She didn't finish her question.

"You know her?" Quince demanded.

"Not well. She knows Karen, that's how I know her."

"You can't be involved…" Cordelia said. "Not in this," she finally finished softly.

"'This,'" Quince mocked her, "is taking our little passengers on a cruise they'll never forget. You're involved in that aren't you, Micky?" He looked at me, probing for any reluctance on my face.

"Yeah, I'm involved with this," I answered, not looking at Cordelia.

"No," she exclaimed. "You can't…not…" Then she trailed off, a look of shock and anger on her face.

You can't react, I disciplined myself, clamping down on the emotions that churned inside me. "Yes, I can. I guess you don't know me very well," I answered. I still couldn't look directly at her. Instead I kept my eyes on Quince. He had to believe my act. But to convince him, I had to deceive Cordelia, too.

Quince asked pointedly, "You got the money?"

I tossed his envelope across the table to him, then called out the names of each man in turn as I handed out their money. Vern got his last. Handing out pay packets certainly made it look like I was involved.

After counting his portion, Quince stood up and said, "Okay, let's go."

"Can't we take the blond with us?" Vern whined. "No one will know if she survives a few more days."

"What are you planning to do?" I asked Quince, trying to keep the agitation out of my voice.

"Fire," he said laconically.

"Wouldn't it be easier to take them with us and dump them overboard?" I asked. Even though my back was to her, I could still feel Cordelia's stare.

"No. No brig on the ship. I can't be bothered guarding them."

"Micky, please," Karen begged.

Quince threw two sets of handcuffs on the table. "We cuff 'em and leave 'em here. Unless you've got a better idea," he challenged me.

I didn't. That was the horrible thing. "Load up the kids," I said, to buy time. Maybe if I got enough men out of here I could chance pulling my gun.

"This child has a high fever. She needs some sort of medical care," Cordelia said. She held one of the girls in her arms.

"What are we supposed to do? Call a fuckin' doctor?" Vern let out.

"She's a doctor. She goes with us," I ordered, pointing at Cordelia.

"You'll watch her?" Quince demanded.

"She's useful. For now. Yeah, I'll watch her."

"The other one stays, then," Quince said, his words leaving no choice. I had won with Cordelia, but I wasn't going to win with Karen. Quince wasn't going to give me that kind of power, even if it meant burning a woman alive.

The children and Cordelia, you still have to fight for them, I told myself. "Whatever." I shrugged. Cordelia turned away. She couldn't stand to look at me anymore.

Quince just nodded. Vern picked up one of the sets of handcuffs.

"C'mon, girlie," he called to Karen as he began stalking her.

"Get the kids out of here," I ordered.

"Let 'em watch," Quince countermanded me. "Let 'em see what happens if they don't behave."

*If you pretend to care, they'll use it against yo*u. The girls would be out of the room by now if Quince hadn't wanted to use them against me. I wouldn't make that mistake again.

"No, you can't!" Karen screamed as Vern lunged at her.

"C'mon, girlie, you can't get away from me," he baited, a savage grin on his face. He grabbed her arm, jerking her to him. "So I hear you like it with girls, huh?" he hissed at her.

Karen used her free hand to claw him, raking his face from his eyebrows down to his chin. Vern let go of her, howling in rage. Some of the other men began mocking him. Several of the children were crying in terror.

Vern lunged at Karen again, tackling her and throwing her heavily to the floor.

I edged away from the fight until I was next to the table. Karen screamed as Vern began pummeling her. While everyone was watching them, I grabbed the other set of handcuffs. And the key that went with it. I put the key in the small change pocket of my jeans; I couldn't risk dropping it, but it had to be close at hand.

"You little queer girlie," Vern shouted at Karen. "I'll teach you." He grabbed her face and tried to kiss her, but she spat at him and jerked away. He began hitting her again.

It was time to stop this. I came around behind Vern, grabbed his shoulders, and yanked him off Karen.

"You stupid asshole," I yelled at him. "Can't you cuff a girl without beating the shit out of her? Just handcuffs, it's weird sex and the building caught on fire. Handcuffs and internal injuries, it's murder. Use your fucking brain." I locked the handcuff around one wrist, then grabbed her under the shoulder and lifted her off the floor. Karen didn't protest. I couldn't be nice to her. I hoped she didn't do anything that would make me hurt her. I hauled her across the room to an exposed pipe, pulled one end of the handcuffs around it, then locked her other hand, leaving her fastened to the pipe.

"There, that's how it's done."

Vern glared at me before sputtering out, "I bet you're queer, too. I bet you want to do it with her."

"I already have, Vern," I said calmly. "Too bad you'll never get the chance."

"Fuckin' dyke," he muttered.

"With you as the alternative, what choice do we have?" I know it's an old line, but Vern had probably never heard it before. "Now, why don't we get out of here?" I needed to give Karen the key.

"After you," Quince said. He wasn't going to let me out of his sight.

"Not going to kiss your girlfriend good-bye?" Vern sneered, his ego in pain.

I started to retort, "Why, so you can get your cheap thrill of the year?" but instead I replied, "That would be fitting, wouldn't it? Better me than you."

I turned back to Karen, at the same time I put my hand in my pocket for a second, then reached up and wiped the sweat off my face. And hoped that moving, with my back to them, no one noticed me putting the key in my mouth. This wasn't what I would have chosen as an ideal key passing ploy, but it was all that presented itself. Karen looked startled to see me next to her again, as if she was wondering how I was going to betray her this time.

"Bye, Karen," I said, not wanting to talk much with a key in my mouth.

She shook her head in disbelief, her eyes wide and terrified. I took her head between my hands. She shrank away from me, forcing me to lean into her. Then I kissed her. Karen didn't fight me, but she didn't respond either, her lids a hard line beneath mine. I increased the pressure, prying her lips open with my tongue. I couldn't risk transferring the key until I was sure it wouldn't slip out and fall to the floor. Finally, Karen began to react. Using my tongue, I maneuvered the key out of my mouth and into hers. She gave a slight intake of breath, but that was all.

I held the kiss a little longer, giving her time to get the key securely under her tongue. Then I broke it off. I wondered what Cordelia was thinking.

"Have a nice life, Karen," I said as I backed away. "Wave good-bye to New Orleans." I pointed in the direction of the city, giving her some indication of which way to head for civilization. I hoped Quince and his boys assumed that I was having a sadistic time of it.

"You want to light the fire now or should Tilman wait until we cast off?" Quince asked in a detached voice. He could be asking if I wanted a roast beef or ham po-boy.

"Let's cast off first. On the off chance that anyone sees the fire, I don't want to be around."

Quince nodded, then said, "You heard her, let's go."

Tilman was the kitchen drunk. Not part of the crew, he tottered along behind us. Several other men led the way, Cordelia and the children between them. I followed, with Quince and Vern behind me.

I had miscalculated, I thought as I watched them walking before me. I didn't think that Karen knew enough to be a threat. But these men were ruthlessly thorough. She could identify Joey. That was enough of a loose end that it had to be tied up. And because Joey had scared her, and I probably did, too, she had turned to the one person she knew she could depend on. Cordelia. No, not her, I suddenly wanted to scream, grinding my teeth to keep silent. I had been the one to suggest that Karen stay with Cordelia. Now Cordelia became another loose end.

We walked silently through another fifty yards of forest until we came to the levee. On the other side of it was a small dock, dwarfed by the broad expanse of the Mississippi River. Tethered to the wharf was a large yacht, probably eighty or ninety feet in length. It was a handsome ship, looking the part of a small cruise boat. As I came down the levee, I read her name, *Earthly Delight*.

"You need to get secured," Quince said to me, with a nod at Cordelia and the kids. "Vern can show you where," he added as he passed me on the gang plank.

"Hurry up, I got other things to do," my good friend Vern snarled. He ducked into a entryway, not waiting for us to follow.

"This way," I said as I tried to follow him.

“And if we don’t go?” Cordelia said coldly.

One of the men was on the dock below us. Other voices were close. I couldn’t tell Cordelia what was really going on. “Just do it,” I said, taking her arm.

She jerked away from me, then picked up the sick girl and carried her into the passage. I ushered the rest of the children in behind her.

We were in a narrow hallway that cut across the ship. It led to a center hall that ran the length of the boat. Vern was waiting impatiently for us at the end of it.

“In there,” he snapped, kicking open the door of a cabin.

Wordlessly, Cordelia and the children filed in.

“Here.” Vern shoved a padlock into my hand. “Keep ’em locked in. Your cabin’s here.” He jerked his head at the one across the hall. “And stay out of our way.”

He pushed past me, “accidently” running his hands across my breasts as he went by.

It wasn’t a smart thing to do, but I lost control. I kicked Vern in the back of the knee, then grabbed his hair, jerking her head back as he went to his knees. I put the barrel of my gun against his cheek, just under his eye.

“Don’t you ever fuck with me again. You behave yourself and maybe I’ll forget what an asshole you are and I won’t tell Joey you’re too much of a fuck-up to have on this boat.”

Vern started to struggle, but I shifted my gun so that it was pointing at his eye.

“Look, sorry. I had a few beers,” he mumbled.

“Just stay away from me and we’ll both bc happy.” Then I shoved him down the hall, but kept my gun out.

Vern stumbled to his feet and with a backward glance at my gun, hurried out. I stayed where I was for a few minutes, making sure he was gone.

Cordelia was standing at the door of her cabin, watching me. “Was that necessary?” she asked harshly.

“Yes, it was,” I defended, although I wasn’t sure I’d done the right thing. Vern might leave me alone or he might be out to get me.

“Why didn’t you use your gun to save Karen?” she spat at me.

One of the other men came in the hall. “Hey, Quince wants to talk to you,” he called to me.

“Is there anything you need?” I asked Cordelia. The man was waiting to take me to Quince.

“Other than the obvious? Karen alive and the children off this boat?”

She glared at me for a moment, then said, "If you have a medical kit anywhere, I could use it." She went back into the cabin.

"I have to lock you in," I said as I started to shut the door.

"Whatever," she answered, but she didn't look at me.

I padlocked the door. It would keep them in, but it would also keep the crew out.

"Hi, my name's Ron," the crewman said. "Do you think I can play with the kids sometime?" he asked as we went back out on deck.

"Uh…we'll see," I said, glad I was behind him and he couldn't see my expression. I had no intention of doing anything other than using Ron's desire against him.

He led me to an upper deck and from there to the bridge. Quince dismissed him with a wave of his arm. I put my hand in my pocket to feel the key to the padlock.

"We're about to cast off," he said. "You and I have to work together."

"Agreed," I said.

Quince nodded. Then he said to the helmsman, "Give the order to cast off." The helmsman shouted to the men on deck and on the pier.

For several minutes there was a flurry of activity as the boat moved away from the dock. Tilman was still standing on the wharf, watching as we eased out onto the river. I hoped Karen had gotten away.

Finally, with the few lights on shore distant points, Quince turned his attention back to me. "You take care of the passengers, the kids, and your doctor. I'll take care of my crew."

"What if your crew doesn't leave me alone?"

"They'll learn that's not a smart thing to do. But a gun going off can cause a lot of damage on a boat. Take yours, unload it, and put it away."

"And let Vern do whatever the hell he wants?"

"I know where the money comes from. Vern seems to have forgotten that. If he forgets it again, he'll make my life hard. Anyone who makes my life hard regrets it."

"Fine. As long as he leaves me alone."

Quince didn't reply. He'd said what he needed to say.

I watched the black water slip by for a few minutes, then I asked, "We're going down the river?"

Quince nodded. "The river's wide," he commented. "The waterway isn't. Here, no one on shore can see the kids."

"I guess that makes sense." Taking the river itself is the long way to the Gulf. Usually ships use the Intercoastal Waterway or the Harvey Canal rather than following the winding curves of the Mississippi. But Quince was right, the river was wide, and under the cover of night, who could possibly see a child waving through a window?

I climbed down from the bridge, then wandered around the deck. I was on an upper deck. It covered about half the boat. In front of the bridge was a small swimming pool surrounded by deck chairs. The deck served as the roof of the passenger cabins. I went down to the main deck, heading past the cabins to the bow of the boat. A lifeboat was on either side of the *Earthly Delight*. I glanced back at the stern to see that there were two there, also. On this part of the deck there were outdoor tables and chairs. The ones on the port side of the boat were under a tarp to keep them in the shade. The tarp made it hard to see the port lifeboat from the bridge.

I considered getting Cordelia and the kids and casting off in the lifeboat. At the moment, I had some freedom. Quince had told me not to use my gun, but he hadn't taken it from me. No one appeared to be checking on my movements. I glanced at my watch. It was a little after eleven. We would probably arrive in Biloxi during the pre-dawn hours. Darkness was perfect for the purpose of this cruise.

If I was going to put out in a lifeboat, it would be much better to do it off Biloxi than here in the river. The Mississippi Gulf Coast was dotted with small towns along some twenty miles of beach. Next to the beach was a busy highway. The Gulf waters near the coast were shallow and calm. The Mississippi River, on the other hand, was riddled with treacherous currents, hidden from the small towns on its banks by the levee. Once those small towns were passed, there was nothing except the river and the swampy delta surrounding it. You would be spat into the Gulf miles and miles from any place to land.

The lifeboat would be a last resort. I continued around the deck. The nice cabins were on this level. There were ten of them. Nice to know I rated one. Or maybe I got it because it was easier to keep an eye on me here, with windows for eavesdropping.

As I walked by the cabin where the children were, I heard soft crying, not just one child, maybe two or three. I thought of going in, but knew I could offer no comfort that Cordelia couldn't do better.

I went down the stairway that led to the crew deck. The cabins were smaller here. Back toward the stern was a kitchen and a mess area. A couple of men were playing cards in the corner. They ignored me. Beyond the kitchen was a storeroom. Next to that was a cramped radio room where a crewman was glancing through *Playboy*.

"I never read it," he said when he saw me. "I just look at the pictures."

I smiled at his attempt at humor. I didn't need to have the whole crew ready to kill me. "You must get bored down here. I don't imagine you send or receive many messages."

"A few now and then. Mostly 'we're in the channel, stay out of our way' shit."

"If I wanted to send a message, what would I have to do?"

"Be real nice to me." He grinned, then continued, "Write it out exactly as you want it, then give it to me. It's best if you can give me a little leeway as to when it needs to go out. Why, you got a message you need to send?"

"No, just curious. I want to find out how things work here."

"Hey, I like these kinds of girls." He waved some airbrushed tits in front of me. "But not those kinds of girls." He nodded his head in their direction. "It's just the money."

"Yeah, you and me both," I replied.

I slipped back out and poked my head into the storeroom. One of the card players turned out to be the cook, who asked me what I wanted.

"Do we have a first-aid kit anywhere? And maybe something for the kids to eat?"

He didn't get up to help me, instead calling out directions of where things might be in between poker hands. I finally found the first-aid kit and also snagged a bag of cookies.

The cook made no objection to my taking the cookies. His only question was, "Do you mind if we drink beer?"

I suspected he was playing me off against Quince, but as far as I was concerned a drunk crew was a happy crew. "No, I don't care," I replied. "Just make sure everyone gets his fair share." Being run aground by a drunk crew and having the Coast Guard rescue us would be manna from heaven to me.

Below this deck, there was one more level. I glanced down the hatchway. It was the engine room.

"Cookies for us?" one of the men down there called to me.

"No, the kids," I replied. "But cook's giving out beer." That said, I clambered back up to the deck level.

I almost barreled into Quince as I headed for Cordelia's cabin.

"Cookies for the kids?" It was almost a sneer.

"The merchandise shouldn't be hungry and sullen."

He nodded as if I'd given him a rationale he could comprehend. "Some of the men are asking about the doctor," he said.

"Yeah? What about her?"

"Why pay if you can get it for free?"

"I want her to take care of the kids."

"Or do you just want her for yourself?"

It's unfortunate that lesbianism is so "in" these days. It seems even evil assholes notice us. "What difference does it make to you?" I shot back.

"Not much. Just want to know what ground rules to set. If you want, I'll tell the men to stay away."

"Yeah, tell them to leave her alone."

"But, remember, you don't outrank me. If I want her, I'll take her." Quince gazed at me levelly, waiting for my smallest reaction, anything he could use against me.

It doesn't matter, Micky. You won't be on this boat long enough for him to ever get the chance. "I have no problem with that," I replied evenly. "I get tonight, you can have tomorrow night," I added, to preempt his suggesting the opposite.

"Fine," Quince shrugged. Then he eyed me and asked, "How does a woman make a woman do it?"

"What do you mean?"

"How do you force her? She doesn't look like the easy type."

I had no idea. But Quince wanted an answer, so I gave him one. "I take the gun that she doesn't know is unloaded and I point it at her head."

"Do you tie her hands?" Quince was playing a game with me, trying to shove me against my limits. He was a man very good at seeing fear and hesitation and using them.

"Are you getting off on the idea?" I threw back at him. "Or is it the little girls you prefer? You wouldn't even need to tie their hands."

For a moment, anger glittered in his eyes. Then he hid it away. "Just remember our bargain. Tomorrow night I'm going to make her scream. Just remember that." Quince stalked off, out to the deck.

I stood foolishly, holding the first-aid kit and cookies, a thin line of nausea curling in my stomach. I had to stand there for several minutes telling myself there won't be a tomorrow night, not on this boat, not with him.

Finally, I fumbled in my pocket for the keys to the padlock.

Cordelia just stared at me as I stood in the doorway. I knew she'd heard everything in the hallway.

"I brought the first-aid kit and something for the kids to eat," I said stupidly. I held them out.

Keeping as much distance as she could between us, Cordelia reached out and took them. "Can't you get any real food?" she demanded. "Some of these children haven't eaten since lunch."

"Look, I'll do…" Someone came up behind me. I turned to look.

"Hi," Ron said. "How are we tonight?" he said over my shoulder to the kids. "Anyone want to go out on the deck?"

"Uh…not tonight, Ron," I told him. "The kids are tired, they need some sleep. Think you might be able to talk the cook into sandwiches or something for them?"

"Hey, no problem, I'm the galley slave on this scow. How about soup and sandwiches? It's gotten a little chilly tonight."

"That sounds great. Thanks," I said.

"Water. Something to drink," Cordelia added.

"I'll bring some milk, too. Growing girls need their milk." Ron counted the girls, then headed for the galley. Another day or two of this and they would trust him, he would be their friend. And then he could easily get what he wanted.

Cordelia was across the cabin, kneeling beside the sick girl. She was taking a thermometer out of the first-aid kit.

"How is she?" I asked as I came into the cabin. I noticed there were six girls, all white except one very light-skinned Creole. Bigotry among child molesters.

"Her fever seems to be going down. It'd be better if she could go to a hospital and we could rule out things like meningitis," Cordelia said in her professional voice.

It was risky to tell her in front of these kids. I didn't know them or their emotional state. What if one of them blurted out something in front of Quince or one of his crew? There was also the possibility that one of the crew might overhear. I had heard soft crying when I was out on the deck, someone standing where I had been might easily be able to eavesdrop on our conversation. Or perhaps the cabins were bugged. The radio man might be listening to more than just ship traffic.

"We'll dock in Biloxi in a few hours," I told Cordelia. "If she's not any better by then, we'll take her ashore."

Cordelia didn't reply. She took the girl's temperature, not bothering to tell me what it was when she was done.

There were six bunks in this cabin with a small couch long enough for one of the kids to sleep on. I busied myself finding blankets and pillows for them all. Cordelia never once looked at me.

Ron returned, carrying a tray loaded with soup and sandwiches, a gallon of milk in the middle of it. "Here we go," he said, placing it on the coffee table in front of the couch. He and Cordelia began passing out the food to the children.

"Ron, can I ask you something?" I said to get him away from the girls. I motioned him out into the hall. "How does this thing work?" I pointed to the head.

"Just like a regular bathroom," he explained.

"Well, I'm going to have to show our guests around, so I need to get everything straight." I asked him about disposing of tampons and condoms, and how much hot water there was and what happened if all the toilets on the boat flushed at once and every stupid question I could think of.

Ron was affable, taking my questions at face value. He showed me the other head on this deck, down at the end of the hall.

Having run out of bathroom questions, we finally went back to the kid's cabin. They had all finished eating and only empty plates were left. I quickly picked them up and placed them on the tray.

I handed it to Ron, and said, "Thanks a lot. I've got to get these kids to bed now. It's almost midnight and they're very tired."

"Okay, be sure if you need anything to let me know."

"Good night," I told Ron as I held the cabin door for him, giving him no choice but to leave.

Cordelia was getting the children into bed, taking off only their shoes before tucking them in. I suspected that her reasons for leaving them dressed were to give them as much protection as possible against groping hands. It might come in handy if we had to jump in a lifeboat quickly. I began helping a drowsy girl out of her shoes and up to the top bunk.

"You need any help?" It was Quince. He was standing in the doorway.

"No, we're fine," I answered.

"Not with the kids." He wrapped a rope around his fist, pulling it tight with his other hand. Quince may have been testing my limits earlier, but under that he was a sadist. People were targets to him, he enjoyed taking aim.

"I don't need any help," I said firmly.

"You sure? She's a couple of inches taller than you, outweighs you by a bit. I don't think you can handle her."

"You don't interfere with me and I won't interfere with you," I said testily. He was beginning to get to me.

"Just offering to help. I bet you won't even be able to kiss her. You can't even make her do that."

"You want to watch me kiss her so you can get off on it, don't you? Your little jerk-off fantasy for the night," I retorted, trying to keep my control.

"Not in front of these children!" Cordelia said angrily. "Take it somewhere else."

"Does 'jerk-off' bother you?" Quince baited her. "These little girls know what the word means. They're jerk-off queens. They know how to do things old-time whores don't know how to do." He smiled as he said it, enjoying the impact of his words.

"You're disgusting," Cordelia spat at him.

"I'm going to be real disgusting tomorrow night. I hope you fight. I really like women when they fight."

"Get out, Quince," I hissed. His breath stank of whiskey. "You get her tomorrow night. Tonight's mine."

"I'll be waiting." He tossed the rope at me and left.

But I didn't think he'd be gone for very long.

"How the hell did you get involved in this?" Cordelia threw at me, her voice a harsh whisper in a vain attempt to keep the girls from hearing.

"It's a long story. Look, let's go to my cabin." I might be able to write an explanation out, so no one could hear us.

"And leave the children alone? You're not the only one with a key. I heard your little bargain in the hallway with that sadist. I saw what you did to Karen. Damn you!" Cordelia was furious, her eyes hard, colder than I'd ever seen them.

"Let's go to my cabin," I said, needing to get her alone for a minute or two. I reached out and took her arm.

She spun away from me. Then I saw it coming, but still couldn't believe it. She backhanded me across the jaw.

Hitting me shocked even Cordelia. She crossed her arms, gripping her hands tightly as if trying to keep them under control. "Get out, Micky! Get out of here! Don't ever touch me again!" She didn't yell, but her voice held such a deep undercurrent of fury that I backed out of the cabin, unable to quit staring at her until I locked the door between us.

I retreated into my cabin, locking its door also, the sting in my cheek a stunning reminder that she had actually hit me. *She thinks Karen's been murdered. She's on a boat with six girls who are being used as sexual pawns in a debauched game. And she just heard me bargain her into white slavery.*

With Quince and his men stalking about, I felt hunted, the vise a hundred times tighter than it ever had been. Cordelia and the six girls were their captives, to be used any way they wanted. A few more shots of whiskey, and I might not be able to control Quince.

Maybe I should have gone to the police back when I had the chance. Given Algernon the choice of leading us where we wanted to go or being arrested. Had I become obsessed to the point where I was no longer thinking clearly?

I might have gotten away from Algernon, but I never would have been able to get the police anywhere near him. I was looking and seeing choices that hadn't really been open to me. And even if it was the wrong choice, it didn't matter. I couldn't change what I had done. I needed to worry about what I was going to do. I still had my gun, but against eight men who I had to assume were armed, it was flimsy protection.

Write a note for Cordelia. Get her on your side, so that she's ready to move when you are. That's the first step. I began looking around the room for a pen and some paper. I found nothing. I was almost to the point of opening up a vein and using my blood. Then I saw another envelope with my name on it. I tore the letter open.

Dear Micky,

O lente, lente currite noctis equi, it began. The Latin looked familiar, but I couldn't quite place it.

> Thank you for all the work you've done for me, Micky.
>
> Joey was too greedy. You are too clever. At two a.m., Quince is going to get a radio message. I hope he's kind to you, although his past history would argue against it.

Then I recognized the Latin. "Run slowly, slowly horses of the night." It was from Marlowe's *Dr. Faustus*, a line Faustus utters as the clock ticks down on him. I glanced at my watch. It was twelve fifteen. The horses of the night were galloping.

The letter continued,

> You were too close to figuring out who I was. I'll miss you, but I couldn't have that. If it makes your death any more palatable, Quince will suffer for it. Like Salome, I'll ask for your head, so to speak, on a platter. The police will meet the boat in Biloxi. They will find your dead body and six young girls.
>
> All the passengers will have to forgo their prepaid cruise. What Better Business Bureau will they complain to?
>
> So that you won't get too bored while you wait to die, I've left the latest batch of pictures for you to look over. It has something of interest in it for you.

I picked up the copy of the pornographic magazine, quickly flipping through it, sickened by the pictures of the young girls.

Then I saw her. Cissy. She was holding a lollipop shaped like a penis, her expression sullen and coerced. There were several pictures of her, as the lollipop moved from her mouth to her vagina.

Over the last one, covering her like some bizarre fig leaf, was a post-it note. It said, "You know you wanted your cousin to do it to you. You really liked it."

I hurled the magazine across the room, then kicked the table over, rage and shame a volatile mixture. I jumped up and started to slam out of my cabin. But I held myself in place by the barest margin, my fists shaking so hard they beat an unsteady cadence into my thighs.

He'll win. If he takes away all your control, he'll win.

The most important thing was to get Cordelia and the children off the boat. With me dead, there would be nothing to stop Quince, Ron, and the rest of the crew from using them as they wished. Quince might believe me if I told him that the police would be waiting for us at our next stop. But I didn't think it would make him keep us alive.

On both sides of the river a road ran fairly close by. If Cordelia could just get the lifeboat to the bank, she could get to the road.

I had a little less than an hour and forty-five minutes. The first thing to do was to check on the crew, find out where they were and how drunk they had become. I took a few deep breaths, put on what I hoped was a calm expression, and went out of my cabin.

Cordelia and the kids could wait. I needed to know what was possible before I approached her. I headed up to the deck, forcing myself to slowly stroll to the bow of the boat. I spotted Ron leaning against the railing. "Are you night watch?" I asked as I approached him.

"Naw. I just like hanging out here watching the river go by."

"Where are we approximately?"

"We should be passing Belle Chase now."

That meant we had about twenty or thirty miles to go before we ran out of small towns on the river banks.

"Should we do lifeboat drills?" I asked, pretending to be casual.

"We never have. I suppose we could." Ron didn't sound very thrilled at the idea.

"Maybe just show me how to work it. I'd hate to have to learn at the last minute."

I led the way back to the port lifeboat, the one I wanted to use. Ron politely explained the rigging, how to lower it, how to release it, so that I at least had a theoretical knowledge.

"Are we going to have six passengers tomorrow?" he asked, his implication clear.

"Uh…no. Only four," I lied.

"I hope the kids get a good night's rest," he said, as he leaned against the railing again.

I sauntered off, trying to think of a way to get him away from the bow of the boat. I gathered that Ron wasn't very popular with the rest of the crew.

No one else was on deck. The helmsman was at the bridge, but Quince wasn't there. I went down to the crew level. The cook and his friend were still playing poker, but the pile of beer cans next to them had grown considerably.

The radio man was still at his post, still flipping through Playboy.

"You getting lonely?" he called when he saw me.

"I was tired of sitting in my cabin. Do you ever get off duty?"

"For you, anytime," he flirted.

"Who takes over when you're not listening in?"

"My bunk's back there." He indicated a bed behind a curtain. "The set makes noise and I go answer."

"Can't escape it even in your sleep?"

"Hardly. I can stay in bed all day and not desert my post."

"I need to stretch my legs a little more. Maybe I'll come back later."

"You're always welcome." He grinned.

I smiled my all-purpose smile and left him to his fantasies.

I looked in the engine room, but no one was there. They were probably asleep. I walked back by the kitchen. "I'm hungry. Can I get something from the kitchen?" I asked the cook.

"Sure, help yourself," he slurred.

I went into the kitchen and rummaged around. I found some matches and lighter fluid. I also took a ball of heavy twine, a knife to cut it with and some dish rags. I stuffed them inside my jacket, trying to arrange them so they weren't too lumpy.

The cook and his friend were too intent on their card game and beer to even notice me as I left. Bottoms up, boys.

I headed back to the bow where Ron was.

"Hi," I said as I came toward him. "You've been real helpful."

"That's okay. Just trying to make you feel welcome."

"One of the girls took a nap this afternoon, so she's still awake. She'd like to visit you."

"Really?" The animation in his voice was pitiful.

"Really. Let's go down to the cabins. I'll bring her to you."

"That's real nice of you."

"Think nothing of it," I replied, turning away from him. I started to walk down the deck to the entryway.

"This way is quicker," Ron said as he opened a hatch. It led to a small set of stairs next to the head. And very close to our cabins.

He let me precede him down the stairs. I led him to a cabin several doors down from mine. I didn't want him near the children.

"We'll use this one," I said as I ushered him in. The cabin was comfortable, but not huge, with a double bed in it. I closed the drape so that no one passing by on the deck could see in.

"Wow, this is great. Thanks," Ron said.

"Oh, don't thank me," I replied. "Ever been tied up?"

"Tied up?" he blinked at me.

"Yeah. Just letting someone else do it to you." I considered dropping the charade and just pulling my gun. But tricking Ron into letting me tie him up would be much easier than forcing him. If he thought this was a fantasy come true, he would wait and wait some more without suspecting anything. What kind of monster was I to play into this aberration? "Why don't you try it, Ron? You might like it," I cajoled.

"Okay, yeah, sure," he responded with a growing enthusiasm.

"Lie down," I ordered and pulled the twine out of my jacket.

"Shouldn't I undress first?" he asked.

"Uh...sure, if you want to." Being naked might make him reluctant to cry for help.

Ron undressed, treating me as a neutered being for whom he had no sexual current and no shame. Then he lay down on the bed.

"Put your hands over your head." I bound his wrists together. "That might feel a little tight, but it'll loosen up in a bit." The lie was preferable to his slipping his hands out. Part of the headboard was bolted into the wall. I tied the twine securely to that.

"It does feel a little tight."

"It'll loosen up soon," I repeated the lie. "Now, your feet." I tied his ankles together, then fastened the rope to the bed frame.

"Which girl is it?" Ron asked me as I finished the knot.

"Uh...which one do you think?"

"Maybe the youngest one. The little blond."

The one I had noticed was still softly crying as Cordelia had put her to bed. "You'll just have to wait and see," I answered, not wanting to give her up, even to his fantasies.

"Will she be long?"

"She's got to get ready, so it may be a while. But she'll be here."

Ron already had an erection. I turned out the light and slipped back into the hallway. Desire sometimes makes us see so much of what we want, that we can't see what we get. Ron was a disappointing man in a disappointing life and this would be one more disappointment.

I glanced at my watch. It was just a few minutes after one. Should I get in the boat with Cordelia and the kids or should I stay? If I stayed I could decoy the crew and guarantee them time to make it to the river bank. If I went with them I could help row and hope nobody noticed that we all had jumped ship.

I'm not a martyr and I didn't particularly want to get killed, but I couldn't see that I had much choice. I could give a very valuable margin of safety to six children and a woman I loved by staying on this boat. Once I got them off safely, I would light a fire, shoot off some flares, and find a place to stay hidden until the Coast Guard showed up.

I went back on deck to make sure that no one was there before I brought Cordelia and the kids up. The only crewperson visible was the helmsman up on his lonely bridge outpost. But he couldn't see the port lifeboat, and hopefully everyone else was drunk or asleep. After taking a quick walk to the stern just to be sure no one was there, I went to get Cordelia and the children. In the hallway, I walked softly, not wanting Ron to hear footsteps and make noise. The muffled throb of the engine and hiss of the boat cutting through water were probably more than adequate cover, but too much caution was better than too little.

Midway down the hall, I stopped, sensing something out of place. First I noticed the stale tang of whiskey, then I saw that the door to the children's cabin was open. Quince had come back.

Could I pull out my gun and threaten him with it? In a small cabin with six children? What if he had a gun? He could easily shoot Cordelia or any of the girls. So much for guns being a deterrent to criminal behavior. I edged next to the door to listen to what was going on. For a moment or two all I heard was an ominous silence.

Then Quince said, "It doesn't matter. I'll take her or I'll take you. But it will probably hurt a young girl more."

There was an even longer silence before Cordelia finally replied, "All right. But not here. Not in front of them."

"How much choice do you think you have?" He used his voice as a knife, slashing, attacking.

"Not tonight, Quince," I snarled from the doorway, unable to watch him taunt her anymore.

He turned to me, a lazy sneer on his face. "I hate waste. You weren't using her. I thought I would."

"Tonight you stay away from her."

"You and your army of kids going to make me? How many captains do you think this 'love boat' of yours is going to find?"

"You don't work for us, who do you think is going to hire you?" I shot back. "You want to get paid, Quince, you go back to your cabin and sleep it off."

"You're not man enough to order me around." Quince was too drunk to see anything beyond his immediate desires, and the most demanding one wasn't sex, but power. "A little trade. How 'bout that? I get her tonight and you tomorrow. She'll be real cooperative by tomorrow night."

"No, we made a deal. It still stands."

Suddenly Quince grabbed my arm, hauled me into the cabin, and threw me at Cordelia. "C'mon, take her, then. Prove you can do it. Don't you have the balls for it?" he mocked me.

Cordelia backed away from the physical contact, but she wasn't willing move much closer to any of the girls, so we remained only inches apart.

The vise was crushing me. I had to get Cordelia and the kids off the boat in the next few minutes. They had to be safely away before that radio message came through. I didn't have time to find the small place where Quince might be reasonable or at least persuadable. That didn't leave me many options.

Desperate women take desperate measures. I drew my gun. Cordelia glared at me, saying nothing, but the rigid set of her lips and the harsh fury in her eyes told me how much she objected.

I didn't look at Quince. "On your knees," I told her.

She didn't move.

"Get on your knees," I said again. I had the gun pointed at the ceiling, but I moved it in closer, forcing it into her direct line of sight.

For one utterly brief moment, she looked right at me, her eyes those of a cornered animal, then her focus went somewhere else, a place where she would not let me reach her.

Slowly, she got on her knees. I reached down and touched her cheek. She didn't flinch, but she remained rigid.

Quince cackled at her submission.

I moved my other hand, the one still holding the gun, as if to grab her head and force it to me. Quince didn't see me take my finger off the trigger. He was totally unprepared when I spun back at him, hitting his temple as hard as I could with the butt of my pistol. His drunken body was unable to react. He took the blow full on. He slammed into the wall, blood pouring out of his forehead as he slid to the floor and laid there without moving.

A bare ghost of relief flitted across Cordelia's face, before she said, "If that gun had gone off..."

"It's not loaded," I lied.

She hurriedly stood up. "Still... What the hell is going on here, Micky? Did you have to do that to me?"

"I'm sorry, yes. If you knew what I was planning you might have telegraphed something to him. I couldn't risk that."

"What about him?" she asked. A doctor to the core, she knelt and felt his pulse. "He's still alive. He might wake up any moment. His pulse is pretty steady. He needs a few stitches in this gash."

"We haven't time. Get the kids dressed."

"Why?" she demanded.

I helped one girl out of the bunk and found her shoes. "In about a half an hour, Quince is going to get orders to kill us." It was just me, but the effect would be the same. "So we have to get off this boat and we have to do it now."

Cordelia just looked at me, unsure of what to think of this latest bizarre twist or whether or not to trust me. Finally, she said, "All right." I guess she felt she had no choice but to believe me.

Cordelia began helping the girls put their shoes back on. Given the previous scene, none of them were asleep.

After I finished tying the last pair of shoelaces, I rolled Quince over and used the remaining twine to tie his hands behind his back. I gagged him loosely so he wouldn't suffocate.

Cordelia just looked at me for a moment, then said, "This is a nightmare."

"One that will be over soon. Let's go." I glanced at my watch; it was a quarter to two. "Follow me," I instructed, adding, "Lock the door after us."

I stuck my head into the hallway to check that it was clear, then I headed to the forward hatch. I opened it cautiously, but no one was on deck. I cut over to the lifeboat, making sure no one was coming from the stern. I unhooked the tarp that covered the dinghy.

Most of the girls were on deck now, Cordelia bringing up the rear. I levered myself up to take a quick look in the lifeboat. This crew wasn't the most meticulous of seamen and a quick visual inspection was better than none at all. It was made of fiberglass and seemed fairly new. I let myself back on the deck and turned to the first girl.

"You get your pick of seats," I said as I lifted her up.

"Am I going home?" she asked.

"You're going home."

"But my daddy will hit me for running away," she said softly. "I don't want to go home."

These are the throwaway children, daughters of no value. "Maybe not home. We'll take you to a place where no one hits you."

She nodded. It was another promise that held no more hope than all the other broken promises.

I lifted the next girl. She was silent, asking no questions, expecting nothing. Cordelia was helping me now, we both put the next two girls in at the same time. Then in silence, the last two.

Cordelia looked at me, as if debating whether or not to let me help her in. I locked my fingers together, offering my hands as a step. She put her foot in it, then hoisted herself up and into the lifeboat. I undid the lines strapping the dinghy to the *Earthy Delight*. Now all that remained was to lower it to the river.

"What the hell's going on here, Micky?" Cordelia asked. "How did you get involved in this? If you needed money, I would have—"

"There's no time," I cut in. "I'll explain later." I looked at her, her eyes barely blue in the dim light, the emotions in them swirling between fear and anger. She was afraid of me, afraid that I would betray her again. But there was no time to dispel her mistrust.

I gripped the dinghy's gunnel, keeping it from banging against the boat. "Don't fight the current," I told Cordelia. "Angle across it. It may take you a while to get to shore, but we're still far enough upriver that there should be towns around. A road runs fairly close to the river. Find it and you're okay."

"You're not coming with us?"

"No."

"Micky, this is no time for stupid heroics. Get in the boat."

"No. In ten minutes they'll come looking for us. And they'll know you're gone. You'll never make it to shore. Unless something keeps them busy." I unhitched the rope and began lowering the lifeboat. There was no time to argue.

"Micky!" Cordelia stood up and reached out for me. Her fingers briefly touched mine. But I didn't stop lowering the boat. There was no time.

Cordelia looked at me for one moment more, then she sat back down in the boat, running her hand along the hull of the *Earthly Delight*, guiding the lifeboat silently into the river. It hit with a gentle splash. With no motor to keep pace, it immediately began falling behind the big boat. Cordelia loosed the rigging, waving me a farewell that she couldn't be sure I would see, before unshipping the oars.

I quickly hauled up the dangling rope as I watched them disappear into the night.

"I love you," I said very quietly.

It was a few minutes before two. I headed back to the stern of the boat, away from the watchful eyes of the helmsman.

Time to keep these boys busy with a few other things than killing me. I took the lighter fluid and dishrags out of my jacket. I found some coils of rope and made those and the dish towels into a pyre. I doused the pile with lighter fluid, threw the can on top for good measure, then backed away. This was going to be the weenie roast from hell. I lit a match and threw it in the direction of the pile. It went out before it got there. So did the next one. Then I tried two matches together. They stayed lit a little longer, but not long enough. Three matches, still no luck.

Four matches finally did it. There was a hiss, then a burst of flame into a dangerous blaze. I raced away from the fire, knowing how volatile lighter fluid can be. I headed back toward the bow, using the forward hatch to get back inside. Underneath the stairs was an equipment locker. I quickly rummaged through it, throwing things on the floor in my haste. I finally found what I wanted, a flare gun.

Shouts from the stern of the boat told me that the fire had been discovered. I started to head back on deck, then I decided to keep all my options open. If my choice was letting Quince capture me or jumping into the river, I would jump into the river. I grabbed a life jacket and put it on. Then I took a second one. The padding might stop a bullet or at least slow it down. Or I might need the extra flotation. Even a life jacket wasn't a guarantee that I could survive the ripping current.

It would be too easy to be caught and confined in the cabins. I headed back on deck. I heard the raspy hiss of a fire extinguisher from aft. We obviously needed to be rescued. It was time to shoot a flare into the air.

I went as far forward as I could then aimed the flare gun and fired. Nothing happened. I pulled the trigger several times in disbelief at my stupid luck. These assholes couldn't even keep their flare gun properly loaded.

Unless a passing ship or someone on shore saw the fire, and decided it was a big enough blaze to pay attention to, my planned-on rescue was no longer likely.

I scurried back to the forward hatch and ran a piece of rope through the hasp, tying it shut. It was one less front from which they could attack me. I looked at my watch again. It was twenty after two. They would soon be coming for me. I gathered rope, some deck chairs, and anything I could find and piled them around the anchor stanchion into a not-very-good barricade. I considered making a run for one of the other lifeboats, but even if I could make it to the river, it would cause them to change course and look for a dinghy. Cordelia and the girls weren't far enough away yet. The shouting voices moved; the fire had been put out.

One voice rose above the rest. "Where the hell is Quince?"

Another seconded him. "We don't have to listen to you. You're not the captain."

Vern yelled back, "I don't know where the fuck Quince is. We've got orders to kill the dyke. Are you a swishy little cocksucker or are you going to help me do it?"

"Fuck you, Vern," the first voice retorted. "I'm not in this for murder."

"Unless you're good for swimming, you're in it as far as it goes."

"We're not taking orders from you," a different voice shouted. "Until I hear it from Quince, it don't mean shit."

A grumbling chorus seemed to second that sentiment. The voices receded as if they were going below deck. Maybe I could hope for a mutiny. These men were probably cutthroat enough to go after one another.

Then there was nothing, no voices, no sounds, only the low pulse of the engines and sounds of the river. I waited, just waited. I glanced at my watch. Only two thirty. Not long enough. The dinghy, pulled by the river's current, might not be far enough away. I had to give Cordelia time to get the children to shore. They wouldn't be safe until then.

I didn't have a plan anymore. Have gun, will fire, was the best I could come up with.

I looked at my watch again. Only five minutes had passed. Why does time go so slowly when you're trapped on a boat with men trying to kill you?

Quince and Ron were out of the action. At least for a while. Without Quince, the men weren't going to obey Vern. It didn't look like he was going to come after me on his own. So far no one had discovered that Cordelia and the kids were missing.

The eye of the hurricane was the only time to move about. And it passed quickly, leaving the howling winds and driving water.

No one was on deck. Just the helmsman in his lonely tower. This crew was mercenary and disorganized; by only looking after themselves they made it possible for me to attack them one by one. The life jacket hindered my movement, so I left both of them behind my makeshift barricade. I carefully made my way midships, walking as silently as I could. No one was about. They were all down where it was warm and comfortable.

I snuck up to the upper deck, waiting in the stairway, watching the helmsman until he looked away. Then, as quietly as possible, I made my way up the ladder of the bridge tower. When I was almost to the top, I took the flashlight out of my pocket and threw it.

While the helmsman was distracted by the sound of it hitting deck, I climbed the last few feet onto the bridge. He turned back and looked at me. My gun was aimed at him.

"Unlike most of this crew, I'm not a killer," I told him. "Unless I have to be. Move away from the steering wheel," I instructed.

"But who's going to pilot the boat?" he asked as he backed away.

"Nobody. We're going to run aground so the Coast Guard will come rescue us. If you cooperate with me, you will be alive when that happens. If not…oh, well," I finished with a shrug.

He looked at my gun and back at me again. "Look, I didn't want anything to do with the kids. I just needed the job, needed the money."

How the guilty confess their sins. "Lie down on your stomach and put your hands behind your back, and you'll live to get another job."

"I didn't know about the kids until I got to the boat," he said as he let himself down.

Get a good enough lawyer and the jury might believe that. I pulled a length of rope out of a pile that was sitting in a corner. I made a loop with a slip knot.

"I'm not a judge, I'm not the jury, and I'm not the executioner," I told him as I slipped the loop over one of his wrists. "But if I have to pull the trigger, I will," I reminded him. He lay still as I tied his wrists. I got another length of rope and bound his ankles. Then I got a big thick rope and put it in his mouth as a gag.

I couldn't stay on the bridge, I was too visible up here. At some point, someone would find Quince. I spun the steering wheel, taking the boat hard to starboard. Since there was no reason for the helmsman to give me accurate information on sandbars, I didn't bother to ask him. I left the boat and the currents to decide which way we should head.

It might take a while for the boat to go aground and even longer for anyone outside the crew to notice. On the shore, I could see the lights of a town. I decided to make noise.

I got another long length of rope and tied it to the cord for the foghorn. Without even a ciao to the helmsman, I went back down the ladder, feeding the rope out as I went.

When I got to the deck railing, I gave the rope a hard jerk. The deep blast of a foghorn shook the deck. The helmsman might survive, but his hearing wouldn't be the same. I tied off the rope to the rail, leaving the foghorn bellowing for attention.

I quickly went back down to the passenger deck, heading to the bow for my barricade. If I had to make a stand, that was the best place. My hunters would have to cross a wide-open space to get to me. And I had some cover.

I dived behind the pile, waiting to hear the shouting voices and pounding feet, hoping to see the running lights of a Coast Guard cutter. But only the blast of the foghorn cut through the night. I looked at my watch again. It was two fifty-five, almost an hour since the lifeboat had cast off. Maybe there were ashore by now. Safe. For a moment, I felt a vast sense of relief; only then did the chill of my situation creep over me. It would take luck to get me off this boat alive. I didn't feel lucky tonight. Instead, I felt desperate, afraid, and worried that Cordelia despised me. I didn't want her to believe that I had betrayed her. Given everything else I had to worry about, it was odd that this seemed so important.

Maybe it was time for me to get in my own rowboat and get out of here. If the noise and erratic course didn't get some cavalry here soon, I would be alone in a hurricane of anger and violence.

Suddenly the foghorn died, the silence heavy and ominous after its shrieking blast.

"Don't play hard to get, Micky." It was Quince. He was using a bullhorn to make sure I couldn't escape his voice. "You know I don't like girls who play hard to get." He and two other men were on the bridge.

I aimed my pistol just over their heads and pulled the trigger. The glass window on the bridge shattered. I fired again, this time aiming at the steering wheel, hoping to damage it. I heard the bullet hit, but I couldn't tell if it had done any harm.

"Goddamn it, bitch," Quince bellowed. "You'll regret that."

Well, actually, I had no regrets. Not where Quince was concerned.

I didn't fire again. I needed my remaining bullets to keep them from crossing the deck to get to me. They would regroup and come at me. Quince might be handing out weapons. I put the life jacket back on. I might not get another chance.

Then, for a few minutes, there was silence, the storm gathering.

Finally, there was a thump and a curse, someone trying to come up the forward hatch.

Quince came back on the megaphone. "I'm going to take you alive, Micky. No quick bullet for you. Just think of all the things I'm going to do to you, to your cunt."

He wanted me to get angry, to fire a shot at his voice, let them know exactly where I was. I pushed the words away, turning his voice into a drone I had to ignore. His voice can't hurt you, I repeated, as some of the brutal descriptions slipped into my consciousness.

A bullet whizzed over my head. They were getting closer. The outline of a figure became visible on the upper deck. He crept a few feet closer. I fired at him. He jerked away; I might have hit him, but I didn't think so.

"We're going to blow your knees off." Vern's voice cut under Quince's monologue. "I'll have a lot of fun ripping your pants off with your knees bloody and broken."

Don't listen, I told myself. I won't fire my last bullet at them. I'll save it for myself. The quick oblivion of a bullet would be better than letting their thick bodies invade mine. Surviving would leave memories. I already had too many of them.

Someone threw something across the deck, hoping to scare me into firing. I ignored it. I couldn't see anyone at the helm. Maybe whoever Quince had left up there didn't want to chance a bullet. It was hard to judge distance and direction in the dark, but it didn't look like we were heading straight down the channel.

Unless the Coast Guard or somebody showed up in the immediate future, my choices were blowing my brains out or jumping in the river. Since it was unlikely that I could avoid being sucked into the propellers, those choices were very grim indeed.

The shadowed figures were slowly reappearing, a ghost of a hand on the port side, a brief glimpse on starboard, noise on the upper deck. They quickly ducked away, then reappeared, holding in place a little longer, coming a little closer.

The figure on the upper deck was the boldest, creeping next to the edge. I picked up the useless flare gun and heaved it at him, his grunt and retreat letting me know I'd scored some damage. The shadow from the port side crept slowly beyond the cabins. Maybe he thought I was throwing things because I had run out of bullets. I could no longer afford the luxury of shots that weren't meant to main or kill.

I aimed at him and fired.

"Goddamn it!" he bellowed, jerking back into safety. Then his hand snaked out and he fired at me. One bullet thudded into the deck. The next was closer, ricocheting off the anchor stanchion.

"Keep her alive! I want her alive!" Quince shouted a reminder.

"I've got a fuckin' hole in my arm," the crewman yelled at him.

"If she's dead, I'll do to your ass what I was going to do to her cunt," Quince roared at him, silencing his complaints.

Did I have one or two bullets left? I desperately tried to count the shots I had fired. Two. But I wasn't positive.

The shadows were appearing again.

The river or my gun. Which would it be?

"Give up, Micky. If you give up now maybe it'll be a quick bullet," Quince offered me. But he was an empty man with no mercy in him.

"You can't win," Vern seconded him, his shadow defiantly standing on deck. "The harder you make it for us, the worse it is for you."

A figure joined him on the other side of the deck. Then the man on the upper deck jumped down to this level. They all slowly came toward me, confident of victory.

"Pull that trigger one more time and you'll find out what pain can really be like," Vern taunted me.

"You lied to me," the man in the middle shrieked. It was Ron. "You left me in that cabin. I'll teach you to be mean to me." And it was pathetic Ron, a blade glinting in his hand, who charged my barricade, his humiliation goading him.

I fired. He didn't scream, didn't moan, simply crumpled to the deck, the long knife in his hand slipping out with only a slight clatter. I had wanted my penultimate bullet for Vern, but I didn't get that choice. I had so few choices now. One bullet and what to do with it. Which second out of a very few minutes, to put the gun barrel in my mouth and pull the trigger.

Another shadow joined them, taking Ron's center position.

"I told you not to pull that trigger," Vern cooed, a hideous joy in his voice. "Now I'm really going to have to teach you a lesson."

Suddenly the boat lurched, its keel digging into the river bottom with a grinding moan. The stern slew about, pivoting on the grounded bow. I grabbed one of the anchor stanchions to keep myself from being thrown overboard. The *Earthly Delight* shuddered like an animal in a trap.

Someone on the upper deck screamed, "My leg. Oh, God, my leg."

And near me, a few yards away, another voice, no longer triumphant, begged, "Help me, help, I can't hold on." Vern had been thrown under the railing, one foot caught on one of the supports, a hand holding to the edge of the deck.

The throb of the engine changed; the helmsman had thrown us into reverse in an attempt to get the ship unstuck. The *Earthly Delight* shivered as if suddenly chilled at what was taking place on her decks. The stern pivoted back, violently shaking the boat.

Vern screamed as he lost his grip. He had no life jacket. The river would be merciless. I watched him slip away with detached interest, not even feeling the horrific joy of seeing him destroyed. For a moment, I imagined that it was my cousin slipping into emptiness in the dark waters. Still, I felt no emotion, no victory. I realized that his destruction would not be my salvation.

"Goddamn it! Get us off," Quince was roaring.

The boat jerked again, groaning and scraping against the sandbar. I still had to hold on to my pillar for support. Quince was having the helmsman turn the still-free stern from side to side, trying to wiggle the boat off the bar.

The stalking shadows had retreated, away from the precarious edges of the deck.

"Full astern! How could you ground this fucking tub?" Quince shouted at the helmsman.

But the *Earthly Delight* remained hard aground and all she could do was pivot her stern a few degrees either way. Quince finally gave up on that and in desperation yelled for full ahead in an attempt to ride over the bar. The boat lurched, the bow digging further into the river bottom, the stern nosing up. I heard a number of crashes below deck from things being thrown about by the lurching of the ship.

"Full astern," Quince yelled, but it was a useless order and he knew it. For several minutes, he let the engine's whine pitch higher and higher. Then they were cut off.

Into the silence, I heard his voice say, "We've got to get her. She can't be alive when the Coast Guard comes."

I checked my life jacket one more time, making sure it was tightly fastened. I clutched the other jacket to me. I could use it as a small raft or throw it away to give Quince another life jacket to fire at.

The relentless shadows reappeared, coming for me.

I fired my last shot at them.

Giving myself no more time for thought or hesitation, I ran to the side of the boat. I leaped onto the railing, using it to push myself off as I dived into the Mississippi. I had chosen the river, preferring the slight chance it offered, or at least the reprieve that I would not be the one to take my own life.

The water was cold and hard. I went under, the force of the dive taking me deep. The life jacket yanked me back up, gasping and sputtering out the muddy water.

But the current spun me about, tumbling me over and over, the life jacket pulling me back up only to be grabbed again by the river. It was much colder than I'd expected. I struggled against the current, thrusting my face above the dark water to gasp in a breath.

A bright light blinded me. I could hear nothing beyond the roar of the river, but I saw the wake of the bullet as it hit the water beside me. When I heard it, the crack of the pistol sounded so far away.

I gulped a breath and forced myself under water. Maddeningly, the current thrust me back up again, into the glare of the light. I exhaled to take another breath and try again, but I was tumbled under before I could get air into my lungs. The river held me under until I had to struggle and claw my way to the surface.

I spat out the brown water as I surfaced, still managing to swallow a nauseating amount of it. The light had lost me and I was again in the dark with the water.

I clutched the second life jacket to me, jamming it under my chin in an attempt to keep my head out of the swirling muck. For a moment I floated easily, the eddies teasing me with their gentleness.

Somewhere I had lost my gun. I couldn't recall throwing it away on deck. I thought I still had it in my hand when I had jumped, but I didn't have it now. I had one of those irrational pangs at losing it, as if it could matter at the moment. But the gun had been my father's, he had gotten it in the Second World War. I had carried it more because it was a connection to him than for any other reason. It really wasn't a very suitable gun, an old .45. But it was gone now, the river had claimed it.

Then the current grabbed me again, pulling and twisting my legs like the limbs of a puppet held by a malicious child. A wave slammed into and over my face, forcing itself up my nose. I couldn't hold the other life jacket under my chin. It spun away, then back, covering my face until I clawed it away in panic. I was pulled under again, surfacing only long enough to get a watery breath.

When I came up again the second life jacket was gone, and I thrust forcefully with my arms and legs in an attempt to get my head far enough out of the water to take a clean breath. I gasped in air, but the river tugged me back, the water again covering me for an instant, before the life jacket pulled my face only slightly above it.

I wondered if you could drown by degrees, a little bit of water in each breath until one little bit became too much. Just the effort of keeping my head above water was exhausting me. It seemed so long ago when I had been back on the boat. Back when I thought I could possibly swim, with the help of a life jacket and make it to shore. Now I knew how utterly impossible that was.

I caught a glimpse of a light playing across the river's surface. They were still hunting for me. And for the few more minutes I would have in this existence, I got satisfaction from knowing that Quince would lose to the Mississippi, the impersonal river would not enjoy killing me.

I thought of Cordelia. I should have said, "I love you," when she had been close enough to hear. I should have called her instead of letting the silence build. But those regrets hurt too much to hold near.

The light swung near, heading for me just as the river pulled me under. I was tumbled over and over again before being spewed to the surface, a deadly lethargy of exhaustion and cold seeping into me. But still I took another breath, still spitting out the water that attempted to accompany air into my lungs.

Bits and pieces of flotsam and jetsam, the debris of a major river, spun downstream with me. A board came threateningly close, the force of the water making it deadly. Something tangled in my legs for a moment before being torn away. I had a nightmare vision of Vern's drowned body being flung against mine, but the shape that passed was only a garbage bag.

The roar of the river increased, as if, bit by bit, it would be all I would ever know—until there was nothing.

The light swung on me again, before the river tumbled me out of it, almost as if they were playing a child's game of hide-and-seek with my battered body.

I heard the bullhorn and my name again. I thought by now I would have been taken away from the ship, away from Quince's voice. I struggled up to look, to see where I was. The river, the shore, everything was blackness around me. I spun wildly, throwing myself around to see behind me, expecting the *Earthly Delight* to be looming there. But only the same black river confronted me. Maybe I was hallucinating.

I heard it again, my name, and the light found me.

If I could get my life jacket off, I would be gone, the river would take me quickly. My hands were numb and trembling with exhaustion as I fumbled with the straps.

The voice repeated my name over and over again, the river dragging me off, then thrusting me back, forcing me to listen. I realized that it was not Quince. "Micky, Micky, wave if you can hear me," it shouted.

I made an attempt at a wave, but the current spun me around, washing another wall of water over my head. I lost the voice as I choked and gasped.

The light was still on me. I couldn't see. Another bullet zinged by. The light snapped off and the river thrust me up enough so that I could see that the light was now focused on the *Earthly Delight*. I heard two distinct roars, the river swirling about me, and another that sounded like a helicopter.

"Micky. We're going to drop a ladder," the bullhorn voice shouted. "Wave if you understand." It sounded like O'Connor.

I managed the best wave I could. I heard the splash of something hitting the water, but I couldn't see it in the dark. For a moment the light flashed on the ladder, then off. It was yards away from me, too far to get to.

The distant crack of a rifle shot let me know that Quince and his crew were still shooting at us. The helicopter needed the light to see where to drop the ladder, I needed the light to see it, but Quince was using the light to fire.

Suddenly the ladder swung by me. It caught me on the neck, then scraped over my shoulder before disappearing out of reach. The river threw me around and under. I couldn't find the ladder when I resurfaced.

"Micky," O'Connor called, but his voice sounded fainter. The sound of the helicopter was receding.

Then the light swung nearby. I reached out for it as if I could grab it and pull it to me. Someone must have seen or sensed my motion, because the light returned and found me.

"Grab the ladder," O'Connor yelled as the helicopter turned back to me.

This time I saw the ladder dragging through the water toward me. I seized a rope side as it twisted by, wrapping it around my arm. The river tried to drag me away, pulling me so fiercely into the current that all I could do was hold on to the rope. I couldn't get my other arm around to hold with two hands. The relentless pull of the water was sucking all the strength from my arm. I couldn't hold on much longer.

Then the river let go, as if saying, perhaps another time. I was able to kick my legs over, getting one through a rung on the ladder. I gripped the ladder with my other arm; the one that had held me felt numb and dead, a bloodied rope burn across my palm and around my wrist. I wrapped myself into the ladder, pulling a shoulder through one rung, winding the hanging rope around my other leg. It wasn't possible for me to climb it, I was too exhausted for that.

The light shone on me again for a moment. I heard the bullets that it attracted whiz by. The light snapped off, and, with a sickening jolt, I was jerked out of the river and into the air. The helicopter was climbing with dizzying speed. The river was now hundreds of feet below me. I could make out lights on both banks. The shape of the *Earthly Delight* was visible, and as the helicopter ascended, it turned into a toy ship.

The height revived my numb arm. I looped it around a ladder rung. I tried closing my eyes, but that was even more sickening than leaving them open.

My sudden transition from the water to the air caused me to shiver uncontrollably. If I let go, this rescue wasn't going to do me any good. I wondered how the hell O'Connor was going to get me off this rope ladder and if he knew he had to do it very soon.

Then my sick stomach noticed that the ladder was moving. Not just moving with the helicopter, but swinging in ways that meant the people inside were pulling me in. It wasn't doing much for my stomach, and I didn't dare lift my head and look up. My vertigo was already more than severe. The ladder lurched again. I felt a runner brush my hair. Then the ladder swung away from the helicopter and its underside and some of the running lights came into view. The ladder careened back, slamming me into the runner. I screamed from both the pain and the shock of it.

"Get her up! Get her up! We're losing her!" someone shouted.

The ladder swung again, this time short and abrupt. Then I felt hands roughly tugging me into the helicopter.

"You okay?" someone asked.

I lay on the floor, catching my breath, and trying to calm my nausea as violent shudders racked through me.

"She okay?" someone else asked.

Someone was untangling me from the ladder. I lay still, panting on the floor, unable to answer. Then I crawled like a drunk crab until my head was resting at the cockpit door. I started retching and coughing up the river water. For a moment, I watched a thin stream of vomit fall away, then I closed my eyes. I hoped it landed on Quince's head.

It felt like forever before the shudders that coursed through me were only shivers from cold.

Someone had a hand on my back, holding the straps of my life jacket to keep me safely inside. "You okay?" he asked. It was O'Connor.

I nodded weakly, then grunted, since I didn't know how well he could see me. I spat one more time, then rasped out, "I'm finished."

O'Connor pulled me back into the helicopter. I was totally limp. He placed a blanket around my shoulders, then used a knife to cut the life jacket straps so I could take it off. He wrapped the blanket completely around me and pulled me across his lap, with my head resting on his arm.

I shuddered, the warmth from the blanket and his body reaching me very slowly.

"The kids…in a lifeboat," I choked out. "Six kids…Cordelia James. Somewhere on the river. Maybe ashore. Need to find them."

"Don't worry, we will," O'Connor assured me. I heard him repeat my message to the copilot who then radioed it in.

That was all I could do. I shivered and tried to get warm.

Finally, when the worst of my shuddering had passed, I asked O'Connor, "How'd you know to look for me?"

"Can you drink this?" was his first response. "It's coffee." He poured some out of a thermos.

I took the cup from him, holding it with both my hands. The coffee was loaded with milk and sugar, something I usually don't like. But milk and sugar were as close as I was likely to come to dinner, so I gulped the warm liquid down, then held the cup out and asked, "More?"

O'Connor filled the cup again, before answering my original question. "Karen Holloway. I hate to say it, but it's a good thing she's a rich white lady, otherwise her story would have been thrown out as too bizarre to believe. We were going crazy trying to figure out where you'd disappeared to when we get the call that someone had picked her up down by Violet. I got her on the phone, got the story, and hopped in this bird. You know the rest."

"What about them?" I asked, a not very clear question.

But O'Connor know who I meant. "A couple of Coast Guard cutters left about the same time we did. We radioed them a little while ago, so they know that you, Dr. James, and the kids aren't on the boat anymore."

I grunted a question, my communication skills rapidly dying.

"Karen Holloway, again," O'Connor answered. "She gave us a rundown of who was on the boat."

"She okay?" I managed to actually articulate.

"Physically? Yeah. She's got a lot of questions to answer about this, but a good lawyer can probably get her off with just a slap on the wrist."

I could think of no more questions that merited shouting over the rumble of the helicopter. All that mattered now was finding Cordelia and the kids.

Chapter 34

I must have dozed, because I was startled into consciousness by the bump of landing and then the sudden cessation of the motor. Still groggy, I slowly sat up. Even my grogginess couldn't disguise all the places I ached. I glanced at my watch. It was filled with water.

"Easy there," O'Connor said, keeping a steadying arm across my shoulders.

"There's no way it'll be easy here," I muttered as I stiffly stood up. I was still wet and chilly, so I kept the blanket wrapped around my shoulders. I stumbled to the door of the helicopter and probably could have gotten out on my own (I like to think so), but the pilot and O'Connor insisted on handing me out to the copilot and the ground crew. The copilot was nonchalant as she grabbed my arm, but the ground crew treated me like something a not-well-liked cat had drug in.

I murmured farewell and thanks to the crew as O'Connor led me across the tarmac to a waiting patrol car.

"You want to go to the hospital?" he asked me.

"I'll be okay. I want to find out what happened to the kids. And Cordelia."

"We can go back to my office and find out. You up to making a statement?"

"Yeah, sure," I mumbled.

I dozed on the drive from the helicopter pad to the station house.

"You sure you're up to this?" O'Connor asked as I stumbled sleepily out of the car.

"I'm going to sleep for a week when this is over, so you'd better get me now," I informed him.

He shrugged and took my arm. It might have been to steady my shambling gait, but I guessed it was to prove that I wasn't some waterlogged lunatic wandering into the precinct.

"We did it," O'Connor announced as we entered the main room. "The suspects are with the Coast Guard and the kids should be okay."

"And some of us are even ready for next Halloween," I added.

There were cheers and applause for O'Connor's news. He led me to some smaller rooms in back.

"I need to go to the bathroom," I said, wanting to get that out of the way before I sat down and endured a long round of questions.

"You're on your own," O'Connor said as he left me at the door of the women's restroom.

I didn't really need to pee, I wanted to wash my hands and face and make sure I didn't have any dead fish tangled in my hair. Draped in the blanket, my hair scraggly, I did look like I should be rattling chains and intoning, "I am the ghost of Christmas past," at least in an amateur production.

I took off the blanket, then my jacket, and shivered for a moment before taking off my sweater. I let the water run until it was hot, then washed my hands and face. I wrung out my sweater before putting it back on. I quickly peed, then put my jacket back on. It probably wouldn't be good for much else, but it did offer some warmth. I was still chilly, so I draped the blanket back on before leaving the bathroom.

O'Connor was waiting for me a few discreet doors down the hallway. I joined him and he ushered me into an interrogation room. It was set up with video cameras, tape recorders, all the latest fun stuff. I didn't really feel up to giving a statement, let alone answering questions, but I had to know if they'd found Cordelia and the children.

"Can I have something to drink?" I asked as I hunched into a chair. "Maybe juice?"

"Sure," O'Connor answered and dispatched tonight's bottom-of-the-rung peon to fill my order. "The FBI's gotten involved in this," he informed me. "Interstate pornography, kidnapping, the whole shebang."

I nodded stoically. The more questioners, the more questions. "Any word on the children and Cordelia?"

O'Connor shook his head. "Do you want me to ask again?" he offered.

I nodded yes and he left the room. Several other police types were setting up the cameras and tape recorders. My fifteen minutes of fame were awaiting me.

The door opened and Danny came in. I wasn't prepared to see her here, although she seemed ready for me. "Danny!" I exclaimed. "What are you doing here?"

"I'm an assistant DA, remember? If you had made it to Alex's birthday, you'd have found out that I've been promoted to the special sex crimes prosecution team. The minute O'Connor started working with us on this case, you landed right in my lap."

I started to say that I had always liked being in her lap, but that wasn't a prudent comment when Danny was in her professional mode and we were surrounded by tape recorders.

"I would hug you," she continued, "but I shouldn't have bought this suit, and I don't want it ruined before I pay it off."

"It's okay," I mumbled. "I've been…sort of a shit lately."

"Sort of, yes," Danny said matter-of-factly. "Although I will admit that since I've been on this case, I've gotten complaints about how out of sorts I've been. And I've only had to deal with it in an office."

"Yeah, well…"

"Besides, this isn't the place to get into personal areas," Danny reminded me. "We're being joined by the FBI, O'Connor and his team, a few more people from my end, and you get to tell us all about the fun you've been having lately." As she said it, Danny reached out and squeezed my hand.

Then the door opened and she let go. O'Connor, the peon with my juice, about twenty other men and one woman entered. Showtime.

I told my tale as best I could, still waiting for word on Cordelia and the kids.

Then the questions began. For the first half hour, I answered them politely. After that, not so politely, then tersely until Danny finally cut in with, "Maybe we need to let Ms. Knight go home and get some rest. She's had a long day."

"Just a few more questions," an impeccably well-dressed white man informed Danny. He was playing territory games. "I know you're uncomfortable, Ms. Knight," he interjected, oblivious that patronizing me wasn't the magic shortcut to my cooperation. "But I'm sure you can see how important this is. We can't allow child molesters and perverts to run around. Now, is it correct that there were only girls, no boys, on this boat?" he asked.

"No, no boys," I answered shortly.

"Any hint of homosexuality?"

"I don't understand your question," I informed him.

He looked at me like I was stupid. "Any hint of sexual relations between men and boys?"

"You're talking about child abuse, not homosexuality."

He was too self-important to see how close his shit was to my fan. "Well, yes, whatever you want to call it, it's the same thing."

"Well, no. Do you know what the word 'consent' means?" I shot back at him. "I am a lesbian. I sleep with consenting adults, I do not coerce or force children into having sex with me." Anger shook my voice. "And I don't care to answer stupid questions asked by ignorant bigots." I stood up to go.

Danny remained carefully neutral. She was black, a woman, and coming out of the closet had a lot of consequences for her.

O'Connor stood, blocking my way. "It's okay, Micky." He turned to my questioner and said, "She's right, you know. I've been married twenty-five years, I don't really understand being gay, but I do know it's not the same thing as abusing kids."

For a moment, there was only silence. At last the self-important man said, "Well, those are all of my questions." He got up to go.

"What's the matter, 'heterosexual' child abuse not good enough for you?" I flung after him.

He straightened his tie and left.

After he was gone, the woman asked, "Any idea who might have orchestrated this?"

"No." I slowly shook my head. I, too, very much wanted an answer to that.

The tape recorders and cameras were shut off. It turned out that the woman was from the FBI, and that the self-important man was a "noted" criminologist who was assisting with the case because his brother was in the state legislature. In Louisiana, no one is safe when the legislature is in session.

After most of the people had left the room, Danny came over and hugged me.

"Your suit," I started to protest.

"You do give the best fireworks show," she said as she let go. "I wanted to say something, but I get so caught up in what it'll cost me and what'll I gain."

"He wouldn't hire me, I wouldn't work for him, so I have nothing to lose. As long as you've got me to mouth off, you don't have to."

"Yeah," she said softly. "Someday, I hope we can all be who we really are." She continued, "Well, you're free to go. Do you want me to arrange a ride?"

"That'd be nice. I try to catch a bus dressed like this, I'll probably get arrested and end up back here."

"I'll see who's around. There's coffee and donuts at the end of the hall."

"Thanks," I said.

Danny smiled, grabbed the notebook into which she had been busy scribbling, and headed off to do district attorney things. I headed for the coffee and donuts.

Halfway there, I glanced into one of the small rooms and saw Karen. I thought of hastening on, not letting her see me. But she was sitting with her shoulders hunched, her hair matted and tangled, her face pale, with whatever makeup she might have had on smearing into grimy pools. Karen had lived in a world that had utterly failed her, and her desolation showed.

"Hi," I said, standing in the doorway.

Her head jerked up. "Micky!" She stood up as if to come to me, but stopped, hesitant and uncertain.

"You okay?" I asked. I didn't go to her. I didn't want to raise expectations that I couldn't meet.

"Me? Yeah, I'm okay. A few bruises here and there. It was horrible wandering in the dark. I think I stepped on a snake, but it may have just been a branch that rolled."

"I'm sorry about...you're probably not going to get your money back."

"That's okay," Karen answered with a rueful half-smile. "I'm sure my accountant will come up with a way to write it off."

"I hope so." Then we were silent. I spoke first. "Why are you still here? You look like you could use a shower and a comfortable bed."

Karen looked down at the floor. "I'm not exactly free to go. They have more questions to ask me."

"Have you called your lawyer?"

"No, not yet," she said slowly.

"Why not? You're going to need to talk to a lawyer sooner or later. Sooner is better."

"I don't know," Karen said with a half-hearted shrug. "I guess I sort of feel like I deserve whatever I get. So I shouldn't use a fancy lawyer to get me off." She sat back down, physically echoing her statement.

"Don't be a martyr," I said sharply.

"Why not? What do you care?" she threw at me, desperately wanting me to disagree. "Did it mean anything to you?" she said in a low voice.

I came into the room and sat down a few feet away from her. "Karen, you're smart, you're personable, and you're throwing it away on that vapid uptown crowd. Some of them will never be better than that. But you can. I hate to see that kind of waste."

"But could you ever care for me?" she asked again softly.

I wasn't going to lie to her, but I wanted to find a truth I wouldn't regret. "I…care, in a way. I can be your friend. I can be the one that grabs you by the scruff of the neck and shakes you until you behave."

"But you could never be my lover?"

"I can be your friend," I repeated. It was the kindest answer I could give her.

"Thanks." She paused for a moment, then asked diffidently, "Are you involved with someone?"

"Uh…yes." I was involved. I didn't know if she still was.

"I guess I knew that. You're too strong and smart not to have someone in love with you—"

"Karen," I cut her off. "For most of my adult life I've been a drunk and a lesbian record holder for one-night stands. I've fucked over a lot of people. I wish I could change that, but I can't. Having a decent person love me is something I don't think I deserve."

"Sometimes I think I'm too much of a coward to try anything but the friends money can buy," Karen said. She sighed, then said, "Last year, my mother asked me to lie about my age. So she could lie about hers. I think I became selfish because that's the only way I ever got anything."

"How you got something from people who don't want to give," I amended.

"Like my mother. And father. I don't think I ever felt that if it was a choice between what they wanted and me, that I would have won. When I was about six or seven, and I guess Cordelia was twelve or thirteen, we had a 'funny' uncle, the Southern type, not really related. He used to corner me in the barn at grandfather's place and make me fool around."

"And you feel guilty about that," I said, seeing where this story was leading.

"No, not that." Karen went off in a different direction. "I finally decided I had to tell my mother. I remember it very clearly. She was at her vanity, putting on makeup, her mouth rounded in a perfect red oval. I stumbled out my story. She looked at me once when I first started, then continued with her makeup, her eyes more and more hidden under the mascara and eyeliner. When I finished, she again looked at me once more, and said, 'That can't be true. Don't tell such stories when you know I'm busy.' She went back to her mascara. I stood there for a few more minutes, feeling humiliated, then I left."

"I'm sorry," I said as Karen paused.

"I got good at dodging him, that was all that I could do. A few months later, he tried the same thing with Cordelia. She told her mother. I remember her father, our grandfather, and several other men, striding across the lawn, the fury on their faces. They confronted that man, I don't even remember his name, but I remember the look on his face when he saw them. Then it was over and he was gone. Just like that. I was always very angry at Cordelia because she was believed and I wasn't."

"But that wasn't her fault."

"I guess I'm still sort of angry at her. She had something I didn't have." I started to speak, but Karen continued, "Yes, I know. The fault was my mother's. If I really were being molested, she would have had to cancel her plans for the evening and do something about it. Much easier to call her daughter a liar."

"Not for you."

"No, not for me. A few years ago, I mentioned that man to Cordelia. You know what her comment was?"

I shook my head, the only response Karen seemed to need.

"She asked me why didn't I tell my mother," Karen said, shaking her head ironically. "It had worked for her."

"Did you explain that you did tell your mother?"

"No, I didn't know if she'd believe me." Then Karen added softly, "Maybe I didn't want to admit that my mother had failed me so completely. Not after Cordelia's mother protected her."

I let it hang. Now wasn't the time to remind Karen of how hard it is to believe someone who tells so many lies.

"I guess I learned that if no one believes the truth, you might as well lie," Karen said.

"And now you've got to unlearn it."

She just nodded in reply.

"There you are," O'Connor called from the hallway. "We just got a call from Pointe a la Hache. Six kids and one doctor. They're going to run them by the nearest hospital for a quick check, then drive them back here."

"Thank God they're okay," Karen said for both of us.

"You know, Karen helped me," I told O'Connor. "When she found out what was really going on, she wanted to go to the police. I told her I was working with you and asked her to keep pretending to be after only money. She put up fifty thousand that she'll probably never get back, just to catch those guys."

O'Connor grunted noncommittally. I don't think he really believed me, but he'd have a hard time disproving it. He finally said, "It could be several hours before they get back. They seem to all be okay. The hospital's just routine. You might want to go home."

"Yeah, I think I'll do that," I replied.

"And I suppose, since you were such a cooperative citizen, you can run along, too, Ms. Holloway. Just don't go too far."

"I'd like to stay and wait for Cordelia," Karen said. "I feel I owe it to her."

"Whatever," O'Connor answered with a shrug. "Micky, we've got a car waiting for you."

"Okay." I got up. I didn't know if Cordelia wanted to see me. I didn't want to find out in a police station in front of Karen. Clearly, she measured herself against Cordelia. For Karen to find out that we were lovers here, in this police station, would be less than tactful. If Cordelia and I remained together, there would be time to tell Karen.

"Thanks, Micky. So long." Karen still looked forlorn and small.

"Hey," I called to her. I held out my arms.

She looked at me, a trace of hesitancy still on her face, before she got up and hugged me.

"Call your lawyer now," I told her. "Don't answer any more questions or they'll find out I lied and we'll both be in trouble."

"Okay," she said. "Thank you."

I let go of her and followed O'Connor as we headed out of the building.

I dropped the damp and dirty blanket on an unused chair. "Don't want to steal government property," I answered O'Connor's look.

He merely grunted and led me to the parking lot.

My ride was a man who looked too young to be wearing a police uniform. He was friendly and chatty, totally unconcerned about my damp butt sitting on his clean seats, but I was too tired to do more than mumble out my address and grunt a few directions.

I thought dawn should be arriving any moment now, but it was still dark when he dropped me at my doorstep. I trudged up the stairs to my apartment. By some miracle, I still had my keys. It seemed a very long time since I had last been here.

I sat at my desk, too numb and tired to do anything for several minutes. Finally, needing to accomplish something, I fished out my wallet. It was waterlogged. I tried to salvage what I could, spreading things out across my desk. I rummaged through my desk drawer to look for a package of tissues. My hand stopped as I reached for them.

Instead I picked up the keys to Cordelia's apartment. This is crazy, I thought, as I stood up and stuffed the keys in my jeans pocket. Well, I did promise her I would show up when she least expected it.

I didn't pause to think, I even left my driver's license drying on my desk. I couldn't stand the idea of her despising me, thinking I had some part in that sordid scheme to sell children. She didn't have to love me, but I couldn't stand her hating me.

I hurried down the stairs, almost running, as if this was the last and most important obstacle of the night. My car, left behind in favor of the rented vehicle, was still parked out front. I got in it and drove to the French Quarter.

A faint glimmer of dawn was visible as I drove by Cordelia's apartment. No one was on the street to stare at my disheveled appearance or wonder as I let myself into the courtyard of Cordelia's building. I fumbled with the keys at her apartment door, unsure which was which, with a nagging sense that I didn't really belong here. Finally, the door opened and I let myself in.

The apartment was still the same, the only visible change yesterday's paper left half read on her couch. It gave me hope as if somehow this apartment, witness as it was to Cordelia's days, could tell me their story. I took its lack of change as an harbinger that Cordelia had taken no new lover and that at least that obstacle wasn't between us.

Rook, her cat, mewed at me, asking to be fed, and despite the interval of absence, recognizing me as someone who might feed her. Almost by instinct I went to the kitchen where her food bowl was and, seeing it empty, filled it for her. Then I changed her water, as if small acts of kindness could make me more welcome here.

I returned to the living room and started to head for Cordelia's bedroom, but instead turned to the spare room first. These rooms had tales to tell. Her bedroom's could wait until last. The spare room had its usual unused expectant look. I went to the bathroom next. Everything there, the soap, the shampoo, the bathrobe, were all familiar. Nothing hinted that anyone new had been here since I was last in the apartment.

Fortified by these signs, I entered Cordelia's bedroom. Her bed hadn't been made, as if she'd left in a hurry. Only one pillow looked like it had been used and the covers were flung back on just one side. These few signs, inconclusive as they really were, gave me a tremendous sense of relief. It was probably why I had rushed over here, knowing that Cordelia was still several hours away. It gave me the chance to make sure there was no indication of another person here without the risk of running into her.

I looked at the clock beside her bed. It was six thirty in the morning. At most it was an hour ago that O'Connor had told me that she and the children had been found. Cordelia might be back here in three hours, but four or more was a better bet.

If I left, I might never come back. If I was here, she had to talk to me.

It might help if I made myself slightly more presentable. Cordelia had a small washer and dryer in her kitchen, so I could even wash my clothes. Three hours was plenty of time for that. I took off my jacket and shoes, hanging the jacket by itself and leaving the shoes next to a heating vent to dry them out. Then I stripped off all my clothes and threw them in the washer. Once that was started, I headed for the bathroom to take a shower.

The hot, scrubbing water felt good. I even washed my hair twice to be sure to get out the foul river smell. As I dried myself off, I reveled in the simple luxury of being clean and dry and warm. And safe, most important of all.

I started to automatically reach for Cordelia's bathrobe. She usually just wrapped herself in a towel after her shower, but I liked the cozy feel of her robe around me, so I had taken to wearing it. Suddenly I wondered if I should put it on, even if I should be here at all. What right did I have to simply show up and barge back into her life? To use her shower and feed her cat as if nothing had happened?

But she had reached out her hand to me before disappearing into the night and although I couldn't pretend that that was a reconciliation, at least it was a tentative bridge between us.

If she wants me to go, she can tell me to leave. And I've taken enough showers and washed enough clothes here that I doubt Cordelia will begrudge me one more go around. I slipped on the robe, wrapping it tightly around me as if I could find some embrace in it.

I took my clothes out of the washer and put them in the dryer. The jeans and heavy sweater would take a while to dry. Then I wandered around the apartment, double-checking my earlier perceptions. Nothing disturbing appeared and Rook seemed content at my presence. I ended up back in the bedroom, sitting on what I thought of as my side of the bed. The clock read only seven-thirty, still several hours before Cordelia was likely to return.

I realized how terribly exhausted I was. *Maybe I'll just lie down until the dryer buzzes. Just close my eyes for a little bit and I'll feel better.* I took off the bathrobe and draped it over a chair. Then I climbed into bed. I pulled the covers up around me and closed my eyes. I didn't think I'd fall asleep, I just needed a few minutes of lying still.

CHAPTER 35

The slamming of the door woke me. I heard Cordelia's voice. Another woman answered her. I was laying naked in her bed. What the hell am I going to do now, crossed my mind.

I heard Cordelia crossing toward the bedroom saying, "They should be in grandmother's secretary." She came into the room and turned on the light, heading for the secretary. She didn't glance at the bed. I managed to pull the covers up over my breasts.

Karen appeared in the doorway. She wasn't as preoccupied as Cordelia. She audibly gasped when she saw me. So much for tactful. Karen was still staring at me, so she didn't see that Cordelia was just as surprised as she was to find me in her bed.

"I fell asleep," I mumbled inanely.

Cordelia recovered first. "Hello, Micky," she said calmly as if my being in her bed wasn't jarringly out of place.

"You're lovers?" Karen exclaimed.

That wasn't a question I cared to answer in front of Karen, so I said, "No, I moonlight as a mattress tester. This is today's assignment."

"But how'd you get in?" Karen asked, still trying to make sense of my being here.

"She has keys," Cordelia said matter-of-factly.

"Oh," was Karen's only reply.

"Here's your spare house keys," Cordelia said as she took some out of a desk drawer.

Karen took them from her. "I wish you'd told me." I couldn't tell if she was speaking to me or Cordelia.

Cordelia put her arm around Karen's shoulders. "You need to get some rest. We have a lot of things to talk about, but now's not the time."

She led Karen back to the living room. "I'll give you a call in the next day or two."

"Yeah. I guess…I know why she's with you and not with me."

"We'll talk," Cordelia repeated. I heard the door open and they exchanged good-byes.

Feeling too vulnerable in bed with no clothes on, I got up and hastily bundled Cordelia's robe tightly around myself. Then the door closed and Cordelia turned the lock.

I came to just inside the doorway of the bedroom. "I wasn't in it with them," I suddenly blurted out, as if Cordelia had accused me of it. "I was working with the police. I only kissed Karen like that to get the handcuff key to her."

"I know. I saw Danny and talked to her. Also, that cop O'Connor. And Karen told me about the key."

Her calm acceptance defused my defensiveness. "How are the kids?"

"They aren't children with easy lives. Child protection's going to investigate a few of the families. I'm going to see if Lindsey will work with some of them, if I can talk their parents into it. One girl was showing what may be the signs of secondary syphilis, which means someone was molesting her a long time ago."

"Shit," I said angrily. "Doesn't it ever stop?"

"No, not really," Cordelia said wearily. "I think at best we prevent a little bit here and there, if we work very hard." She remained where she was on the far side of the room, as if acknowledging that there was a large gap between us that couldn't easily be bridged.

For a minute or two neither of us spoke, then I said, "I slept with Lindsey," the huge space demanding to have all my sins thrown into it.

"I know," Cordelia said neutrally.

"You know?" I demanded, taken aback.

"Lindsey called me. I think she enjoys confessing her transgressions. For the irreligious, ex-lovers function as priests."

"You're not upset?"

"I don't like the idea of you sleeping with Lindsey. It bothers me. I was very angry, more with her than with you, though. She's a genius and she's capable of amazing bursts of compassion and insight, but at other times she can't even bother to look where she's going."

"Are you…still in love with her?"

She paused a moment before answering, "No. Lindsey hurt me too deeply."

"Are we still lovers?" I asked softly.

Cordelia didn't answer at first, then she said, "I don't know. You disappeared on me, Micky. That hurt. Now you've here in my apartment standing across the room from me, your arms crossed, everything about you indicates a barricade."

"I just came here to tell you I wasn't in it with them."

"That's all?" Cordelia demanded.

I just shrugged, terrified to lift my barricades. I couldn't admit how desperately I wanted to revive the time when I was sure she loved me.

"Goddamn it, Micky! I can't be lovers with a woman who turns into a wall."

"I'm not a faucet to be turned on at your fucking convenience," I shot back. "I shouldn't have come here." Fear came out as anger.

"If you walk out, don't come back."

"Good-bye, then," I retorted. Of course, I was still in her bathrobe and my clothes were in the dryer. Neither of us moved.

Cordelia just looked at me, shook her head, then said, "I can't fucking stand this." Abruptly she crossed the room to me. I backed away, but Cordelia grabbed me by the shoulders and said, "Damn it, talk to me. I'll wait for you, Micky, but not forever."

I was backed into a wall, but Cordelia still held on to my shoulders. Caught between her and the wall, I panicked, shouting, "No, let go of me!" I twisted forcefully away from her. "Don't touch me!"

Cordelia backed away, shaken by my vehemence. "I'm sorry. I didn't mean to…"

"Just don't touch me," I overrode her.

"I won't touch you, if that's what you want. But you have to talk to me." Cordelia's voice was uneasy, my rejection of her had been harsh.

I felt brittle and fragile, like the wrong word or look could shatter me. What control I had was only tattered strips. I had, as best I could, saved the young girls, now I was the only one left. "What I want? How kind of you to give me a choice," I spat out. I knew I was being unfair to her, but the anger was erupting, she was here and I couldn't stop it.

"Haven't I always given you a choice?" she asked. But her rationality couldn't extinguish my anger.

"A choice? You'll say you love me if I have sex with you. I even have to pretend I like it."

"Micky. Is that true? I never…" Cordelia fumbled.

"Have I ever said no? Turned you down? Been too tired or had a headache? Whenever you called up, I always came through. Even if I didn't want to."

Cordelia looked stunned. "I'm sorry. I never wanted to force you. I always thought…we both…"

"Maybe for you. You've got money, you're good-looking, you're successful. Maybe you don't understand that not everybody has your choices."

Cordelia looked away from me. She didn't reply immediately. Finally, she said, "It was never my intention to use you like that." She turned from me to hide her crying.

I had hurt her. Proved that I could inflict pain as others had used a similar power when they had it over me. I wondered if they had enjoyed it, seeing the impact they could have in a life that didn't belong to them. I crossed the room and sat down at the table, resting my head in my hands. I felt too weary to stand, too drained to even cry.

I don't know how long we remained as we were, Cordelia softly crying in the corner, me sitting staring at the table.

"I'm sorry," I said to her. "I'm angry and I wanted to hurt someone."

She slowly came over to the table and sat down opposite me.

"Is it true?" she asked softly. "Is any of it true?"

"It's not you. It's me," I said slowly. "Sometimes we've had sex when I didn't really want to. I'm just not very good at saying no. It's my fault."

"Don't take it all on. I can't read your mind, but sometimes I forget you haven't lived my life. You've told me about your cousin. No one forced me to have sex with them when I was thirteen and did it until I ran away at eighteen."

"That's over. It doesn't matter anymore."

"Doesn't it?" Cordelia asked gently. "Why is it so hard for you to take control of your sexual desires?"

"If I wanted a shrink, I'd go talk to Lindsey," I retorted.

"It's still here, Micky. Your past won't just go away."

"Oh, hell. Every ten years you should get a chance to erase the things you can't stand to carry with you for the rest of your life," I said.

"Yes, you should. Spring-clean your memories. Embarrassments from junior high, those college fumbles, a disastrous love affair, all in the trash."

"Yeah. Something like that," I mumbled.

"What would you erase if you could?"

Cordelia's question hung in the air. My answer wasn't an

embarrassment or a fumble. If it wasn't the whole sum and cause of my pain and anger, it was certainly the foundation. "What happened with my cousin," I finally replied. Even that was a denial. Cordelia only knew what I'd told her, the version I'd edited to reflect the person I wished I'd been. It was the part that I had told no one that I wanted to obliterate.

"Did you get along with him before he started molesting you?" Cordelia asked.

"Why do you want to know?"

"How badly did he betray you?"

"I never told you..." I said slowly. "Bayard was friendly and kind when I first came to live there. When he got a puppy, he let me tag along to help pick it out. When he had to run to the store, he took me with him, sometimes stopping for ice cream on the way back.

"I don't even remember it starting. Maybe after a few months, he invited me into his room. It was only the usual kid stuff, you show me yours, I'll show you mine. Then it got to be more than just showing."

After I was silent for a moment Cordelia asked, "A few months? This really began when you were ten?"

"Yeah, when I was ten. I didn't protest and I wasn't coerced. Sometimes...I even started things," I admitted. "I guess I wanted the attention. I'm afraid I...enjoyed it."

"Your body responded physically."

"I responded."

"And you're feeling very guilty about it." It was a statement.

"I didn't fight and protest. I even...asked for it, came into his room on my own. I guess I really did want it to happen."

"You were ten years old. Your father had just died. You were thrown in with an aunt who understood discipline but not love, an uncle who was barely present, and your other cousins who resented you. You desperately needed affection and attention. He gave it to you."

"I didn't have to do what I did."

Cordelia continued, "He hooked you in the guise of childhood play. Bit by bit, he moved the line, there was never a clear space for yes or no."

"I guess I know all this, but I don't feel innocent. When I was thirteen, I tried to stop it. By then I realized that we were doing something we shouldn't be doing. I was worried that I'd get pregnant, that everyone would know. He threw in my face that I had started it and I had wanted it and it was too late to stop."

"He used your guilt as a weapon against you," Cordelia stated.

"I got better at avoiding it. But...I never did stop it completely. Until

I left when I was eighteen. The more I hated him, the more he enjoyed making me…do things." I paused, remembering, then I pushed the harsh image aside. "You're the first person I've ever admitted all of this to. I want so badly not to have been that little girl who was so weak that she took her cousin's dick in her mouth."

"Your vulnerability was not an excuse for him to take advantage of it."

I shrugged, my breath coming out as a ragged sigh. *You really wanted it echoed in my head*. How many times had he said that? *You really wanted it*. Suddenly, I remembered the note on Cissy's picture. Who wrote that note? Who had betrayed me?

Cordelia broke into my thoughts, "I wish I could say 'stop blaming yourself.' You were a kid, he was five years older than you. Your body responded simply because it's a physiological fact that with enough stimulation, orgasm usually occurs. It wasn't because you wanted it or chose it in the way an adult can. You wanted affection, sex was the only way you could get it."

"I wonder if I'll ever really know that. I'm sorry about my anger. I shouldn't direct it at you."

"No, but I do have enough sense to know I've done nothing to deserve that kind of fury."

I nodded, but felt too drained to say anything further.

Cordelia said, "I'm going to get some water. Can I get you anything?"

"Yes, water, thanks," I responded mechanically.

She returned with two glasses, gave one to me, then sat down.

"How did you and Karen end up at the shack?" I asked. Silence was still too threatening.

"Karen wanted to see me. I agreed to go over to her place for supper. That bastard Quince and some of his men were already there. They were really after Karen, but they couldn't very well let me go. They threw us in the back of a truck with the six girls and took us out to the shack. That's about when you arrived."

"What happened after you were in the lifeboat?"

"My arms still ache from rowing. I was terrified we'd end up being swept out to sea. It was dark and I couldn't see many lights. I was worried that we'd get rammed by another ship. If I hadn't had the kids with me, I think I would have sat down and cried when we made it to the bank. Ellen, one of the girls, had a little flashlight on a key chain. It wasn't much light, but somehow we got over the levee and found the road. Then we walked along until a car came by. Two old women were in it—they were out late because a niece had just given birth—so I felt safe accepting a ride. They took us to the police station."

"I'm glad you and the kids made it."

"Thanks to you."

I didn't reply.

Cordelia continued, "I'm starving. I haven't eaten since…I guess lunch yesterday. You can go back to sleep if you want, but I have to eat something." Cordelia stood up and headed for the kitchen. "You're also welcome to join me, although I don't know what you'll join me in." I heard her open the refrigerator.

I followed her. She was staring dubiously into the refrigerator.

"Maybe I should just order out," she said.

I looked. It was pretty dismal. "Eggs," I said, pulling out a half-full carton. "Some cheese, a little onion. Here, wash this broccoli." I handed it to her. I found a cutting board and knife and began chopping up the other ingredients. "Omelet Eclectica," I named it.

"You're a genius," Cordelia said from the sink. "Or I'm very hungry."

"I guess I became obsessed with this case," I said while sprinkling the ingredients into the eggs.

"What happened to those girls was despicable. I know that, but I don't know it the way you do. You couldn't save yourself, but you could save them."

"Is that what you think?"

"A guess. What do you think?"

"Maybe. I don't know. At times, I felt like I had no limits. I don't know if I did the right thing. The boat was only going one stop. The kids would have been rescued then. I don't know if I accomplished anything."

"Karen and I would have been dead if you hadn't saved us. That's an accomplishment as far as I'm concerned."

"There is that." I carefully lifted the omelet out of the skillet.

"That smells wonderful," Cordelia said. "I'm not going to judge you on this one, Micky. I'm alive, Karen's alive, and you're alive. The kids, well, some of them will get help. It's not such a bad place for things to end up." She got silverware out of the drawer. "Let's eat."

We ate pretty much in silence, interrupted only by my getting up to fix toast.

After we finished, I began clearing the plates away. Cordelia also got up, as if to say she wasn't going to let me serve her. She cleared away her dish, then rinsed out the pans and put them in the dishwasher. I took my clothes out of the dryer and folded them, hoping some of the wrinkles would come out before I wore them again.

Then, by some unspoken agreement, we went back and sat at the table.

Not wanting to answer questions, I asked one instead. "Where does this leave us?"

"I don't know," Cordelia said. "I was very angry when you didn't call me after not showing up for Alex's party." I started to protest that I had called, but Cordelia continued, "I know you called and left a message that you couldn't make it, but I would have appreciated a call the next day. It didn't have to be much, just, 'I'm sorry, a very important case has come up and I couldn't get away.' And every few days, calling to let me know you're okay. I can't take you just disappearing on me, Micky."

"I'm sorry," I said. "I just…I thought you'd be mad at me, that you might not ever want to see me again."

"So instead of risking rejection, you took a course of action that would guarantee it."

"I'm not a gambling woman. I like sure things." But it wasn't funny. "Sometimes I just think I'm a clown."

"Sometimes, yes. Sometimes you're a very funny clown and you make me laugh. I'm…just an audience. And an audience without a clown… is lonely."

I looked at Cordelia. Usually we're locked in our own world, our own needs and desires. Cordelia had just let me into a place where she was small and scared. "I'm so afraid of you," I admitted.

"Micky. Why?"

"Because of the…power you have over me."

"You have power over me, too. That's were trust comes in. I won't make foolish promises like forever and always. But I will try to never intentionally hurt you."

"I'm still terrified. I don't think love has ever lasted for me."

"Where does that leave us?" she asked.

"With my barricades still up, I guess."

Cordelia reached for my hand. "I don't want to cut my losses and run. Live with me. It can be at your place if you want. Maybe if we're together, you'll learn to trust me."

"Maybe. Or at least we'll find out fairly quickly that it's not working," I replied, then asked, "Do I have to answer right now?"

"No, of course not. As exhausted as we both are, now is probably not a good time to answer. Within a week? Can you give me that?"

"I think so," I answered slowly.

She nodded, then said, "I'm exhausted. I think I need some sleep."

"What time is it, anyway?"

She looked at her watch. "Three thirty. I've been up since eight yesterday morning." She added, "You can stay, if you like."

"I feel like my brain's too dead to make any decisions."

"I'm going to take a quick shower. I feel filthy. If you leave, let me know. But…it's okay if you stay," she added hesitantly.

I nodded noncommittally. Cordelia got up and went to the bathroom. Sitting alone, I realized that I didn't want to leave. I went to her bedroom. After finding a T-shirt and panties to wear, I climbed into bed. Several minutes later, I heard the bathroom door open. Cordelia came out and called, "Micky?"

"I'm in here," I answered.

She entered the bedroom, towel draped around her. She smiled at me and I knew that she thought I had left.

"I borrowed a T-shirt and some underwear," I said.

"You're allowed," she answered as she got a shirt out of a drawer. She put on her T-shirt and rolled into bed. "Good night, good afternoon, whatever it is." She reached out, took my hand, and held it for just a bare second before she turned away to go to sleep.

Cordelia usually didn't wear anything to bed and she usually sleeps facing me. She seemed to understand the reassurance my fragility needed. There was not much more I could ask for.

I let the tension ease out of me and closed my eyes.

When I woke again, I was very disoriented. The vaguely familiar clock on the bedside said nine eighteen, but it was dark outside. It took me a minute to figure out that it was nine eighteen at night, which neatly explained the darkness. Then I realized that I was in bed with Cordelia and we were at her place. She stirred, bumping into me.

"Micky?" she asked sleepily.

"Yeah, I'm here."

"I thought I dreamed you." Cordelia half sat up. "I'm still exhausted and I'm still hungry."

"Flip a coin. You can't eat and sleep."

"I can eat and then sleep." She sat up all the way. "Pizza?"

"No, too heavy."

"I presume I can talk you into an oyster po-boy." Cordelia knew my weak spot. She got out of bed.

"You can."

"Good," she replied, picking up the phone. She placed our order, then headed for the bathroom.

Cordelia woke up slowly. She might be monosyllabic for the next half hour. I put her bathrobe back on and padded out to the living room. I curled up in an easy chair and picked up a magazine.

When she came out of the bathroom, she said, "I'm not going to be great company. I still feel tired and out of it." She sat down on the couch and picked up the paper. "Will this be dinner? Or have we even made it to lunch yet?"

"I can't keep track."

"I'm going to eat and go back to bed. I think I'm into very basic functions right now."

Cordelia read the paper and I glanced at the magazine until the food arrived. After eating, Cordelia fed Rook and I threw the few dishes we had used into the dishwasher. We brushed our teeth at the same time, a routine already established.

As we entered the bedroom, Cordelia said, "Thank you for staying."

"I was too tired to leave." I shrugged.

"As exhausted as I am, I don't know if I could sleep if I were by myself. Too much…tension lately. I'm very glad you're here." Cordelia lay down and turned off the light.

"Thank you," I said softly.

Suddenly, I wanted her, with a fierce longing. Sex would always be entwined with power, be it destruction or creation. Desire, at its best, held the promise of renewal. I wanted to touch that promise.

I reached for her, a tentative hug. She returned my embrace, her arms tightly around me, no hesitation or ambivalence. Emboldened by her holding me, I rolled on top of her, lifting up only long enough to pull off my shirt. I pushed hers up far enough to uncover her breasts.

"Micky, what's…?" Cordelia started.

"Yes, just say yes," I demanded, asking for what I wanted.

"Yes, of course," she answered. "Of course."

I wanted to be consumed by our lovemaking, to reach a place where it was all that mattered. Cordelia moaned as I kissed her, a deep kiss, our mouths open. I pressed my breasts, my hips into her, wanting to feel the heat of her skin. She moaned again as I spread her legs, my thighs hard against hers. I wanted this intensity, a hard passion that left no room for anything other than itself.

Cordelia's arms were around me, one hand in my hair, urging my tongue deeper into her mouth. I didn't bother with foreplay beyond the press of her body against mine. I entered her, my fingers plunging inside. Not even waiting for her to respond, I pushed her legs open, spreading her across the bed.

I broke off our kissing, sliding down to free my arm. I thrust deeply into her, my fingers sliding in and out, my pace increasing with her rapid breathing.

"Yes, yes," Cordelia gasped as my fingers plunged into her.

For a few moments, that was all there was, my fingers probing and sliding in her, her short gasps of breath and the heat and sweat of our skin where we touched. I was aware of nothing beyond that. The arch of her hips, the tightening of her muscles around my fingers, a breath that held longer, I sensed each increment in our escalating desire. My fingers felt her as she reached the edge of orgasm. I knew she was coming before she cried out, before the spasm clutched my hand, then spread through her body. I kept her riding my fingers, kept her coming until a final shudder told me that she was through.

We lay still for a few minutes. I kissed her softly on the neck, her breasts, my fingers resting inside her.

Finally, she said, "What do you want?"

"This. Not to think or worry about anything beyond these doors."

"Just us. Yes," Cordelia answered.

"Go down on me."

She kissed my neck, then moved to my breasts.

"No," I told her. "I'm ready. Do it hard. I want to feel you everywhere."

Cordelia glanced at me for a moment, acknowledging the change, my desire pushing beyond its former boundaries. Then I felt her warm breath on my stomach, my hips, her hands pushing my legs open. Cordelia made love to me, intense, hard, as I had asked her to.

It wasn't bright and new, the excitement of the unknown that I had felt with Lindsey. Cordelia and I had gone beyond the exploration of the merely physical. I knew her body and her responses, and she knew mine. This is what had so frightened me, being touched in a place that was beyond physical, reaching into areas where trust, and its shadowed twin, fear, were hidden. As I lay on the bed, I knew that it might not last, or remain beyond the night, but I trusted Cordelia, trusted her with my fears and my demons.

She entered me first with her tongue, then when it couldn't probe deeply enough, used her fingers. Cordelia thrust in me and sucked on me, a wall of sensation. Release came quickly, I think I had been ready for a long time, a shuddering climax that made me cry out.

We said nothing, lying in each other's arms. The perfect moment of trust still unbroken. In a few moments, I heard her deep, rhythmic breathing.

I awoke again and the clock on the bedside said three fifty. Cordelia was still asleep beside me. I lay in the dark for a moment. Suddenly, I knew something and, if I didn't move, I would catch it.

First I felt chilled, then exhilarated. I had learned something on that boat. If I could get a few questions answered, I would be able to put together who was behind it all. Not wanting to disturb Cordelia, I carefully got out of bed. I went to the kitchen where my clothes were folded on the dryer.

It was four o'clock in the morning, but some monsters never sleep. I left a note for Cordelia. "My obsession isn't quite finished. Just one more rock to kick over and see what crawls out. I think I can end this." Then, hastily I added, "I love you. Micky."

I got dressed and let myself out of her apartment. I drove back to my place first. For where I was going, my wrinkled clothes wouldn't do.

Chapter 36

Hepplewhite reminded me that I hadn't yet fed her today, early as it was, so I dumped some food in her bowl. I searched in the far reaches of my closet and found my good black wool pants and a winter white raw silk sweater. It would have to do.

I couldn't do much about my car, but I planned to use the servants' entrance.

Traffic was light as I drove uptown, the night misty and opaque. I turned into the gates of the Sans Pareil Club, nosing up its curving drive until I came to the turn that would take me the back way.

A gun or a wire would do me no good here. One of the things a man like Colombé had to wrap around himself was layers and layers of protection. While even his money had limits, none of them applied to me. He could kill me, here or far away, and find out anything he wanted to know about me, including every inch of my past. He could even have someone look up the appropriate quote from Faust.

I drove slowly into the garage, not wanting to do anything that would cause his protection to overreact, letting the video cameras see who I was. Colombé was a man who played games. He could afford to set the stakes very, very high. At least for his opponents. I had to know if I was one of those opponents, or if we both had been caught in someone else's game.

The door opened and Francois came out. "Ms. Knight," he said in his perfect neutral servant's voice.

"Francois."

"What can I do for you?" Nothing was out of place, no hint of curiosity at my being here at this hour.

"I need to see Mr. Colombé. Tell him," I said loudly enough for the microphone I knew had to be about, "that I know something that he's going to want to know, too."

"Why don't you tell me? If it's worth something, I'll give you the money."

"This isn't about money. I have to talk to Colombé."

Francois sighed, a huge emotion for him. "I'll see if Mr. Colombé is interested. It may take a while." The door closed.

Francois made me wait over an hour. He opened the door, gave me the barest glance, and said, "Mr. Colombé will see you now."

He kept his back to me, making it clear that he was leading and I was following.

"Seen Joey lately?" I asked him, just to see his reaction.

"Joey?" he said, without turning toward me so I could see his face. "No, I haven't."

Francois was lying. I wondered if he realized I knew. It didn't really matter. Francois hadn't been a faithful enough servant to any of his masters. He would find out how paltry the rewards of unctuous servitude were.

He silently led me upstairs to the Blue Room and beyond that to the door of Colombé's inner sanctum. He motioned me to enter, then closed the door behind me.

Colombé was sitting behind a massive desk, its rich polished wood offset with gold inlays. He wore a deep crimson velvet jacket, the smoke of his cigar wafting around his head, an ephemeral crown of air and ash. Spread across the desk were piles of coins, old and rare. He swept them casually aside to turn his attention to me.

"Miss Knight, welcome to my late-night sanctuary. To what do I owe the pleasure of your company?"

"Some twenty young girls and a dead man."

"What an intriguing opening. Who is the dead man?"

"You don't know?"

"Should I?"

"Joey Boudreaux."

Colombé blinked as if trying to remember who Joey was. Then he replied, "How inconvenient."

"For you or for him?"

"I suppose you think for him. But Joey Boudreaux was a gnat buzzing around the face of the world. He had as much consequence."

"His life was as important to him as yours is to you."

"Thousands of people depend on me. And thousands more depend on them. I'm too old to feign sorrow for a man I barely knew, and, in what little I did know, could find nothing interesting or redeeming."

"Did you kill him?"

"Is that why you came to see me? To ask that question?"

"Essentially, yes."

"Why do you care?"

"The twenty girls. They were scared and they were abused. The person who did that to them was the person who killed Joey Boudreaux."

"So this is a quest for you?"

"You may call it that. You may mock me for it, but I don't think children should live in terror."

"I shan't mock you. You're the first person in several decades who has dared to question me. Much more interesting than old coins." His wrinkled eyes glittered at me as if I were some new prize to inspect for purchase. "But no, I did not kill Joey Boudreaux."

"The truth? Or just part of your game?"

Colombé's eyes narrowed, perhaps his prize was asking too many questions. "You think I play games?"

"You buy men and women, barely adults, off the street, seducing them with money. You watch to see how far their desperation will twist and bend them. Isn't that a game?"

"I treat my guests well. If it is a game, it is one they choose to play. No one leaves here with less than they came with."

"Unless you count dignity and self-respect."

"I don't take that from them. They sell it."

"What about children? What game is it for an eight-year-old to sell her dignity?"

"Not one I care to play. It is no challenge and therefore of no interest to me. I like winning. But I like winning through my skill, not the weakness of my opponent. Men who play with children are weak men."

"Even if they make a good deal of money?"

"Is that what you think I've done?"

"O lente, lente, currite noctis equi."

"Don't speak in riddles, Miss Knight. My time is more valuable than yours." His voice was querulous, that of an old man. Nothing would slow the horses of the night for him.

"'Run slowly, slowly, horses of the night,'" I translated. "It's from a play by Marlowe. Faustus says it as the last few minutes of his life tick away."

"Great literature has little place in Joey's pathetic life."

I considered telling Colombé that I hadn't thought of Joey, that he was the man who had sold his soul and should fear the horses of the night. His price had been very high, riches and power most men would never touch. As if that made a difference.

"Did you kill Joey?" I asked. Colombé's soul was no concern of mine.

"It was inconvenient for me to have Joey Boudreaux killed when he was. I don't inconvenience myself."

"Why was it inconvenient for you?" I had to force myself to use the word.

"Joey took money that didn't belong to him. I might have killed him after he paid it back, but certainly not before."

"How much did he take?"

"Seventy-five thousand," Colombé said distastefully.

"That's nothing to you."

"Not now. But there was a time when that much money meant the world to me. That's not something I shall forget."

Colombé had not killed Joey. He had his sins, but they were not the ones I wanted to avenge. My questions were answered. And now I knew who was to blame, the man who had less of a soul than Colombé.

"He made a fool of you," I said.

"Who did?" Colombé sharply questioned.

"I'm sure your money can buy you that answer. If you spend a lot of it, you might even get to him before I do."

"You mock me, Miss Knight."

"No, I take you very seriously. That's why I'm issuing you this challenge. There's a person who cheated and used both of us. Let's see who gets there first. But because I've been chasing him longer than you have, I'm going to give you a hint. You might want to talk to Francois."

"Francois? Why?"

"That's the problem with being rich. Your servants become so close to what you have that they begin to want it. Three days ago, I gave Joey fifty thousand. He was desperate for it. If he stole seventy-five from you, why did he need only fifty from me?"

Colombé's eyes gleamed with the chill malice of an iceberg, silent, hidden in the night.

I got up to leave. His money could buy many things. A lesson in the cost of betrayal was one of them. Francois had made his choices.

"That is interesting. You are an interesting companion, Miss Knight." It was his highest compliment, spoken as a god to a mortal.

"Good-bye," I said. "I doubt we'll see each other again."

He began counting his ancient coins as I let myself out. No one was in the Blue Room. One of his tuxedoed henchmen held the door for me as I left, no doubt a video camera cuing him as I approached.

There were a few people in the downstairs area, but I paid no attention to them. Dawn was coming and there were places I had to go. I headed for the back door. Just as I got there, Francois appeared, his servant's mask intact.

"Is everything satisfactory, Ms. Knight?"

"Quite. I think Colombé found our conversation very interesting."

"Oh?"

Francois had to be aware that Joey was just one more skin for this snake to shed. It didn't much matter whether he had gotten the whole seventy-five or just skimmed twenty-five off the top. I considered telling him what Colombé now knew about his betrayal, just to see his mask crumble. But I merely said, "Yes. Good-bye, Francois." And as I had said to Colombé, "I doubt I'll see you again."

"Oh?" His curiosity held him. "You're not working for us anymore?" The smile that appeared on his face was smug, letting me know that I was no better than he was.

"I never worked for you," I replied savagely.

He looked surprised. Soon he would understand. I wondered which master he would serve then.

I turned and walked out the door, then got in my car and drove away. As I passed through the wrought iron gate, I could think of no reason that I would ever return to the Sans Pareil Club. I felt no regrets.

Chapter 37

A gray dawn had appeared while I was hidden away in Colombé's lair. The sun might not shine today. It was a little after seven. The beginning of a Monday morning would not be a convenient time for him, but I no longer cared for convenience.

The parents weren't here yet, and parking was easy to find. A few children were in the schoolyard, their sleepy eyes waiting for the day to begin. I was an adult with adult privileges, and walking into the school door before the official beginning of classes wasn't forbidden to me. I strode purposely, too quickly for any memories these halls might hold to catch me.

He was just coming out of his office as I rounded the corner.

"Warren. May I talk to you?" I called to him.

He looked surprised to see me. He quickly covered it by saying, "Micky, I didn't expect to see you here at this time in the morning." His friendly grin smoothly fell into place.

"No doubt," I supplied.

He headed back into his office and I followed. In the shrouded night, I had been so sure, so confident. Now in the day, in his office with children's pictures covering the wall, everything seemed too normal, too gentle to harbor a monster that taught children the adult lesson of how quickly betrayal can walk into your life.

Kessler sat behind his desk, his expression easy and calm. "What can I do for you, Micky?" he asked kindly.

He indicated a chair opposite him, but I couldn't sit. I leaned against the window, watching the arriving kids. "You gave yourself away," I said.

"Oh? How so?" He sounded puzzled. But the kindness in his voice was slipping away.

"You couldn't resist taunting me about my cousin. I've only told a few close friends about him. And you. Only you could have left that note on Cissy's picture."

"Take off your jacket," he ordered, the kindness gone so utterly, it might never have existed. Without waiting to see if I would comply, he grabbed my wrist, and pulled me away from the window. His other hand searched for a gun or a wire. When he found none, he released me. "What do you want? More money?"

"Justice."

Kessler laughed. "Try again."

"Did you kill Judy Douglas?"

"No. Poor Judy really did fall and kill herself. We had a few more pictures to take. If she hadn't run away from me, she wouldn't have tripped."

"She was running from you. You used her death as a way to terrify the children into silence."

"Not that crude. They were just told that that's what happens to little girls who play when they should be working."

"Do you enjoy frightening children?"

"No, I hate it. But, dear me, a man's got to make a living," he retorted sarcastically.

"Why did you kill Joey?"

"Why not?" he callously replied. "He wanted too much. Too much money, too much power. Children are easy. I thought an adult might be more of a challenge. But Joey never suspected until I actually had the noose over his neck."

"You almost sound disappointed."

"I've never killed an adult before. I looked at it as taking a step up, novice to veteran. His body was a little heavier, that was all. A lollipop or a thousand dollars. They're all easy to fool."

"Francois Brunette. Where does he fit in?"

"Francois, my old college roommate. We were both meant for better things."

"Better than molesting girls?" I acidly retorted.

"I'm not going to spend the rest of my days listening to whining brats and their snarling parents for some two-bit pension. I want comfort. A penthouse in New York. A flat in London."

"Like the plantations built on the backs of slaves. Ten, a hundred, a thousand lives broken for your comfort."

"And what do you have, Micky? A barely running car, a cheap apartment in a bad neighborhood?"

I ignored that. "Why do you think Francois won't betray you?"

"Francois follows, he doesn't care about the direction. He also likes girls of a certain age, fourteen, fifteen. When we were in college he got carried away. She was small and he did damage. I gave Francois an ironclad alibi. We were in the library all night studying. That favor gives Francois the courage to take certain risks. I feed him the information. What teachers desperately need money. Which parents aren't very attentive. He channels that information to the right people."

"Just like that?"

"Well, easier said than done. He makes what I call the dark connections. He finds a Joey. Then Joey du jour finds a photographer who will take the pictures. A printer who will print them. The connections to sell these things. I work in the light. A teacher who can be corrupted. Selecting the children that are most useful to us."

"Useful children. You make it sound like a commodity."

"Don't kid yourself, Micky. These aren't the A students from the nice families. They're yelled at or ignored at home. At best, they'll grow into shallow, boring lives, finding some tubby husband to fix greasy food for. Or they end up on drugs, jail, welfare. No National Merit Scholars here."

"How omniscient of you. You pick the worthless ones, get some use out of them, then throw them back on the trash heap. Like Cissy. Was she worthless?" I shot at him.

"She might be okay. But her father did dump her."

"So you make mistakes. Mix in a few good children with your 'trash' kids," I retorted savagely. At ten, I would have been one of the children he labeled trash.

"You really are after justice," he sneered.

"Why the line from Marlowe?"

"I thought you'd appreciate it." He reached into his desk drawer and took out a gun. "And the horses of the night are gone for you. You've been fun and challenging, Micky. But I wouldn't be chatting like this if I thought you would be around to betray me." Kessler picked up his trench coat, draping it over his gun hand for concealment. "Time to go," he said.

"Warren, you've done such a good job of being bright and innovative, it's a shame to see you descend to the cliché of the gun hidden under the trench coat."

"I thought you were dead, so I'm improvising. Let's go."

"And if I don't? Are you going to shoot me here in your office?"

"If I have to," he said calmly. "You'll be dead and I'll claim you attacked me. Case closed. And if not, who'll believe a dyke detective over an upstanding principal?"

The first morning bell rang, signaling that classes would begin soon.

"Shouldn't we wait until the kids clear?" I suggested.

"No. Ms. Justice won't try anything with children swarming about. Let's go."

"Why the boat?" I pushed. "Why bother with the real thing? That was a lot of work to hire Quince and his crew."

"It was a tidy end. Joey was dead. You were supposed to be killed by Quince. He would have arrived in port with your dead body and six kidnapped kids. And wild stories about someone paying him for it all. I only put a little money up front, so it didn't cost much. It was my grand finale. But not one that would ever be traced to me."

"What an evil mastermind you are," I said sarcastically.

"Now, get going," he ordered.

I shrugged and headed for the door. It would be hard, but not impossible for Kessler to gun me down here. It would raise a lot of questions that wouldn't be comfortable for him, but he might get away with it. Far better to take me somewhere remote and dump my body there. I wished I'd been a little more explicit in my note to Cordelia.

"That story you told me? Was any of it true?"

"About being molested? I read that in a book." He opened the door and motioned me to go in front of him.

Several secretaries were about, but he hurried me past them into the hall. The kids were making their way to class, lockers were clanging, with the children talking above their din. I couldn't try anything in this crowded hallway.

"Colombé knows about Francois," I said. I wanted Kessler rattled and distracted by the time we got out of the building.

"Just walk. Don't talk."

"How poetic. The rhyming murderer."

"Don't talk." He nudged me in the ribs with his gun.

I started to point out that was clichéd, too, but decided that Kessler wasn't interested in knowing that. I didn't talk.

"Micky?" someone called to me over the chaos in the hall. I glanced in the direction of the voice. It was Cissy. She was coming toward us.

"Get back to class, Cissy," Kessler ordered.

She hesitated, but didn't turn to go. "Micky?" she said again, sensing that something was wrong.

"It's okay, honey. Go on back to class," I told her.

"Keep going," Kessler hissed in my ear, again pushing me with his gun.

"Are you okay, Micky?" she persisted.

"Get back to class," Kessler snarled.

Cissy's glance darted to his gun hand. I sped up, hoping to leave Cissy's inquiring eyes behind. I didn't want her anywhere near Kessler's gun.

"This way." He nudged me as we came to an intersection in the hall. "We're going out the back way."

Only a few children lingered in this hall. Some older, beat-up lockers lined the walls.

Suddenly, Kessler howled in pain. Without thinking, I spun around and grabbed his gun hand. Control the gun, I told myself, slamming his arm against the lockers and shoving it upward. If the gun fired, it would go into the ceiling.

"Goddamn it!" Kessler screamed again.

Pinning his gun arm against the lockers with both my hands, I looked back to see what had bedeviled Kessler. Cissy had sunk her teeth into his calf. She was still biting him, her arms grasping his ankle to hold on. Kessler swung at her, but, because I had one of his hands pinned, he couldn't twist all the way around to really hit her.

"Call the police! This man has a gun," I yelled.

"Security! Get security," Kessler bellowed in response. "I've got a lunatic here." He cuffed Cissy across the ear, knocking her to the floor.

Free of her, he turned to me, grabbing my hair to yank my head back. *Don't let go of the gun. If you do, you're dead and probably Cissy, too.* Kessler was a strong, powerful man, several inches taller than I was. A battle of brute strength wasn't one I could win. Tears were starting to run down my cheeks from his grip on my hair, my head pulled back so far I was losing my balance.

Kessler suddenly screamed again and let go. Cissy was biting him, again gnawing the same place on his calf. He swung at her and missed, then swung once more and hit her hard enough to knock her sliding down the hallway.

I slammed my heel into his instep, causing him to howl in pain.

"Help! Get the police!" I yelled. I knew it was perhaps only seconds since we had started fighting, a minute at most. It might take several more minutes before anyone who could cut into our deadly dance would arrive.

Kessler's goal was simple: he had to point the gun at me and pull the trigger. Alive, I was a very dangerous threat to him; dead, he could tell whatever story he wanted to. He had to know that even his security guards wouldn't let him shoot me in cold blood.

Kessler fought back, slamming a blow into my kidneys with his free hand. I kicked at him, landing a blow that was little more than annoying at his ankle.

"Goddamn it, you're going to die!" he spat at me.

He hammered a blow at my face. I ducked just enough to keep him from hitting my nose, but the blow still jolted my head back. Kessler had the advantage. I had to use both hands to keep the gun under control. He had one free hand and I couldn't move out of arm's length. Taking the opening that the punch he had landed gave him, he grabbed one of my arms, jerking it off his hand. The gun shifted down. He yanked it toward me and pulled the trigger.

My ears rang from the loud report, but the bullet went over my head. I could hear yelling and screaming behind us. If nothing else, the gunshot had attracted attention. I hoped the bullet was lodged safely in the ceiling or wall.

Kessler clutched my remaining hand, trying to pry it loose. But he couldn't hold both my hands with one of his. With my free hand, I grabbed one of his prying fingers, jerking it painfully back. Kessler cursed and let go, twisting his finger free. I again held his gun hand with both of mine.

Then he hit me again, connecting with my jaw. He struck a second time, a hammering blow to my ear. His strategy was simple and brutally effective, pummel my face and head until I would have to let go of his hand and the gun.

I couldn't control the gun with just one arm. And I couldn't just stand here and be a punching bag. I tried to kicked him in the knee. He cursed me, not falling to the floor as I had hoped, but at least I managed to break the rhythm of his blows.

"He's got a gun," I heard someone behind us yell.

I kicked again. Kessler grabbed my foot.

"I know karate, too," he snarled as he tried to pull me over.

I jerked and twisted, trying to get my foot free. Kessler yanked on my leg and pulled me down.

"Police!" someone yelled.

Kessler froze long enough for me to slam his gun hand into the handle of the locker as hard as I could, driving his wrist against its sharp edge. I did it again, opening a gash in his wrist. Suddenly, he dropped the gun.

Then all hell broke loose. One of the security guards slam dunked me across the hall to one of his compatriots. She shoved a knee into my back and had one arm twisted until my hand was almost in my hair. (My hair isn't very long.) Nothing like having your nose rubbed into a public school floor to make you appreciate cleanliness.

From this ignoble position I listened to the cacophony of several shouted arguments. At first I tried to add my own point of view, until the security guard, not liking the things I was saying about her boss, convinced me that silence is golden, or at least not painful.

Finally, a familiar voice said, "I'll take her, you take him. We'll sort it out from there."

A handcuff was placed around my wrist and the security guard was convinced to get off my back. Joanne Ranson read my rights as she cuffed the other hand. I was glad to notice that Warren Kessler had a few cops doing the same thing to him.

Joanne started to hustle me down the hall, still holding her police badge.

"Cissy. Is she okay?"

"She had a cut on her forehead, but she seemed all right. The school nurse is looking after her."

"Was she bleeding badly?"

"It didn't look very bad. I only saw her for a few moments."

Joanne put her badge back in her coat pocket. Miscreant criminal that I was, she still kept a grip on my arm.

As we walked out of the building, it occurred to me to ask the obvious question, "Joanne, what are you doing here?"

"Cordelia called me. She was worried about you. I put a call out to look for your car. A radio unit saw it parked here. A lifetime ago, I was a school teacher, so I pretended to be a substitute and nosed around. And you showed up in your usual inimitable style." Joanne unlocked the back door of her car.

"In back? Like a criminal?"

"If I don't treat you like a criminal, they won't treat him like a criminal. At least, until we get around the block," she added as she shut the door.

Once we got away from the other cops, Joanne did let me sit up front, but she left the handcuffs on. "Not because I think you might do anything dangerous, but because you might do something stupid," she gave as her reason.

"Thanks, Joanne," I opined.

"Is this where you've been these past few weeks?" she asked, the kidding gone from her voice.

"Yeah, my own little personal hell. I guess I became obsessed with this case." Then I added softly, "I guess I wanted to save Cissy in the way I wanted someone to have saved me."

We rode the rest of the way in silence.

CHAPTER 38

It wasn't easy to tell O'Connor how I knew that Warren Kessler was guilty.

"You'll admit that in court?" he asked after I'd stumbled out my version of telling Kessler about my cousin and the note he'd left taunting me.

I just shrugged. If I had to, I would.

He didn't have to say it wasn't great evidence, not even good evidence. His final comment was, "Well, now that we know who to look at, maybe we'll find something."

O'Connor also wasn't thrilled to have Joanne around. They didn't get along, and that she was a decade younger than him, female, and outranked him didn't improve their relationship.

"Back again so soon?" Danny popped in to say.

"Can I go now?" I grumbled in response. I knew Warren Kessler did it. I knew it beyond doubt or hesitation. But law isn't justice. Sometimes it doesn't even come close.

"Want a quick update on your friends on the boat?" Danny offered. Responding to my nod, she continued, "Jim Vernon hasn't been found yet. He'll probably float ashore someday. The guy you shot, Ron Acker, is in serious but stable condition. Being around kids is violation of his parole. When he gets out of the hospital, he'll go to jail for a long time. Martin Quince was the only one who decided to take on the Coast Guard. He's also in the hospital in serious condition. He got half his jaw blown off, doesn't have much of a tongue or vocal cords left. The rest of the crew went quietly."

I nodded. Quince's voice stilled was a bit of justice. Sometimes that's all you get. I remembered Camille. My head ached from the pounding it had taken. I felt awake yet tired, all my internal clocks thrown out of sync by the last few days. "What about Kessler? Are you even going to be able to hold him overnight?" I snapped out.

"I don't know, Mick," Danny replied, ignoring my churlishness. "We'll do our best. At least long enough to search his house, car, and office. Right now it's your word against his. With just that, even his bail won't be very much."

"Did I fuck up?"

Danny thought for a moment, shrugged, then said, "At least you caught him. That gives us a chance to find the evidence. We'll do a thorough search and see what we can find. Everyone makes mistakes. We just have to find his. At worst, simply running around with a gun the way he did might put a roadblock in his principal career. That might be all you get, but it's something. We ran down the names you got from Joey. We were able to arrest about half of them with enough evidence that they might not be back on the street in a week. The rest, either no proof, or they've hightailed it out of the area."

"Thanks, Danny," I said. "This isn't a great day in the neighborhood."

"I know, Mick, I know. A little more bad news. Lia Gautier?"

"Yes?" I remembered the name Camille had given me.

"They found her body yesterday."

My only reply was, "Can I go now?"

"I suppose. Don't go far. You're our prime, and so far, only witness," Danny said as she turned to leave.

I was beginning to know this police station too damn well, I thought, as I found my way to the water fountain. As I stood up from drinking, I noticed Barbara Selby sitting on a bench in the hall. Waiting. I guess the police had to question even Cissy.

"Barbara," I said as I came up to her. I didn't sit on the bench, I was too unsure of my welcome for that.

"Micky, hello," she replied, her voice hoarse and fragile. "I saw that… picture of my daughter." For a moment she said nothing more. "I feel like I've failed her completely."

"You did the…what you could," but the words sounded empty as I said them.

"When my child is hurt as she has been hurt, then I've failed," Barbara uttered. "I can never give her back what's been lost. I thought I did…the best I could do."

"I know," I said quietly, aware of how paltry my best had been. Who had I really saved?

Barbara reached out to me. I took her hand awkwardly. "Will she ever be okay? Does it ever stop haunting you?"

I didn't know if Barbara was asking a rhetorical question or asking me about myself. I answered as if it were the latter, "The memory remains. Don't silence her. Don't ever blame her."

"I won't," then Barbara amended, "I'll try not to. I'll try to love her unconditionally. I let them talk to Cissy by herself. It might be easier than… me being there. To talk about some things."

"Sometimes strangers are best. They don't carry the risk of…"

"Your family. Patrick told me about his 'hiring' you."

"Oh. I guess I should have told you."

"I don't know. Cissy didn't come to me. I'm glad…someone got involved. But Patrick, he doesn't understand…how do you explain," she faltered, "explain…this to a boy his age?"

"I don't know. Hurt and shame…how do you explain it to anyone who's never been battered by them?"

"Will you talk to him? I don't expect you to perform miracles. He doesn't understand that this isn't a skinned knee that you just put a Band-aid on to make alright. Maybe he'll listen to you in a way he won't to me."

"I'll try," I offered. "The best I might be able to do is convince him that some things are never over."

"Perhaps next weekend? I need to spend some time with Cissy, and you and Patrick can go do something."

"Yeah, I could do that," I said, wondering what I could tell Patrick. When I was his age…when I was his age, Bayard was no longer content with just playing at forbidden boundaries.

"Thank you," Barbara added softly.

The door that she had been waiting for opened. Two women, one I guessed to be a police officer and one a psychologist, ushered Cissy out.

"Mrs. Selby," one of them said, "You can take Cissy home now."

"Thank you," Barbara said numbly.

Barbara let go of my hand to take hold of Cissy's.

"Hi, Micky," Cissy said.

"Hi," I replied. I knelt down beside her. "Thank you. That was a very brave thing you did. He can't hurt you now. He lied about Judy to make it seem like he was big and powerful, but he's not. He can't hurt you," I repeated.

"Thanks, Micky. I'm not scared anymore." But her voice was small and frightened and I saw her statement for the wish that it really was. Cissy hugged me, then reclaimed her mother's hand.

"Come on, honey," Barbara said. "Let's go home." She added, "I'll call you sometime, Micky. I just have to get out of here now."

I watched them as they went down the hall, not wanting to go with them. Instead, I walked back the way I came, giving Barbara and Cissy time to find their way home.

Another door opened and Warren Kessler, escorted by two police officers, came out of the room. He stared at me, a look of snide contempt on his face. "You're crazy, Micky. I can't believe the kind of lies you're telling about me," he said for the benefit of his spectators.

"I've told no lies," I retorted shortly.

"You're a pathetic man-hater."

"Only certain men," I said, then because I wanted to damage him, to put a hole in his contempt, "Colombé knows about Francois. And about you, by now. You might be safer in jail, Warren."

Uncertainty flickered across his face for an instant. But his arrogance quickly returned. "You know I didn't do it. You know you're just a fucked-up dyke. You're blaming me for what your cousin did to you." His police escort started to lead him away. "You really wanted your cousin to do it. Now you're just feeling guilty," he threw at me.

O'Connor was right—for certain reasons, I could be a murderer. If I went to jail, it would still be better than letting this monster loose. My hatred and anger took over. I lunged at him.

But Joanne stepped between us and roughly pushed me against the wall. "No," she said. "Let the law deal with him."

"The law?" I demanded, watching him walk away down the hall. "I want justice."

"So do I. But that's what heaven and hell are for. Go home, Micky."

"Let me get out of here," I answered. There was nothing more I could do. My best, as Barbara's had, would not save more than a tiny fragment of the world.

Joanne, still holding my arm, led me away. "Cordelia's here. I called her."

I started to say I didn't want Cordelia to see my defeat, but then I saw her standing in the foyer. She was waiting, a tentative half-smile appeared when she realized I had noticed her. Kindness and love aren't replacements for justice, but they still held some chance for redemption.

"Hello," she said as we approached.

"Take her away from here," Joanne told Cordelia.

Joanne let go of my arm, a bare nod as good-bye, then she left us.

"Are you okay?" Cordelia asked, touching my arm briefly where Joanne had been holding it.

"Partly," I replied. I couldn't pretend that I hadn't been battered by what had happened.

"Is it enough?" she asked gently, as we walked out of the building.

"No," I replied slowly. "It's not. Not close. I want my past to turn into just that, past, gone. I hate that it hovers about, clawing at me. And over and over again, it happens to so many others. How many days—lives—do we spend repairing all the damage that's done?"

"As many as it takes, I guess. Suffering and neglect are ongoing."

"Do you ever want to stop fighting?" I asked her.

Cordelia didn't say anything as we walked down the stairs. It wasn't until we were on the sidewalk that she replied, "No. The most frustrating thing is that I have to set limits. I can't be on call twenty-four hours a day, have to have some time for myself just to laugh, read, be with friends. And even if I did give everything I could give, some things are utterly beyond my power to change."

"Men like Warren Kessler. I don't know if I've stopped him. I don't know if I've really changed anything. I wonder what little piece of the world I've salvaged."

Cordelia looked at me, then said, "What you did give those girls, and others who have been hurt the way they have been, is that even if we don't get justice, some of us still look for it. I don't know if you can ask for much more than that." She again touched my arm, gently leading me down a side street. Her car was parked in the middle of the block.

"I don't know," I answered. "If you're decent and you work hard enough, you should be able to defeat evil."

"You don't think we ever do?"

"No. I feel like I've lost, like I shouldn't even bother anymore."

Cordelia was silent for a moment, then she replied, "Destroying something—or someone—is so much easier than creating or building. Or loving. As long as we occasionally win, and some of us always fight, then there's a path to follow. I have no reason to be here if I don't try to follow that path." She unlocked her car and we got in. "Where can I take you?" she asked me.

"Home. Take me home," I said as I settled in the passenger seat.

"If that's what you want." She nodded and started the car.

"Take me home with you," I said. "That's my answer. I want to... follow that path with you."

"Yes," she said, then, "Yes, I'll take you with me." She reached over, caught my hand, and held it. I grasped her hand in both of mine.

Then we let go, and Cordelia started the car.

I didn't look back as we drove away.

Books Available From Bold Strokes Books

The Sublime and Spirited Voyage of Original Sin by Colette Moody. Pirate Gayle Malvern finds the presence of an abducted seamstress, Celia Pierce, a welcome distraction until the captive comes to mean more to her than is wise. (978-1-60282-054-8)

Suspect Passions by VK Powell. Can two women, a city attorney and a beat cop, put aside their differences long enough to see that they're perfect for each other? (978-1-60282-053-1)

Just Business by Julie Cannon. Two women who come together—each for her own selfish needs—discover that love can never be as simple as a business transaction. (978-1-60282-052-4)

Sistine Heresy by Justine Saracen. Adrianna Borgia, survivor of the Borgia court, presents Michelangelo with the greatest temptations of his life while struggling with soul-threatening desires for the painter Raphaela. (978-1-60282-051-7)

Radical Encounters by Radclyffe. An out-of-bounds, outside-the-lines collection of provocative, superheated erotica by award-winning romance and erotica author Radclyffe. (978-1-60282-050-0)

Thief of Always by Kim Baldwin & Xenia Alexiou. Stealing a diamond to save the world should be easy for Elite Operative Mishael Taylor, but she didn't figure on love getting in the way. (978-1-60282-049-4)

X by JD Glass. When X-hacker Charlie Riven is framed for a crime she didn't commit, she accepts help from an unlikely source—sexy Treasury Agent Elaine Harper. (978-1-60282-048-7)

The Middle of Somewhere by Clifford Henderson. Eadie T. Pratt sets out on a road trip in search of a new life and ends up in the middle of somewhere she never expected. (978-1-60282-047-0)

Paybacks by Gabrielle Goldsby. Cameron Howard wants to avoid her old nemesis Mackenzie Brandt but their high school reunion brings up more than just memories. (978-1-60282-046-3)